A LAWLESS NOVEL

WILLIAM SUTTON

Lawless
and the
Devil
of
Euston
Square

EXHIBIT A
An Angry Robot imprint
and a member of the Osprey Group

Lace Market House,
54-56 High Pavement,
Nottingham, NG1 1HW
UK

www.exhibitabooks.com
A is for Anarchy!

First published in 2006 by Crescent Books, an imprint of Mercat
Press, under the title *The Worms of Euston Square*

Published by Exhibit A in 2013
1

William Sutton asserts the moral right to be
identified as the author of this work.

A catalogue record for this book is available
from the British Library.

UK ISBN 978 1 90922 324 0
Ebook ISBN 978 1 90922 326 4

Set in Meridien and Historical FellType by Argh! Nottingham

LAWLESS & THE DEVIL OF EUSTON SQUARE

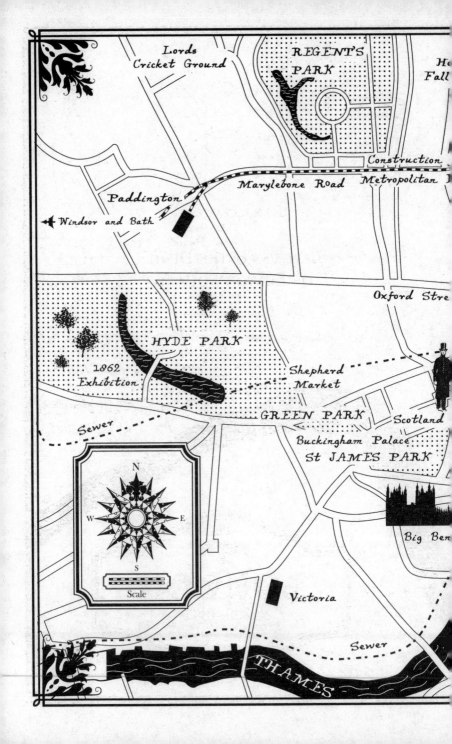

THE FIRST PERIOD
[1859]

The Watch Man — The Worm — The Spout
The Hydraulic Devil — The Night Porter
The Bugle — The Cadaver

THE WATCH MAN

I was alarmed to hear the creak of the constabulary gate in the wee small hours of my night shift. After three months in London, I was inured to the vulgar ways of street hawkers summoning their customers: water bearers clapping, coster-mongers wailing, all manner of whistling, yodelling and rattling. But this was the dead of night, and my heart began pounding as I put down my newspaper.

I shaded the desk lamp and stepped up to the window.

Through the shadowy lamplight I made out a small shape, methodically swinging the gate back and forth to produce that fearful creaking.

I hefted up the window. "Do they not use door knockers where you come from, laddie?"

"Hulloah!" the shape replied. "Coming out to play, Lilly Law? Shift your dish, will you?"

I glared at him.

"Hofficer," he went on with mock pomposity, "there is a hincident at Euston Square, and your hassistance is required."

"I don't care if there's a bonfire in the British Museum—"

"There'll be a bonfire up your lally crackers if you don't shift 'em."

I was impressed with the bairn's cheek. "Is it customary in

11

these parts for small boys to be summoning members of the constabulary?"

"Customary is exactly what it is, Captain Clocky." He sighed, as if to emphasise the depth of my ignorance, his breath forming clouds in the air. "Especially as where Wardle is concerned. You coming?"

"Hold your horses–"

"Or shall I say you were out?"

"Inspector Wardle? Of the Yard?"

"God help us. Don't they parlyaree inglesey where you come from?"

"We speak a damn sight better English than yous do." At this, he laughed, which I found even more annoying than his remarks. I was puzzled. "Wee man, you don't even know who I am."

"You're a Scotchman, and you're the Watch Man. Am I right or am I a Dutchman?"

My father told me not to stare. He said it showed ill breeding. But I was always third-rate at following father's precepts, and I stared at the boy. His hair was plastered across his forehead and his waistcoat a breeding ground for lichens. Yet, despite the whiff of sewer life about him, he had a jaunty grace. His eyes were a brilliant blue and his grin so charming it was impossible to dislike him.

"The great inspector," he said, "requests the use of your habilities. We had heard they was considerable, hard though that is to credit on current showing."

"Look, wee man. How do you know who I am? How does Wardle know?"

"Word travels fast here. You'll see. Everybody knows everybody else's business."

THE WORM

My companion introduced himself as Worm, of the Euston Square Worms, public company as yet unlimited, and off we set. He had an engaging way of steering me through the potholes and horse dung with the merest nod or touch on the elbow, as if I were the child and he the adult; as if he thought that I, a provincial, might not have encountered traffic. True enough, I was not used to such disorder on the streets at this hour of the night, nor the dank smell that assailed my nostrils. Though little did that matter now.

My chance had finally come. Three months I had been in the capital, without a hint of adventure. But Wardle's name was in the paper every other week. The *Times* called him "the second sharpest mind in the country". The stage of great events lay before me. Step forward with confidence, and I might find myself amongst the principal characters of London – of the world, no less.

When I applied to join the police, the Superintendent at Brunswick Square scrutinised my references thoroughly. I had been forced to swallow my pride and beg father for a good word from the Clockmakers' Guild. As I saw it, repairing watches required subtle deductive powers. For their owners invariably lied about how they came to be broken; nobody likes to admit they have dropped their quarter repeater in the bath. I thought it would be clear that I could be trusted with tasks beyond deskwork. The Superintendent rather saw it as proof that I could fix watches. Eager to make a good impression, I stayed up, fixing his mainspring by candlelight, until I could hear the Chapel Street marketeers setting up for the day. How bitterly I came to rue this effort. Within the week, watches were arriving from senior officers from Wapping to Westminster. My Superintendent set me to work on them all, only too pleased to notch up so many debts of gratitude. Even Mrs Jemmerson, the tea lady, brought in her grandmother's mantel clock, offering the payment of an extra biscuit at elevenses. I realised I had been hot-headed in quitting my apprenticeship; in father's workshop, all that mending would have earned me double my constable's wage.

Worm sauntered along, tipping his hat familiarly to the shadowy night people. As we emerged onto the broad thoroughfare of the Euston Road, he wrenched me back without warning, into the gutter. Foul play, I thought, staring about me in alarm. On the instant, a plush chaise careened past my nose, its shutters down, as if fleeing a crime. Water sprayed off the roof, as the well-appointed cabman urged the horses towards town, and the trill of reckless laughter sounded within.

Worm stared after it, eyes narrowed. He helped me to my feet, drew a grubby handkerchief from his waistcoat pocket and dabbed at my cape. "Dreaming of them high lands, was you?"

I breathed in deeply, frowning down at his ministrations. "What does a wight like you know of the Highlands?"

"I been about." He stuck out his chin. "Me and the Professor, we went to Bath once. Beautiful, them green fields. Cows and that."

"Cows?" I smiled. "I'm surprised you deigned to come back."

"Had to," he shrugged. "Professor got the scarpering spooks out of the city."

"Who's the Professor when he's at home?"

"One of the Worms. You'll see soon enough, if Wardle takes a liking to you. We do a lot of work for him."

He ran through the services offered by his association. Available at the shortest notice, competitive rates and unrivalled knowledge of the byways and backwaters. Services guaranteed, references from professional gentlemen across the capital.

"Finding things as is missing, somewhat of a speciality. With a sideline in unfinding things as may be better off lost."

I chuckled and looked at him more closely. The boy had a head for business. He would go far, given the start. "All above board, is it?"

His eyes grew indignantly wide. "I may have been known to sharp at skittles, but do I look like a hoister or a jolly?" Whereupon he fished inside his waistcoat and, with a theatrical flourish, handed me my own wallet.

I clutched at my pocket and took it back with ill grace, checking that my pennies were still there. "Thanking you kindly, I'm sure."

"You're a novice, you are. Guarding the public? Don't make me laugh. They'll eat you alive here." With a sigh he stepped out across the thoroughfare. "There is them as has no respect for the traditions we work in. Them as regards us as vermin and would gladly see us put down. But me – I'm in the habit of forgiving them their ignorance. Besides," he grinned, rubbing his hands, "what is life without a few enemies?"

I could never quite tell whether he was in earnest or not.

"Never mind that now." He pointed across the square, up towards the grand entrance of the station. "Have a peep at this."

I followed his gaze and burst out laughing.

THE SPOUT

Far across the broad square, a great fountain of water gushed up high into the air, in front of the grand new entrance to Euston Station.

It took me some moments to make sense of the scene. The square was bustling with people, as if the spout were the centre of a vast street fair. Could that be the case? Had the station owners arranged this impromptu spectacle to celebrate the completion of their great entryway? The masons' strike had long delayed so many building projects; and railway shareholders rubbed their hands at any publicity, however scurrilously gained.

"Good God," I said, shaking my head.

Worm was less impressed. "Ain't the first spout I seen, nor the biggest neither. One down by the river last week, nearly washed Parliament away. They're a menace, them hydrollah-rolical devils. Shift your mush, now, the old cove's waiting."

Worm ushered me on across the great road. The spout had extinguished half the gas lamps, but even in that dim light I could see that I must be mistaken. The grand colonnade was still not finished. The massive central portico was swathed in scaffold, and the central alcove waited to be filled by a great circular clock.

The spout was emanating from a strange contraption that stood square in front of the scaffolded columns; a vast winch, or a crane. The water shot up from the body of the machine, a box the size of a house covered only by a flimsy tarpaulin. The great vertical beams of the crane extended triangularly upwards to a pinnacle that surpassed the colonnade's monumental height. From the apex of the framework dangled a confusion of pulleys and cranks. Just below, swinging on colossal cables, some great piece of masonry was so buffeted by the water that I feared it would never reach its destined place atop the columns. Up and up the water gushed, into the dark night air – one hundred feet, one hundred and fifty – before it fanned outwards from the upper reaches of the machine, descending in a broad arc, like a rain shower on the station's mighty entrance.

All around was the hubbub of a ghoulish market. Bookmakers gave odds on the spout's longevity. Tea-sellers called out prices. Biblers were reading aloud, largely for their own benefit, and proffering leaflets from the Society for the Suppression of Vice about the ways of Satan – as if the assembled company were not well enough informed already. A swarm of night-time people, beggars, sweepers and fallen women, chattered in amusement. An unlikely herd of cattle off the late train was enjoying this last diversion before its final march down to the Farringdon market. This dash of country colour Worm ignored, as we pushed our way through the crowds to the far corner of the square near the station.

A short man in an overcoat stood beside the night porter's hut, scanning the crowd intently. As we approached him, I felt a tug at my sleeve.

"Lucifers, lucifers!" said a tiny child. With a debonair flick, he lit a match on his coat button, but it went out at once. Biting his tongue, he tried again, and again.

"Numpty," Worm hissed, "take a stroll."

The overcoated man turned abruptly. "What do you want, Worm?" he said in the cantankerous tones of the north of England. "I'm busy."

Worm tilted his head in my direction.

"I'm Lawless, sir." I held out my hand. "Campbell Lawless."

Worm sighed. "He's the Watch Man, like as you asked for, old cove."

Inspector Wardle of the Yard barely gave me a glance. He tossed a sixpence to the boy, and turned back towards the spout.

Worm checked the coin with his teeth and flipped it into the air, where it vanished. "Come on, Numpty," he said, pulling the sixpence out of his friend's ear. "While you stand agog at my dexterity, old chum, opportunities are going a-begging. That brolly man needs a helping hand..."

Wardle was a good deal older than me, a man as short as his overcoat was long. His hair was white, his hands thrust deep in his pockets, and perspiration glistened on his brow.

I stood upright and steady, trying to restrain my curiosity. At length I felt so uncomfortable, I made an effort at conversation. "Fairly comical accident, sir."

"You won't see me laughing," he said. He glanced darkly across the crowd. "Accident, you reckon?"

True enough, it seemed a strangely elegant disaster. I looked over the crowd and considered the spectacle. The great station buildings lay quiet to our left, closed to passengers for the night. In the boarding houses fringing the square, a surprising number of lamps were burning. Closer, the fair people of Euston made an ugly mob. They crowed and shouted, buying and selling, eating and drinking, while a shocking number of children amused themselves around the great hulking machinery, splashing in the puddles. On night duty we charged beggars and borough councillors for misdemeanours perpetrated under the influence. Could this be a drunken jape, only on a bigger scale?

Wardle narrowed his eyes. "There's a man hurt. Porter's watching him for now."

"How bad, sir?"

"Worse for wear, let's say."

"The machine blew up on him, did it?"

"Else he fell. Meddling somehow, like as not."

"Maybe he was trying to finish the building job. With the masons' strike, you know. Only he botched it..." I trailed off. The inspector hadn't asked for my theories.

"We'll deal with that soon enough," said Wardle brusquely. He turned to me at last, looking me up and down. "You know clocks, do you?"

I caught my breath, dismayed.

"Do you know them, yes or no?"

"I do, sir. You want me to fix your mainspring?"

"Might and all." He did not smile. Not quite. Instead, he walked all the way around me, as if I were a tree. Then he pointed up at the pinnacle of the crane. "Up and have a look, then, before any more meddling's attempted."

I peered up at the crane. Now that I looked more carefully, I could see: it was no monumental stone hanging there. I could make out the face of a gigantic timepiece, dangling aloft in front of the columns, held in a timber frame: the station clock, reading twenty to two, the time of the late train, an hour past.

"Oh, do keep away, won't you?" A bearded man in tails struggled out from the crowd, trying to shoo away children from the machine. They kept darting around him, yelping with delight. The man looked around, tugging at his beard, until he spotted us. "Who is in charge here? Officer, is it you who are in charge? I say! Could we keep these people away? My equipment has suffered enough tomfoolery for one day, don't you think?"

Wardle looked at him.

The man scratched at his forehead, where his bony temples protruded from uneven hair. He made an effort to collect himself. Deciding that I was more amenable than the inspector, he approached me first.

"Roxton Coxhill," he assured me with a damp, enthusiastic clutch. "Gerhart Roxton Coxhill. Bloody awkward bloody name. Friends call me Roxton. Simpler, eh? Otherwise you end up with Gert or Coxers, or Gertie boy, which won't do at all. Call me Roxton, do. And you are?"

The inspector intervened. "Wardle. We've met."

"Have we? I don't recall."

"Inspector Wardle, Scotland Yard."

"Ah, yes! Good. Capital, in fact. Just the man. Quite clear what's happened. Porter's asleep, some fool's been tampering with the apparatus. It's a bloody disgrace and a considerable embarrassment to me, and I shall be pleased to see it dealt with pretty damn quick. Now can we clear this rabble?"

"Mr Coxton–"

"Roxton Coxhill."

"Your contraption," Wardle snapped, "has left a man injured–"

"Serves the villain right, don't you think?"

"Who is to blame, Mr Coxton, I can't say. But this spectacle is not helping any of us. If your equipment is so ill-maintained that any Tom, Dick or Harry can crack it open–"

"Steady, now!"

"You may be liable," Wardle soldiered on, "for damages. Criminal negligence. Wouldn't you say so, Watchman?"

I nodded, quietly impressed with Wardle's doggedness.

"I see. Quite." Coxhill cast a sidelong glance at Wardle, as if to size him up. He turned and looked up at the crane, as if he were staring into the future. "It's a question of confidence, you see. They're trying to ruin confidence in me."

Wardle glowered. "We'll investigate that for ourselves. The minute you turn it off."

"Shouldn't bloody well be on, that's what's so galling. Can't see how it is, not at this hour of the night. My reservoirs will be quite emptied."

"Reservoirs?"

"Yes, it's revolutionary engineering. Reservoir's two miles away, up by Hampstead, but three hundred feet up, you see. All that weight of water, concentrated into pistons no more than an inch and a quarter across–"

"Shut down your bloody machine," said Wardle, "and let

my constable make his own judgement."

"Quite." Coxhill looked around uneasily. "You see, I would, of course." A boy with an upturned nose was standing quietly behind us, spinning a top along a length of string, from one hand to the other. Coxhill swatted irritably at him, but the little chap ducked away and made good his escape. "It's just that my fellow should be here, by rights. Dashed nuisance. He'd have the thing off in two ticks. He's a veteran of Sevastopol, don't you know."

Wardle snorted. "Watchman, shift that crowd. Then up and look at the clock for us."

I stared at the crane. There was a ladder fixed to its side, but it must be sodden. Coxhill leapt in. "Oh, I hardly think that safe, Inspector."

"You would warn us, I'm sure, if there were any danger of it exploding."

"Of course, Inspector. Not that it will. These idlers, though. If we could clear them away... Ha! Here's Hunt, with the chaise. Marvellous."

A stylish carriage, embossed with florid lettering in gold leaf, pulled up behind us at the edge of the square. A bull terrier of a man leapt out and marched over to us. He seemed ill at ease in his starched shirt, suit and tie. "What's this bloody monkey business, sir?"

Coxhill coughed, to draw the man's attention to us. "This is Hunt. My right-hand man, you know."

With a glance at his master, Hunt turned to us with a military bearing. "Hunt, HECC. At your service."

Wardle looked unimpressed.

"Excuse me," I frowned, "but what is the HECC?"

Roxton Coxhill smiled. "You've surely heard of the Hydraulic Engines Corporation of the Capital?"

I indicated that I had not.

"Well, you soon will. Won't they, Hunt?"

"They will, sir."

"I'd say we're attracting considerable interest, wouldn't you?"

"That's right, sir."

"Considerable. There's talk in the City, you know." Coxhill tapped the side of his nose. "Next big thing. Investment mania. It'll outstrip the railways, mark my words."

Wardle looked at the spout. "With equipment like this?"

"Early days, Inspector, early days." Coxhill stuck out his jaw. "You'll see. These machines of mine can lift an elephant, or cut a man into thrupenny bits." His eyes gleamed. "They're giving us statutory protection. I have the Prince of Wales' assurance. A Royal Seal is on its way."

I couldn't help but picture a portly seal, with Coxhill's whiskers, flopping up the Euston Road towards us. He went on, his poise entirely recovered. "Now, Hunt, my good man, help the poor constable by turning the thingummy off, while I have a nice chat with the inspector."

THE HYDRAULIC DEVIL

The colonnade stood high and proud, like the entrance to a Greek temple. The crane in front of it towered above the crowd too, the height of twenty men. I buttoned up my greatcoat, pulled my regulation oilskin tight around my neck, and strode forwards.

For the first time in my career, I felt the rabble's hostility to the uniform's blue-and-white striped cuffs. The crowd was gathered before the metal railings surrounding the two patches of withered grass at the heart of the square. As I asked them to move, they turned their backs. They eyed me with suspicion, or with loathing. For a moment, my courage failed. My first chance to shine, I thought, and I'm not able for it.

Then I noticed another constable in the crowd. And another, and another. Of course. There was a series of fixed posts along the Euston Road. I even knew a couple of the fellows by sight, from walking home after night duty. They were watching, already helping, quietly cautioning people away from the spout. Once I realised this, the mob seemed to resume its aspect of genial indifference. Most of them at least stayed well back. A few children played games closer to the machine; the odd merrymaker splashed around with an umbrella, but never for long.

Soaked already, I approached the body of the crane. I raised the tarpaulin to reveal a door. I turned the handle tentatively, half expecting a flood to knock me off my feet. To my surprise, it opened as easily as any door, and I peered into the gloomy engine room.

At the mess of sopping levers and cables, gear shafts and cogs, I frowned. I am no engineer, nor do I wish to write a manual for saboteurs and activists. Yet one part of the apparatus appeared distinctly makeshift. Cogs affixed to the timber ceiling fed slender wires from the hydraulic levers to the pistons and cylinders at the machine's heart; several pieces resembled watch parts, albeit on a massive scale. From these emerged twine cords and a rope that passed through a duct in the ceiling. It must be there that some valve or pipe had come into play as a vent for the pressurised water. Hence the spout.

I little understood the levers, but I could surely work out how to shut off the machine. That would earn me points in Wardle's book. He was right, it hardly seemed an accident.

I heard the slosh of footsteps behind me.

"Oi! Want to get yourself killed?"

I turned to face the terrier's glare. "I've to look at that clock up there."

Hunt glanced aloft, wiped the water from his eyes, and grinned at me. "On you go then."

"While your machine empties the London waterworks on us?" I narrowed my eyes. "I'd rather switch it off first."

"I'll deal with that," he said.

"Will you now?"

"I will," he replied, pushing past me, "with your inspector's say-so."

I stepped back reluctantly.

"Have their guts for garters, I will," Hunt muttered. "Bloody tampering monkeys."

I looked over towards Wardle, but he was nowhere to be seen, doubtless collecting the evidence, examining every detail, interviewing every suspect. I would have to take the terrier's word for it.

"Clear out of it, copper. I'll have it sorted in two shakes."

I left Hunt on his tiptoes, peering into the machine. He growled under his breath, as he tugged at one lever after another, favouring force over finesse. Remarkable that I could form such a dislike for the man in the space of such a short exchange. I should have guessed that he understood hydraulics no better than I.

I withdrew to the side of the machine, where the narrow ladder was fitted. It looked like a relic of the siege of Sevastopol. I looked up at the streams of water coursing down over the scaffold's upper platforms. I am no more fearful of heights than the next man, but I did not relish the prospect of climbing that ill-functioning contraption while it spouted like a victory fountain. Yet I must impress. I must keep my wits about me. Others might deal with injured men and malfunctioning machines, I had been chosen to glean something from the maltreated clock. I had been summoned by an inspector of the Yard, no less.

I turned to the colonnade's scaffolding, leaving Hunt to his mischief. This ladder looked hardier. As I ventured my ascent, the fine insistent spray became a regular torrent, cascading down upon me. From the first platform I could see the gleam of some kind of silver piping, wedged atop the body of the crane where the great cables emerged: the source of the spout.

Steadily I clambered upwards, grateful for my oilskin cape. The timber was devilish slippery and my hands numb from cold.

It was some minutes before I reached the upper platform. The wind on high was biting. With runnels from my hood dripping over my brows, I thought it wisest to crawl across the sodden timbers on hands and knees to inspect the piece.

The crane's apex rose up above the level of the scaffolding, a few feet out from the platform. Dangling from the winches, just above me and out of reach, the clock juddered and swirled with the force of the spout. An elegant piece it was, fine workmanship evident in the tidy lettering: the IIII perfectly balancing the VIII.

But from my vantage point I could see only the face of the clock. To garner more information, I would have to examine its reverse. I could see no alternative. I would have to clamber across onto the crane.

I reached out, but it eluded my grasp. Sacrificing elegance for safety, I lay down flat on my stomach. I could feel the water soaking through my clothes as I inched my way to the very edge of the platform. I swung a leg out into space, and grabbed hold of the crane. With a fearful lurch, I tugged myself across the gap and onto the next ladder.

The crane swayed for a moment, and there was an outburst of applause from below. When it stopped swaying, I glanced down. I wished at once that I had not. They had doubtless offered odds on my chances, half the crowd were rooting for me to conquer the summit. The rest would gladly see me impaled on the railings of the square. A fine end that would be.

My heart was pounding. I noticed silhouettes in the windows of the boarding houses. I shivered, feeling myself part of a lurid show, but who had organised the piece I did not know. Coxhill and Hunt wanted their machine rescued from ignominy. Wardle needed some revelatory detail from my scrutiny; probably the inspector was already extracting confessions from the injured man. All I could do was play my little role, dangerous as it was. I felt strangely alone. Then I caught sight of someone waving far below. Worm stood with a thin-faced man in a bowler hat. For a moment I thought it was Hunt, but the terrier was still making mischief at the base of the crane beneath me. Worm and companion looked up at me in friendly fascination. Amongst that sea of avid countenances, I was reassured to make out his amicable features. I took a deep breath and turned to my task.

The clock swung some feet above me, sloshed hither and thither by the streams of water. Gingerly, I climbed a couple of rungs, praying that the sodden wood wouldn't give way. My left boot slipped. I clutched on for grim death, ignoring the shouts from below. I held my breath, climbed two more rungs, then wound my arms and legs through the crane's framework to hold myself firm.

I reached out to pull the clock's timber frame towards me. A precarious prospect, but it was lighter than I expected, and I easily drew it close. I strained to read the clockmaker's name, inscribed in minuscule print on the casing. I had it all but deciphered – Allnutt & Gatz of Clerkenwell, or maybe Allnutt & Franz – when the timber frame jolted.

I looked down in alarm. I had better hurry, before Hunt did

something foolish. I gently rotated the framework to examine the back of the clock. I felt in my cape pocket and breathed a little prayer of relief. Watchmaker habits die hard. I had with me the screwdriver-cum-wrench that I used for odd jobs and on-the-spot repairs. Father considered this a slovenly approach. Each timepiece, he said, requires the implement most apt for the job. But this was no time for niceties. I hooked my arm through the clock's packing frame, and tugged it closer still. I was surprised to see that the water seemed to be coursing right through it. A station clock that could not withstand the elements made no more sense than a house without a roof. My curiosity was piqued. The back panel was just accessible between the timbers. I set myself to undo the corner screws of the panel, anticipating that familiar reverie of puzzling at cogs and querying springs until the parts should connect and the clock's secrets be mine. The casing I saw was beautifully effected. Yet how slackly the screws were driven in. Father had a point: to inspect such a clock's workings, by rights, a man should require a full set of tools. This panel was too easily shifted. Indeed, there were already scratches around the screw holes. Strange, on a brand new clock.

I swung the panel round to lay bare the clock's innards and gasped in surprise. The mechanism had been removed. The pendulum was there, dangling from the barrel that was affixed to the great wheel, as you would expect. But the rest of the wheelwork was nowhere to be seen.

Could it simply never have been installed? Unthinkable. Granted, they would have to put the clock in place before lowering the pendulum and setting it in motion. But to wait until it was perched thirty yards aloft before installing the rest? That would be not just awkward, but downright stupid. Stupid too to leave it hanging in mid-air, with the platform right there beside it. Why not pull it to safety onto the scaffolding? Or into its rightful place, crowning the colonnade?

I stared at what was left of the workings. The key to the mystery lay before me, if only I could fathom its intricate augury. I determined to note every detail. It might have been by chance or design that the clock showed twenty to two, but there was nothing to propel the hands. The frame had been neatly opened, and the most delicate parts of the gearing mechanism – pinions, spindles and motion work – were gone. Judging from the scratches on the casing, the mechanisms had been extracted in some haste. Coxhill might well complain that his hydraulics had been tampered with, but the clock had seen equal mischief.

The pulley above me creaked. The spout sputtered momentarily, and the fountain began to die away: a blessed relief in my precarious post, though I was already soaked. Cheers arose from the crowd as the dying spray blew out over their heads.

Then the pulley jerked again. I drew back instinctively, wrenching my arm out of the clock's packing frame. With a chafing rasp, it began to drop. My reverie broke, and I clutched myself to the crane. Hunt had managed to shut off the water supply, but the brakes on the cables were hydraulic. In turning off the water, he had released the winch as well.

The clock fell away from me, ever so slowly at first. My first thought was, would I be held responsible? There was no way I could have held on to it, all by myself. More likely it would have dragged me to my death below.

I opened my mouth to call out, but it was too late. The world seemed to fall silent.

The clock gained speed as it fell, tumbling down onto the body of the crane. When it hit the ground, I turned my face away. Not from any danger. More a kind of shame at the destruction of a beautiful thing.

The crash echoed over the mob, rebounding off the grand hotels across the square like a great explosion. I looked down to see the merrymakers shrink back, as shards of glass scattered wide, glimmering in the dim light; a second sound reached me, of the pieces splintering, like the fizzing of a frantic Roman candle.

The mob redoubled their whooping. Within moments, children darted out from the crowd to claim their spoils. By the time I descended, there would be damn all evidence of the clock left. Everyone applauded one last time, as if it were the finale to a fine show of fireworks.

THE NIGHT PORTER

The porter wore a beard as tangled as if he were fresh off a whaler from the Southern Seas. "On my watch," he moaned. "A body, on my watch."

"A body?" I stared at the bundle of blankets piled in the corner. Wardle had not said the man was dead. I considered for a discreditable moment taking a blanket for myself, for I was soaked to the skin and shivering.

"One half instant I close my eyes, and there she blows. There she blows! Poor cove's blowed himself clean apart, so he has."

"Calm yourself, man. Tell me all that has happened since you came on duty."

"This repair man, it was, see. Early evening, he turned up. Weren't expecting him none, but he was that pleasant–"

"From the hydraulic company, was he?"

"Nobody never tells me nothing." He screwed up his brows. "Anywise, the fellow went about his business in exemplatory fashion. Full of wit and the argot, he was. Spoke Thieves' Latin and costermonger's Aye-talian. We had a time, we did. He was highly sympathetical, not like most, that don't see the hard road I travel on."

These effusions seemed a trifle excessive. There was an aroma in the air which made me suspicious. I spotted a bottle beneath the man's chair. Sterner enquiries revealed that it was a gift of poteen furnished by this same repair man. They had shared a toast, or two, to Queen and country. In fact, when pressed, the porter had no clear recollection of the repair man at his work at all. It was not even clear what the man was meant to be repairing.

"Was it the crane he was fixing, or the clock?"

"The clock?" A haunted look came into his eye. "I've kept watch over that accursed piece this sixmonth. Ticking, tocking. Tocking, ticking. Drive a man mad."

"Here?" If he were telling the truth – and I doubted he had the wit to lie – then his phantom repair man must have whisked the clock away, removed the mechanism and then winched what was left on high. I glanced around the rotten little shed. "Why in God's name did they keep the clock here?"

"Should have gone up long since, but for the lock-out, see. Glad to be rid of it."

"The lock-out?"

"That's right. George Potter and his Most Worshipful Association of Master Carpenters. A nine-hour day he wants, and woe betide them as flaunt him."

"You mean the masons' strike?"

"What stone you been hiding under? He's took out all the guilds, since them nine stonemasons fell from the scaffold up the Westminster Palace Hotel."

I thought of my escapade up the crane and shuddered. "Do you see the masons' hand in this?"

"Bain't got the foggiest, me." He gave a theatrical shrug. "Like as not it's the Imperial after the Independent again."

"The what?"

"Gas Wars, I mean to say."

"Ah yes." The gas companies were in the habit of blowing up each other's pipes in territorial disputes. There had been an explosion at the Imperial Gas Works, down by King's Cross, not two weeks previous. "You blame the gas men, do you?"

"Did I say that?" He stared wide-eyed. "I's just mentioning, sir. No more, no less. You won't hear no rash alligators from this particular quarter."

"Nothing would surprise me," I murmured, "after the drop you've taken."

"Oh, sir. Have mercy," he blinked. "I never touches it, me, in the normal run of things, not on duty at least, I don't. I's dutiful to the extreme case. Only, this evening–"

The door flew open and in barged Hunt, huffing and puffing as if to blow down the station. "Bloody gauges and levers. I'll string them up, I will." His trousers glittered with glass, but he was not chastened in the slightest. He turned on the porter. "Here, is it you that's let some monkey tamper with our machine?"

The porter seemed to fear him terribly. "I got a wife, sir, and children–"

"Shut up." Hunt prowled back and forth across the tiny space. "Blithering fool. This the coward that blew himself up, is it?"

"A body, on my watch!" He hid his face in his hands.

"Got what he deserved. Undermining our business. Let's have a look-see." Before I could object, Hunt pulled away the heap of blankets.

A musty odour arose from the body. All manner of charges I had drawn up in the bleak hours of night duty, but I had not seen anyone killed. The last corpse I had viewed so close was my mother's, when I was a child.

The dead man was middle-aged, perhaps older. His face was stone grey, with dark blotches that looked like bruises, though they might have been dirt. His clothes were clean but shabby. Was this really the orchestrator of tonight's entertainment? He didn't look like a militant radical, nor a master thief.

Hunt stared at the body and turned quite pale. It seemed strange that I, the novice, should be unperturbed by the corpse, while this beast fresh from a Crimean battlefield stood mesmerised.

Although there was no doubt that the man had breathed his last, I felt obliged somehow to confirm it. I said a quick prayer, then bent over him. My stomach lurched to feel his neck so chill and hard. I felt ashamed to think I had been exulting in the mystery of that night with him lying there cold and dead.

Yet where were the signs of his death? There were no traces of blood; his limbs seemed regular and in good order. His clothes were sopping wet and his features rigid. But his hair looked clean, and his mouth was serene and smiling. I was particularly struck by that smile.

Was he an unskilled labourer, who botched his attempt to work the crane, after dampening the porter's vigilance? Had he meddled with the clock and fallen, blasted by the water burst? Could it have been a booby trap?

At the sound of Wardle's voice outside, I went smartly to the door. Coxhill was with him, talking earnestly to two men with notebooks.

"Compensation?" Coxhill was saying. "Pshaw! It should be we that receive compensation. Litigious bloody society we live in. It was the end of ancient Athens and it'll be the end of us."

"Ah, Watchman," said Wardle. He looked past me into the hut, then manoeuvred so as to block the newsmen's view.

"Sir," I said quietly, "the man's dead, sir."

"Is he, now?" The inspector glanced back at Coxhill, eyes narrowed, but he was fully occupied giving the papers something to write about.

"Inspector," said one of the newsmen, "can you spare us a moment?"

Wardle turned back to me brusquely. "And the clock?"

"Yes, sir. Somebody's been tampering–"

"Gunpowder? Explosives?"

"No, sir, but somebody's taken–"

"Enough."

"But, sir," I insisted, desperate to show off my discovery. "Half the clock's been–"

"I said, that's all for now, son." He looked past me; Hunt was still staring at the body. "Don't be giving nothing away. Not till we know who we can trust."

"Inspector?" whined one of the newsmen.

Wardle jabbed a finger up at my lapels. "Written report, on my desk, Friday."

I hesitated. "My superintendent, sir–"

"Which station?"

"Brunswick Square, sir."

"I'll have a word."

"Thank you, sir." I blinked at my good fortune, to be included so firmly in the enquiry. "Should I take the body somewhere, sir?"

He looked surprised. "What's that?"

"For post-mortem, or something of the sort?"

"Why not?" he said, nodding to himself. "Mr Coxhill, step inside, would you?"

"Inspector?" The reporter raised his pencil in anticipation. "Jack Scholes, local rag. I understand someone is injured?"

"Blown himself up, has he?" said Coxhill, pushing past me. "Damned fool."

Wardle eyed him cannily. "Watchman, take that body down yon college mortuary. Ask for Simpson, he's our man nights." He lowered his voice. "I want to know how he died. And when. Exactly when. Don't take half-cock answers, mind. I'll have another word with the toff and his guard dog." He turned to confront the newsmen, gritting his teeth as he shut the door behind him.

"Dash it all, I can hardly bear to look." Coxhill was blathering away to himself. "Blighter's family are bound to try it on. It's too beastly."

I watched him closely. "Am I to understand that this is your own repair man, Mr Coxhill?"

"Repair man? Our machines don't need repairs. No, no." He tugged at his beard. "Not one of ours, is he, Hunt? Hunt! I say, do buck up."

The terrier looked away from the body, subservient again. "Never saw him before in my life, sir."

All of a sudden, the night porter piped up. He gaped at the corpse, then he stood up, clapping his hands in surprise.

"Hulloah!" he said. "That ain't him! When me and your inspector was dragging him in, I didn't see it, I was that upset." Drunk, you mean, I thought to myself. "No, sirs, I didn't see it in the dark and the wet and all, but that ain't the same fellow. My man had these intensitive eyes. Trust those eyes with your life, so you would. I'd know him anywhere. This! This is a different codger entirely."

Euston Evening Bugle

9th November, 1859

LAST TRUMP SOUNDS FOR LONDON

The metropolis is doomed. Veteran reformer, Mr Edwin Chadwick, prophesies the imminent demise of the capital in his pamphlet published today, "Smell is Disease."

How wonderfully smell concentrates the mind. For years Londoners have been dying in their cohorts of cholera, typhus and worse. Yet it took the "Great Stink" of last summer to convince panicked parliamentarians to stomach the cost of the Sewers Bill. Poor Mr Disraeli, clutching a handkerchief to his sensitive nose as he ran from the chamber!

Still, our reliance on Progress and Capital to cure our maladies seems increasingly vain. Thus far, the Metropolitan Board of Works' monumental expenditure has effected only an embarrassment of traffic jams and a shortage of bricks. The stink lingers on.

DEVILS AT EUSTON SQUARE

Last night, a water-powered crane – called an "hydraulic devil" – burst outside Euston Station, killing a vagrant. A sizeable crowd applauded, as passengers from the late train were greeted with an impromptu fountain. Inspector Wardle of Scotland Yard insists that readers of the *Bugle* may go safely about their business. Nonetheless, the use of hazardous machinery in defiance of the builders' strike must be cause for alarm.

Another alarming local development sees the Metropolitan Railway sink a preliminary shaft at Euston Square next month. In approving the short-sighted plans of the Hon Mr Charles Pearson, championed by that misguided publication, the *Clerkenwell Horn*, the Traffic Select Committee has ignored the *Bugle*'s manifestly superior proposal. Our "Crystal Way" would have spanned the city with road, rail and pedestrian tiers, triumphantly solving congestion in a feat of engineering to make the world gasp.

"Shameless profiteering will lead London to the same dismal end as Rome and Babylon," predicts Mr Chadwick, in his Sanitary Committee pamphlet. "We stand in need of drains, not trains."

The *Bugle* awaits with curiosity the collapse of tunnels, annihilation of property, and subterranean fumigations that must inevitably result from Pearson's infernal undertakings.

ROYAL CELEBRATIONS

None of which can dampen the frolics of the younger royals. Albert Edward, Prince of Wales, returned to Windsor Castle this morning.

Following a spirited start to his university career, rumour has it that he is to be created a duke. Tonight Prince "Bertie" sets aside a raucous social schedule to celebrate his eighteenth birthday with the Queen and the Prince Consort.

Amongst such banquets and honours, may the ills of the capital remain to him but a distant murmur.

Anonymous Telegram, 8th November

"To Roxton Coxhill & His Rotund Friend":
     GUY FAWKES WAS A GENIUS.

THE CADAVER

It was perhaps unwise to take a cab, especially as my wage was only nineteen shillings a week, lodgings not included, and Wardle had made no mention of reimbursement, but I had no idea what an interest London cabmen take in matters that don't concern them. I didn't feel I could ask the man to help me shift the corpse; at least, not without a substantial tip. Fortunately, Worm & co. offered their services.

Worm organised his chums with a grim efficiency, and a sort of tact, which made my earlier eagerness seem all the more inappropriate. He called upon Numpty the matchseller, and the Professor, a precocious tyke with an upturned nose. How three children and I lugged a stiff, wet corpse from the hut to the cab and the cab to the hospital without attracting the suspicion of morbid bystanders I will not relate, but Worm and his tired companions made a fitting sort of cortège. The Professor put on as brave a face as you could wish to see; but I did repent of involving them in such dark business when I saw the poor wee fellow brush away a tear.

Worm refused the coins I offered. "On the house, Watchman," he said with a wink. "Just bear us in mind, eh? Taxing time you've had tonight. Teetering on top of that thing like a tomtit up a tree. We was that worried, we could barely look. Good luck, eh, Watchman."

While I waited for Simpson, uncomfortable in my vigil, I took the notion to check the dead man's pockets. There was nothing to identify him. No personal effects. Just a couple of coins. There was no more I could think of to do.

I sat down, dead tired of a sudden. The last time I had been in hospital was when I gashed my thumb in father's workshop. My recollection of the Edinburgh Royal Free was incomparably bright and clean beside this dark, shabby locality.

Twenty minutes later, a corpulent man with starched cuffs breezed in.

"Another cadaver? Wonderful. *Caro data vermibus*. Flesh given to the worms. Ca, da, ver, you see. It's an acronym, of sorts." Simpson glanced up at me for the first time. He raised his eyebrows at my sodden clothing, then turned back to the corpse. "Not a classical scholar, I take it? Never mind. You're Wardle's new man, are you?"

I coughed uncertainly.

He made the briefest examination, glancing at the face, the chest and especially at the feet, nodding knowledgeably. It was hard to credit that this informed him of anything. "What's the purpose behind bringing me a tramp?"

"He's dead. Is that not sufficient?"

"People die every day, Constable. That's not reason enough to waste my time. Wardle rarely requires inquests for vagabonds. What is it he wants to know?"

I frowned, recollecting my instructions. "When and how he died."

"Let us not be coy, Constable. If you wish, we shall lay bare his innards. If not–"

"I do not need to know what he ate yesterday, if that is what you mean."

"Yesterday?" he laughed. "This fellow did no eating yesterday. But come, have you a specific query?"

I restrained myself from a sharp reply. "How did he die, man?"

"Bruising. Severe. To head and chest. Internal bleeding." He thought a moment. "I would hazard that cerebral failure preceded cardiac, but it's impossible to be sure, so long after the fact."

I stared at him. "What caused these injuries? The man was

involved in an accident. I want to know what happened."

"I am a doctor, Constable, not a clairvoyant."

"Was violence done to him?"

"I cannot say. The bruising suggests that he fell heavily, but I cannot rule out the use of blunt instruments."

"I see. When did he die?"

He wafted a hand through the air. "We cannot know exactly."

I mustered my patience. "Could you see your way to giving an estimate, doctor?"

"If that will suffice."

"It will have to."

"In my opinion, this man died close on one week ago."

"One hour ago, you mean?"

"I said one week, Constable, and I meant one week."

I looked down at the cold, grey face. I believe my heart started to beat faster. "Dr Simpson, the accident – the incident – took place barely two hours past."

"As you will. I have given you my professional opinion."

"On what do you rest that opinion?"

"To explain such things to laymen like yourself can be rather tiresome."

"I would appreciate an attempt."

He checked his pocket watch in irritation and appeared to come to a decision. "In these uncommon circumstances, we may be able to confirm the time of death. Can you spare a quarter hour?"

Outside the hospital, he hailed a cab. We hurtled through the lamplit byways, past the Brunswick Square constabulary, between the Foundling Hospital and Gardens, all the way to the Free Hospital on the Gray's Inn Road. He paid the fare without a word, which I was glad to see, as my pockets were bare.

Strolling in as if he owned the place, Simpson bustled me through tortuous corridors, signally less kempt than the establishment we had just left. He moved rapidly for such a large man, and we arrived in an oppressive dormitory, filled with groaning and moaning. As my eyes grew accustomed to the dark, I made out dreadful shapes, cramped close together in an atmosphere that smacked of the grave.

"Ah, Bunny," Simpson greeted the portly matron. "Fetch me the ward book. I want to check a time of death from last week. Beggar's name escapes me. But I do recall he had a club foot."

"That'll be Shuffler, sir," the woman nodded obligingly. "The tosher, that good Mr Skelton brought in."

"I believe you're right, Bunny. He certainly smelt like a sewer."

As she retreated to a side room, Simpson glanced at his watch again and tutted. He addressed me sharply. "I would place the man's death last Thursday evening."

"You're convinced it is the same man?"

"My recollection of your man's odour may be circumstantial evidence, but the club foot, you will grant, is hard to refute. If he was alive to suffer the accident of which you speak, it was a miracle beyond belief. You see, I visit this ward on Thursday mornings, and I saw your man here, Thursday last. He had already suffered the injuries that killed him. He was quite at death's door, I tell you, and suffering rather. Even without the present evidence of nascent putrefaction, I would doubt that he lived through that night. Bunny will look up the details. Kindly inform the college hospital whether the Yard will require the body, else they will deal with it as normal."

"Doctor, I need to know how the man died. You're telling me that tonight's events had nothing to do with it. What am I to think?"

"Those questions, Constable, may come within your ambit.

They have little to do with mine. I leave you in Bunny's capable hands – and I suggest to you strongly that you quit this place and hurry home to your bed, if you don't want to catch your death. Good day."

THE SECOND PERIOD
[1860]

EUSTON EVENING BUGLE

30th June, 1860

ALL IN DANGER OF BEING BURIED ALIVE

The city's influence stretches from Suez to Saskatchewan, and from beneath the Thames to the Himalayan heights. Yet these far-flung victories, claims Mr Edwin Chadwick, are outweighed by shameful deteriorations here at home.

The *Bugle* accepted Mr Chadwick's challenge to tour the Empire's least salubrious frontier – our own East End.

Cruel irony lurks in Green Street and Pleasant Place. A century back, the names may have been apt, as the last of the Huguenot fugitives reared dahlias in summer houses laced by Virginia creeper. Today this antheap of alleys is lined by ruinous tenements reeking with abominations. The wells of Clerkenwell are poisoned and the only greenness in Bethnal Green is that of putrefaction. One alley sees eighteen families served by a rotten pump, ruined with rusty nails, which functions weakly for twelve minutes a day, save Sundays. The struggle for this tap makes for battles every bit as bitter as Balaclava.

An Inspector of Nuisances took exception to Mr Chadwick's report that a shed of sixty cows stands against a shoemaker's house whose children are dying of putrid fever. Pigs are also kept close by. This Inspector declared vehemently that there are but fifty cows, that the shed is at least eighteen feet from the house, and that it is many moons since pigs were kept there. The cost of bribing such soulless functionaries is negligible to the miserly landlords who prosper thereby, little troubled by continual deaths. Are the wonderful sanitary schemes, which taxpayers are funding, nothing more than costly failures?

With what abandon, meanwhile, Parliament sanctions daredevil schemes such as Charles Pearson's diabolical railway. Pickaxes, hammers and steam drills make a mayhem of the New Road, and those who have nothing watch even the little they have – their homes – swept away. The police turn a blind eye to the Local Management Act, and thousands resort to illegal lodgings, teeming with disease and death.

INDECENCIES OF PROGRESS

Beneath a poisonous mound of ill-built walls, through which weeps dank, unwholesome matter, Mr Chadwick showed us a family cowering in a windowless dungeon. Naked but for black rags across their middles, in darkness at the height of noon, they had not the means or inclination for the most ordinary observations of decency. So continues the round of vice, filth, and poverty, destitution without parallel in Calcutta or Peking. There is nothing picturesque in such misery, however our popular novelists may depict it.

Mr Chadwick called out to the woman, "How many children have you?"

"Four," she replied.

"Have you lost any?"

"Five, and one more given over by the doctor."

Where are they to go, these wretches, reared in the dark and the dirt? Whither those dispossessed by the advance of Progress? How can we purge our metropolis of this fearful multitude? For, after all, nobody can be held responsible. In the Great Battle for Life that every day confronts us, there are bound to be casualties. Suffering and Evil are nature's admonitions; they cannot be got rid of. Diseases are nature's way of separating the grain from the chaff.

We must be thankful for small mercies. Let us reflect that, despite the continuing fevers afflicting thousands across the capital, nobody of significance has yet died.

INFERNAL SCHEMES & RESURRECTIONS

From these filthy ashes, at least an occasional phoenix rises. George Shillibeer gave us the omnibus thirty years ago. Undercut by the London General Omnibus Company, with their modern fleet packing in passengers, old George has resurrected his ailing business. Shillibeer passengers will henceforth travel alone and always arrive "late". The demand for funeral services is always on the increase.

Letter to Roxton Coxhill, Received Late 1859

> *To Roxton Coxton Foxton Bloxton and friend:*
>
> *We take your foul act as a declaration of war.*
> *Your loathing servant,*
> ....
>
> *(signed in unintelligible symbols)*

The Wilderness

Writing my report for Wardle was an ordeal. Why did I suffer so over it? I had written reports galore during night shifts, but this was a far cry from those simplistic charges. This was a mystery. A report for Scotland Yard had to be more weighty, surely. More accurate; more brilliant.

That night I wrote my text, and rewrote over and again. I would frequently finish a long passage with a sense of triumph, only to be appalled when I sat back to check it over. Not only were my sentences poorly constructed, full of solecisms and non-sequiturs, but I seemed to be recording irrelevant details, or obvious ones. I would comb through, pick out the few phrases worth salvaging, and begin again.

I may not be a fluent stylist, but I am careful with details. I knew from my work with watches that one cog misaligned may throw an entire mechanism off-kilter. Besides the facts, I limited myself to the most clear-cut deductions: that the man who had beguiled the night porter was surely the saboteur; that, contrary to appearances, the body was placed there already lifeless; that the saboteur was therefore still at large. Why the corpse was placed there, I refrained from speculating. I also restrained myself from labelling Hunt's behaviour as odd, reluctant to give in to personal opinion; but I tried to leave no doubt that he was to blame for the clock having fallen. Nor did I mention the Worms' help.

Late on the Thursday afternoon I found my way down to Scotland Yard, exhausted. I was disgruntled to find Wardle out, on special duty at Windsor. I reluctantly left the precious document, copied over in my neatest hand, with his assistant, a sour-faced sergeant called Jackman. Later that evening, my Superintendent called me in to check if I had dealt with "that other business". I was elated to know that Wardle had indeed had a word, as promised.

After delivering the report, I heard nothing.

What did I expect? Compliments from on high? A sensational trial? I was not so naïve. Yet I had carried out the tasks entrusted me. I thought I had made a good impression. As weeks turned into months, with still no word, I found myself going over and over my actions of that night. Where had I erred? Had I given away information that should have been kept secret? Was it inappropriate to engage the Worms' help? Perhaps I should have been sceptical of Simpson's revelation, confiscated the ward book, taken the matron's details.

I scanned the press. I saw only one piece about the spout, which seemed less concerned with the facts than with trumpeting its author's ill-founded opinions. The HECC launched their shares on the market with some fanfare, though no sign of that whiskery Royal Seal. There was little mention of "the second sharpest mind in the country". Instead a Superintendent Foley in Wiltshire stole the limelight, solving the Road Hill House killings. Such sensations set the country alight momentarily. Then everyone returned to Mr Dickens' magazine, protesting how moving was his *Tale of Two Cities*, and how significant, though I wished it had been a Tale of Two Pretties or Two Ditties, as it had no jokes like his old books, leastways none that I could understand.

Nights were the worst. As a junior officer, I spent two months out of three on night duties, sometimes at the desk, with the fire always aglow, but more often freezing my socks off down at my fixed post by Holborn. At least, with my woollen underclothes, I was accustomed to the Edinburgh winters. The poor souls passing me by seemed never to have seen the like of it. The winter was so bitter, sometimes they cried out with the cold. If a poor roustabout stole scraps of timber to try and keep his family alive, they all ended up in the House of Correction. Meanwhile a toff who stole a cab, knocked over a girl and lamed the horse could laugh off the charges, secured from scandal by his bank balance and fine friends.

I coughed and spluttered through the palpable fogs. Glossop, nose raw from sneezes, told tales of other officers: the Superintendent's rheumatic pains, Plympton's bilious attacks, Rout's fistula. The whole city had the ague.

Those months after the spout hardened me to London life. A restless, hungry feeling ate away at me, not just from the din and the stink and the fevers. How little my life had changed. If I was lonely, I had brought that loneliness with me. If I was disappointed, it was because I had entertained unreasonable hopes. I had come south expecting London to amaze me. I soon learned that few of the streets were paved with gold, and that to grasp one opportunity demanded a multitude of sins.

I remember one night-reveller fondly. Mr Wetherell was brought in by a publican as a suspected gentleman thief, having offered the entire establishment drinks on the house. In fact, he was celebrating his early retirement from the underwriting trade.

I dismissed the publican, and Mr Wetherell told me how he had found his business increasingly fraudulent and deceitful.

"Insurance," he said, "is a form of corporate gambling whereby the little man loses everything and the big fish get away unscathed."

We passed the wee small hours toasting his leaving – his hipflask held a finer malt than mine – until he left for the morning train.

I foolishly mentioned his story to Glossop. The carrot-haired northerner regarded me strangely. Previous to this, he had considered me "holier than thou". Now he looked at me with admiration.

"Bloke did you the handsome, did he?"

"What?"

"Doing the handsome, Yard Boy. Greasing the palm. No shame in that. Common practice, especially with gentlemen. Half a sovereign in't nothing to 'em." Thenceforth, he would flash me complicitous grins, thinking I had descended to his level.

In the late spring, I was sent to fix the clock at the Cold Bath Fields House of Correction. The warden was strangely fond of boasting how Coleridge had immortalised the place:

> As he went through Cold-Bath Fields he saw
> A solitary cell.
> And the Devil was pleased, for it gave him a hint
> For improving his prisons in hell.

I somehow found myself signed up for charitable visits to an inmate with the unfortunate name of Josiah Bent. Rather than chat about his rehabilitation, Josiah preferred instructing me in the ways of London's underclasses. He was a night-soil man: that is, he collected the excrement stored by the needy in cellars to sell as fertiliser. His trade, first ruined by guano imported from South America, was banned in the reforming fervour of the Fifties. Josiah worked on. What else could he do? Now he was in the jug for it, and his family destitute.

Josiah spoke in the dialects used by lowlifes to avoid being understood by "straight" folk. He tried to teach me to "roker Romany", mixing cadgers' cant, the argot and thieves' Latin.

"Suppose I want to ask a codger to share a glass of rum with me," he would ask, "what should I say?"

I scratched my head. "Erm, would you like a big bass drum?"

"Too straight, my friend, too straight." His eyes lit up, as he imagined himself back in a dockside tavern. "I should do better saying, Splodger, let us share a Jack-surpass of finger-and-thumb. And what might the splodger reply?"

I knew the parlyaree for good. "I might reply, Bona!"

"You might." Josiah nodded unconvinced. "Or you might say, It's on doog, Josiah, on doog."

"No good!" I translated, pleased with myself for spotting the backslang.

"Yes. The esilop have lifted my tol–"

"The police have taken my lot."

"– and I ain't got nanty dinarly to my name."

"What?"

"Nanty dinarly. C'mon, my friend!"

"No money?"

"That's it, my friend. 'Don't worry, Scotland,' I'd say. 'I'll shout you a top of reeb and don't think of it. Now, let us return to the subject of the sixty orders of prime coves.'"

These were my lessons on the underworld trades. Grave-robbers I had heard of. As a small child, whenever I was caught by my father playing on the street in front of our house, he fell to yelling at me. Beyond our gate lurked demons, goblins and trolls. The devil himself! How would father feel then, mother gone and me infernally kidnapped? "D'ye hear, Campbell?" he would say. "The De'il will tak ye awa' and ye'll ne'er be met with agin." I realise now the old man was afraid. In a city of medical students desperate for corpses, a smothered child was a tidy alternative to midnight digging. Edinburgh was famed for resurrectionists and bodysnatchers.

When Josiah spoke of these trades beyond my ken, his voice thrilled, as if he were reciting Shakespeare. "Smashers, swigsmen, coiners and bloods. Dubsmen, cadgers, footpads and cloak-twitchers! Omitting neither patterers nor merry-andrews, which ain't crimes but might as well be. Then there's your mudlarks, down the Thames at low tide, like magpies scouting for valuables. The grubbers does the street drains and culverts, and toshers the same down the sewers."

Toshers? "Mr Shuffler, the tosher," the matron had said. Perhaps I should not have told Josiah about my brush with high crime, but it slipped out before I considered that. The spout left him none the wiser, but his eyes lit up when I described the clock with its workings removed.

"Churching jack, we call that," he said nostalgically. "Common ruse. Remove the ticker's insides. Some rum clocky gives it a fresh ridge – that is a new casing – then you can lumber the thimble – pass on the goods – without fear that some charpering feint will sell you up the flue. Quality loge will fetch a fine price any day of the week."

Walking home that night, I considered dropping by the Free Hospital. I could check the ward book, send Wardle more details. It might be significant who had brought Shuffler in, or who had removed the corpse. Yet it seemed a kind of desperation, and I kept my peace.

When I finally mustered the courage to ask the warden about the injustice of Josiah's imprisonment, he burst out laughing. Josiah Bent was inside because he had beaten and robbed an old widow. Somewhat ashamed of myself, I stopped visiting.

THE THEFT

A matter of days later, I sat on the early watch, head in my hands. It had been foolish to leave Edinburgh; I had given up my solid career as clockmaker's apprentice for a vapid dream.

Then the constabulary gate creaked.

My old home in Edinburgh had an iron gate just like the constabulary's. My father hated to be distracted; it was for my inability to concentrate that he was always upbraiding me. After my mother died, it fell to me to peek out the window whenever the gate creaked. Were it a customer, I would make myself presentable, quick as a flash, and invite them in. It was a task I hated, and I grew to hate that creak.

It was a taller, leaner Worm who summoned me that morning, swinging the gate in that irritating manner. He had grown up an unreasonable amount in those six months, and he seemed more guarded – or perhaps just weary. "Long time, no vader, Watchman."

I enquired after his company, the Euston Square Worms, thinking he'd be pleased I had remembered his patter.

"We don't call ourselves that no more," he frowned. "Sore point, but thanks for asking. Companies is old hat, you see. Co-operative ventures, that's where the future lies. Anywise, you're wanted at the Yard. The old cove."

"Wardle?"

"The same," he grinned.

I nodded slowly, trying to overcome my surprise. "One thing, Worm," I said. "How was it you that knew me, that first night?"

"Simple. All those watches you fixed? It was me delivered them." He doffed his cap as if to take his leave, then thought better of it. "Before you charper off, old cove, I've a query of my own. That hydrollah-rolical gaff, mind. What did the old crocus have to say about the corpuscular, if you get my word?"

"What business is that of yours? Off to study medicine?"

"Just asking," he shrugged. "No hoffence hintended, hofficer."

"None taken, wee man." A thought struck me. "You didn't know him, did you? Club foot, name of Shuffler?"

"Merely hinterested, hofficer."

"Hmm. You'd make a good detective, young Worm."

"Give us a job, then."

I laughed. "Put it this way, it wasn't the spout that killed him."

"That what the doc said?" He peered at me, eyes flashing with the same old light. "Full of bluff and flam, these apothecaries. A Scotchman at Scotland Yard, eh? Fit in nice, you will. Shift your crabshells now, or you'll get an earful."

The dullard at the front desk in Scotland Yard stared at me like I was speaking a foreign language. I repeated myself, as slowly as humanly possible.

"Wardle? He's ahhht," he shouted, and went back to his illustrated magazine. I stood my ground and light finally dawned. "Aoh, Wardle's new man, is ya? It's a theft, isn't it?" He passed me a slip of paper marked with a Lambeth address. "You'll want a cab. Nelson Square traffic'll be somfink terrible this time of day." He contemplated the fiendish puzzle. "Parliament Square worse, with the works on the clocktower. Ah!" he cried out, as if he had deciphered the Rosetta Stone. "Leg it to Charing Cross, grab a hansom on Waterloo Bridge, you'll be there like the wind."

Leaving the dullard and his wind behind, I walked up Whitehall as in a dream. My Superintendent had sent me off with his blessing, as if he was expecting the summons. Glossop was crestfallen that I had been requested ahead of him. Now this Yard subaltern had recognised me. Was I to be part of it all, at last?

I had been in London nine months without once crossing the river. From the hansom, I saw a London quite new to me. Fine buildings gleamed as far as the eye could see along the riverbanks; below them, ramshackle slums tumbled down to the turgid sludge.

As we crossed the bridge, the stench was shocking. For a moment, I thought our horses had defecated, but it was worse than that. This was the notorious Stink. In the pale summer sun the water was filthy brown. Far below us, ill-clad children splashed in the shallow water: Josiah's mudlarks, like little magpies in search of treasure. I could not help but imagine legions more, all struggling to get to the surface, suffocating in those treacherous shallows.

Lambeth too was like an open sewer. We travelled slowly, crossing and recrossing roadworks, where teams of navvies seemed to be digging down to hell itself. I paid the fare grudgingly, fearing that Wardle would have long quit the scene of the crime.

Inside the house of Charles Pearson, MP for Lambeth and solicitor for the Corporation of London, all was calm and peace. The portly housekeeper showed me into the drawing room, where a scene of quintessential English hospitality met my eyes.

"Watchman," said Wardle absently. "About time." He sat hunched over in his overcoat, stranded in the middle of a chaise longue, clutching a cup of tea in both hands. It seemed the wrong moment to correct his misunderstanding of my name. "Go on, Mr Pearson."

The honourable gentleman turned back to his wife. "It's hardly life and death, dearest, and I have pressing business with the Metropolitan."

"Charles, we have been burgled," she said. "Most peculiarly burgled."

"My dearest, nothing has been taken. The servants would have noticed."

"But, Charles," said Mrs Pearson in exasperation, "one of the servants may be the culprit." She looked at Wardle tellingly.

"Well," Pearson wafted a hand in the air, "they're servants, dearest. They have a right to steal from us."

"Do be serious, Charles."

"Better they steal from us who trust them than cause bother stealing from others."

"Really, Charles, one can be too flippant." She sighed, but she clearly shared his affectionate indulgence for their servants. "We ought to call upon the City Police Force."

"Inspector," said Pearson, "should we call the City Police?"

Wardle grimaced, as if woken from a reverie. "With respect, sir, you might as well call upon the royal menagerie's parrots."

I watched in a state of awe. Wardle smoothed out none of the northern roughness from his voice for these people, and yet he seemed to speak their language. He was anatomising the couple's exchange, I was sure of it. He appeared impassive, but actually he was sifting it all for details overlooked, or suppressed.

"You see, dearest?" Pearson sprang to his feet and reached for his briefcase.

"One moment, sir." Wardle held up a hand, half-rising.

"My house has been burgled, Inspector," Pearson interrupted charmingly, "I own it, I lament it, I rue it. But nothing has been taken, nobody has been hurt, and so–"

"You are sure, sir, that absolutely nothing of import has been removed?"

"You have something in mind, Inspector?"

"Something less obvious." Wardle affected a casual gesture. "Papers. Receipts."

Pearson considered. "My business work I keep at the office. Parliamentary documents at the House. The Metropolitan's are secure in this case."

Wardle frowned. "The underground scheme? Is that proceeding, sir?"

"Proceeding apace, if I do say so myself."

"After twenty years of bargaining and begging," added his wife.

"We sank the first shaft in February," said Pearson, eyes twinkling, "and already we have a mile of tunnel cut, and the New Road relaid on top of it – or the Euston Road or whatever they call it now."

"So," Wardle nodded, "the devil is to have his own railway."

Pearson laughed. "They won't call it the devil's work when they get from the City to Paddington for tuppence. Picture a labourer who toils all day at the cattle market, say, then has to walk all the way home. It's no wonder he beats his wife and terrorises his children. Don't you think, once he travels in luxury, he may retain a little kindness to spread around the hearth?"

"Of course, dear," said Mrs Pearson. She had heard all this before.

"There's a moral side too. If they can afford bigger premises by living further out, then these operatives can have their bed in a different room from their children." He coughed significantly. "I'm sorry to be beastly, dear, but these things must be spoken of."

Wardle gave no sign of being moved. "You anticipate profits?"

"Profits? I anticipate mania. Buy property in the suburbs. Underground trains will redraw the map of London. Every city in the world will want them."

"And you'll be digging up our roads for the next fifty years?"

"On the contrary, Inspector, we will be open within the year. Unless we wait for the Prince Consort's new Exhibition."

Mrs Pearson turned in my direction. "I still say it's a pity they didn't choose the high-level train. Gleaming bridges arching over the city. Think of the dramatic views."

"Through the smog, dearest."

"At night, then."

"Poor views, in the dark, dearest."

"But honestly, Charles, under the ground! The odour from the horses!"

"They're trains, dearest, not omnibuses."

"Sulphurous fumes, then. We shall be smothered. Why not put the filthy things on the streets?"

"That will come, dearest," said Pearson, struggling to maintain his good humour. "They're laying rails on the streets next month, special omnibuses running in trammel lines. I'm pushing for one up the Kennington Road." He coughed, suddenly gaunt, and leaned over to kiss his wife's hair. "Really, I must fly. I am frightfully late already."

"Trains under the ground," she sighed as he left. "My mother told me I was marrying a dreamer. Whatever next? They'll be sailing to the moon, given half a chance."

Wardle set down his teacup and leant forward. "Mrs Pearson, we must establish exactly what has gone."

The housekeeper was called. Between the hours of eleven and six, without sign of forced entry, several bits of furniture had been moved around. A miniature "Tom Thumb" chair and footstool were missing, and a few coins from the kitchen jar. The housekeeper hesitated.

"Spit it out, Mrs Laing," said Mrs Pearson.

Mrs Laing took a deep breath. "Happen as we's found, Old Joseph, that is, being who found it, wrapped up in canvas by the mantelpiece clock, as has stopped, mind, what Old Joseph found there, that he's put in the larder, madam, which I say ain't right–"

"Mrs Laing."

"It's a bone, madam!"

Wardle frowned.

"Mrs Laing," said Mrs Pearson, "please keep to the subject. The mantelpiece clock is hardly the inspector's domain, and, heaven forfend, a bone! Pray what do you mean?"

The housekeeper prayed indulgence that she meant what she said and she said what she meant.

Wardle narrowed his eyes. "Why do you say it's not right, putting it in the larder?"

"I won't make stock from it," said the good woman. "I don't know where it's been."

"What I meant was," Wardle continued gently, "what kind of bone is it?"

"Oh, I see. It'd be a rib, sir. From a scrawny old pony, I'd say." She thought a moment. "Or a big old dog."

"I should like to see that bone, Mrs Laing." Talking quietly, Wardle led the nervous servant out, and left me with the lady of the house.

"Officer," said Mrs Pearson bright-eyed, "did none of us offer you tea!" She stood to pour me a cup, and I realised that, despite her elegant bearing, she was shaken. "Whatever do you make of it? You haven't said a word."

It was true. In my eagerness to appear attentive, I had been too nervous to speak. I had to cast around to come up with a theory. "A bone," I said, feeling a fraud, "may be used to pacify a dog."

"We have no dog. Nowhere to walk them, you see. Charles says that one day we will walk along the riverbanks for pleasure, the water clean as a mountain brook–"

"And all the traffic underground?" I said. For a moment I was anxious that my joke was inappropriate, but she smiled.

"No doubt. But until that day, no dogs for us." She went

over to the window. Her grey hair gave her a most
distinguished look, when another woman might have made a
show of dyeing it. "They say William Blake used to fish in the
Westbourne, you know."

"Did he really?"

A look of doubt crossed her face. "You know Blake?"

I smiled. "We weren't personally acquainted, ma'am."

She eyed me quizzically. Realising that I was joking, she
seemed to relax. She gazed back out at the road covered with
the dust of the digging works. "All these great works and
schemes. Lambeth is getting its own bridge, you know. We
shall become fashionable if we're not careful."

She appeared to me the height of fashion, but it seemed
inappropriate to say so, even though we were indulging in
small talk. It was a strange thing I had noticed on night duty,
people seemed uncertain how to place me. Perhaps it was the
combination of my accent with being a policeman, an
equivocal profession that drew from the labouring types up to
the beleaguered upper-middle classes. Uncertain of my
provenance, people often gave me the benefit of the doubt and
treated me almost like a gentleman. It would have annoyed
my father no end, proud artisan and guildsman that he was.

I coughed. "The thief may have been unaware that you have
no dogs."

"Not if it were our own servant. The inspector suspects the
servants."

"Did he say so?"

"Not in so many words, but we are not in the habit of
handing out keys willy-nilly."

"I'm glad to hear it."

"Yes, but if nobody has broken in, then the servants…" She
hesitated.

"You find it hard to credit?" I said quietly.

"One always hopes one's servants are–" She narrowed her eyes. "Nonetheless, the inspector suspects, I'm sure of it."

I hesitated to disagree with the second sharpest mind in England. Yet there seemed no harm in reassuring her. "Let us not leap to conclusions."

Mrs Laing popped her head around the door. "Madame? The inspector asks permission to check the doors and windows."

"Granted, of course." Mrs Pearson and I exchanged a look. Wardle was one step ahead of us.

With the aid of the excellent Mrs Laing, we combed the house. I knew I should take notes, but in the rush to obey Worm's summons I had of course forgotten my pencil. I asked to borrow one.

"Watch out, Mrs Laing," said Wardle. "I've lost grand pianos that way."

Mrs Laing thought this so hilarious that she broke out into giggles every few minutes. I marvelled at Wardle's acuity, as the excellent woman, smiling now, spoke freely about all sorts of household matters. What with the roadworks, they were not in the habit of opening windows unnecessarily. The nursery, the bedrooms, and bathrooms were sound, and besides any commotion would have been heard. The kitchen and servants' quarters held quieter spots, but the doors had been locked.

The servants greeted us with expressions of panic and fear. Wardle gave them no hint that they were under suspicion, instead evincing quiet interest in their work. One by one, they relaxed and spoke of familiar matters. I noted down the comings and goings of the household. Wardle kept silent as far as possible, watchful as a hawk.

"You'll need a lamp for the cellar, sir," said Mrs Laing, tugging at the stout door, "and a peg for your nose." She turned her face away, as an earthy aroma arose, accompanied by a fearful banging. "God-awful racket. All that digging. Mr Pearson says it's for the good of the city and we must grin and bear it, but it drives me barmy, I don't mind telling you."

Wardle screwed up his nose. "Any opening to the street? Coal hatch, delivery chute?"

"None, sir."

He nodded briskly. "Needn't brave the dark, then."

Which left the chimneys. As the inspector peered up the drawing room flue, Mrs Laing allowed herself a smile. "Saint Nick about early this year, sir?"

Wardle did not smile. "I've known many little snakesmen in my time," he said, "but you'd need a trained chimpanzee to get in this way. Such a chimp would leave a trail of soot. Even if it cleaned up after itself, it could never get a chair up there."

Mrs Pearson was right then. He did think this had been an "inside job".

"Mrs Laing, I'd be glad if you'd keep an eye on the staff for me."

"Oh, I ain't doing no spying on my fellows, if that's what you mean," she said, but she was clearly relieved to be judged trustworthy.

"Not at all. Just in case anyone's behaving strange. All right?"

He asked Mrs Pearson to be similarly watchful, and arranged to keep in touch over further developments.

Further developments? I couldn't see how we could solve the crime once we left. We were hardly likely to stumble upon the Tom Thumb, nor could we expect the servants to turn each other in. I was surprised to be leaving without any notion who had committed the crime. I hadn't even an inkling how it was committed.

What else was I expecting, though? Wardle was surprisingly

polite and reassuring, different from the gruffness I had witnessed at Euston Square. A good policeman, I reflected, must recognise when his words count for more than his actions, and when the contrary is true.

He must also have noticed things I had not. Did he have suspicions? Surely. Yet to spout guesses, as I would have felt obliged to do, would only have undermined his authority, and forewarned the culprit. So he had kept his thoughts to himself, elaborating his thesis neither to the Pearsons, nor to me. Yet we left a satisfied and composed household behind us. It was a fine display of detective work from a thorough professional, and I felt privileged to be in attendance.

As soon as we had left the house, his hands plunged into his pockets. When he headed for the riverside tavern, I hesitated, anxious that I hadn't sufficient money.

"My treat, Watchman," he barked gruffly. "I haven't forgotten what it's like living on a constable's wages."

It was true, I wasn't accustomed to eating out. My landlady, Mrs Willington, left a cold platter for me daily in the larder; the rest of the time I got by on scraps at the station and from the market.

Inside, Wardle turned his back on the spitted pig the landlord was keen to show off. "The chicken and spinach. Dose of ginger pudding to follow."

Too nervous to think about food, I asked for the same. Glossop would have chosen the most expensive dish, no doubt, and asked for double helpings.

"Ginger," nodded Wardle. "Clears the head." He made for the corner snug, away from the gamblers and the snoozers, and we sat in silence. "So," he said finally, as the barmaid brought plates piled with pie and bread. "What do you think?"

I glanced at the barmaid and back at him in some confusion.

"About the crime, Watchman."

I blinked. Here was my chance. I had to come up with a theory. But I had nothing better in my head than Mrs Pearson's surmise. "One of the servants," I hazarded.

"Oh, yes?" he said, tucking in. "Why?"

I looked at him blankly. "They needed money?"

"No, no, no." He didn't look up from his plate. "Why do you think it's one of the servants?"

I coughed. "If entry hasn't been forced, the theft can only have been done by someone already inside the house."

He frowned. "Not necessarily."

My heart was pounding. Stupid, really. I would have thought I'd developed some kind of self-confidence by now, but here I was, acting like a schoolboy who hasn't done his homework. "Somebody with a contact in the house, then. Who knew one of the servants."

"Or the family."

"Yes."

"Or someone who happened," he went on, mouth full of pie, "to have a key. Delivery boy. Service man. Local keycutter."

I was on firmer ground here. "Mrs Pearson was quite clear, sir, that there were no other keys."

"Was she now?" He wiped his mouth thoughtfully. "Good. Mrs Laing too."

As he fell to thinking, I searched for something intelligent to contribute. I was annoyed with myself for being so green after all this time.

"Whoever it was, Watchman," he said, suddenly quiet and intent, "Why did they take such a risk?"

I considered. "Maybe a servant is in need of ready money."

"A few shillings?"

"They couldn't find more. They stole things to sell."

"A footstool? There's things easier to shift."

"They weren't thinking clearly. They took it on the spur of the moment."

"And left the clock?"

I felt my cheeks smarting. Had I really made such a fool of myself?

Wardle began mopping up his gravy with a monstrous doorstop of bread. "Possible. If they're that desperate, we'll have them soon enough."

"How, sir?"

"It's not so hard to instil confidence, Watchman, and confidence inspires loyalty."

"Right, sir. I'm sorry, sir. I don't follow."

"Mrs Laing took to us." He sat back and belched contentedly. "The lady of the house didn't much like the cut of my jib, but you charmed her good and proper. Good work. If there's anything amiss, we'll hear of it."

I nodded, somewhat taken aback.

"Happy household, do you think, Watchman?"

I thought of Mr Pearson's gentle words and Mrs Pearson's elegant smile. "Yes, sir."

"Would you risk your position in a household like that for a few pennies and a joint stool?"

Had Mrs Pearson been mistaken? He didn't suspect the servants after all, unless there were other gains that would have made it worth the risk. Think, Campbell, think. Wardle had asked about documents. "They wanted something else."

"Like what?"

"Something easily stolen, but valuable, in the right hands."

Wardle pushed away his plate and snapped his fingers for pudding. "Go on."

"Something of Mr Pearson's. He's an important man."

"Well connected too."

"Some kind of industrial theft. Someone paid one of the servants, bribed them, whatever you want to call it, to steal something important. There's money to be made in stealing plans. Designs. Even ideas."

"Not spur of the moment?"

"No. On the contrary. Well-planned. They'd need to know exactly what to look for. They'd need to know Pearson had the documents in the house. So what went wrong?"

Wardle licked his fingers methodically. "Who says it went wrong? We'll see. I'll wager Pearson discovers something has gone missing after all."

"Why steal the cash, then, sir? Why the chair?"

He just looked at me.

The barmaid plopped the ginger pudding in front of us and I snapped my fingers. "To make it look like an ordinary break-in."

"Good, son. And the bone?"

"To throw us off the scent. Make it look like they didn't know the household." Now I was talking with my mouth full. "Hadn't we better speak to him, sir?"

"I'll have a word. He seemed very confident of his security. But if they didn't get what they wanted, I'll wager they'll have another go within the week. Can't solve crimes before they're committed." He drew the pudding towards him. "One other notion. Is our thief a dolt or a fool?"

I felt more confident now. "Well, he left no trace, and he has the household thrown off the scent. Smart enough, I'd say."

"Who is the cleverest man in that house?"

"Mr Pearson, I imagine. Sir! You're not suggesting that–" I looked around, and lowered my voice. "That Mr Pearson is our thief? He's stealing from himself?"

He stirred his pudding around with quiet relish. "I was chasing a theft a few years back. Irish financier, dabbled in politics. Two hundred and thirty thousand pounds went missing from a Tipperary bank he happened to be manager of. Tricky one, that."

"He did it himself?" I stared at my pudding. "Did you get him, sir?"

"In a manner of speaking. He took prussic acid on Hampstead Heath before we could send him down. It was me that found the suicide note tucked away with his papers."

I blinked, trying to imagine it all. "But, sir, Pearson?"

"Keep an open mind, son. Like as not, we'll never know." He saw my look of surprise. "Don't misunderstand me, son. Nothing we can do, that's all. I've forty years of cases in my head. What does it help to fret about them? Drive yourself barmy."

The second sharpest mind in the country started shovelling pudding into his mouth. I sat spooning at mine, agog at his way of thinking, blunt and incisive.

"Like being a copper, do you?"

Taken aback by the question, I hesitated.

He coughed, and spat a lump of pudding back on to his plate. "That bad, is it?"

"It isn't quite what I was expecting, sir."

He put his hand in his pocket and pulled out an object wrapped in canvas. The bone. His face clouded over a moment, then he thrust it back in his pocket, unopened, and looked at me squarely. "What did you expect? Violence? Mystery?"

He was right, of course, however I would have liked to deny it. If he could tell as much from my hesitations as he'd gleaned about the crime, there was no point in hiding anything. But I had rid myself of illusions now, trying instead to find some kind of dignity, or satisfaction at least, in my everyday tasks. I sighed. "I may have had a few foolish notions, yes."

He thought for a moment, picking strands of ginger from his teeth. Then he smiled, which caught me quite off guard, and raised his glass. For a moment I thought he was about to propose a toast, but he simply finished his beer and said, "Thought of joining the Yard?"

After that lunch, I was tired. I had started my shift at Brunswick Square before six, which meant rising at four, near enough. The walk from Lambeth back to Scotland Yard wasn't so far, but the examination Wardle had put me through in the pub left me exhausted, and I was glad that he kept silent most of the way. He led me to his office, sat me down and gave me some paper.

"Don't need a literary masterpiece, mind." He sat down at the larger desk and prepared his pipe.

I was enthralled to be there, in his office, if a little confused as to what was going on. But, as I tried to focus on my task, I felt muddle-headed and stupid. I glanced over at him every so often. He had gone into a kind of reverie. So that was genius at work. I sat there dumbly, struggling to get the pen to work.

The thing seemed so unresolved. At Brunswick Square, things always seemed clear-cut. Someone damaged this, someone stole that. Anything more complex was sent up to the Superintendent. Now, although I had been to the scene of the crime myself, everything seemed temporary. I forced myself to jot notes before attempting to put anything coherent on paper. Three times I started and bungled. My greatest achievement came near the day's end, when I worked up the courage to ask him where the paper was kept.

Wardle made nothing clear. Every so often, he wandered out of the office for fifteen minutes. On one of these occasions, a cheery face popped around the door.

"All right? I'm Darlington. Next door. How you doing?"

I introduced myself, glad to be greeted as if I belonged there. I admitted I was struggling with my report.

Darlington hopped into the office. He was a bright-eyed sort, always hopping and popping and hovering in doorways. He looked over what I had written and made a face. "I'd have another go, old man," he said, tugging an old report from the filing cabinet. "More like this, see?"

I flushed with embarrassment, staring at it. The style was simplistic; the details were minimal. "I don't mention suspects?"

This seemed to trouble him. "I wouldn't."

"No theories? Nothing speculative?"

"Want to solve it all at once, do you?" He laughed. "No, my friend. I'd stick to solid facts. Write it, file it, let the big man worry about the rest. Good to have new blood around, though. Oops, here's himself." And, as swiftly as he'd appeared, he vanished.

"That Darlington prying already?" said Wardle. "Watch out for him. There's to be nothing told him or anyone else, not without my say-so. All right?" Selecting some papers from his desk, he made ready to leave. He glanced over my pages of scribbles. "What's all this, eh? Justifying God's ways to man?"

I managed an anxious smile. I was finding it hard to concentrate. After all, I had no idea where I stood. Would I be working with him again? Or was this it, another one-off, then back to night shifts at Holborn?

Wardle paused at the door. "Tomorrow I'm out at Windsor. Get your things and settle in. I've sent word to Brunswick Square. Finish up that report and go home."

Nobody to Blame

At eight o'clock next morning, I bade farewell to Brunswick Square and headed for the Yard. One day fixing mainsprings on night shift; the next, assistant to a renowned detective. Within the week, I signed papers awarding me the rank of sergeant and the princely sum of £58 per annum. I was to assist Wardle principally with legwork and paperwork. The tag in my jacket was changed from Holborn to Whitehall, and I swore a silent oath that he shouldn't regret his choice.

There was a certain interest in me as an outsider. Though not unheard of, bringing in someone from outside meant passing over the constables within the Yard. I chose to say as little as possible. This proved wise. Darlington decided that my silence hinted of secret experience; he broadcast impressive rumours about past successes, of which I was not permitted to speak. He frequently asked about my work with Wardle. The questions were harmless, born of curiosity and fun, but I thought it best to parry them, remembering Wardle's injunction that first day. Darlington thought this secrecy a hoot. "You tight Scotsman," he would say, "aiming for the top, are you? You'll be in the foreign service before long!" He was also kind enough to invite me out every so often. I occasionally went for a drink after work; but I refused weekend invitations, afraid that if I got to know him off-duty I would be found out as a fraud and a new boy. He soon decided that I was a cold fish and stopped asking.

Every so often, Wardle would summon me along to a case, in the main little different from Brunswick Square affairs; but it all seemed grander to me. I took to making assiduous notes so that future reports might not cause me so much anguish.

These outings gave me the chance to see the great man at his work. Throughout, he would keep his hands thrust deep in those coat pockets. Shaking hands he did rarely, as if wary that some ague might assail him. Writing was anathema to him. When there were notes to be taken, it was I who took them. Though some found him a difficult little man, he always seemed to get the answers he wanted. He was disarmingly dogged, though a man of few words, those few words were intense enough to make you feel he knew all about you. It was thus bootless to conceal what he already knew. Impressed from the first, I strove to anticipate his requests and to please him, though it took me a time to fathom his methods.

He required from me a daily synopsis of events across the capital. Studying the newspapers thus became dignified as work. I took pleasure in keeping up with current affairs, and skimming the cream off the news for him. The papers were full of triumphalist trumpeting and apocalyptic clamour. Election fever swept the nation every five minutes or so. The columns were full of questions: the Irish Question, the Reform Question, the Slavery Question. People wrung their hands over the Whitechapel garottings, only for that to be eclipsed by new scandals about Middle Eastern canals or East Midlands cotton.

The leading articles exalted rationality and condemned passion and profiteering. The other pages glamorised the same, especially the theatre reviews. Mr Darwin's book was *de rigueur* on the coffee table, though I never met a soul who read it. Anticipation of the underground train gave way to boredom. And the Queen's array of mid-European quacks sparked rumours that her forefathers' madness was descending upon her.

Besides all this, Wardle had an ongoing task for me. "I want to put my house in order," he told me. "There's years of rubbish in these cabinets. When I retire, I want everything left straightforward for the man who steps into my boots."

So, on quieter days, I set to work whittling down the paperwork from forty years of cases. Of closed cases I was to throw out everything but the final report. If a case was not closed, I was to close it, that is, tidy up loose ends and write the report.

Some cases solved themselves. Complaints were outdated, debts invalidated, or infringements irrelevant. Some gave of obvious action. Missing persons were frequently no longer missing, and if the necessary letters were written and answered, they could be tied up in a matter of days.

Other cases were less clear. I learnt that many investigations are never concluded. This took me aback at first. I gradually came to realise how much tramping about town each scrap of paper in the files represented: questioning here, corroborating there. It was no wonder there were so many loose ends.

Only when bewildered could I trouble Wardle, and he would always choose the simplest way to be done with it. I learnt to propose my own plan of action for each case. At the end of quiet days in the office, I would run through the files while he stood at the window, gazing out into the grubby courtyard at the heart of the Yard buildings. New reports drew an approving murmur. To my plan for cases outstanding, he would listen impatiently, snapping, "Nobody weeps over the likes of them, Watchman. Spare us the Celtic indignation and lighten the burden."

It was a peculiar process, dispensing with history thus. I would flick through the material painstakingly transcribed and fastidiously labelled by Jackman, dash off a summary reprise, then throw out the rest, refiling the nice, slim envelope in a drawer marked "Cases Closed". Not that I didn't make mistakes. Unsolved murders, I quickly learnt, he was content to leave open.

"Bodies have a way," he said "of lingering. You never know when a skeleton'll fall out the closet and point a bony finger at someone."

Nor had it occurred to me to take into account the persons involved. A caution for drunkenness against Billy Broad of Barking could go straight into the wastepaper basket; but, should Baron Burlington of Belgravia's china vases turn up in a Sotheby's catalogue, we would need the full details of their disappearance. I got a roasting for throwing out a theft at Charles Dickens' house.

"Use your nous, Watchman. A public figure. Writer. Experienced with the courts. Suppose he pops in, writing some new serial, and asks us to check the files?"

I fished the papers out of the bin and left the Dickens theft open.

It was a happy time for me. Wardle stomped in and out, shrouded in gravitas, which impressed me greatly. I never could work out quite how he was so busy. Either he was involved in cases of which I knew nothing, or else, through years of grind, he had earned himself one of those positions of such respect that nobody knows what your responsibilities are any more.

I worked at the smaller desk – nonetheless a broad affair with drawers and an inkwell. He decreed that I start working back through the files from the previous New Year; more recent cases might yet admit of progress. Christmas had been busy, and it took several weeks to sift through December of '59, trying to find a sure-footed style for my reports.

We soon fell into a routine. On Fridays, we lunched together at the Dog and Duck, and he went home early, leaving me to put the office in order. The rest of the week, I chose between wandering out to a street stall and sandwiches in the back room, where Darlington bombarded me with stories about the Yard. He told me that Wardle was an expert in unmasking frauds and cracking gambling rings. That Irish financier investigation, for instance, was the famous Sadleir suicide, an undercover coup that scandalised the business world; the story went that the man had left such a revelatory suicide note, the police had been obliged to cover it up and forge a less explosive document. Darlington saw this as a touchstone of Wardle's genius. His own department was much more mundane, he complained, and I realised he envied me my post.

Thus occupied, I managed for nearly a month to resist looking up the spout case, more through fear than self-denial. If Wardle caught me looking at it, it would be obvious I had ditched chronology for curiosity. I had no greater dread than stepping out of line and finding myself back at Brunswick Square under Glossop's mocking eye.

One Friday, when Wardle had gone to the doctor with a pain in the gut I found myself pulling out the envelope marked *"Euston Square, 9th November"*. It was marked as closed. Seized by excitement, I flicked through it urgently, the porter's statement, and Roxton Coxhill's; my own report, in pristine condition; Jackman's summary. Of Wardle's previous sergeant I knew little, beyond the sour impression I'd received when handing in my report. From his paperwork he seemed a dab hand in calligraphy, but no visionary with the bigger picture. A few comments around the Yard had given me the impression that he had departed under a cloud. "Wardle's new boy? Good luck. You'll need it." I didn't ask for details.

Filled with excitement at the prospect of unravelling the mystery, I scanned through Jackman's summary. I found myself none the wiser. Rather than solve the riddle, he seemed simply to have ignored it. He had left out everything of importance, labelling it an industrial mishap, with not a question mark in sight. My indignation rose as I read the travesty of a report over and over. It mentioned that the corpse was sent for post-mortem, but there was no mention of

Simpson's revelation. In fact, Jackman mentioned none of the peculiarities, the clock sabotage, the mysterious repair man. There was no new evidence whatsoever, and the companies involved were exonerated from blame under the tag "accidental damage".

The complacency of the thing left me breathless. I stomped around the office in indignation. Was I simply to despatch this case into obscurity, like all the others? True enough, I had thrown away cases still more inconclusive than this, but it would not do to worry about that. I stood at the little window, as Wardle often did, the details of that night flooding back to me, when the door opened and in stomped the inspector himself.

"Afternoon, Watchman. You're working hard."

"Sir! Are you quite well? I thought you were going straight home."

"You don't get rid of me so easy, son." To my horror, he sat down at my desk. I hurried over to tidy the papers away but he raised a hand. "Sick of filing, Watchman?"

"Can't keep me from the filing cabinet, sir."

"Careful now. Push too hard and that brain of yours might start to function." As he glanced over the papers, my heart pounded, but he sat back with a satisfied look. "This may be a grind, son, but I'm pleased to see it done well." He nodded that special nod he kept for approving my plans. "Keep your head down and we'll get through the lot by Christmas after next."

All weekend I could barely sleep. I tossed and turned in my little garret, dogged by unquiet dreams. Why did it trouble me so? Partly because I'd spent so long musing on the solution, partly excitement. I had watched how Wardle would pick up on little details and expand them into theories. Here was me, aping the great detective's method, going over unexplained details with obsessive, if unproductive, scrutiny.

By Monday morning, my head was muddy and I felt on the verge of illness. Wardle eyed me strangely, and my cheeks burned under his gaze. I had the job I'd wanted so long, and he was pleased with my work. Why should I care about a case long closed, that meant nothing to anybody? Better to stick to the task in hand. I tried to put the spout from my mind; but I could not.

I formed a plan. Rather than rile him with a special song and dance, I would evaluate it on the same basis as any other case: that is, with a view to closing it. From that angle, my scruples were hard to justify. Property had been damaged, yes, but none of the injured parties had pressed charges. As long as they stood to receive insurance payments, what did it matter whether it was caused by a vagabond or an activist? If the man had been killed there, the Crown would have to take an interest, but it was hard to pinpoint where the illegality had occurred. Yet if I could get Wardle's approval, I could later stumble on the anomalies Jackman had suppressed and open up Pandora's box.

While Wardle was in the office, I worked speedily through the intervening files, back to early November. Whenever he was out and about, I spent an unreasonable amount of time reading over the spout file. Only then did I notice that Jackman's sheet was dated 10th November. That was the day I delivered my report, but I delivered it late afternoon, before my night shift. Too late. No wonder he'd looked at me sourly.

I spent the week planning my strategy. I decided to slip the spout into the last session on Friday, hoping Wardle would give it the nod and head home. To put him in a good mood, I had accumulated several closed cases, which we sped through rapidly.

"Then we come to Euston Square, early morning, ninth November."

"Night you came along?"

"Yes, sir." I hesitated. "Seems a little murky. Thought I'd do a few interviews. The night porter."

"Why?" he snapped.

I bit my lip. I had gone over and over these justifications. "For a sober report, sir. He was drunk that night, but only he met the mysterious repair man. Then I'll try the HECC."

"Oh yes?"

"Perhaps Coxhill has enemies. I'd like to hear what his engineers have to say about the sabotaged machinery. Maybe there have been other mishaps."

"They'll be the last to tell you that."

"Then the clockmaker."

"The clockmaker?"

"Yes, sir. Might have a notion who would want to steal the mechanism. I noted the manufacturer's name."

Wardle raised an eyebrow. "I see your thinking, son. No need for it, though. Any more? Or can we have lunch?"

That was all. I looked down at the file. "You must admit, sir, it was peculiar."

Wardle frowned a moment. "Job's full of oddments and novelties, son."

I nodded, embarrassed. Of course, with those twenty years of files, he was weary of wonders, and shrugged them off. But I was tired, and I couldn't seem to let it lie. "Begging your pardon, sir–"

"You want to be the hero of a thrupenny novel, son. Natural enough. But don't make work where there is none. There's nothing to show it wasn't an accident. Nobody was hurt–"

"The man was dead, sir."

"Don't give me that look, Watchman. Simpson said the

tramp was dead beforehand."

I stared. So he at least had read my report.

Wardle sighed. "Let's assume that Simpson was right. Someone was playing a joke. Who?"

I cast about for the most convincing theories I had come up with in the wilderness. This was a test, and if I had to show off how much research I had done, where was the harm in that? "I thought maybe the builders' union."

He nodded warily. "Go on."

"Or the Chartists. All that business about Drains not Trains."

"Not the Fenians? Or the Luddites? The Anti-War League, the Anti-Poor Lobby?" He was teasing me. "Look, Watchman, something irregular was afoot, I grant you."

"Wilful sabotage, it seemed like."

"Maybe. If it was political, they'd tell someone. Otherwise why bother? I've seen so many syndicates and unions in my time, I take it with a pinch of salt. People don't think they're alive unless they're complaining. Why give them anything? As soon as they get it they take it for granted, complain it's not as good as it used to be, or could be, or ought to be." He scratched his head. "Like as not, it's something much simpler."

"Yes, sir?"

"I'd wager that it was a kind of message from one criminal gang to another. A message we're not meant to understand. No reason to suspect it'll happen again."

"I see." Would we leave it at that? Abandon a case that I had an uncanny instinct to pursue? Otherwise, could I disobey my new master, like a mischievous schoolboy doing exactly what his teacher has told him not to? "Is there nothing to be done, sir?"

"Stop worrying," he said with a penetrating look, "and get some sleep."

Perhaps he was not teasing after all. Behind his bluster, he seemed not just amused by my anxiety, but somehow pleased by my insistence.

"Before the clockmaker, though," he went on, "what about that ward book?"

"Sir?"

"Matron might have known something."

I looked at him eagerly. Was he giving me the go-ahead after all? "Yes, sir, she did. She recognised the dead man."

"So?"

I hesitated. "That's all I know."

"How much did you give her?"

"Sir?"

"Tends to loosen the tongue, the jangle of silver. Can be expensive, investigating. Find yourself short, you know where to come."

I looked at him in surprise. "Thank you, sir."

"Unless it's for a girl, mind." He stood up, thrusting his hands into his pockets. "There are two ways to get on in the police. One is to be brilliant. The other is do what you're told. If you can't do the former, best keep to the latter." He narrowed his eyes. "Get some rest over the weekend, son. If you have got yourself a girl, that's your business. Only don't come to work and expect to catch up on your beauty sleep."

"No, sir. I mean to say– That is, I haven't …"

"I don't want to know. Let's skip lunch and go home, eh? And Watchman, write your bloody reports quicker."

COVERT INVESTIGATIONS

I took this to mean that, provided I kept up with the filing work, my free time was my own look-out. After all, as Darlington told it, Wardle had been catapulted to fame through a resourcefully solved case back in the Forties. Why shouldn't I do the same? Moving Wardle's suggestion to the top of my list, I started my investigations that afternoon.

Without the doctor to open doors, I had trouble convincing the woman at the hospital front desk that I was bona fide. When I told her I was a sergeant of the Yard, she pointed me off down a dark corridor with a smirk. When I came back to her, lost, for the third time, she abandoned me to the devices of a hoary old porter. He refused to take me anywhere until he'd wormed my mission out of me.

"I simply wish to speak to the matron known as Bunny. Do you know her?"

"Might do. What shift?"

"She was on nights. In the paupers' ward."

"Best come to the paupers' ward at night, then."

"Will she be there, do you think?"

"Don't pay me to think, mate."

I gritted my teeth. "What do they pay you to do?"

"Shift the dead, mate, and the half-dead, and them as would be better off dead."

"Do you remember," I asked slowly, "a dead man with a club foot? Name of Shuffler. Mr Shuffler."

"Whenabouts?"

"November."

He burst out laughing. "Come off it, mate. I drag a legion of stiffs out of here every day, and their conversation don't tend to be memorable. It's only when nobody's taking them I have to worry. When they start to smell, then we call the stiffsman. Not so keen, he is. It's a pittance they pay."

"Very well, but this woman Bunny seemed to know Mr Shuffler."

"Best speak to her then," the man replied insolently. And off he went.

Outside, a Bibler harassed me with pamphlets: *Satan in Your Hairbrush* was one, *Satan in the Teapot*, another.

All the way home, I kicked myself. There was no place for my polite timidity. Wardle would never have been palmed off so easily. Back home, I planned my questions, thinking hollowly of Simpson's words, "The hospital will deal with it as normal." What had happened to those arrangements the first time around? Who had taken the body? What was the name Bunny had mentioned, the man who had brought Shuffler in?

Late that night, I returned, blustering past the secretary and trusting to memory to find the ward. Sure enough, I found myself back in that dismal place, amidst the oppressive groaning and moaning. The smell of disinfectants could not conceal the stench of illness.

A plump nurse with a pale lamp approached me. I asked, in a whisper, for Bunny.

"Useless asking me. I'm new."

"Perhaps you can find someone who can help me."

She fetched another nurse from the shadows. This second girl was bony, with a wart on her nose, and she carried a baby in her shawl, wrapped up tight as if she didn't want me to see it. I repeated my question.

"There's no Bunny here."

"Do you know where she's gone?"

She stared at me unreceptively.

"I need to know about a man who died in November."

"November?" she said and laughed. "Do you know how many ruffians pass through these doors?"

"Nurse," a voice called out from the dark, hoarse with pain. "Come to me, please."

Before the girls could turn away, I slipped a couple of coins from my pocket and toyed with them. Their manner changed instantly. The fat girl, all politeness now, said, "We deal with so many, your honour, we're just glad to see the back of them."

I tapped my foot impatiently. "Where would they take the corpse for burial?"

"Hard for paupers to afford burial in this town," said the thin girl.

"What happens to them, then?"

"There was that train out from Clapham," the fat one piped up. "Cemetery express."

The thin one laughed again. "And that vicar. Stacked coffins ten deep in his crypt. Made a mint, he did."

"Good God," I said. "How big was the crypt?"

The fat one put a hand on my arm. "Whenever it was full, he dug out a cartload and dumped them in the river."

"That's how they caught him," nodded the thin one. "Cart tipped over at Ludgate Circus and out rolled all the skulls."

I took a deep breath. "Please, I'd like to see your records for November."

They looked at each other as if I were speaking of ancient history.

"I believe you keep a ward book." I tossed the plump girl a sixpence and she scurried off. I turned to the other. "And Bunny?"

"Don't remember," she scowled.

I held the second coin between my fingers, wondering how Wardle would play it.

She smiled suddenly. "Don't mean Mrs Bunhill, do you?"

"Perhaps," I said. "Friendly faced woman. Dr Simpson seemed to know her."

"Know Dr Simpson, do you?" she said.

"Tell me about Bunny. When will she be in?"

"It's Mrs Bunhill I knew." She snatched at the coin and I let her take it. She hesitated. "She went off sick."

I clenched my teeth in annoyance, as the fat girl returned.

I took the book impatiently and held it up to her lamp, flicking through the pages.

"When did she go off sick?"

"Months back. She must have found something else," the thin girl went on.

"If she's still alive," said the fat one. "Sir, are you quite all right?"

I stared at the book. If only I'd come when I'd first thought of it, I might have found Bunny. It was too late now. The page I wanted, the page that Bunny had shown me so fleetingly months before, had been torn out.

THE CLERKENWELL CLOCKMAKER

"The Euston clock?" said the little man at Allnutt and Ganz. He squinted across the counter with an injured air. "How could I forget? Those vandals!" He jabbed at his chest. "It's an indescribable pain to me. A torment! I was no good for weeks. The shock of it, you see. No good at all."

I nodded. "I'm from Scotland Yard, Mr Ganz, and—"

"I thought you were from the Guild." He peered up at me, his enthusiasm melting away. "How disappointing. Your lot haven't turned up any answers, then? One of my finest mechanisms. Quite destroyed."

It seemed strange to think that this unappealing little man was the creator of that elegant piece. "I can understand your frustration. But I'm still hoping to track down the culprit. I take it they told you the clock was tampered with."

"Ha! They brought back the pieces. Not a one worth saving. Vandals! Barbarians! And no intention of replacing it."

"No, sir. I mean, before it fell, it had already been damaged."

"Poppycock. A drop of water? Wouldn't have touched it. I made that clock to survive the worst thunderstorm in a thousand years, I did."

"I'm sure you did, Mr Ganz," I said through gritted teeth, "but that's no defence against somebody opening the back panel and stealing the main movement."

"Stealing the movement?" Ganz rolled his eyes, as if to ask what did I know of mechanisms and the language of his trade.

My father used to roll his eyes the same way. I suppose the indignities I suffered were no different from most sons. But as I grew older, I found these criticisms hard to take. Father had finicky, dextrous fingers, but my hands, from an early age, had grown large and awkward. The last straw came when I was fumbling at a silver French Oignon quarter repeater. I knew that I was clumsy, and took care to remember my own strength. With Father glancing over my shoulder, however, reminding me how important the customer was and how valuable a job it was, I lost my rag. I tweaked and tugged at the repeater, and damaged it beyond repair. It was that, along with certain other troubles, that sent me packing for the south, his criticisms ringing in my ears. Worst of all, I half-believed his criticisms: that I hadn't the patience for difficult tasks; that I always wanted the thing solved at once.

"Look," I eyed Ganz squarely, peeved to be taken for an ignoramus, "it was I who was inspecting your clock, when some fool dropped the crane arm and smashed it." I went on to describe his clock in detail: how the motion work was coupled to the long hand drive mechanism, with an extending arm back to the main movement – which was signally absent.

At my talk of wheels and pinions, gears and spindles, a hint of respect flickered across his face. Then his mouth twisted to one side. "I didn't know that the police studied sprockets and mainsprings."

I had no desire to go into my connection with the Clockmakers' Guild. "Mr Ganz, this was no mere stealing of trinkets by children. You cannot tell me that a barbarian could so neatly remove so large a mechanism."

He pursed his lips. "It isn't the first and it won't be the last."

"You harbour suspicions?"

"I suspect the lot of them." He harrumphed. "You know how it goes."

"I assure you, I don't."

"The populace are such asses as to think they can purchase respectability for the price of a Deutsch wooden clock. I'll lay odds some manufactory's churning out cheap copies of my pieces as we speak." He broke off abruptly. "I don't wish to speculate. It's a matter for the Guild."

"Are they investigating it?"

"They should be, if they weren't obsessed with Big bleeding Ben." He laughed, a short derisive laugh. "Not up a year and cracked already. What do they expect, giving contracts to some parliamentarian's cousin?"

"Mr Ganz. The Euston clock."

"Must you torment me with it? My finest work and it will never be seen."

"You're not making a replacement?"

"The London and North-Western Railway," he said, through clenched teeth, "has decided against it."

"You were paid for your work, though, were you not?"

"That," he burst out, "is not the point! It was a showpiece. There's stations going up all over the world. They ship them out, you know, every nut and bolt. I'll wager there's already Hottentots and Pygmies telling the time from my clock, or flagrant copies of it."

An idea began to form in my mind.

"It's indescribably painful to me," Ganz went on, "to think

of such trolls and Visigoths hacking it apart, pillaging my ideas to boost their profits."

"You suspect a corporation of orchestrating the charade?"

"And I wouldn't be surprised if the railway owners are on the board of directors." He shot me a look. "Your own commissioner, like as not. They're all in on it."

I began to wonder whether Mr Ganz's sense of persecution might be a trifle exaggerated. Nonetheless, I scribbled my name on a card, beneath the Scotland Yard legend. "I'll see what I can find out. If you come across any more clocks similarly tampered with, would you contact me?"

BAD BUSINESS

On the Monday, I arrived at the HECC yard before eight in the morning, hoping for a brief word with Coxhill. It was a small detour and I aimed to get to work more or less on time, knowing that Wardle tended to come late Mondays to avoid the rush on the train. I was uneasy conducting these investigations without the inspector's approval, but it seemed foolish to upset him with it until I'd uncovered something. Someone, it seemed from the ward book, had something to hide. Could it all be a diversion? Like the bone at Pearson's, perhaps the corpse and the spout made it look like an accident, when after all they were simply stealing Ganz's clock.

Arriving at Coxhill's yard reminded me of my first arrival in London, a year before. As the train had groaned towards King's Cross, I had looked out at that wasteland, dotted with the flotsam and jetsam of the railway mania. On patches of unclaimed land, unscrupulous landlords had thrown up death traps of rotten timber. I had glimpsed those hordes of indigent incomers, their days and nights tormented, who would never escape the roar of the trains.

It was here that the premises of the Hydraulic Engines Corporation of the Capital were situated. At first I thought I had turned through the wrong gate. I don't know what I was expecting. A hum of activity, perhaps, smelters, smiths and panel beaters amidst vast clanking machinery. Instead I found a muddy circle of machines, like the stones of a druidical cult, and in their midst a solitary grey-haired workman.

He looked at me quizzically. "Lost, are thee?"

"This is the HECC, is it not?" He didn't deign to nod, but I was encouraged enough to go on. "I was after a little chat."

He wrinkled his nose at my oil-skin cape. "Don't like thy face."

"I beg your pardon?"

"We don't speak to Scotsmen where I come from."

I took a deep breath. "Where would that be?"

"You'll be wanting the manager, if you're so full of questions." He pointed to a squat structure standing desolate in the mud. The lower doors were open, revealing a mess of machines. Attached to the side of the building, a rickety staircase led up to an unfinished timber door. I went over to it hesitantly.

The workman watched me with an amused look. "He'll be in later," he grinned. "Happen as not, leastways. That is, he does sometime come in, on a Monday."

At that moment, the HECC chaise swept in through the gate, with Hunt up on the driving board. Roxton Coxhill descended, a little unsteadily, mumbling good-byes, and Hunt drove off again at speed. Coxhill was dressed, somewhat incongruously, in tails, as if he had come straight from a night on the town. Disraeli had declared that we were a nation divided, but I found it hard to believe that this was how the other half lived.

Coxhill looked around, rather wildly, and the workman made himself scarce. Spotting me, Coxhill started, then recovered himself, with an effort that seemed all the greater for his attempt to conceal it. He then marched over and welcomed me as if I were his long lost aunt. He smelt of smoke and perfume.

"Sergeant! It's fine to see you. Yes, fine." He ran a hand through his wispy hair. "Don't look so surprised. I never forget a face. Especially those working with Inspector Waddle." He ushered me up the steps and into his office, a single room with a closet and a window looking down onto the yard. He sat down heavily at his desk, took up an ivory letter-opener in the shape of a small animal, and began ripping an old magazine into squares. "Your man's highly esteemed by the royals, you know." He nodded sagely. "Please, please, sit down. Make yourself at home. Our premises may seem rudimentary, but you know how it is. From mighty acorns and all that. May I say, we are glad to have your watchful eye protecting us in these early days."

Somewhat unsettled, I told him not to mention it. I was not convinced that he remembered me at all.

"Ah, but I do mention it," he insisted, stringing the squares of paper together. "Because I value it, you see. The early days are the most vulnerable. The hounds of commerce delight in preying upon the little creatures, so to speak, picking them off for sport. Do you think George Hudson could have become the Railway King, without some helping hands in high places?"

He pronounced "railway" more like "whale way". I smiled awkwardly, for I seemed to recall that Hudson's fame had long since turned to notoriety.

"It is now that we need your assistance. And let me make it clear that we shall not forget our friends when we reach the top. Now, Sergeant, you must try our new water closet. Just installed. It really is the go." He clamped his hand onto my shoulder and led me over to a strange closet in the corner. "Look at that quality. Cistern made of glazed stoneware, piping of impermeable clay, and a guaranteed flush with every pull. Here's some paper, if you need."

"Thank you, no."

"Don't be alarmed. It's not for general use. Workmen have an outdoor privy, so you won't catch anything – unless it should be from one of our lady visitors." He laughed a devilish little laugh and went in, clutching the paper. "Anyway, if you don't mind…"

In he went. I looked around the office, thinking that I ought to note salient details of the furnishings. On the wall was Reynolds' new map of London, marked with strings of coloured pins. A luxurious sofa boasted a bearskin rug, complete with snarling head resting on the arm. On the desk lay some books, among them *Self-Help* by Samuel Smiles and a biography of George Stephenson, the inventor of the locomotive.

Beside the books stood a framed daguerreotype of two bright-eyed girls in theatrical costumes. It was this I was inspecting when there was a fearful gurgling of water behind me. I turned in alarm to see Coxhill approaching at speed, his bony temples oily with sweat and his ginger beard hanging limply from his chin, as if it might fall off. He took up *Self-Help* and declaimed.

"'Heaven helps those who help themselves.'" He breathed in deeply. "A marvellous work. Explodes the belief that talent is thinly spread. We all have our talents, but few of us have the energy, and the confidence, to make the most of them. Borrow it, Sergeant, if you like. I draw constant inspiration from its pages. Ah, I see you've spotted our hoofer friends. As young ladies go, I recommend them. The liveliest sort of girl, and by far the best value. Perhaps I offend your sensibilities.

You're more literary sorts, you Scotch. My father taught at Heidelberg University, you know. That's how we know the Saxe-Coburgs."

"Mr Coxhill–"

"Do call me Roxton, please." He sat down again and tugged at his beard.

"I was hoping, sir, to clear up a couple of questions. From the night we met."

He shot me a glance with his birdlike little eyes. "Ah, yes. A bad business, that."

I went on. "Did you discover who the impostor repair man might have been?"

He drew out a pipe from a drawer and began to prepare it. "The chap who blew himself up? No idea."

"No, sir. The other man. Your repair man, or so I was given to believe, if you recall, by the night porter."

"That old seadog? Had him dismissed. Soaked, he was." He lit his pipe and inhaled deeply. The thing had a visibly calming influence on him. "We weren't at fault, you know. The machine was tampered with. Your man, Waddle, said it."

"No doubt, sir. I just thought you might have looked into it. How they did it, if not who."

"Bloody Fenians, don't you lot reckon?" He gazed out at the machines in the yard. "A feckless crowd, aren't they, those Irish?"

"I'm not at liberty," I said, "to reveal our lines of enquiry."

He leant forward. "Sergeant, I'd be grateful if you would make known your conviction that we were not at fault. The HECC must be seen to be spotless. I realise such a request lies outwith the bounds of duty, but I'm sure I can trust you to scupper any rumours you encounter."

I frowned. "May I speak to the man who repaired the machine?"

He seemed not to hear me. Turning in his chair, he gazed up at the map. Jabbing the end of his pipe at it, he spoke in a voice full of excitement. "The greatest city in the world, Sergeant. London." He let the word resonate around his mouth, as if he were tasting fine wine. "Do you know what London is?"

I looked at him.

"It is a city crying out for power. Gas is all well and good for street lights that are the envy of Europe. But machinery? Look! Here are the docks, needing engines and cranes. Here are the theatres, wanting safety curtains. Mayfair hotels, installing passenger elevators. Construction all over, roads, railways; statues erected; bridges thrown across the river. London is hungry for new sources of power." He sucked again at his pipe, the peculiar aroma of the smoke beginning to fill the room. "And I intend to satisfy that hunger."

I opened my mouth to speak, but he was in a world of his own.

"How shall I do it? I shall do it – through pipes." He spoke in hushed tones, with eyes glinting, as if the subject were sacred. "Blood vessels for the city, pumping life through veins and arteries of Bessemer steel, beneath the feet of the unsuspecting citizens. As Frankenstein brought his monster to life, so we shall vitalise London."

"With hydraulic power?"

"What other power can spread its tentacles so wide? The force required by the great engineering feats for which our nation is renowned – nothing can supply it but hydraulic power. It is an invention of genius." He beamed in self-satisfaction.

"This piping, sir, will contain water at high pressure?"

"Hundreds of pounds per square inch. We're laying the prototype network. I tell you, Sergeant, every era thinks it's the apex of modernity. But this one truly is. Could old

Stephenson have dreamed that his engine would revolutionise the country? No! But now we can move an army from Land's End to John o'Groats in a day." The birdlike eyes gleamed darkly and he went on in a thrilled whisper. "It's only twenty years since William Armstrong invented the hydraulic engine. We can barely begin to dream how it will affect our lives. We're installing an hydraulic elevator in Marlborough House – for the Prince of Wales, you know. With support such as that, it won't take long to finance our network. We're to receive a Royal Seal, you know. I have the Prince's assurance."

I could not help but picture once more that circus seal with its whiskers, gliding along the whaleway, powered by Coxhill's hydraulics. "Mr Coxhill," I said, "if your crane proved so vulnerable, how could such a network be safe?"

"People die crossing the road at Oxford Circus, officer. Hydraulics are safer than gas, more robust than the combustion engine. Have no doubt. These cranes are playthings beside the network I am planning to create." He lowered his tone. "The railway mania is over, Sergeant. Finished. Power," he intoned, his voice brimming with conviction, "is the next thing, and I intend to be in the vanguard. Our network will power everything from printing works to hat-blocking presses. The Royal Mint, why not? You should consider investing, you know."

With my £58 per annum, thought I? With all this chatter, though, I would be late for work. I had learnt next to nothing from him. "Mr Coxhill–"

"Roxton, old chap. Do call me Roxton."

"Of course," I replied uneasily. "One last thing, sir. That night, at Euston. How did you get there so quickly?"

"Why," he replied ingenuously, "didn't you know? I was on the late train."

I stared.

"Still, no serious damage done," he said. "We must turn

these little setbacks to our advantage." He stood up and squeezed my shoulder meaningfully. "I do thank you for your concern, though. Must you be going so soon?"

"I must. Sir, if I could talk to the workman who repaired the machine?"

"That chap?" he said. "No longer with us, I'm afraid. Tell you what. Are you heading into town? Will you accept a little something to entertain you on your trip? It's a little trifle of my own composing. Privately printed, but I think nonetheless worth your perusal." He drew from a drawer a sheet printed with stanzas and pressed it into my hand. He began to declaim the verses aloud, rhythmically, insistently. I tried to control my dismay, as he droned on, looking not at the paper but into the middle distance, and giving no pause for interruption.

> Th' unexplorèd worlds of commerce do I hold in thrall.
> At their lattice opportunitous I glance,
> I seize – Oh! – pluck the fruits, while others' fructuous ignorance
> Lets squandered prospects fall…

"Thank you," I leapt in at a pause in the recital. I realised he was waiting for a comment on the poetry. "I… I shall look forward to studying it later."

This seemed to satisfy him. "You're a good egg, Sergeant. You really must come and dine at the club some night. Yes, I'd like that." He clapped me on the shoulder again, like we were old chums, and bade me good day.

THE MODERN AGE

As I strode, dissatisfied, across the circle of desolate machines, I spotted the solitary workman. He was sipping a bottle of beer, sitting inside the hollow arm of a machine very much like the crane from that night at Euston Square. I went over to him.

"Still here?" he said. "Himself answered your questions, did he?"

"He read me poetry," I said. This seemed to amuse the man, and I was emboldened to speak further. After all, I had already missed so many opportunities, and if he knew hydraulics as I knew clocks, it might shed light on the spout. "There's one or two things you might help me with."

"He don't like me talking about company matters."

"He said it was all right."

"Did he now?" The man looked surprised. He peered out towards the office. My heart sank to see Coxhill gazing down upon his little kingdom, puffing contentedly at his pipe.

The man seemed reassured. He shook my hand and invited me into his makeshift room. "My name's Pat, my home's Cumberland, and all Scotsmen are my enemies," he grinned. He offered me a swig of beer, and seemed delighted when I asked him to explain the workings of the machine.

"We pipe it down from the reservoir, mile and a half away. It's a good three hundred feet up. That's one hell of a weight of leverage driving the pistons in the cylinders."

I barely comprehended his explanations, but I felt ten times more comfortable with Pat than with his master. "Many problems with the equipment?" I said.

"See this band, the hood on the driving rod here? That's India rubber, only it's shrunk too small for the socket, and we're losing pressure."

"Right. There must be lots of teething problems with newfangled equipment."

He laughed. "Not so new, nor so fangled. You should see the new designs they're making down the docks, boy."

"Why, the machines you're building are outdated, are they?"

He pursed his lips, glancing at Coxhill's office. "We're not so much building them, sir, as buying them."

"Oh yes." I frowned. "And that's profitable, is it?"

"If you buy them broken, it is. This is an old Edward Elswick accumulator. Him in there buys 'em broke, I make 'em work and Hunty boy paints HECC on the side."

"And they work?"

"More or less."

"You've had incidents?"

"If you cut corners, there's bound to be problems."

I suspected Pat was understating the case. "Anyone hurt?"

He hesitated. "I'd best be getting back to work."

"All right, all right." I took a deep breath. "But speaking theoretically, if someone were hurt, would you have to pay compensation?"

"Theoretically, I wouldn't know about all that. I only hear talk of all the money pouring in. Not that I see much of it out here."

I smiled. "How long have you been with the company, Pat?"

"Two years. Glad of it, for all I moan." He tried to settle himself to examining the piston, but the words kept tumbling out of him. "Not like the old days, you know. My parents worked two fields in Cumberland their whole lives. What was so wrong with them old times? Someone ran short, you all helped out. Me now, I been a weaver in Preston, canal man in Manchester, railwayman in Crewe, miner in Derby and a longshoreman down Greenwich." He tugged at the perished rubber, and it came off in his hand. "You go where the money is, you learn your trade, work your fingers to the bone. Two minutes later, it goes arse over tit, and you're out on your ear. Here I am in hydraulics. But I don't put my heart into it. Not worth the sweat, just to get laid off when the next mania comes along."

I was late for work. "Pat. There was a crane damaged at Euston last winter."

He shot me a sideways glance. "That what this is all about?"

"Did you fix it?"

"It were a puzzle, that one, at first. Hats off to him, he knew his business. Must have been an expert on the old Elswick."

"Who, Pat?"

"The fellow that bollocksed it, of course. He took some pains. Otherwise it wouldn't have kept spouting so long, would it?"

"Wouldn't it?"

"He had the aperture worked out that finely, see, to maximise the pressure. Drained half our reservoir. See, on top of the outlet pipe, he'd attached this–" He paused, holding in a chuckle. "Lovely idea, really. He'd attached a rose."

"A rose?"

"You know, a garden rose."

"I am familiar with the flower."

"No, no. You city types. No knowledge of nothing. A garden rose is what you put on a watering can. Turn a jet of water into spray. A fountain, see. Must have looked comical, I imagine. Tell you one thing, though. I'd be surprised if it killed someone. Might have knocked you sideways – knocked you off of the crane, maybe – but there weren't no blast. More like taking the lid off a pot. The reservoir water pumps in here, see, at the bottom. Through the pistons, generating the torque to work the crane pulleys. Then it's channelled upwards, through this pipe. Your friend just removed the valve. Released it into the air. Couldn't have bollocksed it better myself."

There was a noise in the yard, the chaise pulling up again. I frowned. "It must have been dangerous, though, setting the thing off?"

"Oh, no. He weren't even there when it went off. He'd attached a clockwork mechanism to release it."

Clockwork, I nodded to myself.

"Flaw in the design, really," he went on. "He knows his Elswick, that man. Knows it like the back of his hand." His face clouded over. "Excuse me. I... There's something needs finishing."

I turned to find Hunt striding towards us pugnaciously. I raised a finger to my lips, passed a coin to Pat, and stood up to leave.

Hunt insisted on giving me a lift in their chaise. I was none too keen on accepting favours from Coxhill, but I would otherwise have been late for work. Hunt showed me the interior, replete with superfluous luxuries: brandy and sherry, napkins and neckerchiefs, telescopes, fans and flannels.

"We been to France in this, you know. And very comfortable the master found it."

After this display, however, he made it plain that I was to ride up front with him. I thought at first this was simply because he did not take me for a gentleman. It soon became clear what he wanted.

"Nice chat, had you?"

"What's that?"

"What business have you speaking with HECC employees?"

I recalled Wardle's comment at the spout: "Give nothing away," he'd said.

Hunt gave me a look and increased his grip on the reins, steering us through the traffic at a fearful lick.

I held on tight, eyes half closed, thinking over what I had just learnt. Pat had been in no doubt that the sabotage was both deliberate and careful. And Coxhill had arrived on the late train. Why should the spout have been planned to coincide with Coxhill's arrival? Unless, as Wardle had suggested, it was some kind of message. The image swam before my eyes of the saboteur, swiftly fashioning cogs from the clock into a release mechanism to set off the spout. I thought too of Pat, migrating ever southwards as industries collapsed behind him. At least I had a trade to fall back on. Although, if Ganz was to be believed, clockmaking too would soon fall by the wayside beneath the march of progress. Perhaps, in joining the police, I'd done the right thing after all.

I decided to counter Hunt's prying with questions of my own. "I hear there's been a few problems with the engines."

"None worth speaking of," he growled.

"But there have been mishaps, besides the time at Euston?"

"Other monkey business? Nothing that springs to mind."

"Does the company, to your knowledge, have enemies?"

His cheek twitched as he shook his head. "Nobody I know."

"Has the company ever had to pay out compensation? Due to an accident, maybe?"

He whipped the horses and they sped up. "Ain't been no accidents."

"Mishaps, then. Like the one at Euston Square."

Hunt kept his eyes on the road. We were scything across town at a speed that made me hold on to my hat. "Ain't been mishaps either," he said firmly, then added as an afterthought, "Officer."

THE LIBRARIAN

I was late for work, and it was lunchtime before I could collar Darlington.

"Old man," I said, "how would you go about checking the records of a particular company? You know, to see if they were trustworthy."

"Investing your savings, eh?" he said brightly. He looked

sheepish for a moment, then whispered, "I got a bit of railway scrip. Hasn't brought in anything yet, but fingers crossed. Tell you what. I'll grab you a saveloy from the sausageman, and you pop down to the Yard records office."

The clerk in charge was a pie-faced buffoon with a cleft palate. At first he feigned that he understood not a word I said. I mentioned Wardle's name, twice. Still he seemed to resent this appropriation of his time. He wanted forms signed in triplicate. "Besides," he said, "what makes you think such reports exist? If we were to keep track of all the shenanigans of industry, I'd need an office the size of the British Museum."

I turned tail and ran.

In those days, with nothing to hurry home for, I had the habit of wandering home by a different route each night to my garret off the Pentonville Road. The performance licensing laws had just been relaxed, and I noticed new theatres, music halls and gentlemen's clubs opening all over, on the Strand, in Covent Garden, as far as Holborn. I observed Captain Fowkes' Conservatory rising beside Hyde Park, ready for the next Exhibition; it was even bigger, they told me, than the Crystal Palace, which had long since been removed south of the river. They said you could see it on a clear day, but there weren't many of those.

That night I chanced to stroll homewards via Museum Street. The British Museum was still open and I recalled hearing word of the public reading room there. I found the spanking new rotunda squeezed into the central courtyard. At the doorway I was stopped and asked for my pass. To acquire this precious item I would need from my employer a recommendation stating not only that I was to be trusted but also, as it was a "library of last resort", what was my momentous purpose.

All the next day, I was nervous, working up the courage to

ask Wardle. Fortunately, that very afternoon found him in expansive mood.

"I've a business meeting on the morrow, Watchman. Take the morning off, and I'll see you after lunch."

"Thank you. Sir, I was toying with a notion…"

"Spit it out, son."

"I'd like to join the British Museum Library. Only you need a reference, from a respected member of the public."

"Would a police inspector be sufficient?"

"I believe so, sir."

"No slacking with the deskwork, though," he said. He took the application form and signed it with a flourish. "You won't solve crimes in there."

"Are you in need of assistance?" The dark-haired librarian was trying valiantly not to laugh at me.

I looked up at her, tongue-tied. At first glance I had taken her dark hair as a sign of Mediterranean background, but closer inspection of the pale face framed by those dark locks revealed a face so quintessentially English that I forgot my manners and stared. I had been standing in pure amazement among the canyons of bookshelves. My first plan was to leaf smartly through the *Illustrated London News*. If I should spot anything of import, I would then turn to the *Times* for the day in question. In that labyrinth of books, however, I had not been able to locate the illustrated magazine. Now the old copies of the *Times* kept getting the better of me, and I was spending more time folding than reading. If only I had asked Pat for dates.

"I didn't realise," she said, a sparkle in her eyes, "that the police force was so forward-thinking as to employ mutes. How modern."

"I am," I assured her, "possessed of the power of speech."

"How fortunate. Do tell me what I can help you with."

"I wanted to start with the *Illustrated London News* for the last year."

"I think what you have there is the *Times*."

"I realise that. I was unable to locate the magazine."

"The stack."

"The stack?"

She pointed at her feet. "I'll go and dig them out for you. All the best stuff is underground. Helps it mature. Nothing else while I'm at it?"

"There is another– No, thank you."

"Why is it that men," she said absently, "find it so problematical to ask for help?"

"It's… It's police business, you see."

"Is it really?" she nodded conspiratorially. "You'd better let me show you to a desk."

She promptly reappeared with the magazines, and made me promise to ask if I required further assistance. Glancing through that pile of print took much longer that I had expected. I was blinking with weariness when I looked up to find her at my desk again.

"I'm impressed," she said, "that the police consider literacy an asset. Or are you just looking at the pictures?"

I smiled grimly. "They should invent machines for doing this. I'm just looking for a couple of words."

"They'll have such machines soon enough. Haven't you seen Mr Babbage's difference engine? It calculates sums all by itself. It was in the Royal Panopticon of Science."

"The royal what?"

"Panopticon. In Leicester Square. It's been converted into a music hall now, of course. The Alhambra, you know. So much for popular science." She sighed, as if that were an elegant summation of the spirit of our age. "In a few years," she went on, "my job will be done by automata. Yours too, no doubt. We'll all be out of work."

"And free to do as we please?"

"With no income. It's difficult to enjoy a place like London without a bit of money in your pocket."

"That must be what I've been doing wrong."

"Why, do you not like it here?"

I made a tight face and she laughed. A moment's silence fell between us. "Right," I said. "I'd better get down to some reading."

"You had indeed." She paused. "Are you sure I can be of no help? The library's quiet today. I might help finding those elusive words, if you tell me what they are."

"I can read on my own, thank you," I said, which was ruder than I had intended.

"As I said, I'm astonished that policemen can read at all. Is it a requirement? Only we don't see many of you in here."

"How are you so sure who's a policeman and who isn't?"

"I take quite an interest in the readers. It's my job. We've got a revolutionary over there, you know. Set Europe alight in '48."

I followed her gaze. A man with a thunderous beard was buried in his studies, clutching his head in his hands. He didn't fit my image of a dangerous revolutionary. "Do the authorities know?"

"Oh yes. They know all about him."

"Why don't they do something? Have they evidence?"

She disappeared for a moment behind her desk and reappeared brandishing a small cream-coloured book, and pointed to one of the author's names embossed on the cover.

"Marx?" I said. "Never heard of him."

"You will. He sits in row G every day, unless he's at some rally."

"Is he the leader of a secret organisation?"

"I suppose you could put it like that."

"How exactly did he set Europe alight?"

She simply tapped the book. "Workers of the world unite," she said. "You have nothing to lose but your chains."

I snorted. "Doesn't sound so dangerous."

She glanced skywards in exasperation. "He ignited the imaginations of the dissatisfied and dissident throughout the continent."

"Do people take books so seriously," I said, "as to start revolutions?"

"You don't like books, I take it? At least, you don't think them important."

"Quite the contrary, but I don't think that's the type of book I would enjoy."

She laughed pleasantly. "Prefer the theatre, do you?"

"I do like a good show."

She raised her brows. "I saw the Siamese Twins in the West End."

"Did you?"

"It's the Singing Mouse at Savile House next week. Come along, if you like."

"That's very kind." I hesitated. "I... I'm not sure when I can get away from work."

"Not your kind of show?

"Not exactly." I felt something of a fraud hinting that I had a taste for high drama. My frequenting of Edinburgh theatres had less to do with Shakespeare than with certain actresses I admired.

She leaned forward and spoke in a low voice. "Won't you tell me what you're looking for, Sergeant? I'm quite an expert at solving mysteries."

"Thank God one of us is. Where did you acquire this expertise?"

"Mr Wilkie Collins' serial in *All the Year Round* – *The Woman in White*. Have you been following it? Oh, and this, of course." She brought out another little book from behind the counter. *Tales of Mystery and Imagination* by Edgar Allan Poe. "You can learn a lot from Mr Poe."

"Really? I must purchase a copy."

"Would you like to borrow mine?"

Some notion of confidentiality kept me from accepting her offer and I struggled manfully on without assistance. As the time pushed towards midday, I decided I might be better off back in the office with a cup of tea. I went over to the librarian's desk and placed the magazines in two piles in front of her.

"I've finished with those," I said. "I tell you what, I'll just take these home and look through them tonight. I'll bring them back tomorrow, if I may."

"Tell you what," she mocked, pointing to a printed sheet at the side of the desk. "You certainly may not. Have you not read your Reader's Agreement?"

I frowned, casting my eye down the list of rules. The admissions clerk had impressed upon me the importance of reading this agreement before he would hand over my precious pass, valid for one month only, as a trial period. I had sworn, though, to kindle neither fire nor flame within the library's bounds, and considered my own researches more pressing.

"There is a reason they call this the Reading Room," she went on, nostrils flaring. "If you want to borrow books, join Mudie's Lending Library. They've just moved to New Oxford Street."

"You were going to lend me Mr Poe."

"Mr Poe belongs to me!" She looked at my pile of unread

magazines and seemed to take pity on me. "Are you sure I can't be of help?"

I bit my lip. "I'm concerned, you see, about confidentiality–"

"You misunderstand. Can I help you read the rules? If they take you as long as the illustrated magazines, you'll be here all week."

At this, I laughed so loudly that the bearded revolutionary looked up and harrumphed. Soon I would have to be back at the Yard. I decided to take her into my confidence, at least partly. I explained that I was searching for newsworthy events in the world of hydraulics.

She listened, her head tilted towards me. A mischievous smile played across her lips.

I broke off my explanation. "What is it?"

"Nothing at all." She glanced down sheepishly. "Only it sounds like something from Mr Poe's book. I must confess, I think I have caught the detective fever."

Her rate of reading put me to shame. When she noticed me glancing in amazement at her skimming through page after page, she shrugged it off. She explained briefly that she was studying for a degree at Bedford College. She narrowed her eyes as she told me this, expecting some quip about women and further education. In fact, I was envious, though I refrained from expressing it. When I had become apprenticed to my father, many school fellows had gone on to the law college and the medical school. I could not have made sense of such subjects, but one could now study languages other than the classics. One of my friends was studying English Literature, which seemed a grand excuse for four years of idling. What would he do all day, I wondered? Read novels?

We had been working in near silence for half an hour, when she grew excited, flicking back and forth through several items before announcing her discovery. "I have something," she announced. "An incident."

"Go on," I said quickly.

"November last year. Euston Square."

"Ah. This incident I already knew of."

She paid me no heed, recounting details in a rapturous whisper. "Strange," she went on, her brows darkening. "Most of the papers speak of an impromptu fountain. They make it sound rather jolly. But this local rag is altogether darker. They say a hydraulic crane burst."

"I know–"

"And a man died." She glanced rapidly from one paper to another. "They're most unforthcoming. No sign of an inquest. Is that suspicious, Sergeant?"

I opened my mouth, but decided against explaining, for now, at least.

Working backwards, we found little more. A theatre in Haymarket had proudly announced the installation of hydraulic curtains for their spring season. And, just ten days before the spout, there had been some kind of hydraulic burst down by the river, on the new embankment they were beginning to build. These reports were muted. There was no sense of danger, nor mention of which company was involved.

As sunlight beamed into the cupola, I looked skywards. One could lose oneself forever. All the wisdom of the ages was stored herein, and all the nonsense too. Who was to say which was which?

She mistook my gaze for disappointment. "There must be something else we can check."

I shook off my daydream. "Yes. Perhaps some other information on hydraulics. Learned tomes. Technical periodicals."

She glanced over to the desk. Her superior was half asleep.

"Come on. Let's see what we can dig up." She led me back through the open shelves to a little curved door in the wall and we descended a spiral stair, two floors down under the ground. Here stood a labyrinth of shelves, curved and angled so as to use the space as fruitfully as possible My mind boggled at the arithmetic: each shelf held x volumes, each bookcase y shelves, there were z bookcases; for all I knew, there might be other basements in other libraries, stores and warehouses across the country, just as replete.

She led the way with silent assurance, and selected several volumes without hesitation, which she showed me for my approval. I nodded dumbly. As we went back up the staircase, I couldn't help but burst out, "Do you know where every single book is kept? How can that be?"

"Natural brilliance." She laughed a cool fresh laugh. "They only take on the most brilliant staff at the British Museum Library."

"I've no doubt of it."

She giggled, looking at me with something bordering on pity. "No, no. It's just that, only last year–" She stopped in her tracks and turned to look at me. "Someone else was asking about exactly the same subject as you."

At the librarians' desk, she started riffling through boxes of files.

"What are you doing?"

"Don't you want to track down the previous reader of these books?" She stared at me. "Don't you see, this might the fellow you're looking for?"

"I didn't say I was looking for anybody."

She looked at me.

"Besides," I said, "there could be a thousand building engineers trying to grasp the basics of the new technology. I hear it's going to be the next mania."

"What is?"

"Power," I said uncertainly. "In pipes. So I've heard."

"I see." She bit her lip. "If only I could recall his name."

"Do you remember him?"

She half-closed her eyes. "I can just about picture him. Striking chap. Round-faced. Gentlemanly."

"How long ago was it?"

"I don't know. A year, perhaps. As I recall, he was studying all sorts of things. Hold on a second." Her eyes opened wide. "I know who will remember him."

She bustled through the desks towards the bearded revolutionary. She bent over his table and spoke discreetly. The man looked up at her in consternation. He retorted with some sharp Germanic phrases and returned abruptly to his reading. She stood there a moment, mouth agape, then retreated rapidly.

"It's perhaps fortunate," she said, "that my German is weak. Otherwise I might have had to eject our revolutionary from the library."

We both laughed, a little too loud. Over at the desk, her superior had woken up. She gave me a look, and I realised I ought to be behaving more formally.

"I would like to reserve those hydraulic tomes for my next visit, if I may."

"You may certainly," she replied. "May I see your reader's card? Thank you, Mr– Sergeant Lawless."

"Why, thank you, Miss– You have the advantage of me."

She flashed me a smile, then glanced at her superior. Like a sloth from hibernation, he rose from his place and drifted somnolently towards an inner office.

"You've been an inestimable help," I burst out, gripped by a sudden emotion. I searched for an appropriate suggestion.

"Can I not prevail upon you, that is, might you consider an invitation, to discuss this further, of course, to go out for lunch with me?"

She feigned shock, though her eyes were smiling. "First a show, now luncheon? Sir, do you think it prudent for an unchaperoned lady to accompany a police officer to a Bloomsbury tearoom?"

"I have no idea what is prudent, and I suspect that, if you are honest with me, you do not give a fig for what is prudent and what is not."

She smiled hugely. "Give me two minutes."

Of course, I had meant lunch another day, for Wardle was expecting me at the Yard early afternoon. Before I could explain the misunderstanding, she had dashed off. I called out. "Miss–? Librarian!"

She popped her head around the door.

With acute embarrassment, I began, "I'm afraid you've misunderstood me... That is, it's my mistake, for which I beg your pardon, must humbly, but I must hasten back to the Yard, else I will be in trouble, you see, with my inspector."

She looked sceptical. "Keeps you under his thumb, does he?"

I laughed emptily, then lied, "He's expecting a report on his desk this afternoon."

"That's all right," she said. "Actually, I've already missed my lunch hour, helping you with your reading."

"I'm sorry." I frowned. "You're right, you know. I would like to find your student of hydraulics. If by any chance you see him, could you ask his name?"

"I can do better than that. I can look through the readers' cards."

"Is that allowed?"

She grimaced. "Librarians are not bound by the same oaths

as a doctor, although we feel a compunction towards the readers that prevents indiscretions. If the matter is important, however... It is important, I take it?"

I assured her that it was.

"I'll find it." She smiled conspiratorially again. "Shall I write to you through the penny post?"

"No," I said. Wardle might ask questions if he saw letters arriving for me. "I'll send a boy." Worm and his subalterns tended to present themselves at the Yard every so often, available for chores. We arranged that one of the Worms would ask for her at the entrance a week hence. I must say, I rather enjoyed giving the impression that I had a legion of urchins at my disposal. "I'll tell him to ask for Miss..."

"Villiers." She held out her hand. "Ruth Villiers. I shall rack my brains, and the filing system, to discover the suspect's name. The *suspect*! How exciting it all is. You have given me detective fever, Sergeant Lawless, and no mistake. I am sure I shall not recover until we have fathomed the depths of your mystery."

She passed me the Edgar Allan Poe book. I pocketed it and hurried out.

GIVE IT UP

"What kind of time do you call this?"

After my exchange with Miss Villiers, I was terribly late. To my dismay, Wardle was sitting at my desk, on which I had left the spout report, expecting I would be back long before him. There was a strange aroma in the air and I felt as if I had been found out.

"Meeting go badly, sir?" I said as casually as I could.

He turned to me, tight-lipped. "This needs to be filed."

"Yes, sir." I thought of Miss Villiers' eyes, bright with the fever. "I'm hoping there may be further developments–"

"Developments? You go down the British Museum and come back with developments? If you're an academic, back to the library with you. If you're a sergeant of the Yard, sit down and start filing."

I laughed weakly, but he did not smile. I had made mistakes before, but this was my worst roasting yet.

"The case is closed. Says so here. Should further evidence arise, we only need the final report."

"That report's full of omissions, sir."

"I don't care if it's full of woolly mittens. It's the final report, and it's stamped." He took the other sheets from the envelope – the depositions, interviews and my old report – and crumpled them in his hand.

I stood there dumbly.

He threw the papers into the basket and stood up abruptly. "Now, if I'm not mistaken, you're a little behind in your work, Sergeant."

I sat down meekly and pulled open my drawer. I set some paperwork upon the desk. Reaching for my pencil, I felt the Edgar Allan Poe book in my pocket. Wardle paced over to the window and stood gazing out into the dark yard. I stared at the papers but my head was throbbing with the shame of his accusation. "Sir," I burst out. "A man died and we gave no account of it."

"A tramp, Watchman. Are we to panic over every old man who dies in the city?"

"Sir?"

"Do you know how many people are murdered every day in this city?" He strode across the room and opened the door. "Darlington!" he called out. Within moments my bright-eyed friend was hovering in the doorway. Wardle looked at him sardonically. "Darlington, in all London, how many killings per day?"

"I'll ask the inspector." He bounced out. There was a guffaw of laughter from next door, and Darlington was back. "He says the devil himself don't know, sir."

Wardle turned to me. "No more do I. What would you say, though, Darlington? Five? Ten?"

"At least, sir."

"How many of these crimes admit of a solution, Darlington? Half?"

"Oh, less, I would say, sir."

"A quarter?"

"I don't know, sir. One in ten, maybe. One in twenty."

"Thank you kindly." Wardle closed the door and turned back to me.

"I see." I swallowed, nervous to reveal the extent of my illicit investigations. "It seemed so strange, though, sir. Someone has gone to the trouble of defacing the hospital ward book."

He looked at me sharply. "You've been at it, have you?"

"There were so many loose threads. I hoped I could tie things together." I decided not to tell him about the mysterious hydraulics student at the library, not until I was sure I had something significant.

He glanced at his pocket book. "Watchman, I have a yen to take a walk. Will you accompany me through the parks in the direction of Paddington? Don't look so startled. We'll finish early, inspector's prerogative."

He maintained a grim silence, as we threaded through the Whitehall traffic. On attaining the peace of St James' Park, we passed a dairyman, milking his cows to serve fresh milk to well-to-do nannies. The hot-potato man was having a field day with a regiment fresh in from the east. All conspired to ignore a singing beggar, whose sign proclaimed that he lost his legs in the Crimea; his rendition of "My Love Is Like a Red, Red Rose" recalled to me evenings in Edinburgh taverns and I gave him a farthing. The leaves were already turning brown, and there was a hint of autumn cool in the air as we headed toward the Palace.

"You've a stubborn streak, Watchman," said Wardle.

I kept my silence, but I was relieved, for he seemed to have repented of his anger.

"That's no bad thing," he went on. "You've spotted certain omissions in that report. What you consider serious omissions. It's doubtless led you to form a poor opinion of my previous sergeant, and of me to boot. Oh, yes. We inspectors must accept responsibility for our charges' shortcomings. That's one of the perils of duty. Not that there aren't perquisites to balance. Allow me to explain. Our reports do not..." He sighed. "Not necessarily – contain all the information we've garnered."

I looked at him in surprise.

"You reckon we were lacking in zeal. Didn't pursue the routes presented to us. Swept things under the carpet, even. Let me tell you, I do not take lightly a public menace such as that bloody spout." He frowned. "But I have satisfied myself that it was not engineered by any of the obvious suspects."

We passed the Palace and headed up Constitution Hill.

"See, Watchman, you don't spend a lifetime in the force without making contacts. Contacts with guilds. Partisan organisations. Political, commercial, questionable. We asked more questions than you might think. The mighty George Potter, for instance. You know him? Activist, trades unionist, author of the famous Document. I know George. I know his bloody father and all. It was nothing of theirs. How would it help them?"

Humbled, I simply nodded.

"We made enquiries, all right. Only, as my sources are, shall we say, private sources, I'm reluctant to name them. Not in reports of unfathomable incidents. The devils we know of, I checked up on."

"And the devils we don't know?"

"We'll see them in hell."

He fell silent again as we went up through Green Park towards Hyde Park Corner. I gazed in wonder at the grandeur of Mayfair's fine hotels, its stately homes and gentlemen's clubs. The further we distanced ourselves from the Yard, the more Wardle relaxed. He walked with a jauntier step. He looked around him at the trees and birds. Quite against his usual practice, he spoke freely and at length. He even took one of his hands out of his pocket.

"Wherever there's people with money and people without, there'll be killings," said Wardle, as we crossed into Hyde Park. "And that's everywhere in the world I ever heard of, outside of El Dorado, though I'll wager they have their own axes to grind even there, over who's the most blissful and why. Come to that, I don't like the sound of a place where they're all so bloody blissful. Sounds like a recipe for jealousy and discontent, which are the two greatest springs of crime that I know."

He frowned as he spoke, as if he was trying to frame for me some of the hard-won wisdom of his years in the job.

"Understand this, son, there's more petty retributions each day than you can dream of. Accidental deaths happening on purpose, if you take my meaning. Some things don't add up all neat and pretty. You have to live with that. When a toff meets an untimely end, I grant you, there's trails to be followed; bank accounts, deals, unsavoury affairs. I could tell you some stories. These lowlife killings, though, that's a different story. Nobody knows anything, do you get it? As in, everybody gets the message, but nobody breathes a word. Not to outsiders, especially the likes of you and me. That's why it pays to keep little chaps like Worm and his crowd on your books. There's times even he won't tell what he knows."

We came to a riding path, spread with cinders. He stopped as a handsome couple rode past at a canter, a whiskered gent and a lady in a mantle of shimmering green.

"Your man," Wardle continued, "he's no more important than the rest. As to how he ended up in our files, rather than floating down the Thames at high tide with the rest, I can only think that some of the city's criminals have a more finely tuned sense of humour than others. I've no intention of paying them the compliment of my interest. What that fellow did to end his days there, I do not know. You could spend your life investigating it, I warrant you, and end up knowing less than you do now. They only kill their own, for the main. I say, let them get on with it. Haven't we enough work without inventing more for ourselves?"

"Yes, sir. But if they commit further crimes?"

"We catch them then."

"Yes, sir." I was persuaded by Wardle's down-to-earth clarity. He knew the ropes in a way I never would. I must simply trust him. At least he did understand my frustration; appreciated my doggedness even.

Still I felt disgruntled. As we left the park at the Lancaster Gate, I felt the frustration rise within me again. I had caught Miss Villiers' detective fever, I suppose, and I simply wanted to know what had happened. "Isn't it worth at least asking the questions, sir?"

"Maybe so," he said, a sterner note creeping into his voice, "but that don't mean you can go upsetting businessmen and interrogating employees without my say-so."

I looked at him in dismay. I knew suddenly that his meeting

that morning had been with Coxhill. The unusual aroma I had smelled in the office was Coxhill's special tobacco. All my secret enquiries – Wardle must know everything, and suspect worse.

"It's irregular. Bothering busy industrialists on a whim, especially on a case that's closed. I won't stand for it. I've defended your actions this time but I don't want it repeated. Clockmakers and whatnot, all well and good, but use some judgement if you're going to harass gentlemen. Clear?"

I nodded. But I felt a strange elation. "Sir, you met Coxhill? You must suspect them of something."

He gave me a look, somewhere between respect and irritation. "Come on, Watchman."

"Shouldn't we investigate them further?" I said. "Their own engineer was quite plain that there have been mishaps and will most likely be more. Why did Coxhill deny it?"

"Protecting his interests." Wardle's face was grim. "Who knows with that Coxton? Strange fish, he is. I'm not stupid, Watchman. I don't need you stirring up problems where there's none. Making them nervous. Is that clear? You've gone at it like a pig at a tatty."

"Yes, sir." I hung my head. We had arrived at Paddington. I followed him towards the ticket hall. Yet I was damned if I was going to give it all up so easily. "Still, the timing can't have been pure chance."

"What's that?"

"The spout went off when the late train came in. Surely that means someone was trying to embarrass him. Scare him."

"How do you mean?"

"Coxhill was on that train, sir."

"How do you know that?"

"He told me, sir."

Wardle's mouth twisted to one side. I didn't know if he was

exasperated or impressed. He nodded slowly. "Perhaps so, son. That's why I'm keeping an eye on them. But you've got to learn, it's not like fantastical stories in the penny press. You can't expect it all to make sense. Often as not, you don't get to the end of it." He sighed. "You have good instincts, son. But don't delude yourself. We're fortunate enough to live in a civilised country, on the whole. But if someone wants to commit a crime, it's damned hard to stop them. Any fool can buy guns, or gunpowder, and–"

"Blow up the Houses of Parliament?"

He grimaced. "Leave treason and plots to the history books. You can pass your days sweating if you like, imagining all sorts of fearful crimes. That's not our work, though. There's nowt to be done till there's something needs done. Keep your eyes open and your ear to the ground, son, but get some sleep. You look ruined."

He bought me a platform ticket and himself a ticket home to Windsor. I wondered if I should suggest that we share a pitcher of ale in the station saloon bar. But his patience had worn thin and I was loath to aggravate him further.

We stood waiting for his train. "How long is it," he said, "that you've been in the police?"

"A year, sir, all but."

"Give it one year more and your imagination will stop running away with you. Too many bloody thrupenny novels, that's what I reckon. Though I'll confess," he said, his tone softening on a sudden, "there was a paper I liked as a lad. The *Terrific Register*, it were called. We'd each put in a penny, buy one copy between us. Most outlandish stories. I'll never forget them. Folks buried alive; trapped in tunnels; rivers of fire under the earth. Pure fiction, of course, though it were dressed up as fact. Good, if you get a thrill from that sort of thing, like all lads do. Do you think they keep that in the British Museum Library?"

"They say," I smiled, "they have everything ever published."

"Do they really? That's what our taxes pay for, is it?" He sniffed and looked on down the line. "How old are you, son, twenty-three, twenty-four? Your day'll come soon enough. I had a big success round that age. There was six children, all their throats slit, and their mother, a wet nurse, hurt too. Mary Ann Brough was her name. The papers were shocked. Everybody clamouring for justice to be done. I took the time to talk to the woman. Nobody'd thought to do it. She told me plain enough. Killed them herself."

"Killed her own children, sir?"

"Six of them. Told me why she did it. Couldn't get any peace. She were shattered and they wouldn't give her no rest. Nobody believed it at first, but she confessed it, clear and simple, come the trial." His train rolled up to the buffers beside us. "Since then my star's been in the ascendant. There's no hurry, see, not for a bright lad like you. Bide your time. Put in the hours. Don't throw good time after bad. You'll learn soon enough. It's not like the papers."

As the train pulled out, I turned away, surprised to find myself dejected and tired. I walked off to find a bus home. Passing the cheap hotels of Paddington, with their cargo of cheap women, I felt all of a sudden lonely. In the dim lamplight, I pulled out the book Miss Villiers had lent me: *Tales of Mystery and Imagination*. Wardle was right. I mustn't let my fancy run away with me. He had checked things. He knew what he was doing. He had better connections than I ever would. If there was a conspiracy or a cover-up, he would have found it. The case was closed, and he was right: I ought to drop it.

Message from the British Museum Library, delivered to the Yard by the Professor:

FOR THE ATTENTION OF SERGEANT LAWLESS OF
SCOTLAND YARD

Dear Sergeant Lawless,

Found it, after countless hours fiddle-faddling through filing cards. A catholic taste in books the chap has too. Of course, I do not even know what he has done. I hope I am not consigning the poor fellow to the gallows.

I trust that no Caledonian custom of illiteracy shall be allowed to grip your soul and you will deign to grace our sturdy desks with your formidable shadow once again. That is, if I cannot prevail upon you to invite me to the Singing Mouse.

Good luck and God speed. Do, please, let me know what transpires, if you pity a poor librarian her interest in affairs none of her business.

Yours,

Miss Ruth Villiers

POST SCRIPTUM

Will I receive a reward? Or do you keep that for yourself?

POST POST SCRIPTUM

Have I have quite forgot myself? Forgive me. This little ginger mop who styles himself the Professor is in rather a hurry. Before you are quite burnt up by curiosity and impatience, I will tell all.

His address is 42 Red Lion Street, which I believe to be by the Victoria Road in Clerkenwell. His name is Berwick Skelton.

THE THIRD PERIOD
[Early 1861]

The Bugle — Comedy Routine & Popular Song
Passages Marked in Periodicals — The Skeleton Thefts
The Rose & Crown — A Note from the Library — Lord's
The Family Marx — The Haymarket Hoofer
The Elocution Teacher

20th April, 1861

WHAT A RIOT

The height of fashion this spring is not fine French clothes, nor a fully accoutred carriage. The clamour is neither for railway shares nor the debut ball of yet another European princess. Infidelity with an actress is passé; royal parties a bore; likewise throwing down the gauntlet to popular novelists in the Garrick Club. This season, to become the talk of the town, one simply must be burgled.

Is it the old highwayman fever, society swooning over some latter-day Dick Turpin? Not so. Today's thieves have abandoned the old melodrama in favour of a terribly modern mysteriousness. They enter in the dead of night, armed with a single bone to pacify the dog, and make off with the household's most elegant item – a footstool here, a decanter there – leaving the police baffled. No doors have been forced, nor windows broken; nobody hurt; nobody seen. The city's finest houses are on tenterhooks. Hostesses faint; lords offer rewards; youngsters miss school from staying up late to catch them red-handed.

Bravo to the chivalrous culprits. You have set society aflame.

In this topsy-turvy modern world, not only do the rich pray to be robbed, but convicts disdain their victuals. Prisoners in the Cold Bath Fields House of Correction caused panic yesterday when, in protest at their provender, they rioted. The *Bugle* secured an interview with one inmate. "The slop is filthy," declared Josiah Bent, "and the portions minuscule." The *Bugle* refrained from suggesting that, if Josiah wished to be the master of his mealtimes, he had better have stayed outside the walls of such an institution.

The warden of the prison remained sanguine. "Our inmates are perfectly well provisioned. Trumped-up ideas those Reformists inculcate into the lower classes, making people ungrateful for the mercies shown them. Well-meaning amateurs they are, deluding the poor with expectations of grandeur, and lamentably, for it leads only to dissatisfaction. They should acknowledge such nonsense for the tripe it is and keep their mouths shut."

Comedy Routine & Popular Song performed by the Great Mackay at Evans Music hall, Covent Garden:

(Enter Great Mackay dressed as a toff. Upstage, weeping, sits Little Mackay, mostly undressed, as the lady of the house.)

GREAT MACKAY: Ladles and jellybubbles, good eventide and God bless ye. What pleasure it is to receive ye–
LITTLE MACKAY: Boo-hoo-hoo.
GREAT MACKAY: Cough, cough. As I was saying, to receive ye at–
LITTLE MACKAY: Boo-hoo-hoo.
GREAT MACKAY: For the love of God, Mrs Mackay, what have you got your bloomers in a twist about tonight?

LITTLE MACKAY: Oh, Mr Mackay.

GREAT MACKAY: What is it, my petal? What ails my sweet?

LITTLE MACKAY: I'm so ashamed.

GREAT MACKAY: (*to audience*) Do you perceive her meaning? I don't!

LITTLE MACKAY: (*weeps and hides her face*)

GREAT MACKAY: What should I do, sirs and madams?

VOICE FROM AUDIENCE: Give her some nice flowers, Mr Mackay!

GREAT MACKAY: Good idea. My darling!

(*He produces from under his hat a bunch of cloth begonias. She bursts out crying. Great Mackay stuffs them back into his hat.*)

GREAT MACKAY: Look what you done, clever clogs.

2nd AUDIENCE VOICE: She wants pearls, Mackay!

GREAT MACKAY: Good idea. My darling!

(*He pulls from her bosom an enormous string of oyster shells and presents them to her. Little Mackay redoubles her weeping.*)

3rd AUDIENCE VOICE: Give her a Crapper!

GREAT MACKAY: Good idea. (*From the flies descends a picture of a Water Closet*). A certain flush with every pull, my darling! (*sound effect*) Airtight seal to prevent noxious aromas, and gas receptacle for combustible ends.

(*Little Mackay walks melodramatically downstage and looks up to the gods. Mackay follows. Upstage appears a shadowy figure.*)

LITTLE MACKAY: I have flowers in the garden. I have pearls coming out of my ears. I have chamber pots wherever I turn. But, my darling, everybody I know has been– (*she holds back the tears*)

GREAT MACKAY: To Brighton?

LITTLE MACKAY: No. Everybody but us has been–

GREAT MACKAY: To the Queen's garden party?

LITTLE MACKAY: No! (*wails*)

GREAT MACKAY: My darling, what can it be?

(*As he steps forward to comfort her, the shadowy figure creeps centre stage. We now see it is a skeleton figure. It picks up the pearls.*)

LITTLE MACKAY: Everybody but us has been robbed!

(*Skeleton figure whips the hat off Great Mackay's head. Makes a run for it, banging his leg against the chair. He hops off.*)

GREAT MACKAY: Lor' lummy, what was that?

(*He runs back centre-stage and picks up the skeleton's shin bone.*)

LITTLE MACKAY: Oh, my darling, you do love me after all!

(*She shows the bone to the audience, and swoons away. Enter hoofers. Music and skeleton tap dance.*)

GREAT MACKAY: (*sings*)

Who's that slipping through the fence
When the gardener's asleep?
Who's that lifting your sixpence
When you are counting sheep?
It could be highwaymen,
It could be a monkey.
It could be a bywayman.
Could be a flunky.
They'll speedily remove from your stately old home
Your most stylish possession, leaving just that old bone.
With all their stealthy coming and going,
It's a fabulous Skeleton Theft.
Oh, let me tell you,
It's that scandalous Skeleton Theft.
You've been the victim of the
Fabulous ... Skeleton Theft.
Oh yes.

Passages marked in periodicals by Reader 1381, British Museum Library:

"The proletarian question is the one that will cause a terrible explosion in present day society if society and governments fail to fathom and resolve it."

ALPHONSE LAMARTINE, poet and leading figure
in Paris Commune of 1848

"Monopoly and the hideous accumulation of capital in a few hands... carry in their own enormity the seeds of cure... Every large workshop and manufactory is a sort of political society, which no act of parliament can silence and no magistrate disperse."

JOHN THELWELL, *The Rights of Nature*, 1796

"It is true that labour produces wonderful things for the rich – but for the worker it produces privation. It produces palaces – but for the worker, hovels. It produces beauty – but for the worker, deformity... It produces intelligence – but for the worker, stupidity, cretinism."

KARL MARX, *Manuscripts*, 1844

"Let it come twice again, severely – the people advancing all the while in the knowledge that, humanly speaking, it is, like Typhus Fever in the mass, a preventable disease – and you will see such a shake in this country as was never seen on Earth since Samson pulled the Temple down upon his head."

CHARLES DICKENS, writing about cholera,
Household Words, 1854

THE SKELETON THEFTS

Wardle turned away from the gaggle of newsmen outside Sir Joseph Paxton's house and climbed into the cab where I sat shivering.

"Bloody papers these days," he growled. "Barely asked about the crime. Full of nonsense about this blasted fever sweeping the country again."

My breath caught in my throat. "Cholera, sir?"

"Election fever, so they call it." He cast a withering glance behind us, as our driver headed off, weaving between the newsmen and the roadworks lining the Bayswater Road. "What business have they, asking me who I might vote for?"

I breathed out with relief. "People value your view, sir. As a pillar of society."

He snorted. This was the third theft now, all of a piece, which suggested that we had it wrong at Pearson's, and Wardle was irritated. Worse, the press were banging on the door when we had barely begun our investigations, as if someone in the household had tipped them off.

"Waste of time and money, elections," he grumbled. "New issues every time, and they never address any real problems. If you ask me, they should have done with them chattering politicians. Like dancing bears, they are. Choose a proper king."

"Sir!"

"Oh yes, I'm a royalist. I make no bones about it. We've had a few duff ones, I'll admit. Mad ones too. But this German is a prince among men and no mistake." With that, he fell to staring out the window. The rest of the journey we sat in silence.

It was a new year. My excitement at joining the Yard wore off, as surely as the seasons turned. By the time the Professor brought Miss Villiers' note – some weeks after my day in the library – I had given up on the spout. Wardle was right. The possibilities were infinite, the evidence negligible.

Yet that name pulled me up short. Where had I heard it before? That night, in the hospital. From the matron, Bunny. "Good Mr Skelton," she had said. An incontrovertible connection: the man who had brought Shuffler to hospital was a student of hydraulics.

It did seem extraordinary. I had been chosen, however, not for extraordinary duties, but for mundane ones. Indeed, perhaps it was good for me, that knock-back from Wardle. I must determine to be a useful, obliging sergeant, like Darlington and the rest. I was enjoying increased wages, more regular hours. There was even time to slip into the theatre of an evening, if I had the inclination. Why risk Wardle's wrath? Why throw my chance away?

The Edgar Allan Poe book lay by my bedside like an unfulfilled promise. I read a couple of the tales, but found them fantastical. I felt I owed Miss Villiers an explanation, but somehow I kept putting it off. Before I knew it, Christmas had come and gone. I kicked myself for my ill manners. In January, I scribbled her a desultory card reiterating my lunch invitation, and asked Worm to deliver it; but I heard nothing back.

The next day, Wardle stomped in late and threw the papers on my desk. "Bloody newsmen, eh?"

I read the headline in surprise. "Skeleton thefts?"

"Sensationalism. Make the public restless with their jumped-up claptrap. A name for everything they have. Their Great Stink and their Road House murder. Skeleton thefts, I ask you."

I skimmed through two or three quasi-fictional accounts of the theft at Paxton's. Contrasted with rather jocular references to Wardle were weighty evaluations of Paxton himself. Designer of the Crystal Palace. Botanist, architect, engineer. Liberal MP, inventor and railway promoter. "I don't understand, sir, why they make one little theft so important, just because he's well known."

Wardle snorted. "He's got his finger in a few pies. They all have, that railway lot. Remember Hudson? Owned half the papers. That's how he had the clout to get the filthy things built. I'll give you two-to-one on, Paxton's got money in a couple of these rags." He must have noticed my expression of shock. "How long have you lived here, Watchman? Have you not noticed how money talks? If they say it's good, it's because they're selling it. If they say it's bad, they haven't got shares in it – yet. Simple as that."

I stared at the papers, as if they might turn into a pumpkin. "Sir, shouldn't we warn Hudson to invest in guard dogs?"

"Why's that?"

"The thieves clearly have a partiality for railway developers." Wardle gave the bark that served him for laughter. "Hudson lost his pile in '47. The week of terror, they called it. He's still in exile for fraud, far as I know, despised and debt-ridden. Still, there's something in what you say."

So Coxhill's hero-worship was indeed misplaced.

"Tell you what, Watchman." Wardle put his hand to his brow. "Do some digging around. See where Paxton's interests lie. And the others, why not? Not least which papers they back. Publishing nonsense like this! There's times I'd like a little something to shake in their faces as a warning."

I could think of no better place to look into Paxton's holdings than the British Museum Library. I had forgotten, though, that my reader's card was only valid for a month. They would not permit me to enter, nor renew my pass without a further recommendation from Wardle. I asked for Miss Villiers, thinking she might put in a special word for me. She was unavailable. I tried to write a note, but the appropriate words eluded me.

I hurried away down Museum Street, gritting my teeth at the awkward prospect of asking Wardle again, when a voice called to me from a doorway.

"Sergeant Lawless?" Out came Miss Villiers, wrapped in a long coat that would have suited the Tsarina. "It *is* you! I thought you'd vanished quite away. You're rather overdue with that lunch you promised me."

She waved away my mumbled apologies with a disdainful gesture, taking hold of my sleeves and dragging me into the tea room.

"I see." She arched her brows. "You are in too much of a hurry to stop with me."

"I'm working," I protested, laughing. "At least, I really can't stop long."

"Well, don't let me delay you, officer. I wouldn't like to be guilty of keeping a detective from his work through some womanish fancy for tea and cakes."

I demurred, of course, explaining all at once how helpful she had been, how sorry I was, what an awkward situation I now had, and so on and so forth.

Before I could object, she ordered a pot of tea and scones. Thus obliging me to stay at least a while, she gushed with questions like water from a Highland spring. "Have you found the chap? I've been watching like a hawk, but not a peep. I was worried that my indiscretion had led to his arrest. Of course, I'm jumping to conclusions, assuming he has committed a crime. Otherwise, why should you be looking for him? And why should he hide himself?"

I was so relieved to see her, and not to be in her bad books,

I quite forgot my usual reticence. It was no longer police business, I reasoned to myself, and thus no longer confidential. So I spoke of the spout, of the repair man and the cadaver, and of my first investigations. "We have not apprehended the man," I confessed finally. "Nor have we solved the case. Indeed, the inspector has no intention of making further enquiries, and I am bound to comply. You are right, though, in thinking I suspected this man of doing something, if not criminal, at least highly irregular. I'm sorry I left you in the dark. Only, with my work and Inspector Wardle–"

"This Wardle of yours." She gave a look of mock disdain. "Has he no curiosity?"

"He is not a character out of Mr Poe." I smiled. "I must return your book."

"No hurry. I have books enough at my disposal." She idly stirred her cup of tea. "That address, though. It's a public house, did you know? I just happened to be passing through Clerkenwell one day."

"Just happened to be?" I nodded. "Did you ask for our man?"

She looked offended. "Sergeant, would it be proper for a young lady to enter a public house alone?" She laughed. "Besides, I suddenly thought it suspicious. What kind of chap would give as his address a public house?"

"That could admit of a simple answer."

Her eyes sparkled. "Someone with something to hide?"

"Someone who lives in a pub," I countered. "It's not uncommon for gentlemen whose resources run low to hire chairs in taverns." I thought better of telling her that I myself had stopped in a corner of the Old Red Lion before securing Mrs Willington's garret. "There needn't be a mystery behind every detail, you know. That's what you learn when you work in the real police force."

"Is it?" She flared her nostrils. "Why, then, pray tell, should our Mr Skelton have stopped using the library?"

"Are you quite sure he has?"

"Yes." She stared at me. "Unless he comes in disguise."

"Have you checked with your colleagues?"

She made a face. "They would consider it most inappropriate for me to ask. As the youngest librarian, and a single lady, I must consider my every action scrupulously."

"Could you not check his card? See if he has been consulting any books?"

"I might be able to do that," she nodded, "and you might find the time for a visit to the Rose and Crown in Clerkenwell."

I hesitated.

"It's at the corner of Red Lion Street and Victoria Road," she said, holding back a smirk, "in case you'd forgotten, Sergeant."

"I shall visit it," I promised, "if only to clear away the cobwebs of a mystery that was never a mystery. I wonder, might your bearded revolutionary help us?"

"It may have been he that warned our man to stay away. Still, I may try to pick his brains, if I can do so surreptitiously." She raised her teacup. "Here's to detective fever."

"And the passing of that fever," I nodded, "with as few casualties as possible."

The Rose & Crown

"ALL PATRONS ARE REQUESTED" – announced a placard by the stairs to the tavern – "BEFORE ENTERING THE SALOON TO LEAVE AT THE BAR THEIR KNIVES AND PISTOLS, OR ANY OTHER WEAPON THEY MAY HAVE ABOUT THEM."

I had changed out of uniform before leaving work. I went wrong in the backstreets skirting Liquorpond Row, but I came

suddenly upon the Session House which stood at the head of
both Victoria Street and Red Lion Street, its door daubed with
the words "Closed Prior to Demolition". Across the square, like
the gatehouse of the labyrinth, stood the Rose and Crown.

I decided I must bide my time. Accordingly, I bought myself
a pint of watery ale and listened in to conversations, as the
place began to fill. A miraculous assembly it was too. Since the
troubles of '48, Edinburgh had had its share of European
emigrés, but never had I seen anything like this. Besides the
navvies labouring on the canal and the Irish from the
underground train, there were French and Germans,
Dutchmen and Greeks. Spanish fishermen; Norwegians in the
ice trade; Italians from the Sadler's Wells, their earrings
twinkling as they twirled their moustaches. There was a Moor
with a crimson cummerbund; a Slav girl selling posies; there
was even a Chinaman, with his pigtails rolled up under a
British Navy cap. These diverse specimens of humanity formed
energetic circles around small tables, as a ragtag trio struck up
one jig after another, as if disconcerted that nobody was
dancing. At the bar, a weasel of a man with a mop of oily hair
was eyeing me warily. I retreated to the corner furthest from
the hearth.

At the table nearest the musicians a heated discussion arose.
On a sudden, a fellow with a broad smile slammed down his
tankard and called out. "Come on, boys. Give us 'Fast Fade the
Roses of Pleasure', will you?"

The discussion was momentarily stilled, as the fiddler spoke
to the drummer. "Begging your pardon, sir," he said in soft
Irish tones, "but we don't know it."

"Lads, lads," the man insisted. "Come on and strike it up
for us."

"Honestly, sir. Only that it's not a part of our repertory."

The man insisted, his smile tightening. "Look, boys. I'm a

musician, too, you know." There was laughter at his table. He stood up, rounding upon them. "What's that? I'll play rhythm with your bones if you ain't respectful. Will you play 'The Roses of Pleasure' or won't you, boys?"

The man's companions eyed each other meaningfully, as the musicians conferred. "We can do 'The Last Rose of Summer'," said the fiddler, "or 'The Roses of Picardy'."

"Damn you," the man exploded, his smile devilishly wide. "You come here with your outlandish tunes, but you don't learn the old songs." With a roar, he swept his table clear of glasses. "Damn your eyes," he shouted above the clatter, and he seemed ready to leap at the musicians, if his companions had not risen as a man and pinned him against the wall. They lifted him up, as if it were the commonest thing, and carried him over the broken glass, across the straw-covered floor, and out the back of the tavern.

Hesitantly, the band struck up again and everyone went back to their chatter. When the barmaid brought me another pint, I caught her by the sleeve.

"If you please," I began, meaning to sound offhand, "have you a fellow living here by the name of Skelton?"

She showed me a face as stony as if I had spoken Greek.

I fumbled in my pocket and drew out Miss Villiers' note, staring at the name I had read so many times. "Yes, that was it. Berwick Skelton. Don't you know him?"

She scurried back to the bar, and a series of whispers were exchanged. Eyes darted in my direction, and I heard the weasel of a man ask, "Who is it wants to know?"

I found myself stared at by a hundred eyes full of mistrust. A panic went through me. The weasel man knew very well it was I who had enquired. Yet he gave no sign of coming over to me. I took a sip of my ale and rose to go up to him, where he was leaning against the bar. Three seafaring types, however, were seated at a table in front of me. Large as whales and quite as intractable, they gave way not an inch, and I was obliged to call out from where I stood.

"I'm looking for–" I began. "Would you know if–" I faltered. It seemed strangely impersonal to call him Berwick Skelton; Mr Skelton sounded formal; Berwick too familiar. Besides, I was giving myself away with the way I was speaking: far too polite, like a toff or a foreigner. I tried to roughen my tones. "A mutual friend told us I'd find this particular fellow here."

"Did they?" the weasel nodded. He looked slowly around the room, as if our chat was a show for the benefit of the whole tavern. He turned to the barmaid, restraining a smirk. "Sal, do you know anyone by the name that the gentleman mentioned?"

The barmaid went about her business, stony-faced.

The weasel looked disappointed. He looked around the tavern again. "Has nobody heard of–" He looked at me. "Forgive me. What was the name again, sir?"

Feeling trapped as a mouse in a cage, I said it again. "Berwick Skelton."

How can I describe the ripple that surged around the room? Around every table, they glanced from one to another. There was none of the posturing that would accompany such a scene in a theatrical melodrama. No facial histrionics, no whispered questions. How, then, was I so sure that they were all, every last one of them, only dissembling ignorance?

"I'm afraid," said the weasel, running a hand through his unkempt hair, "we can't help you, officer."

My heart sank. He knew me for a policeman. Was it so obvious? I should have dressed differently, spoken differently. I should have prepared some elaborate alibi.

"A drink for the officer, Sal. Whisky, is it? You are a Scot, if I ain't mistaken."

I could not give up before I had begun. I returned his gaze. "Thank you."

The weasel gave a nod. As if by magic, the musicians struck up anew. Conversation resumed, and the seafaring types allowed me to pass.

"The thing is, officer," said the weasel as I joined him at the bar, "you have to be careful round these parts. Don't get me wrong. Only we've had, shall we say, a little awkwardness with colleagues of yours of late."

"I'm sorry to hear of it," I mumbled.

"Well," he said with a dismissive gesture, "it's just unfortunate. You may have seen how they're digging up the roads around here. Progress, you see. Underground trains, iron ships, whatever. I'm all for it. Sadly, though, some of the lads have had their houses quite swep' away. There's talk of leafy suburbs being built, for us to remove to, you see, though I for one would rather stay here, where I was born and raised."

"Of course."

"Only it appears some very important businesses have purchased the land. Corporations. Practices of law and medicine and oculism. They want their premises up and running as soon as possible. Who can blame them? Accordingly, they've engaged the police to exert a little persuasive force. Only as nobody's told us the whereabouts of these leafy suburbs as yet, there lurks that doubt in our minds, you see. As to whether the leafy suburbs actually exist."

"Yes," I mumbled. "That's a problem, I grant you."

"Come, come. It ain't your fault, is it? Nevertheless, dear chap, you'll understand, it's disappointing when the police – our protectors, as we're told – start knocking our houses down. Which is why a copper strolling in here does not meet with the most generous reception."

There was a shout from below. "Ho-ho!"

I turned to see the smiling man, reeling drunkenly back in, to the hilarity of all.

"Ah," said the weasel. "The music lover returns. But you can see, even if we did happen to know of what you were enquiring, which we don't, we might be less than inclined to divulge it."

"This the copper, then?" The drunk man lurched up towards me. Something about his features was oddly familiar. "Been 'specting you, we have. What you after, eh?"

Seeing no harm in it, I mentioned Skelton's name again.

The drunk frowned. "John," he said to the weasel, "do we have a gentleman under that particular monicker in these vicinitudes?"

"Don't know that we do, Smiler, old mate. What would you suggest the officer do?"

"I do not know, John, my old friend, my old charpering homie. How about you ask down the Academy?" Somebody behind me laughed. The drunk turned on them reprovingly. "A lot of gentlemen are Academaticians, you know."

"Ask the hoofers," somebody called out, "down the Haymarket."

This drew chuckles all around.

"Ask Charles Dickens."

Further laughter.

"Ask the Prince of Wales."

This brought a bellow of laughter.

"Ask his fiancée."

"If you can find her!"

"I am sorry," said the weasel impassively, as the chorus of guffaws grew more and more raucous. "The lads do get carried away. But rest assured, nobody knows nothing."

At this, the drunk roared with laughter.

The whisky rasped at my throat, but I drank it down, threw a few pennies on the bar, and hurried out.

Note from British Museum Library: Berwick Skelton's Studies:

Dear Sergeant,

By gosh, you were right. What a job he must have had of it, avoiding my hours. So it appears that he knows. That is unfortunate, I admit. Yet, if he does not want to be found, that means he has something to conceal. Wherefore we want to find him all the more.

I have checked his card and the fellow's been reading as much as ever. His recent areas of study are:

a. Engineering journals. Besides hydraulics, he has a predilection for tunnels.

b. Dissolvent literature. Social pamphlets, political pamphlets, the *Poor Man's Guardian*, the *Black Dwarf*, the *Beehive*, pretty much everything my poor father would wish me to steer clear of.

Now I may be mistaken, but I believe he has taken a couple of cuttings. (Imagine! I suppose it shows a deep interest, if a lack of community spirit.) An engraving from the *Illustrated London News*: a depiction of the Queen's outing through the filthy Thames Tunnel in 1843. Also, a section from one of Mr Dickens' angrier editorials in *Household Words*. Until I locate another copy, I cannot say precisely what he excised, but it was the conclusion to a fiery piece in Chartist vein.

That comprises his reading for the past year. If you wish, I shall look through everything he has taken out

since he joined in '58. Glancing down the titles, there
is a deal of literature, though I notice also some issues
of the *Red Republican*, which published a translation of
the bearded revolutionary's inflammatory pamphlet.
When I have summoned the confidence to brave his
beard, I will be in contact again. Kindly send the
Professor in a week.

Yours feverishly,

Miss R Villiers

LORD'S

I was disheartened by my debacle in Clerkenwell, and could
neither bring myself to ask Wardle for a new recommendation
to the library, nor to write to Miss Villiers with such a rotten
report. She sent her note by penny post to my garret, to avoid
arousing Wardle's suspicions, and it quite put the spring back
in my step. The same day, at lunchtime, Worm's friend, the
Professor, turned up at the Yard with a further letter, addressed
in a spidery hand:

Esteemed Police, namely Lawless,

*Remembering your injunction that you should like to know
more about my mechanisms, the injury and larceny thereof,
please to come today to the sporting green of Lord's new cricket
ground, St John's Wood.*

*I have been called upon by the Marylebone Cricket Club to
do some repairs in situ and wish you to understand that the
mechanism installed there was a species of prototype for the
clock you admired at Euston, now destroyed.*

If you should care to come along, I should be glad to see

*light shed upon these obscure, nefarious dealings. I shall be
there at lunchtime.*

Yours in all sincerity,

B N Ganz, Esq

ALLNUTT & GANZ, WATCHMAKERS OF DISTINCTION

I certainly did care to go along. I was pleased to think that
an inquiry made so long ago might yet bear fruit. But how to
tackle Wardle? I hurried in without a strategy, and was taken
aback to find him at my desk, consulting the newspaper's
sporting pages.

"Spit it out, youngster," he barked. He always knew when I
had something to say.

"Reading about the cricket, sir? I'd like to go to this Lord's
ground."

"A Scots cricket fanatical?" His eyes narrowed and he started
making a peculiar noise. It took me a few moments to realise
that he was laughing. It was the first time I had heard him
properly laugh. "Full of surprises you are, son."

"I used to watch it as a child, sir, in Edinburgh." I had no
more watched cricket than I had been to the moon.

"I was unaware that you Scots enjoyed sporting activities,
beyond sword skipping and log tossing." A faraway look came
into his eye. "Oh, I was a useful bowler, when I was young
underarm, mind you. Never made my peace with it since they
messed with the laws. It's all bloody round-arm these days, like
ladies. Or out-and-out chucking. I blame the locomotive trains.
People think time is money and speed's of the essence. Foolish
claptrap. Where's the subtlety in it, I ask you? Where's the guile?"

Terrified he might interrogate me on some intricacy of the
game, I just grimaced.

"Nothing pressing to be done here." He frowned, a rueful, indulgent frown. "I won't join you. Another time, perhaps. Go for the day, if you like."

To my surprise, the Professor was still outside, spinning a top back and forth on a string. He stuffed it in his pocket and doffed his cap. "Good day, officer."

"Good day again, yourself. Professor, tell Ganz I'll see him there, would you?"

"I could, sir," he intoned. He had an impish tone, the Professor. The nasality of an archbishop, with great elongated vowels. When he said "rather," it sounded like "rawther;" in place of "can't" was "caun't," like the heavyweight, Big Ben Caunt; Lord Palmerston more like "Paw-miss-tin". He hesitated. "Only as how he didn't rightly ask for a reply." He had read the note, of course, and he was eager to come with me. "Worm should be along any minute. He's a cricket fiend."

Worm fell in beside us in the Regent's Park. He presented me with a sweet pastry that he had doubtless pinched from a street trader. "Didn't know you played, old cove."

"There's a lot we don't know about each other. Beautiful day, though, isn't it?" I said, ruffling the Professor's hair, which made him crinkle up his eyes in annoyance. "Makes you glad to be alive, boys."

"Oh, now." Worm shot me a reproachful look. "I wouldn't go that far."

It was comical to watch the two of them together. The Professor was a charming wee fellow with a snub nose and gritty red hair, who clearly thought the world of Worm, and Worm took advantage of this to the hilt.

"Give us a ha'penny," said Worm. The little fellow complied reluctantly. Worm held the coin up in the sunlight. "Observe closely."

With a click of his fingers, he made the thing disappear. I applauded.

"Bleeding heck," cried out the Professor, stamping his feet with a peculiar dignity. "Why is it always my ha'penny? Why couldn't you have asked the hofficer?"

"Cut the stamping, you daft bat," said Worm. "It's a fair spell before you're due boots."

The notion that these urchins planned their expenditure far in advance impressed me no end. Nonetheless, on reaching the gates of the ground, I proffered the entrance charge for the three of us. "These junior officers," I explained, "are helping me with my inquiry."

"A likely story," said the gate man, frowning severely. "Helping themselves, more like it. There's been enough petty thefts this month to feed an army. And fires."

Before I could reason with the fellow, Worm piped up, "We don't want into your poxy ground. Who's on the card, anyhow?"

"Lillywhite," said the man reverently. "Wisden, Grace, and Tear 'em Tarrant."

"What do you think, Professor? Worthy of our friend's hard-earned pennies?"

"Worthy?" the man laughed. "These are the most famous men in the 'ole country."

"Excepting good Queen Vic," said Worm, "and her princes." With a snap of the fingers, he retrieved the lost ha'penny from out of the Professor's ear and presented it to me with a whisper. "Sneak us in, can't you?"

"I think you'll find," said the Professor with a huffy expression, "that Mr Charles Dickens is even more famouser than that lot."

"I'll watch them," I promised the man. I paid for the boys, and returned the Professor's ha'penny, as I thought my income a little steadier than his.

As we passed under the canopy of the spectators' stand, I was astonished to see a portly, mustachioed gent running hell-for-leather towards me, as if fleeing a crime. He bent over, thrusting his tightly-clad white backside in our faces. He picked up a ball and proceeded to hurl it into the distance with a grunt to rival the Highland Games practitioners. This performance earned him a round of genteel applause, which he accepted with a self-deprecating gesture.

"Look at that arm," Worm marvelled. The man's limbs seemed to me unremarkable.

"That's one of England's finest athletes, is it?" I asked. "To be honest, I was expecting some frivolity with horses, or at least hoops and mallets."

Worm clucked at my ignorance and led me over to the clubhouse, which he called the pavilion. This was crowned by a clock the image of the Euston one, only smaller. As we approached, we were assailed from the balcony by a familiar wheedling voice. "Sergeant!" Roxton Coxhill hailed me. "Do come up, won't you?"

The slovenly guard attending the stairs opened a single eye. "Members and players only," he mumbled. "You members or players?"

"All right, Jenkins," Coxhill's voice came down the stairwell, "he's with me."

The Professor and Worm slunk silently up the wooden staircase, the guard too weary to object, and we entered a long dining room set for a great luncheon. The walls boasted trophy cabinets, bats, balls and stakes bearing illegible signatures. I examined a daguerreotype of a solemn group of fellows wearing outlandish blazers. They brandished their bats as if they were still boys, which would have seemed amusing if they were not now most likely running the country.

"Glad to see you, old chap," said Coxhill, grasping my shoulder. "Do accompany me on a circuit around the boundary. I have some information of interest to you."

"Information?" I nodded. "I must find the clockmaker. Have you seen him?"

"I'll just fetch my pipe."

The boys had cornered a whiskered cricketer. He was dressed in cream flannels, padding affixed round his legs and his gloves sewn with rubber spikes.

"You're E M Grace, ain't you?" said Worm. "I heard your cover drive is hexquisite."

"I heard," said the Professor, anxious not to be outdone, "that you bowl the ball from behind your whiskers. So as they won't see the spin, of course."

"Of course," the man laughed.

"Would you like to see a trick, sir?" the Professor said. Ignoring Worm's dismay, he soldiered on. "Observe this ha'penny. I put it into my ear, and, with a shake of the head, it vanishes–" A look of doubt crossed his face. He shook his head again, and stuck his finger in his ear. Looking rather alarmed, he consulted Worm in an urgent undertone.

"God Almighty." Worm peered in the Professor's ear, cursed under his breath, then cuffed his friend about the head. "Why can't you stick to your spinning top?"

"It's called a diavolo," retorted the Professor.

"Spinning top, I said," Worm hissed. "Blimey. Is there a doctor in the house?"

By good fortune, Grace himself was a medical man. While he inspected the Professor's ear, Worm confided in me. "Professor's never got the hang of it. You have to distract their attention. That's where the magic lies."

There was applause outside, and Grace looked up in exasperation. "You'll have to go to the Children's Hospital. I haven't the equipment here, and I have to bat." He pulled on his gloves, and strode manfully out.

"We'd best be going," said Worm, looking thunder at the Professor, who steadfastly avoided his gaze. As Coxhill emerged, pipe in hand, Worm dragged his friend away with a scowl. "Oi," he shouted as the Professor stomped off down the stairs, "I told you. Easy on them boots."

Coxhill took my arm in a vice-like grip. Barely lunchtime and he smelt of liquor. He led me out to walk around the boundary rope. It seemed a shame to keep this vast expanse of green for these strange antics, when it could have been a park or a golf course.

I hoped I might get something useful out of Coxhill. But he took it upon himself to explain the game to me, breaking off only to applaud, and I could barely get a word in. All I could see was men in the distance, evidently having epileptic fits and practising their golf swings.

When we passed in front of the more expensive seats, the assembled society of straw boaters, petticoats and parasols so drew Coxhill's attention that he barely spoke to me at all. I was surprised how lax the general behaviour was. People lounged on their benches as if they were in their private back gardens. Fine ladies shouted out like fishwives. And all sorts of intimate conversations seemed to be held in every corner, while nobody paid the slightest bit of attention to the game. Of course, Coxhill thrived on this. He shook hands with top-hatted gentlemen, plumped himself down beside unattended ladies with hampers, and offered tips to sharp gents with field glasses. Every so often I glanced back at the clubhouse in hopes of spotting the clockmaker.

"Disraeli is right, you know," said Coxhill, leading me on past the cheaper seats. "Individualism is all but dead. It's only we entrepreneurs who keep the flame of ingenuity alight.

Lovely shot, Mr Grace." He applauded, and gestured that I should do likewise. "As I was saying, my father practically owned the White Conduit Club."

"I thought they called this the Marylebone Cricket Club."

"Quite, quite. One must get accustomed to the newfangled names. One turns one's head for a moment and the city has transformed itself. Marvellous, I suppose, though a tad disorientating. They used to play down at White Conduit Fields, you see."

I explained that I was a newcomer to London.

"It's an age ago now. Down at the old Great Northern terminal. It was father sold the land to the railway barons. Made his fortune."

"I thought your father was a teacher."

"That's right, old chap." He looked pleased that I had remembered. "A brilliant man. Taught at Heidelberg University, you know. That's how we come to know the royals, you see. It was Albert who introduced him to Mama. Dear Mama." His voice quivered and he fell silent, staring into the middle distance. His grip on my arm tightened, until the crack of splintering wood broke the spell, and he turned back to the field. "Well bowled, Charlie. Marvellous!"

I stared out into the middle. I tried to picture Wardle as a youngster, hurling a ball at a man with a bat. The image eluded me. Instead I found myself recalling my own father's fury when I came home from school sports with a chunk gouged out of my index finger and was useless in the workshop for weeks. "What did your father teach?" I asked.

He stared at me in puzzlement for a moment, as if he had forgotten where he was. "Engineering," he declared vigorously. "A genius with machinations of every kind."

"Was it he who founded your hydraulic enterprise?"

"Not a bit of it," he rejoined. "The HECC is the product of

my genius, if I may so put it, and mine alone. You know, father wouldn't have got on in the modern climate."

"Mr Coxhill–"

"Do call me Roxton, old chap. Father was too much of a gentleman, you see. Too cautious. Of course, there are hazards with up-to-the-minute knowhow. That's the territory. But one must be bold. Take risks. Should there be little losses, well, why else does one insure oneself?"

I looked at him. This must be it. A flood of verbosity he had poured out, but there might be sense hidden in it. I breathed in sharply. "You mentioned that you had some information."

"Time enough, old man." The teams began walking off the pitch, though I had seen nothing conclusive in the play. Coxhill hastened towards the clubhouse, hurrying to shake the hand of an energetic young man. "Jolly good, young Charlie. You really ought to up sticks and throw in your lot with us southerners."

"I should, should I?" said the man. His voice was so familiar it was uncanny. "Well, I'm off south, all right."

"I say, Constable, come and meet this young fellow. I daresay it's him you've come to see, no?" Coxhill tapped the side of his nose, before vanishing in a haze of social niceties.

The young cricket player regarded me with a sardonic look that threw me quite off my guard. "Pleased to meet you. I'm Charlie Wardle."

My jaw dropped open. I introduced myself in subdued tones, and he led me back up the steps to the dining room.

"Work with the old man, do you?" His eyes narrowed. "Has he sent you?"

"No, no. He gave me the day off."

"Oh yes? How d'you like working with him, then?"

I fetched around for an appropriate answer.

"Say no more," he smiled. "Someone's got to do to it, eh?"

I laughed. "Do you not see eye to eye?"

"We have our differences," he grinned. "He says I'm a republican agitator, I call him a lily-livered loyalist. Still, if you're not for reform when you're young, they say you've got no heart."

The bewhiskered medic, standing in the changing room door, overheard us and tutted. "You are misleading the officer by omission, Charlie." He turned to me. "They go on to say that if you're not against reform when you are old, you have no brains."

"Do they, Dr Grace?" Charlie grinned. "I'd rather have heart than brains any day."

"That, Charlie, is why you are still bowling and I am still batting."

Charlie invited me to lunch with him. I found a quiet spot in the corner while he went off to change his boots.

"Forgive me," I said when he returned. "Are you not on the same team as the man with the whiskers?"

Charlie snorted. "The two changing rooms are not for the home and away teams, they're for gentlemen and players."

"I don't follow, I'm afraid."

He laughed. "I'm not surprised. In simpler terms, I get paid and he doesn't need to. Toffs and peasants, see? You've got a lot to learn about cricket. Tuck in."

Charlie Wardle was thoroughly engaging and I took to him at once. He was a textile worker, skilled, yet he had lost one job after another. He blamed the mechanised factories, which he called prison camps, run by faceless committees and shameless entrepreneurs.

"Where's the end to it? They buy things up on a whim, then cast us aside when they're done without fear of retribution. It's madness. Father's never forgiven me."

"What for?"

"Moving to Lancashire. And the Preston strike. I went to gaol, see."

"Because of the strike?" I looked at him in surprise, then recalled the news. "Ah, the riots too?"

"I'd take part in it all again, if it came. Which it will. Cotton's drying up, with this bloody war in America. They'll have civil war again here, if they don't watch. Which side will you be on?"

"That depends," I said. "We Scots were a bit taken aback last time you chopped the King's head off."

He laughed. "Look, I'm for reform. I may even be a republican. But father, he thinks that makes me a Chartist, or some kind of communist. He's all out-dated. He wouldn't know a communist if one smacked him in the nose."

I recalled Chartism from Miss Villiers' letter, but the word communist was new to me.

"Look what we're up against. Thousands of years of feudalism, held together by aristocrats whose only interest is keeping the wealth in the hands of as few as possible. The newspapers pretend the issues are dead, but that's just propaganda. D'you know there's a war going on in this country?"

"Money talks," I said. "Industrialists buy papers in order to control information." It occurred to me that I was parroting what his father had said to me.

He looked at me with a new respect. "Point taken. But why need anyone go hungry? That's what they were asking in '48. The powers that be don't like the sound of that." He jabbed at his potatoes belligerently, putting on a pompous voice. "Keep them in their places. Down the mines. Off and fight Johnny Russian." He spoke in an undertone. "All these people, if they've knives and forks on their tables but no food, well, they'll end up cutting something. Wouldn't you think?"

I gestured around us. "Should you really be hobnobbing with the other side?"

"Know your enemy." He cut into his pie and watched the juices flow out with satisfaction. "And you don't half get good fodder here."

"A fairweather reformist."

He laughed again. "I spout off about ideals and ideologies, yes. But I've no illusions. Whatever presses men together, even if it's exploitation, can promote liberty. But you have to educate the hopeless, marshal the disinherited. Organisation's the key."

"Organisation," I nodded, reminded of Worm and his long-term planning for the Professor's boots. "That's how you'll transform society?"

"Maybe" he grimaced. "Not me, though. I'm sick of the old satanic mills. I'm off to Australia. It's Stephenson I have to impress now."

"The rocket man?"

"Heathfield Stephenson." He pointed out a gent smoking on the balcony. "Captain of the All England Eleven. That's the other thing father can't forgive me for. I'm a better cricketer than he ever was. They're touring Australia this winter."

"Going to start a peasants' revolt?"

"They don't have peasants in Australia." He chuckled. "Not yet, at least."

"What'll your father say?"

He considered for a moment. "He'll be glad to see the back of me."

I might have said the same of my own father, were I the one headed for the Antipodes.

"Five minutes, gents," called E.M. Grace.

"Is that clock still broke?" exclaimed the man with the moustaches. "Can't we afford a bloody watchmaker? I thought the club owned half of England."

Charlie gave me a look.

"Clockmaker Jew fellow's up there now," Coxhill called out. He pointed to a ladder up to a trap door in the ceiling. "Fixed in two ticks, I'm sure."

As Charlie excused himself from the table I frowned. "Off home now, are you?"

"You're joking." He smiled. "Game's barely started."

"You go out and play another game?"

"The same game, and tomorrow and the next day, like as not."

"And I thought golf was tiresome." I stretched. Now I understood why Wardle had said I could stay all day. "One last thing, Charlie. Among your reforms, and strikes and organising, you haven't come across a chap called Skelton, have you?"

"Skelton?" Charlie looked at me. "No, don't know anyone by that name. Excuse us, I'm needed out on the field."

As the players muddled out, I popped my head up through the trap door into the clock turret.

Ganz was there, muttering to himself. He gestured at the three faces of the clock. The hands were still there, but not much more. "I'll murder 'em. Little hooligans."

"Taken the main movement, have they?"

"The main movement?" He scowled. "They've took the escapement and the motion work as well. Bandits. You slave your life away, designing and crafting, then some little Visigoth purloins it to pass off as his own."

He was so livid, he would not be spoken to. I could have told him that I recognised the handiwork, from that night at Euston Square.

I resolved to tell Wardle a little fib, that Charlie had asked after him in kindly fashion. After all, Wardle had been looking at the sporting pages; he must have known his son was in town. But he never asked about it.

"I tell you what, Cameron, old man."

I could not recall telling Coxhill my Christian name, but I decided against correcting his mistake. He had piqued my curiosity with his promise of information.

I had passed a lazy afternoon, trying to make sense of the game. Half of the players lounged in the clubhouse, lazy as pigs, while the other half ran around after the ball like headless chickens. The sun shone down. To while away the time, I had reluctantly accepted Coxhill's offer of an ale or two from the clubhouse bar; as soon as the drink was bought, though, he was apt to disappear off with a new acquaintance, leaving me to my thoughts.

As the match drew to its mysterious close, I found myself accepting his offer of a lift into town, against my better judgement. Hunt regarded me with veiled hostility as his master led me up to the luxurious carriage. I admit, I took a perverse pleasure in riding within while he sat up front in the dust and heat.

"You and I are going out on the town. I won't brook a refusal. I simply must show you the ropes. Bright young thing like you. Hardly seen life at all, I'll wager."

I smiled uneasily, but he was obdurate. We simply must and we simply would go out. It was irregular, all right, I told myself, but he was in such garrulous mood, who could tell what I might learn?

"Have you been to the Evans? Thought not. You simply must try the devilled kidneys. We'll take in the show! Bertie and I have the use of a private box, y'know."

"Must cost a pretty penny."

"Everything has its price, my friend. Most useful for

entertaining, though. You can imagine. There's a late spot too, I know you'll enjoy. Don't fret. I've a jacket here to lend you. Fit well enough. Hunty boy! Straight to the club!"

I think that I have never heard a man so talkative say so little of substance. Yet he had friends aplenty. He was greeted with striking joviality at his club, where he lent me a jacket and tie and we changed rapidly. At Covent Garden, as we descended into the vast, dimly lit music hall, peopled with the most flavoursome crowd, a steady stream of nods and hulloahs assailed us.

"Now, Cameron," he said, rubbing his hands together. "Let us secure some refreshments."

An important looking man hurried over and mumbled to him apologetically.

"Dash it all, is the box taken?" He peered up into the darkness in annoyance. "Table by the wall, then. Less likely to have our pockets picked, what?"

As I strove to cast off my reserve, Coxhill summoned to our table a stream of tidbits and delicacies such as I had never seen. I would have felt even less comfortable in my uniform, but I have never liked wearing borrowed robes. His jacket was of undeniably fine tweed, but it was too short in the sleeve, and made my arms seem like a baboon's. He had enjoined me to leave my things at the club, but I preferred to keep them with me, fearful of finding myself stranded in Piccadilly Circus at five in the morning.

Despite my protestations, he made clear I was not to put my hand in my pocket. So I tucked guiltily into a seemingly endless round of chops, kidneys and every type of potato, while he pointed out to me some personalities in the audience: Thackeray, the *Punch* Brotherhood, and Wilkie Collins, the author so admired by Miss Villiers. As he accepted some snuff from the waiter, I decided it was time to engage him on more serious matters.

"Mr Coxhill, you mentioned some information–"

"Not over dinner, old man." His eyes widened. "Come along. Enjoy yourself."

I held back a sigh. I must proceed patiently, I told myself, be more canny. "You were telling me about the hazards of modern business."

"Insure to the hilt," he said, sniffing up the powder, like some anteater from the Cape. "Father considered insurance a gamble, though. Did I mention my father? He taught at Heidelberg University, you know. That's how we know the royals."

I glanced at him in dismay. "And insurance–"

"He didn't hold with it, you see. I'm not averse to the odd flutter myself. Nor is a certain prince of the realm I happen to know. I'll tell you a story. Just last week, I was trouncing the young rascal at billiards in Marlborough House. We had a tidy sum wagered on it. I fluff a shot, and Bertie pipes up, all excited: Roxy, Roxy, you are too drunk, he says, too drunk. Tum Tum, says I, anticipating my triumph, I may be too drunk, but you are too fat. He tells the valet to prepare my luggage and only goes and chucks me out. Worst of all, he claims that the debt's invalidated. Invalidated! The cheek of the boy, I ask you."

"How interesting," I managed. There was a surfeit of royal tittle-tattle in the papers, and I had little appetite for more. "But insurance–"

"The lowest sort of gamble, father called it. Wouldn't wash today, you know. It's a dead man who doesn't insure himself for his life, as it were." He nudged me in the stomach, and gave a sort of a sideways grin. "I suppose it is gambling, of a sort. But we all like a little flutter, don't we, old man?"

"The machine at Euston," I said casually. "It was insured, was it?"

"Oh, yes. Dashed hard to get the blighters to pay up. Ah, the show, at last. Hush up a little now."

I held my tongue, frustrated, as the curtain rose on a stage veiled in gauze, or rather the mists of the past. A man in a dressing-gown, standing for turn-of-the-century costume, clutched a pile of swaddling clothes, while painted signposts were carried across the stage as he travelled widely, amassing a fortune. Then a demon sprite skipped up, murthered our traveller most foully, and stole his fortune. The gauze was snatched away, and the actor removed his historical dressing gown to characterise the swaddling clothes grown to a man.

This offspring likewise travels the world, past those same signposts, in his thirst for revenge. He finds the demon sprite on an egg-box throne, lording it up over a tribe of dancing girls. Our man becomes his trusted courtier, meanwhile becoming enamoured of a strapping Amazon wench. The sprite, hitherto indifferent to these women so proximate and fetching, promptly weds the wench himself. Whereat resinous flashes play in the wings, and a cannon ball is rolled around.

In this terrible storm, our dejected hero sees in a green limelight the dressing gown that was his father, which plays out for him his unjust fate. The stage becomes luminous with blue fire. The egg-box throne falls, discovering the stolen riches. At a chord from a solitary violin, the sprite doubles up and our man runs him through. He weds the wench, who seemed well worth the effort, and the dancing girls erupt in a hymeneal dance, with high kicks, drawing the stoutest applause.

"Some port, there, my man!" Coxhill turned to me, his eyes gleeful. "Capital, don't you think?"

"Yes. Yes, of course. You were telling me, though," I hesitated, "about that crane at Euston."

"Hard to get them to pay at the best of times. Worse when

there seems something rotten in it."

"That's right," I said, trying not to sound too eager. "You thought someone was trying to damage confidence in your company."

"Did I?" He bit into a quail's leg. Oil ran down his chin. "I don't recall."

"Do you have enemies, that you know of?"

"Glory be, old chap, one can hardly start a concern of this magnitude without ruffling a few feathers."

I spluttered on my port. The image of the dead man from the spout flashed before me. And he spoke of ruffled feathers. I looked at him more closely. "Does anyone spring to mind?"

"One hopes not," he said, playing down the idea with a carefree smile. "One hopes not."

I thought of the mysterious repair man. "Mr Coxhill – Roxton. I do urge you to think. Could there be someone, within your own ranks even, who holds a grievance against you?"

"I understood it was activists. What have the bloody Fenians against me?"

"Your man, Pat, said the saboteur had a knowledge of the machines."

"Pat? Don't mind old Pat. He's on his last legs."

Like your engines, I thought. "You haven't had any trouble with claims? Compensation for injuries, I mean."

"The odd chancer, yes. Nothing worth speaking of. As I said, it goes with the territory." He laughed and drank down his glass. "There was one old comedian who tried it on. Put on a limp, claimed it was our fault."

"Did you pay him off?"

"No, no. Hunty-boy sends 'em packing. Good-o! Here's the song and dance girls. Have a cigar, old man."

The tragic actor now metamorphosed into the Great

Mackay, the *lion comique*, bestriding the second half's miscellany of skits and songs like a colossus. I found myself giggling even at the most third-rate of the performers, only to realise that Mackay was standing idly upstage brandishing a rubber chicken. When he turned to singing, we laughed at "The Dandy Dogs-Meat Man" and "Threading My Grandmother's Needle"; tapped our feet to "Dainty Miss Skittles" and "The Woman in White Waltz"; and wept to hear "The Soldier's Tear" and "Sweet Betsy Ogle".

There was even a skit on the skeleton thefts, which might have galled me but for the wine with which Coxhill kept plying me, and the metamorphosis of the Amazon wench into Mackay's society wife. She was a gorgeous thing indeed, with a cascade of blonde hair and a bosom that would have sunk the SS *Great Britain*.

"Ha ha!" roared Coxhill. "Our Scotchman is of flesh and blood after all. My, we shall have some entertainment tonight."

There was a deal of horseplay in the audience behind us, and ideas exchanged in the most colourful language. By the end of the show, I was somewhat the worse for wear. Coxhill whisked me back into the chaise and within moments we were descending a stone stairway to a smoky cellar.

"Where are we?" I said in alarm.

"Gambling hell, old chap," he announced. "My favourite one. The odds ain't too tight, you know, and the extras cheap too."

Wide-eyed, I stared around at a cross-section of debauchees more louche than I imagined in a den of vice in Naples. Coarse faces leant heavily over small baize tables, while the more refined puffed amicably at extravagant hookahs.

"Don't fret," said Coxhill with that sideways grin. "You look quite the greenhorn."

"I fear I've had a drop too much, Roxton. I'd like to go home, if you wouldn't mind."

"Don't be a bloody ass, old man. Sit down and enjoy yourself. The club's next door, near as damn it. You can catch forty winks there, if need be."

Sure enough, I did begin to relax. Coxhill found us a spot under a vaulted arch, and I squeezed in, reclining deep into the Moorish cushions, while he sat up at a gaming table. I did not join in, too befuddled to follow. By the time Coxhill passed me a pipe, I was ready to enter into the spirit. The smoke soaked into my head, and I observed the assembly with mounting amusement.

"Tell you what," he said. "Time to call on Madame Lorraine and her Academy."

He spoke to a waiter, and ten minutes later an older lady, eyes dark with make-up, came and kissed us on both cheeks. Coxhill bantered with her in a low voice, and she soon vanished away, giving me a broad smile and a pinch on the cheek. He cashed in his chips with the waiter and sat back heavily. "Now, old man. I wanted to tell you."

"The information!" I laughed. "Good God, I'd quite forgotten." It struck me that all Coxhill's posing and posturing was just an attempt to match up to the world, to match up to a father doubtless every bit as domineering as mine. I giggled to think that behind that unprepossessing beard was a young man barely older than myself. Indeed, I had begun to find everything amusing, and was quite unprepared for the grave tone he adopted.

"I'd like to give you some shares in the company, old man. What do you say?"

I looked at him as if I had been hit square on the head. Even in my cups, I was cautious with money. "Roxton, you lunatic. A policeman's income is–"

"Tosh."

We both laughed.

"I've no savings," I said. "I'm in no position to be dabbling."

"Look, old chap, I'm offering you them for a song."

"Really. I can't be gambling." I paused for a moment, then said, as if it were a brilliant discovery, "It's against my religion."

Again, we both fell about, as if my foolish joke were the witticism of the year. When we had recovered ourselves, Coxhill wiped his eyes with his handkerchief. "Well, really. You Scotch! Cameron, old man, you're the darnedest haggler I ever met. All right. Have the bloody things for free."

"What?"

"Come along. I'm saying you can have them for nothing. A hundred of 'em. Value? God only knows. Now, what do you say to that? Will that see us right?"

"You're too kind, man." I shook my head warmly and gestured around us. "But it's not my place to be receiving perquisites from your good self. I mean, there's no need to buy me off!"

I laughed, as he gave me a look of the most exaggerated admiration. He clamped my arm in that vice-like grip again, as if he was holding on to my decency for dear life. "My dear fellow, you cannot know how admirable I find you. I'm in awe of your sacrifice, quite in awe. We've been through a rough trot of late, but still I couldn't do it myself. Forego riches and consequence. Contribute to society at the basest level. It must be something akin to being a monk, would you say? Not that you're holier than thou, but... Well, I have the most profound respect for the lot of you."

A thought struck me as he sniffed valiantly. "I say, Roxton, old man. You don't happen to know a fellow called Skelton, do you?"

"One of your lot, is he? Where would I have met him?" His

eyes darted about, looking into the darkness behind me. "Ah, here comes the Academy."

He turned, as a troupe of brightly dressed ladies began to circulate around the dim cellar. With a resounding chortle, Coxhill grabbed a buxom girl and sat her upon his knee, holding up his cards for her to kiss.

I suppose I was no longer quite myself when Madame Lorraine's Academy arrived. For I soon ended up leaving with a wee fair-skinned girl. She took me up to a small back room. It must have been very late, as there was already a glimmer of light from the grubby window high up in the wall. All the details I cannot recall, nor do I wish to. I remember, though, she wouldn't say a word at first. She had her hair pinned up, and I had the devil of a job to persuade her to let it down. I never saw such a pretty thing as those red-brown curls tumbling down over her bare shoulders. She said her name was Eloise. I don't think that was in earnest, for she was about as French as I am. She washed herself unashamedly in front of me, before and after, and put on a cheap perfume, as if to cover her sins. Afterwards, she lay down exhausted and fell into a light sleep.

I rose in the light of early morning and hastened to put on my clothes – my own, not Coxhill's – amazed to find I had had the presence of mind to keep the bundle with me. The poor girl awoke to see me in my uniform. She was seized by fear at first, then, when I had managed to calm her down, she pulled me back towards the bed.

"No," I said softly. "I must be going."

"Don't worry. Your friend has paid in advance, sir, up till noon."

"My friend?"

"Him with the filthy beard."

I sat by her and stroked her hair until she dozed off again, her eyes shut tight. I looked at her, as my befuddled mind began to clear. My friend? He had made every effort to befriend me, showering me with attentions. As if he thought that I came from the upper echelons of Scottish society; that I had somehow given up hopes of inheritance and business in order to tackle the ills of society, like the Temperance people and the Society for the Redemption of Fallen Women. Yes, we seemed to get on well enough, though I had little expected to be befriended by his likes. Still, Coxhill was not such a bad egg after all. I must refrain, I told myself, from drawing conclusions on insufficient evidence and personal whim.

Yet a sense of shame washed over me as I slipped out into the soft morning light. I was galled to feel I had obliged myself to him. I tramped slowly towards the Yard, clutching Coxhill's jacket. Disappointed in myself, I resolved to avoid him as far as possible, hoping the wind would blow the smell of smoke from my clothes, even if it was powerless to drive the fatigue from my face, or undo my blunder in accepting his disquieting largesse.

THE FAMILY MARX, AS RELATED BY MISS VILLIERS

I called unannounced at our bearded revolutionary's apartments. Amidst a hubbub of wailing infants, his wife icily explained that he was out at a meeting.

"A political meeting?" I asked.

She gave me a look so frosty that I made haste to assure her I was a friend, interested in her husband's work, even well disposed to it. (I felt this to be reasonable half-truth. His activist pamphlet is rather too modern to form part of my studies, but I found it striking, if a little awkward stylistically.)

The ice melted, and out poured her tale of woe. Their exile

from Germany. Elation at the revolutions of 1848. Gloom as the uprisings were quenched all over.

"Social upheaval," she said, with an air of long-suffering appeal, "may be sparked by a work of genius, such as Karl's, but to stoke the fires of lasting change requires a lifetime of selfless dedication, study, and meetings upon meetings upon meetings."

I accepted her bubbling invitation to step inside, deciding that this loquacious lady might be rather more indiscreet than her husband.

"It is a noble thing, Miss Villiers," she said (I am translating, of course, from the German), "this spectre haunting Europe. To unite the workers of the world may be inevitable, as Karl tells me, but it is also terribly fatiguing, and such a cost of postage as you would scarcely believe." She explained that they disseminated her husband's work through sympathetic organisations and offshoot cells across the continent.

"Mr Marx's publications must provide a steady income, surely?"

At that moment, several infants flocked into the room. Mrs Marx spoke to them rapidly in a dialect I could not follow. Out they went again, and she sat back down, rolling her eyes in exasperation. "Frankly, Miss, no."

"I see. Can these organisations not raise money to help you?"

"Karl is adamant," she replied, "that money raised from the proletariat must finance revolution, not our dinners. Mr Engels has secured offers of publication in American magazines, but Karl won't hear of it." She cast down her eyes. "In fact, if it was not for Friedrich's kindness, and the success of his Manchester factory, we would have starved already." The poor woman raised her hand to her face, stifling a sob. "Karl makes it so difficult for himself, writing the way he does.

If only he would write a bestseller, like Mr Dickens. I feel sure he could."

"I had not thought," I said, surprised, "of Mr Dickens as Mr Marx's equal."

"Oh, Karl has the highest regard for him. He says that Mr Dickens has issued to the world more political and social truths than have been uttered by all the professional politicians, publicists and moralists put together."

"But your husband's reputation is beyond any popular novelist's."

"Karl has kudos, I know, Miss Villiers. But kudos does not pay the bills."

Again the children flocked in. This time, she permitted them, and with military precision they gathered about her in a picturesque group. She looked up at me with forlorn eyes, and I finally realised that she was appealing to my generosity.

I had been trying to draw the conversation towards Berwick Skelton, and it was most awkward to be mistaken for a potential patron. I must turn her misapprehension to my advantage. "Rest assured, Mrs Marx, the legions who take inspiration in your sacrifices will doubtless come to your aid. Indeed, the man who introduced me to Mr Marx's writings, a certain Berwick Skelton..." I paused, and sure enough, recognition lit up her face.

"You are involved in the Reform League?"

I gave a sort of equivocal quiver of the head.

"So nice a man. Such a pity. How is he?"

I blinked innocently. "I was hoping you might be able to tell me."

"Still no sign of him at the League? Oh dear."

I feigned a look of assenting concern.

She sighed. "We need them, tireless comrades such as he, to lead sympathetic bodies around the world. It is Karl's belief that just a few selfless men of genius at the head of the proletariat could fashion the world anew."

"And Mr Skelton?"

"That girl." She made a face. "Did you know her? I suppose even the finest revolutionary minds can fall prey to temptation. It is fortunate that Karl's weakness is for wine and not women. I expect him back from the tavern any moment, Miss Villiers. He will be pleased to meet you."

At the prospect of the bearded revolutionary's arrival, I panicked. Enough equivocal language, I decided. "Mrs Marx, you have been most kind to a poor unworthy student–"

"A student?" she said, her frosty tone returning. She looked me up and down, dismayed that she had wasted attentions upon me, clearly no benefactress. "I see. You must excuse me, then, but Karl will be angry if he finds the little ones still up. Do call again."

THE HAYMARKET HOOFER

"Don't you see?" said Miss Villiers, pouring a second cup of tea. "Every detail matters."

She had sent a most persuasive note, hinting at grand discoveries made in Highgate. I bought her lunch in a Museum Street tea room. She entertained me with an unflattering portrayal of Mrs Marx. Although her discoveries were limited, her approach seemed most impressive, beside my debacle in the Rose and Crown. She quizzed me and quizzed me about the mockery I had incurred there until I could stand it no more. "What does it matter, what they said when they were laughing at me?"

"They mentioned the Haymarket–"

"Not exactly mentioned."

"What did they shout? Tell me again."

I sighed. "Ask the hoofers down the Haymarket, they said. But the man was laughing all over his face."

"At his own audacity, perhaps. Hoofers are dancers, aren't they? They have hydraulics at the Haymarket Theatre. Don't you remember?" She looked at me triumphantly. "Mrs Marx hinted that our man had girl trouble, and your lot shouted about his fiancée. Add it all together and it may amount to something."

"They also mentioned Charles Dickens and the Prince of Wales."

"Maybe they are involved too."

"Your imagination knows no limits," I said.

She smiled. "What else? The Academy. What could they mean by that?"

I had not until then connected the man's catcall with Madame Lorraine's Academy. "A lot of gentlemen are Academaticians," he'd said. I flushed. "I have no idea."

"No matter. I will try the Reform League. You must go to the Haymarket."

"Must I? And what if I am received as I was in Clerkenwell?"

She sighed. "What other avenues can we explore? The night porter at Euston?"

"Sacked. At Coxhill's behest, I believe. They have no trace of him, which is galling as he actually spoke to our man."

"The hospital matron?"

"Gone too."

"And the ward book page with her. Strange. It's not exactly that we can't find people. More that, when we find them, we don't know how to make them talk. Those men in the pub, for instance."

"Said they didn't know him."

"But you didn't believe them. Why should they lie?"

"People have a million reasons for lying."

She flared her nostrils and gave me a penetrating look. "Maybe so. We must seek ways to persuade them not to."

The manager at the Haymarket, a supercilious man with theatrical moustaches, kept me waiting for some time. Miss Villiers' conviction had given me a much-needed jolt. Since my visit to Lord's, I had been seized by a feeling of unholy impotence. Yet she might be right. I had been in a room full of people who all knew my man. Perhaps some of their jibes were more significant than I realised. If the Academy was not without sense, why not the other things? Miss Villiers had gone to Highgate on the most speculative off-chance, and it had borne fruit, if only a little. Standing in the foyer of the Haymarket Theatre, by a hoarding that proclaimed Shakespeare's return, I went over my stratagems.

The manager's face soured the moment I mentioned hydraulics. "I believe you have them installed in the theatre?"

"Did have. Bloody liability. Cost a fortune, never worked, went and burst."

"An explosion?"

"At the bleeding finale. Gushing down off the safety curtain, like a river. Quite the precipitous evacuation, we had."

I frowned. There was no way, I supposed, to find out if Coxhill was present at that mishap, as he had been at Euston, short of asking him. The other connection I could pursue here and now. "Was that a dancing show? I believe you have hoofers."

"We're under new management. Going upmarket, if you must know. No larking about with orchestras and that. All these new halls spending fortunes to outclass each other. With Shakespeare, you just need the odd clap of thunder, the odd lightning flash."

"And the words, I suppose, which are cheap, at least."

His face soured further. "I must be getting on."

"In that case," I said with a regretful look, "I may be back later, with my inspector, to discuss a couple of items from the Licensing Act–"

"Oh, what is it you want, officer?"

"Your hoofers. Only to speak to them."

"They were snapped up by the Evans, if you must know. Look for 'em there."

In the few minutes it took me to reach Covent Garden, I puzzled over the multiplying coincidences of the case. Glancing down the alleyway beside the music hall, I chanced upon three girls arriving in high spirits.

"Hulloah, there, ladies."

The tallest, a full-bodied woman, called out. "What can we do for you, officer?"

"Is the stage door this way? Only I'm looking for the dancers."

"You've found us," she said. Her voice crackled darkly. "What of it?"

My nerve faltered as I recognised her. It was the marvellous Amazon of the show. Her tumbling locks were tied up beneath a bonnet, but that voice of hers was unmistakable. The two shorter girls eyed me with suspicion and amusement in equal measure, as nervous of me as I was of them. I asked my question quietly, as if the name were a charm – a spell, a key – which I was scared of uttering too many times, for fear of wearing out its magic before I unlocked its secrets. "Do you… Might you know a man – Berwick Skelton?"

The tall girl turned away, while the short ones burst out giggling.

"Who doesn't know him, officer?" said one.

The other made a face as if this was the most daring comment she'd ever heard. She pointed back at the tall girl. "It's her you'll want to talk to, though."

The two scurried down the alley and tugged at her shawl. The Amazon looked back with a strange dignity. "I ain't got the foggiest what he's talking about," she said and turned on her heel.

The others clapped in excitement.

I strode after her. "Please," I said. "I must speak with you."

"It ain't me you want." She fixed me with her dark eyes, and my plan to be tough melted clean away.

"Please. I beg you most humbly."

She glanced round. Her friends were huddling at the stage door. "Oi," she called out. They disappeared into the doorway. "This is no good. Got a teviss?"

I gave her a shilling.

"Here, girls. Now, bugger off while the copper and I have a chat."

Her friends tried to stifle their giggles. They grabbed the coin from her hand and vanished with some leery comment that brought a scowl from the tall girl.

She strode in through the door and led me into a small room with a shelf of wigs, a mirror and a rail of extravagant costumes. She sat down and began to put on make up. "What kind of a reputation this'll get us I don't know. Bringing a copper into me dressing room. What is it you lot want this time?"

The statuesque tilt of her head and a dismissive tone in that velvet voice left me at sea, and I fumbled for words. "You know him. You know Berwick Skelton."

She frowned quizzically. "Are you for real, mate?" Her laughter was warm and infectious. She looked me up and down, appraisingly. "Who's sent you along here?"

"Nobody," I said quickly. "I've come on my own account."

"I'm sick of the lot of you." She looked down her aquiline nose into the mirror with sudden decision. "I have to get ready. I got a good job here and I likes to look me best."

I must choose how to play my hand. I couldn't let her send me away so quickly. But this was not the moment to speak of the spout. That would make it seem like I was pursuing him for a crime. I had no veiled threats to drop, as with the Haymarket man. I reached into my pocket. "Look, you gave that shilling to the others. Here's one for you."

"I don't want your filthy shillings."

"I'm sorry." I frowned in dismay. "Please, if you ever had any fondness for him–"

"What's he done?"

"I just want to find him."

She turned her big doe eyes upon me. "You're a strange one. All right. As long as you don't mind me getting into me things." She went across to the rail and pushed her way through the rich fabrics as if she was walking through a forest. "Yes, I knew Berwick."

My heart thrilled, and I realised that I had begun to doubt that he existed. I almost burst out and told her how relieved I was. "Do you know where he is?"

"Oh yes. He's sat in the upper circle, waiting for you."

I started up in confusion.

"I'm having you on, copper," she laughed. "What d'you think this is, a drawing room farce?" She picked an outfit off the rail.

"I'm Hester, by the way."

I introduced myself in turn, feeling foolish. "Tell me about him, Hester."

"What, like his life story?"

"Why not?" I realised I could see her in the mirror, changing her clothes. I averted my gaze. "Were you close?"

"I think," she said tightly, "it's my old friend Nellie that you're after."

"Nellie?"

With a rustle of cloth, she popped her head around the end of the rail, jaw set firm and bare shoulder peeking out. "You really don't know nothing, do you?"

"Oh, I don't know what I know, Hester." We both laughed. "Is Nellie in the show?"

"Nellie," she grinned, "no longer graces the stage with her little tootsies. She has, shall we say, alighted in higher circles."

"As Berwick's fiancée?"

She puffed out her cheeks. "Let me say straight away that I have lost touch with Nellie, not seeing eye to eye with her, you might say, but as far as I know that particular agreement is no longer binding."

She gave me a smile. Disappearing back among the gowns, she began to speak more freely. She had been best friends with Nellie since they were knee-high. She spoke of their early days on the stage, dancing down at the Hoxton Hall. Even then, she said, Nellie was the darling of the audiences. Hester painted her friend as a charmer, who revelled in playing off against each other the million men chasing her.

"I was the shy one," she said, emerging resplendent in her rather sparse Amazonian costume, red frills and feathers all over it.

The door burst open and one of her little friends popped her head around the door.

"Bugger off," Hester growled. The friend vanished. "What's so funny, copper?"

"You don't seem so shy to me," I mumbled.

"You can bugger off and all."

"No, no. It's just that I... I've seen you perform."

"Oh, yes? Juliet or Cleopatra? I do so love the classical roles. Don't look so confused. I'm pulling your leg."

I grinned. "And out of these millions of men, she chose Berwick?"

"They chose each other. Nellie wanted to go up in the world, you see. Which of us doesn't? And Berwick was always headed somewhere. You could see that from the start."

"Tell me. What is he like?"

She looked at me, as if I she could scarcely believe that I didn't know him. As if it amused her and, at the same time, she pitied me for it.

"He was a lovely one. Full of brains. And a way with words he had. Ask anyone."

"Where's he from?"

"There was different stories. I heard he was an orphan. Nellie said his family were gypsies and they'd left him in London to grow up into a trade. Others said he was the illegitimate child of some lord, abandoned at the Foundlings' Hospital. Could have been, he had that air about him. He had family in Clerkenwell, I think. They'd know the truth of it."

"What do you believe?"

"Don't know," Hester said with a wistful grace, as she fixed her hair into a high bunch. "Does it matter? He did have something faraway in his look. She loved that, the thought that he was destined for great things. Oh, he had stars in his eyes when he saw us dance. He wooed her good and proper, like a gentleman would have done, and that's how he won her. Whenever she stepped out with him, it was like he couldn't quite believe it. Like he thought it was his birthday every day. Silly boy. He was worth her weight in gold. Could have been somebody too, with his brains. Nellie was ever so impressed. Not that she told him. Then along comes another, money jangling in his pockets. Nell takes one last look at

Berwick's old waistcoat, and his sideburns, and his old bowler hat. And she drops him, like she dropped all the others. Yes, she drops him and goes off with the toff. And that was the last I saw of them."

"And now? Where are they now?"

"Your guess is good as mine."

"You're not friends any more?"

"Look, to my eyes, Nellie behaved badly. Berwick deserved better than her, and she treated him like dirt."

"Hester, forgive me. Did you have an interest in this fellow too?"

"No," she said sharply. "He was a nice-looking fellow. Well-spoken, and gentlemanly. A lot more gentlemanly than a great many gentlemen I've encountered." She stood and, before I could speak, she kissed the top of my head. "And you're a sweetheart too, but you must be off or I'll be in trouble."

I stood up, my mind spinning. "The toff that Nellie ran off with," I said, knowing it was indiscreet to ask, and maybe irrelevant. "Who was it? Not a man called Coxhill?"

Hester's eyes narrowed.

I stopped short. "You know Coxhill, then?"

"I knew I'd seen you before." She looked at me closely. "Last week, wasn't it?"

I laughed an awkward laugh. "Not Juliet, nor Cleopatra. You're very good."

She brushed off my compliment. "Uniform suits you better."

I thought of my arms sticking like pins out of Coxhill's jacket, and my cheeks burned with shame. "Hester, I have to find Berwick. I can't say why, but can't you tell me where Nellie lives?"

"I tell you, petal, your lot know more about it than me. Go on now, scarper."

I thanked her. Enthralled with these discoveries, I decided

to stop in at a tavern to collect my thoughts. Yet in truth I still had nothing substantial to go on. After a couple of ales, the notion took me to step into the Evans and watch the end of Hester's show over again. I huddled into a corner, keeping a wary eye out for Coxhill. There was no sign of him, thankfully, though I did spot Jack Scholes of the *Euston Evening Bugle* looking around sharp-eyed and taking notes. I was not sad to miss the first half, but when the dancing girls appeared for the finale, I gazed in awe at Hester, resplendent and lustrous in the reflected lamplight, kicking up her skirts and twirling magnificently. Near the end, she seemed to catch my eye, though perhaps I was imagining it.

As I slipped out ahead of the rush, an usher gently touched my jacket. "Sir, I have the information you were asking for."

"The information?"

The usher screwed up his eyes in concentration. "Yes, sir. Miss Hester kindly requests that I recommend to you the elocution teacher employed on occasion by herself and her friends. A certain Groggins, sir. Groggins, of forty-four, Shepherd Market."

The Elocution Teacher

There was trouble waiting for me at work the next day. I glanced, as usual, into Darlington's office, to find him sticking pins into a large map on the wall.

"Playing war games?" I joked.

"Murderous games, old man," said Darlington gleefully. "I'm on the Whitechapel garottings."

"Woe betide the lunatic when he meets you and your drawing pins."

"It's the pattern, old man." He lowered his tone with

gravitas. "We're establishing his *modus operandi*. Speaking of lunatics, though, your man's on the rampage."

I hurried in to meet my fate. Wardle was at his desk, snorting like a bull, newspapers scattered everywhere.

"You're early, sir," I said weakly.

"What have you got? On Paxton and the rest."

I took a deep breath. My mind had been so full of my own investigations, I had made no progress with the thefts. "I'm finding it hard to get solid information."

"I'll give you solid information. I'll give it you all right. Paxton does own the *Bugle*, or good as. He was a shareholder in Dickens' old paper, too. What about the others?"

"Nothing that I've found, sir, not as yet."

"If you're not too busy swanning about the theatres of London, you might find time to uncover something." He picked up *Punch* and threw it at me. "Because there's a mite more to be checking now."

I squirmed beneath that formidable gaze, trying to think if I had mentioned my trips to the Evans to anyone in the Yard. But there was nothing to be done but pick the thing up and sit down to find out what he was talking about. It didn't take long. The newsmen had unearthed a string of other thefts over the last year, details comparable to our skeleton thefts. Now I understood the music hall sketch. They were calling it an epidemic. "But, sir, how can we have missed all these?"

"Look where they happened."

I scanned the article again. The City, most of them at least, that was the jurisdiction of Wardle's *bête noir*, the City Police Force. No wonder he was disgruntled. "I'd better gather information on this lot."

"Bloody right," he nodded. "Copies of all the reports, mind."

"All, sir? Right. Will they let me have them, sir?"

"They'd better. Check the other boroughs while you're at it."

I nodded efficiently. "Right, sir."

"Then I want connections. They can't all own newspapers. This bloody rag. Might ask where their information comes from."

I stared at the article in frustration. "And yet there's next to nothing been taken. Such a fuss about nothing."

"Someone's walking into the finest houses in London easy as you like. That's hardly nothing."

"Unless you were right at Pearson's, sir, and they're bribing people on the inside."

"Where's the sense in it? If it's for documents, they've got a bloody library by now." He thought a moment. "It's in the details, I'll tell you that. We need to know exactly what's gone missing in each case. Then we'll see it."

We worked in silence for several hours. Then a further thought struck him as he got ready to go out.

"I've a feeling I had another case not so different from all this. Can't place it, though. Write to my old sergeant, Jackman."

"Right, sir." It would feel odd writing to Jackman: like sending a note to my own ghost. "His address?"

"I don't bloody know. Ask in the front office." He left impatiently.

I smiled. Jackman had worked with him for years. But then he didn't know where I lived either.

Shepherd Market had seen no kind of market for hundreds of years, but the smell of roast mutton emanated from the elegant tavern where a barmaid pointed out Groggins' door. I knocked for some time. Indeed, I would have given up, had the barmaid not assured me that Groggins was in, only might not answer if he was teaching.

Sure enough, come seven o'clock, the door opened and a

breathless Irishman greeted me cordially. "Sheridan Groggins, tutor in Elocution and the Dramatic Arts. Is there a problem?"

"No problem. Just a few questions." I was watching him closely. He was an energetic, highly-strung sort of fellow, but seemed more at ease when I added, "About a certain Berwick Skelton."

"Ah, is it Berwick?" He glanced up the stairs behind him, then turned back to me with a quizzical look. "Could you give me two moments to dispense with my pupil? If you'd stay out of sight, I'd greatly appreciate it. Without wishing to be rude, we none of us want to be thought of as the sort that has dealings with the police."

He gave me a smile so charming I could hardly refuse. I hurried around the corner. A minute later, I heard him hail a cab. It passed me by, a fine lady peering out of the window.

Groggins invited me directly up the four flights to his apartment on the top floor. He threw open the French windows and stationed me out on an elegant tiled terrace.

"Quite a view you have," I said, gazing out over Piccadilly towards Green Park. "Teaching elocution must bring in a few pennies."

He grinned. "It's a disreputable trade, officer, in that I tutor mostly actresses, debutantes, politicians and bishops, with a smattering of European royalty."

"Are they not reluctant to learn English with an Irish accent?"

"Have you not heard?" He proceeded to elongate his vowels outrageously. "We Dubliners and you Edinburghers have the most fashionable English in the four kingdoms. Ah, Sergeant, don't be alarmed now. Your accent's quite unmistakable. Though I would hazard that you have spent, what, eighteen months here in the capital, which is roughening up your rounded tones. Do you not enjoy being a foreigner in your own land? Sure, it's terrible hard for the eejits to place you, which is a tremendous advantage. As none of them can tell to which stratum of society we belong, they are obliged to treat us with a degree of courtesy which I consider most gratifying. Do you not find the same?"

Groggins talked as if he would never stop, of his family's migration to London, his own entry into the Dramatic Arts, and subsequent prosperity from tweaking the vowels of the rich and the garish. "And they love me for it into the bargain, officer."

Yet, even while he was talking about himself, I had the feeling he was sizing me up. I cut him off, and asked was it true that he taught an actress named Nellie.

"Why?" he said sharply.

Taken aback, I fetched around for an answer.

He softened his tone. "As a teacher of voice, one feels a certain compunction–"

"I mean her no ill. I'm simply looking for Skelton. I have a couple of questions I need answered."

"What has the rascal done now?" he grinned. "It's strange, you know. We all used to ask what was it that he was going to do."

"I'm sorry, I don't follow your meaning."

He laughed an enigmatic little laugh. "No, I suppose you don't. I've only the highest praise for Berwick, Sergeant, though our acquaintance was slight. Aside from recommending me to some pupils of the highest calibre – and the highest income – he comported himself charmingly, estimably, beyond reproach. Were I a man of his talents, I would feel myself quite justified in behaviour full of conceit. Yes, I taught Nellie, and a more enthused pupil I do not hope to find."

"And this Nellie was connected to Skelton... romantically?"

"Connected?" he laughed, stepping in off the terrace to a little table covered with bottles and glasses to open a bottle of port. "Oh, I'll say." Without further bidding, he launched into an account of their entanglement: the Rise and Fall of Berwick Skelton, a tragedy in three acts. Framed in the proscenium of his French windows, Groggins made quite the theatrical tale of it.

She was a vivacious hoofer who dreamed of becoming a West End Lady. He was an idealistic young fellow with rather more elevated aspirations. Not content with the keen wit that made him the darling of the Clerkenwell lasses, he worked hard to become something more than another bore in a tavern. He read. He joined societies. He wrote articles, short, fiery pieces for the alternative press.

"I've had occasion to pass off his ideas as my own in polite conversation. It's extraordinary how tellingly people react to a little social indignation." He poured out two glasses and set down the bottle. "A beautiful couple they must have made, Sergeant. The brightest flower in the whole of East London, charmed by his wit and quietly confident that he was the man to lead her whither she wished to go."

"Which was where?"

"Sergeant, when one is the coach of voice, one is something of a *confidant.* Nellie likes to fascinate. She seems an endless riddle that doesn't give of a solution. But she does love things that sparkle. She loves the bright lights. Diamonds. Pearls." He handed me a glass, holding on to it just a moment too long. "Don't form an unkind picture of her, though. She's no fool. She is drawn to sparkling people as well. She loves quick ripostes, duelling talk, and all the artillery that goes with good conversation, weapons as satisfying as a good port, Sergeant, only cheaper."

"And she came to you to learn how to wield those weapons?"

"Ostensibly she came to fill out her voice. To take out the Hoxton and put in some Kensington. She thought that would be enough, along with her looks. She wanted to escape from the dancing halls and secure a few balcony scenes. I don't pretend to be anything more than a teacher of voice, Sergeant. But occasionally people come to me as a sort of finishing school. Behind it all, you see, she wished to keep up with Berwick."

"To keep up?"

"Yes. To be ready. For him to lead her into polite society, you see."

"And did he?"

"He could have, you know. Theirs was an uncommon rise. But no. That was where it all fell down." He frowned, staring out over the town as the lamps were being lit. "Berwick was no fool. Nellie wanted to make-believe she belonged there, but he never tried to hide his origins, he knew their value. Picture it, the editors of the progressive press toadying around him – just what they've always wanted, a brilliant mind, raised out of the sewers, self-taught, expressing the thoughts of the people more eloquently than the people would themselves. Look here, say these editors, we have our ear to the ground. We are attuned to the *vox populi*."

"He wrote for them?"

"He did, though you could be forgiven for suspecting that they were interested less in his ideals than their newspaper sales. Still, Berwick and Nellie soon found themselves moving in captivating circles. You know, the Garrick Club, the *Punch* brotherhood. They found it intoxicating enough, I'd say, the both of them."

"As do you, Mr Groggins?"

He laughed. "I flatter myself that I see through the shallowness of such things. But there's no harm in a little shallowness, I tell myself. Still, we were talking of the doomed couple."

"Why doomed?"

He began to sing in a fine warbling tenor:

The pretty horse-breakers ride out in the Row
And cause crowds to assemble wherever they go
But the one who is easily queen of them all
Is dainty Miss Nellie who holds us in thrall.

"The Row?" I said.

"Rotten Row, Hyde Park," he explained. "Nellie was never the settling kind, you see. Hard to be quite content when your dreams come true. Not that she didn't like Berwick. She did, I'm sure of that. But he was a very intense young man. He wanted to achieve, to change things, whereas Nellie is free of conviction. She was bound to tire of his intensity." He smiled phlegmatically. "Mr Disraeli tells us we are one land divided into two nations. Berwick, now, he wanted to end all those injustices, while Nellie– ah, Nellie likes things as they are, only of course she wants to be on the other side from where she grew up."

"So she dropped him?"

"She moved on."

I was surprised to find myself feeling sorry for Berwick, so carelessly betrayed. "And he?"

Groggins sipped at his port. "A few years back now, he turned up here when she was meant to be having a lesson. Only she'd gone down with her new fellow to the Thames Tunnel. The anniversary fête, you know. I let slip that she was there, though I made no mention of her fancy man, as far as I recall." He gulped down some more port, as if troubled by the memory. "'Groggins,' he says to me. 'Groggins, if that

self-satisfied interloper compromises her honour, I will entrap
him in that tunnel. I will shut him up, and I will let in the
filthy Thames to drown him. I will make it a warning to them
all. We are not the playthings of the rich.' That's what he said.
He was a most equable man, Berwick, but there was a fury in
his eyes that day that frightened me."

"Was her new man well-heeled?"

"Doubtless he was."

"You don't know his name?"

"There are limits to the questions one asks. Nellie sometimes
hinted at dishonourable behaviour. Shameful practices in
gentlemen's clubs. There are still strata of society where people
think that just because a girl is a maid or an actress she is, if
you take my meaning, available. It's quite shocking. You'd
think we were still in the eighteenth century."

For the first time, his frivolous tone was alloyed with steel,
and I suspected that he was not as free of conviction as he
would have me believe. "A sad end," I said. "And now?"

"He's vanished, as far as I know."

"And she?"

"It's many months since I have seen her. I assumed she'd
been whisked off to some continental *chateau* or *schloss*. One
cannot complain. In this line of work, pupils come and go. One
takes an interest without involving oneself too much. Now, if
you will excuse me, I am expecting another pupil."

I sighed. As I was taking my leave, a chaise deposited a lady
more or less identical to the previous pupil. I walked back
towards town. Another cul-de-sac. I learned so much without
coming any closer. Nobody knew their whereabouts, unless
they were all lying. Of course, why should anyone want to tell
me anything? I must change my way of thinking. Become
tough-minded. Plain-spoken. Blunt. I must make it in their
interest to tell me what I wanted to know.

As I headed back across town, I bumped into Worm. It was a time since he'd presented himself at the Yard, and he'd treated himself to leather patches on the elbows of his jacket in the interim.

"What you been up to?" said he, with a half-hearted grin.

"Seeing an elocution teacher. A man who teaches you to speak properly."

"Oh, yes? Curious accent you have. Pity to change it, though. Cost a pretty penny too, I'd imagine?"

"Beyond my means, and yours. But you speak well enough, you wee rascal."

"That's kind of you, old cove."

"Here, what's wrong, wee man?" I said, taken aback by the doleful tone in his voice. "Has somebody died?"

"No reason, old cove," he smiled brightly. "Just the general grimness of it all."

THE FOURTH PERIOD
[MID TO LATE 1861]

The Bugle — Passages in Lending Library Books
Dirty Laundry — Mens Sana in Corpore Sano
I Weep Continually — A Prince Amongst Men
Philandering Princes & Crazed Cuckolds

EUSTON EVENING BUGLE

1st July, 1861

SETTING THE THAMES ALIGHT –
WHY SHOULD THE TAXPAYER PAY?

The constant cries of so-called liberal thinkers for the government to spend, spend, spend on issues undeserving of public attention have reached a shrill pitch in the wake of the Tooley Street Inferno.

Granted, the destruction of eight six-storey buildings, despite the presence of fourteen fire engines, merits a parliamentary inquiry. Granted, too, the image of the brigades disputing whose responsibility it was, while long-suffering fire chief, James Braidwood, and others burned to death, is gruesome. It is, however, ludicrous to hold that a single Metropolitan brigade might have saved the day. What incentive for a service that receives wages regardless of its efficacy? A service answerable to financial backers has long proved itself effective; a brigade answerable to God is a utopian nonsense.

The prudent among property owners already pay vast sums to insurers, who are in panic over the two million pounds of goods and property destroyed in the blaze. If the payments prove the highest ever recorded, all well and good, those insurers must drill more efficient brigades.

Rumours are rife of warehouse managers sighing in relief at the blaze. What with the cotton crisis, they had insured the stock to the hilt, anticipating record profits. But the sales bonanza never materialised, and the insurance will pay far dearer for the lost stock than any Savile Row tailor would have. Meanwhile, the value of stock laid aside elsewhere will also rise. The *Bugle* suggests to the parliamentary committee that suspicion will only by allayed by tough-minded convictions for fraud, or arson.

FROM FIRE TO FLOOD

The late Dr John Snow of the Middlesex Hospital, who styled himself an epidemicist, claimed that much of our drinking water simply revisits disease upon us. Tracing numerous deaths to the pump in Marlborough Street, he demanded fanciful government investment in free drinking fountains, fed from reservoirs in the Walthamstow marshes, of all places. Snow's henchman, Henry Mayhew, who writes for the agitatory gazette, *Punch*, is now imploring the government to cleanse the river. He claims to have found in Father Thames dead dogs and kittens, dung of stables and pig-styes, kettles and flower-pots, chemical substances from breweries and gasworks, and slaughterhouse offal. The *Bugle* is nevertheless assured by the Sacred Guild of Water Bearers that the source of the cholera, which killed sixty thousand Londoners in 1848 and 1849, remains moot. If the river is to blame, they point to the vast investment in Bazalgette's sewers. His processing plant east of London at Crossness is already running its first massive engine, built by James Watt and to be named "Albert Edward", which nomenclature will surely delight the Prince of Wales.

COLONY'S LOSS IS SICK CHILDREN'S GAIN

More pleas to help the unhelpable. Charles Dickens gave a reportedly rousing address to raise funds for the Hospital for Sick Children. Perhaps the popular novelist should look a little more to his own affairs. He repeatedly turned down a lucrative offer from Spiers and Pond of the Café de Paris in Melbourne, Australia, for a reading tour. The rebuffed entrepreneurs have instead invited H.H. Stephenson's All England team to tour the colony, where they plan to cash in on the public's obsession with cricket, the latest euphemism for gambling and gaming. Dickens, meanwhile, will mount another royal command drama at the Gallery of Illustrations to raise funds for the hospital.

Should we not remember Samuel Smiles' dictum that "No laws, however stringent, can make the idle industrious, the thriftless provident, or the drunken sober"? The claims of the Association for the Preservation of Infant Life, that unwanted children are being murdered for the sum of £12 by unscrupulous widows, though serious, are not credible. In the last twelvemonth, the four hundred and sixty-four cases of suspicious child deaths investigated have produced just fourteen prosecutions and seven convictions, presenting no reason to amend the Bastardy Clause of 1844. After all, if Mr Darwin is to be believed, the Survival of the Fittest is only part of the Great Struggle for Life. Thus, for mankind's sake, all these sickly unwanted children would be better off left to fend for themselves.

Passages in Mudie's Lending Library Books Marked with Cipher Annotations:

... Brutus and Caesar: what should be in that Caesar?
Why should that name be sounded more than yours?
Write them together, yours is as fair a name;
Sound them, it doth become the mouth as well;
Weigh them, it is as heavy; conjure with 'em,
Brutus will start a spirit as soon as Caesar.
Now, in the names of all the gods at once,
Upon what meat doth this our Caesar feed,
That he has grown so great?

Cassius, *Julius Caesar*, WILLIAM SHAKESPEARE

Princes, the dregs of their dull race, who flow
Through public scorn, mud from a muddy spring,
Rulers who neither see, nor feel, nor know,
But leech-like to their fainting country cling,
Till they drop, blind in blood...

England 1819, P.B. SHELLEY, writing of
the House of Hanover

DIRTY LAUNDRY

It was on my way to Charles Dickens' house that I stopped in at Brunswick Square and had an unpleasant run-in with Glossop, the carrot-haired companion of my first months in the police.

Wardle had fallen into a dismal funk. They were still thieving, up in Hampstead, over in Bayswater, and right under our noses along Whitehall.

"And what have we got?" Wardle exploded. "Nothing. They'll be taking Victoria's petticoats next."

Several puzzles baffled us. The list of the robbed made impressive reading: industrialists, parliamentarians and literary men, the well-heeled and the well-known. There were a couple of gentlemen's clubs, a music hall, a brothel and a lunatic asylum. It made sense, of course, to rob the wealthy, yet, having gone to so much trouble, why take so little? And how did our thieves get in and out without leaving a trace?

At first, Wardle stuck doggedly to his theory from Pearson's, that we were sniffing out industrial saboteurs. While it was unlikely that servants in each household were executing identical crimes, it was nonetheless possible that a contact paved the way in each case, passing crucial details to the thieves and allowing them access. We gathered lists of tradesmen and the like, but no recurring names jumped out. What kind of mind would it need to orchestrate the thing? When Wardle started demanding full guest lists for the month prior to robberies, I realised he was considering the notion of gentlemen thieves, who might be best placed both to steal ideas and to sell them on, if one can sell ideas. Continually we asked if any blueprints or manuscripts had gone astray. Continually the answer came in the negative, and we remained confounded.

I had also failed to find Wardle his bargaining chip with the *Bugle*, but I had confirmed that they, like every newspaper in town, were owned or part-owned by railway barons. The press had got bored of the story, though, thank goodness, which took the pressure off a little.

Reports of other thefts kept drifting in from other boroughs, some so minor they were barely noticed, others unmistakably like ours, with pennies taken and a piece of furniture, and a bone left behind. Everyone dragged their heels in sending the information I requested, especially the recalcitrant City Police.

And then there were the bones. Why leave a bone in houses that had no dog?

"Can we not have someone look at them?" I asked Wardle. "Find what kind of bones they are, or where they're from?"

He shot me a withering glance. "What's the use? If they're dog bones, the man's from the Isle of Dogs? If it's a cat, he's a Manxman? Come off it, Watchman. This isn't an after-dinner puzzle, and I don't need poxy zoologists soliloquising over skulls in my office."

Though I knew he had no time for newfangled ideas, his derision stung. There were days he arrived grumpy and morose, with little will to work on the thefts. I often wondered what other cases he had on the go, hidden from my eyes.

Then a terse note from Jackman arrived, proposing that I check on the theft at Dickens' house. It struck me as odd that a man who had worked with Wardle for years sent no word of greeting to his old inspector. I went straight to the cabinet. The Dickens theft was two months before Pearson's. The file mentioned only petty cash, but Jackman hinted something about a bone.

On my way to Tavistock House, I took the chance to drop in at the old constabulary. Coxhill's blathering about the importance of insurance had piqued my curiosity. I wanted an address for Mr Wetherell, the retired insurance man I'd saved from the over-zealous publican. Perhaps he could shed light on the HECC's dealings.

"Enjoying life at the top, Yard boy?" Glossop smirked, flicking through the files. He had clearly been preparing quips for months.

"Surviving," I replied. "How are things here?"

He ignored me, concentrating on writing out the address in laborious script.

"Oh, come on, Glossop. Out with it, if you've something to say."

"All high and mighty, are you now?" He pushed the address across the desk with a filthy look. "I know why you got the nod."

"I'm sorry?"

"Why it was you got promoted."

"And not you, Glossop?" I had to hold back a laugh. "Is that your meaning?"

"I asked the superintendent," he insisted. "Your great inspector asked for someone biddable. He wanted someone easy to order about and they gave him Campbell Lawless. Because you're weak-willed. Ha!" He wiped his nose and looked at me squarely. "I'm doing fine too, thanks, since you ask."

I took the address and walked out.

Dickens' residence was in disarray. When the butler opened the door, after a long wait, servants were flitting hither and thither and I could hear voices raised. With my heart accelerating at the prospect of an interview with a famous man, I asked if might speak to Mr Dickens.

"No, sir."

"Is he out of town?"

"No, sir."

"Where is he, then, may I ask?"

"Mr Dickens is at home, sir."

The man was beginning to irk me. "Then why mayn't I speak to him?"

"Mr Dickens is writing, sir." He spoke as if the subject were distasteful to him. "It doesn't do to disturb him. Could you come back in the afternoon?"

With so much traipsing ahead of me, I had no wish to return

to what was most likely a dead-end enquiry. "Is Mrs Dickens available?"

The butler's jaw tightened. "I am instructed to say that Mrs Dickens is down in the country."

"No family members at all?"

"Miss Dickens, Miss Dickens and Miss Dickens are at home, sir."

"Then, I pray you, ask the eldest's indulgence for an interview."

He sighed, as if he wished I would vanish. "Is the matter pressing, sir? Only the house is rather occupied at the moment and the Miss Dickenses are not of age."

"The matter is urgent," I said.

No sooner was I ushered into the reception room than I fell under that spell which entrances us members of the public when first confronted with fame. Was this the desk at which the great man thought of Pickwick? No, that was of course upstairs, for he was writing at it. Were those the windows against which he pressed his nose as he dreamt up David Copperfield? Of course not, for this house was bought on the proceeds of that novel.

"Officer?" The young woman who interrupted my daydreams was not beautiful, but appealing in the flush of her excitement. "I am sorry, but you have been needlessly summoned. Really, all's well. You needn't have come. A storm in a teacup. Father will be appalled at the hullabaloo when he comes down."

"The hullabaloo?"

She bit her lip and sniffed nobly. "It was just my mother departing, again. This time I fear it is for good."

The butler, till then silent, coughed.

The girl looked round in annoyance, but returned to me with a charming smile. "I'm sorry. I have forgot my manners.

Catherine Dickens. And you?"

I took her hand. "Miss Dickens. I am Sergeant Lawless, of Scotland Yard."

"Scotland Yard?"

"I have come on quite another business, about the theft, a year and a half back. But if I can be of help in your current crisis–"

"Oh, it's nothing, really. A misunderstanding on all sides. Come now, sit down."

"Thank you. I need to confirm some details. Did you discover anything further missing, beyond money?"

She sat opposite me, warmth returning to her face, as if glad to be distracted from domestic cares. "Money? I'm not sure there was any money taken."

I frowned. "Nothing at all, then."

"I recall father was concerned about his manuscripts. He used it as an excuse to take an office in Camden, which only roused mother's suspicions. Ridiculous, of course."

"And were manuscripts taken?" I asked quickly.

"No, no. Father was quite deluded." She turned again to the butler. "Perkins, what the deuce are you fretting about?"

Perkins was a man whose features seemed carved in stone. "Miss Dickens, I would suggest that such matters should wait till your father is available."

"Perkins, father has expressly stated that in mother's absence I am the lady of the house. Kindly comply with his wishes." She gave me a sweet little smile as if to assure me that, despite her severity with the servant, she was a sweet young thing.

"Miss Dickens," I went on. I was becoming irritated. "Have you noticed any suspicious behaviour on the part of any servants?"

"Suspicious?" She inclined her head, eyes narrowed in

deliberation. "Perhaps I have. Perkins, wouldn't you say Agnes has been out of sorts?"

A certain stiffness of the lip gave the impression that Perkins had just swallowed something unpalatable. "Agnes, Miss Dickens?"

"Come, Perkins. I have seen her slipping out after dinner, in fancy new frocks."

"Is there a crime in that, Miss Dickens?"

"Don't hedge so, Perkins. You know something. I do believe you are blushing."

"Not at all, Miss Dickens." He coughed as if the topic were distasteful to him. "I am given to understand that she is courting. With a Frenchman."

"A Frenchman? Heavens!" Miss Dickens shot me an amused look. "That hardly explains her new clothes, though. How does she afford them? Perkins, you look furtive. You are not lending her money, are you?"

"By no means, Miss Dickens."

"Sergeant?"

It was exactly the kind of thing Wardle watched for. I sighed. "Can we speak with this Agnes?"

"Perkins, call Agnes, will you?"

The man hesitated. "The girl is not fit to speak with the police."

"Fetch her, Perkins. And you are dismissed."

The butler bristled with indignation, then departed.

Miss Dickens looked troubled. "You will be kind, I hope? Agnes is no thief, Sergeant. She will die of anxiety if she thinks herself suspected."

"I'm afraid you will have to trust me. I will try not to scare the girl."

"Oh, Sergeant. I humbly request that you do not dismiss me, now the thing looks interesting, just because I am of the distaff side. You see, we are devotees of Mr Wilkie Collins, who declares no mysteries are more enthralling than those that lie at our own doors."

I was fool enough to allow her to stay. Despite my suggestion that she leave the questioning to me, Miss Dickens plunged in and asked Agnes how she could afford her new clothes. I cringed, thinking we would learn nothing. To my amazement, the poor girl started chattering about resignation and her shame and what would become of her. It was all we could do to calm her down enough to explain.

The crime to which Agnes confessed came as a surprise. A few years back, she had let out space in the cellar to a family of indigent relatives, newcomers to town. They insisted on paying her the few shillings they could afford for her troubles. These she had saved up, until this fellow came along. Her relatives had avoided notice by coming in through the servants' entrance after dark and leaving before morning, of which deception she was sorely ashamed. Yet she assured us that her cousins were the most honest souls in Christendom. Besides, they had left three years ago, well before the theft I was investigating.

"She's a good girl, and methodical," said Miss Dickens when we dismissed the maid, "but I am afraid what father will say."

We recalled Perkins.

"Did you know about our subterranean tenants, Perkins?"

Perkins' stony features betrayed nothing. Only in a certain hesitation in his voice did his embarrassment show. I began to think he might be the one, the inside contact of Wardle's theories.

"Come on, man," I said. "We have no ill intentions against you. But you are responsible for the household. Do you not see that access to the cellar means access to the house?"

Seeing himself suspected, Perkins finally yielded. He had

known about Agnes' relatives. But that was not all. Such
goings-on, he claimed, were prevalent throughout London. It
was nigh on standard practice. He couldn't claim he was proud
of it, but he made no practice of taking a percentage, as many
butlers did. The girl had asked him most properly and most
piteously, thrown herself on his mercy, in fact, when her
cousins had been freezing down by the docks. Though Agnes
had dealt with the minutiae, he felt that no breach of trust had
occurred. "Of course," he said, marshalling his dismay, "I am
prepared to take full responsibility, should it come to that."

"Leave that for now," I said, gripped by a strange excitement.
I must inspect the cellar. This could be the key. "Perkins, tell
me. Was there anything unusual found after the theft?"

"There may have been."

"Good God, man, there either was or there wasn't."

"It's the household, you see, sir. We've been in such
disarray. But, yes, I admit it. I myself discovered it, some time
after the theft."

"What, man? What?"

"It was behind the mantelpiece clock, you see, tucked away,
where nobody could see. You could fault the staff, under
normal circumstances, but I shouldn't want anyone taken to
task in this case."

"For heaven's sake, it is not my concern to cause you
embarrassment over household chores. What did you find?"

"Why, sir." He looked pained. "An old bone."

I descended the narrow stairs with my mind whirling. Could
all the houses have had invisible lodgers? If a whole family
could come in and out of a house without the master's
knowing, what other scallywag or mountebank might enter
likewise?

Perkins gave me a lamp. "If you must inspect the cellar, sir, of course you may, but you should remember that it is not only the coal vault but a former cesspit. Since all the new sewerage work, I do not know what is attached where, nor how any of it functions."

The stairs were strong, though a broken handrail almost saw me pitched in among the musty old barrels and boxes. I ducked under a stone arch, my nose clogging with coal dust. God Almighty, it broke your heart to think of humans condemned to live in this dim prison.

I stooped under the next vaulted arch and peered under into the darkness. The stink all but made me retch. Besides my lamp, weak light filtered through glass bricks high above. I must be under the street already.

I stiffened at a noise, drawing back the lamp so suddenly that it went out. The noise had seemed unmistakably human, like someone licking their chops. Were there new residents since Agnes' cousins? Covering my mouth, I hunched down and waited. As my eyes grew accustomed to the dark, I saw straw spread over the floor and a wealth of thick clay pipes disappearing into a dark corner.

A sudden movement caught my eye, darting into the blackness. There was a small splash. I sprang forward, raising my hand to protect myself from the low vaulted arches. But the intruder had vanished, swiftly and silently. In the furthest corner, where several pipes disappeared into the ground, I felt metal beneath my feet. I dropped to my haunches and ran my fingers over a grate. I braced myself against the wall and tugged at the metal. To my surprise, the thing opened with barely a squeak. I squeezed through, feet first.

I dropped down into low, foul-smelling conduit, inclining downwards. I was certain I could hear movement ahead. The only way to move was on all fours. I splashed down towards a dim light. The base of the conduit was curved, and I found I could avoid the worst of the watery sludge beneath me by crawling with hands and knees wide apart.

Soon enough, I reached the end of the passageway and the source of the light: a second metal grate, stout and vertical like a portcullis. I peered through it, keenly hoping for a sight of my quarry. What I saw amazed me. Stretching into the distance in either direction was a great brick tunnel, oval-shaped, perhaps nine feet by six. Lit at intervals, it carried a steady flow of dark liquid. The cellar dweller must have already outpaced me. I cursed myself for coming so close and failing. Then the noise came again, further along the tunnel. I could see no one, but it sounded only yards away. They must have climbed through to hide out of view.

I tugged at the grate. It was fixed in place and much heavier than the first. Again I tugged, then pushed, but to no avail. Convinced that my quarry would hear these exertions and flee, I gave way to a desperate energy, reaching through the gaps in the metal to try and find a catch to release it. Finding a sort of latch, I pulled the thing back with such force that I fell backwards with a splash. My fingers twisted painfully as the grate swung open. As I lay there in the filth, shocked, it began to swing shut once more. I threw out my foot to intercept it. It closed upon my knee with a fearful momentum, and I could not help but cry out. Forgetting my twisted fingers, I pulled at it with both hands. The metal rasped over my knee. I wriggled through the gap, my leg smarting fearfully. The portal was set high up in the great tunnel's wall, and I did not jump down. Instead I sat there, looking up and down and cursing my clumsiness. Insulted in my nostrils and sullied with filth, I was dumbstruck. I pictured a network of passageways, like an invisible city beneath our feet. And if someone could escape Dickens' cellar this way, where else could they gain access?

Waves of pain seared through my knee. I felt myself on the point of swooning, as numbness spread up over me. Then I heard the noise again. That same slobbering sound, just below me in the tunnel. There, beside the dark flow, looking up at me with an insolent confidence, was my quarry: a large rat.

"Sit still," Miss Kate enjoined me, dabbing at my injuries with a hot compress of poppies. "Lie back, now. This is quite the most excitement we have had for years. At least since the archbishop knocked the chancellor flat."

"Since what, Miss Dickens?" I said, wincing. I could still move my fingers, and the gash on my leg did not look too serious. Yet the kneecap had swollen monstrously, and I felt ungainly as the elephant in the Royal Menagerie.

"Oh, call me Kate, please. It will cost you less effort." Miss Kate had taken to her job of nurse with gusto. The trivialities she spouted were perhaps intended to divert attention from my injuries. All I wanted was to be left in peace. "At leapfrog, you know. After-dinner disportment."

My return to the surface had taken some time. I had come to my senses to the sound of a voice above me. Somehow I had crawled back up towards the house, and there was Perkins, thank God, to pull me back up. How I came to be lying on a dog blanket upon the drawing room ottoman with my bandaged leg raised on silk pillows, I had no idea.

Miss Kate lost no time filling me in on what I had missed. Far from sacking Agnes, her father had applauded the girl's ingenuity. If she had taken a liberty, she had done it out of kindness. "But then," she rattled on, "father always felt tender towards the downtrodden, and harder towards his own. A case in point: our annual drama. We perform it ourselves, you see. Family and friends, in the Smallest Theatre in the World, that is, right here in this room. The thing has turned serious now.

Not that father was ever anything but serious. He is a harsher director than the moustachioed generals at the Charge of the Light Brigade. That, however, is not my grievance. Our presentations began to draw wider notice. What did he do? He ingloriously curtailed his daughters' careers. Yes! He threw us out with barely an apology and stooped to casting in our stead professional actresses." Miss Kate pronounced these words with the utmost disdain. "He claimed that he did not want us presented to Her Majesty in the light of such a trade as acting. Poppycock. Our latest extravaganza is to be presented to the Queen in a few months. Despite my memorable performance in the Christmas version, I am now relegated to the department of stage properties and make-up. What an insult!"

I was trying to think clearly. All the houses that had been robbed, could they all have cellar dwellers? Or simpler, could they all be accessed by the new sewer? But Miss Kate's prattling put a new thought in my mind. I struggled on to my elbows. "Miss Kate, tell me. How did your father engage these actresses?"

"Oh, he goes on little jaunts, you know. Mr Collins likes to scandalise me with tales of frequenting the louchest nooks and crannies of the West End theatres."

"Did he engage the services of an actress called Nellie?"

"Sergeant, all actresses are called Nellie. Can you add a distinguishing feature?"

I laughed, but I sensed something serious in her manner. "All right. She had a friend, a fiancé, I think, called Skelton. Berwick Skelton." The pressure on my knee increased and I looked at her keenly. "Might you know the fellow?"

"I might."

"I do ask you to think carefully."

"I should like," she said, pursing her lips coyly, "to consult my diary, Sergeant."

She was playing games, damn it, trying to keep my interest.

"So as not to furnish you with incomplete information," she went on, more eagerly. "Are you in a hurry for details? I shall do some detecting and report post haste."

I nodded and lay back down, irritated. I had no place there, with this silly girl fluttering her eyelids. She didn't know Skelton, not with anything more than a passing acquaintance. Still, it was another coincidence. She babbled on and I stopped listening to the words themselves.

"Good God," said a familiar face poking around the door. Charles Dickens made an anguished face at the sight of my bandages. "Are you quite all right, Sergeant? Oh, Kate, we must move back to the country, away from these perils. Is that the time?" he said, glancing at the mantel clock. "Barbarous. Do call on us again, officer. Good day."

Kate shook her head. "He knows very well that clock stopped years ago."

I started. "When exactly did it stop?"

She frowned. "A couple of years back."

"After the theft?"

"I don't recall. Perhaps."

I tried to rise but there was no strength in my leg. She brought the clock over to me. It took only a moment to check. Sure enough, the clock's workings were removed. Not an unusual practice, as Josiah Bent had taught me. Yet I could not shake off the feeling that this was a house where I had encountered too many coincidences.

Mens Sana in Corpore Sano

"Who dragged you out of the river?" said Wardle when I hobbled back into the office. "We can't have officers trooping around covered in filth."

I started in on my new theory, talking of the great sewer and how we would have to check all the houses over again, but I was overcome by a great weariness.

"Pull yourself together, lad, you're gabbling," he said evenly. "Go and clean yourself up."

I stood there, my leg throbbing with pain. I had to make him understand. I rolled up my trouser leg, explaining all higgledy-piggledy about the grate and the rat and the interconnected passageways.

Wardle took one look at my leg. "Hobbling Joe, eh? Go home, then, if you must, and get better. I need you fit. Write to some of these bloody constabularies while you're at it." He returned to the work in front of him. When he realised I was still standing there dumbly, he looked up sharply. "Go on, off with you."

On the walk home, the leg bore my weight well enough, but I could not straighten it at the knee, so was forced to swing it round from the hip like some sort of hunchback. How often before had I seen the beggar singing in St James' Park? As I hobbled past, he looked in worse condition than ever, and I realised I should consider myself lucky to have legs at all. I stopped and offered to buy him a hot potato, thinking to save him some trouble.

"Potato my arse," he scowled. "Give us the penny ha'penny."

That day, he seemed the captain of the legions of maimed and mutilated. On the torturous climb homewards, I noticed cripples and madmen in every corner, entreating without accusation the carefree passersby. Outside my lodgings, I encountered the costermonger. He had the kindness to tell me I was white as a sheet, and gave me a bag of apples for free. I retreated to bed, feeling I had exhausted myself, trying too hard, and to no end, for I was too gentle on people, and I suffered for it, running back and forth across the city for answers I should have demanded the first time.

Sleep crept deliciously over me.

I awoke in the night in panic. With no strength to go for water, I reached for an apple. The foul taste pulled me up short. I had not pulled my shutters to, and in the dim light from the street, I could see worms wriggling in the apple's core. I threw it down in disgust and fell back into a series of dreams. In one, I could hear an enormous creature, a mole or a worm, tunnelling beneath me till the whole house began to quake, with smoke and alarming noise. As the ground sank away from me, I found myself floating there in the newly clear sky. I looked up to find that a stage magician was holding me there, levitated in midair. I was afraid, but I looked up to find his saintly face smiling down at me, and I was filled with contentment. In another, I pursued an unseen quarry along a bold new road until I dropped from sheer fatigue, only to find that it was I who had been pursued all along, and they were upon me at once, their little fingers tickling me, scratching, clawing.

Thus began a cycle of terrible dreams and feverish wakenings. I lay there in the half-light, listening to the cries from the market. How would I gather the strength to go for help? What if I should sleep and never wake up? It made me wonder, what kind of life did I have? Who knew who I was, or cared? They might recognise me in the local tavern; the landlady would miss me if I didn't pay the rent. But if I simply vanished there was nobody would miss me, nobody to notice. Wardle might spare me a thought, but he didn't even know where I lived. Even if some secretary dug out the form where I had written my particulars, would anyone take the trouble of sending out to see what happened to me? In the Great

Battle For Life that the papers constantly talked of, people disappeared all the time, little mysteries that stirred the meagrest interest, Londoners being fully absorbed in their own concerns. My dreams turned blacker still.

On the third day, or perhaps it was the fourth, I summoned up my strength to call for help. But my body felt indescribably heavy, and my legs gave way beneath me. I fell to the floor, crying out with pain and desperation. I must get to the stairs. I must get help or I would vanish away. I crawled towards the door but it seemed far beyond reach. My head dropped to the floor, overwhelmed by nausea.

I awoke to find water pressed to my lips. A familiar voice was speaking, gentle words which comforted me like a blanket. I fell back into sleep. I awoke again in terror that my succour had been but a vain dream. But beneath me was not the hard wooden floor, but my bed, with sheets soft and fresh. I found fresh water beside me and a glass of brandy which burned through my aching limbs. I knew I must get to a doctor. But I had heard stories enough to scare an executioner about Humbug von Quack, MD, FRS and all the rest of the letters in the alphabet, whose motto was "cure or kill". My thoughts turned to Simpson, but how to get to the hospital I could not imagine. It was then I had the strangest of all the dreams. It was as if I were visited by a ministering angel. I heard a girl's voice, felt a soothing cloth upon my forehead and a cool breeze. A far-off melody drifted in through the open window: one of the old songs. A chorus of voices joined in, and to that distant harmony I drifted back to sleep.

"You've had a close call, nor are you out of the woods yet."

I looked up to find the corpulent frame of Simpson hanging over me.

"Merciful God," I rasped. "Did Wardle send you?"

"Wardle?" He gave a short laugh. "No, no. I came in answer to your note."

"I... I wrote none."

"Did you not? Perhaps your urchin friends forged it." He laughed again and glanced behind him. "I must be going. Put him into a cab to the Middlesex, would you, Worm? Here's a florin."

I raised my head weakly. "Worm?"

"The same," he returned in sprightly fashion from the stool by the window.

"Was it you? You who helped me to bed?"

"Landlady helped," he shrugged. "Though she was less concerned with your welfare than with loss of rental."

"I'll give notice if I intend to pass on."

Worm and the Professor bundled me into a cut-price trap, doubtless taking their cut of Simpson's cab money, and I found myself enduring the worst journey of my life. Smiling eagerly, the idiot headed under the railway and through the gasworks, the roads evidently littered with potatoes. It was the bumpiest route in Christendom, and I soon lost my joy at seeing the world again. It should have been a short ride, but we ended up in Camden Town. Might as well take me straight to Highgate Cemetery, I thought. Racing back down across the Euston Road, the cretin contrived to collide with a pony and trap. We could have been killed. More dreadful to me was the prospect of waiting hours to give evidence to a policeman. When I stepped shakily down to find Glossop striding towards the scene of the crash, I almost wished I had been killed. He looked at me in shock, and I realised how grim I must appear. I explained where I was headed. To his credit, he packed me into another cab without a word, and I arrived at hospital with my faith in humanity restored.

Over the next week, Simpson made clear it to me how narrow my escape had been. My fingers were merely sprained, but I had suffered considerable damage to the tendons above my kneecap. They might heal, given time, but I would always limp. More seriously, the gash had introduced an infection, poisoning my blood with a kind of pox which had swollen the leg so badly they considered amputation.

"You have been in the sewers, I take it?" he said sternly. He seemed to imagine I had been working down there with the Worms, and he was cross. "Rat syphilis is not the worst of the dangers of such work. I will not speak now of the necessity of using gloves and other hygienic measures. Only remember, young man, you have had a miraculous return from the underworld."

As I regained my strength, Wardle appeared, with a bag of sweetmeats and a half bottle of whisky. I was so glad to see him I almost wept. This time I managed to communicate to him, more coherently, the notion that the sewers might offer thieves access to houses.

"I see." He nodded quietly. "Make some enquiries while you're lazing round here. Write to the boroughs, will you?"

"No resting on my laurels, then, sir?"

"I've brought paper and pen. What more do you want?" He looked away for a moment. "You get well now. The Yard will deal with the bill."

I did not realise till after he had gone that, with my injured hand, I could do no writing. It struck me that it could only be Worm that had written to Simpson. If he had done that so effectively, why not employ him as my secretary? On his next visit, I struck a deal for his services. Soon we were drafting letters to constabularies all over the city, demanding details of thefts and requesting checks of houses' access to the sewer network. A fine secretary he made. For, although he lost no opportunity to cheer me up with jokes, sleight of hand and other merriment, the days he spent at my bedside were highly productive, and among the most pleasurable of the whole charade.

It was two weeks before Simpson gave me a clean bill of health. I shook his hand, keenly aware that he had saved me. "Can I call on you again?" I asked tentatively. "I have some questions about some bones I'd like answered."

"Yes, yes," he nodded brusquely. "Good day, now."

I Weep Continually

Though still troubled by fevers, I began retracing my old routes to and from the Yard even before I went back to work, for Simpson had told me to exercise the knee mercilessly. In those weeks, I observed Nelson's lions under construction, watched the bold new thoroughfares cut across town, and saw the Hungerford Market torn up to make way for another train bridge.

So it was that, one warm October Thursday, the day before I was due back at the Yard, I found myself standing again before the Rose and Crown. The pub seemed now the final fortress against an oncoming invader, as the rookeries to one side and the other of the road were cleared before the underground railway's advance. How had I so lightly walked away, I asked myself, when I was so sure that everyone in the tavern knew Skelton?

I knocked on the scullery door. A maid answered in kindly fashion, with no trace of hostility.

"Do excuse me," I said. "I'm a friend of the Skeltons."

"Go on up, sir," she answered. "Only as I'm a-baking the

tarts. Master'll have my head if I don't be watching 'em like a hawk." She nodded, most prettily, to a door at the back of the kitchen.

I thanked her, trying to betray no surprise, and climbed with some difficulty up the dark stairs. At the top was a store room. Beside it, a door stood ajar.

"Excuse me," I called out, knocking lightly. "It's a friend of Mr Skelton."

A woman's voice, full of world-weariness, replied imperiously, "*Entrez!*"

I found myself in a room laden from floor to ceiling with paraphernalia of all kinds. It was as if a whole house had been squeezed into it, so that furniture and fittings which once complemented each other were now piled in precarious optimism. The centrepiece was a great brass bed, shrouded in green gauze, wherein lay a grand old matron, her grey hair scattered across the pillows.

"You seek," she said in the rich tones of a foreigner, "the which Mr Skelton?"

"Berwick," I replied. "I'm looking for Berwick."

"I am his mother. His poor long-suffering mother. Madame Skelton."

My heart leapt and I swayed for a moment in amazement. It was as I had said to Miss Villiers, the simplest reason a man might give a tavern as his address was that he lived there. "I am pleased to meet you, ma'am."

"You are a man of the police, I see. Berwick has done something grave?"

"No, no," I assured her. Not exactly, I thought, not yet. But what he might do, and why, I wanted desperately to know, so desperately that I thought little of deceiving an old woman. "I'm just an acquaintance. An admirer. You see, we... I am concerned about him."

She turned her eyes dolefully to the window. "I wish to hear more. Close the shutter. Remove the veil. You will take beer, or I shall call for tea?"

I did as she bade, struck by her manner, like the lady of a fine house, not a room above an East End pub. As I drew back the veil, I couldn't help but think of my own mother's illness. I remember, as a child, being scared of going in to her; she was so weak, it felt like you were alone in that cold, dank room. Madame Skelton, however, exuded life, though marooned in this invalid bed. Stories etched in the lines of her face, she filled the place with her presence, and that indomitable voice.

I poured her a draught of beer from a pitcher on the bedside table, beside a framed drawing of a little girl, and sat down by her. As she drank, I studied the drawing. "Berwick's sister?" I asked.

"Yes." She wiped her mouth with the sleeve of her gown. "You have siblings?"

"None. Does she live here too?"

"The cholera took her, in '42. Before you were born," she smiled.

"I was a boy," I nodded. "It took my mother the same year."

She reached out and squeezed my hand.

She took the notion that I was one of her son's acolytes. It soon became clear that nothing delighted her more than talking of her family. She folded back the top of her coverlet, an old-fashioned tapestry showing gentlemen and damsels cavorting on quaint stone bridges, and proceeded to unfold before me the fabric of her past. In another place, I might have been impatient. But after my sickness, the whole scene was permeated with a feverish reality, and I sat mute with wonder as she spoke lyrically of her family.

Her husband was an enterprising Irishman, who rose through the ranks of Brunel's engineering team, and became an important draughtsman. The great projects he worked on took him the length and breadth of the country, culminating with the Great Thames Tunnel. That brought him back to London and to her, the daughter of refugees from the French Revolution.

"Can you imagine the astonishment with which the Tunnel was greeted?" she exclaimed. "They had to invent twelve new techniques of the tunnelling! Ah, short memories people have. There were celebrations across the city, I tell you. Your Queen commissioned a special train for to ride through it."

"You must be proud."

"He is gone now." She gestured towards an engraving hung above the bedside. "It finished him."

In the dim light, I examined a cheap print of an underground feast. It bore the legend OPENING BANQUET, THAMES TUNNEL, 1843.

"Was he killed in the tunnel?"

"Injured. A small compensation they paid, despite that he innovated in the tunnelling. Times were not easy, but he was a good man was Mr Skelton. Even in his illness he made charitable visits to Poor Houses, you see. It was there occurred the infernal explosion of gas that robbed him from us."

She fiddled with her pendant. I glanced around the room, realising that every piece of paraphernalia was likely imbued with family recollections. Next to the engraving hung a certificate so faded, I could only make out a florid signature, the words "Red Lion Club", and an extravagant wax seal.

"Little Berwick, he suffered without his father. Nevertheless, he was a great comfort to me. Well behaved, studied sincerely, was diligent and useful." She glanced fondly at a desk beneath the window, as if her son was sitting there now. After the husband's death, they were unable to keep their house – their apartments, she called them – and they had gone from bad to worse until the slum clearances of the Fifties left them quite homeless. It was Berwick who arranged this room, for he knew the landlord. "Since then I should have been happy. I could have resigned myself to our fall, if only my Berwick had not gone – how do you say – off the rails?"

She fell into a coughing fit, raising her hand to indicate I need not worry. I walked over to the desk to give her a moment's privacy, hoping that she would tell more. On the desk stood a fine clock, engraved: "John Skelton, from Isambard Kingdom Brunel". I recalled Josiah Bent's tales of how, for a small fee, a clocky will rechristen jack, that is inscribe a stolen clock with a new engraving; though what reason had I to doubt that the great engineer had thus commended her husband? There was an ink bottle and quill, ready to use, as if Berwick had just gone out of the room. Shivering to feel myself so close to him, I put out my hand to lift the desk lid.

"Go ahead," she said. "There are some of his *pensées*."

At her invitation I drew out a finely bound tome. Inside were pages and pages of densely inscribed writing, but I could make nothing out, except for the odd phrase. One page was entitled "The Shameful Slums of the East End". The rest seemed at first illegible, then I began to wonder if it were in some code.

"You are puzzling, are you not?" she laughed. "His father taught him all kinds of secret writing. Go ahead, look below."

Though I was chafing to study the book more, fascinated by that dense vision of code, I slipped it back into the desk. Beneath lay a box of toys, Noah's Ark with animal figurines; a toy train; a miniature theatre complete with tragedians and comedians glued to the stage, their melodramatic poses filled with love, anger or anguish. Was it then that I felt the first stirrings of admiration – of affection – for this man I had never met? Seeing his childhood squeezed into a single piece of furniture. Thinking of the happy child turned forlorn, growing up with tireless efforts to make himself someone his mother could be proud of.

"That theatre," Madame Skelton hissed, a shadow falling over her features. "That was the ruin of him. He was doing so well. The writing. The meetings. Such fine ideas he had. The finest of minds. He could have been a Member of Parliament. He would have got for us some sort of justice. She gestured at the mess around her, tired now, or a little drunk. Enthralled by all she had told me, I repented of having tricked her.

"Where is he now?" I asked.

"Ask the little vixen," she retorted. She drank down her beer and poured herself another draught. "She blinded him to all that was best. I told him, I said she was just one of those Haymarket tarts, but he had high-up ideas of her good breeding, just because she put on airs, and had aspirations, and acquaintances in high places."

"But where is he?" I repeated gently.

She pulled the edge of the coverlet towards her. "He was a good boy, always interested in fine things. Lofty things. Everyone loved him so, he could have chosen any girl." She laughed emptily. "I lost my house and my husband to progress, my health to consumption, and my son to a trollop. We are a benighted clan, officer, are we not?"

I smiled ruefully, thinking for a moment of my father, still in our Edinburgh flat, marking the passing of the seasons alone. I sat back down at her bedside. "When did he leave this place?"

"When? Does it matter? Long ago."

"How long?" I insisted.

"Too long. One year and a half, perhaps."

Soon after the spout. "And you don't know where he is?"

"They tell me he has gone." She turned to me fiercely. "It is untrue, I tell you. I see him. Sometimes, in the early mornings–"

The door burst open and in strode the weasel of a man from that day in the tavern. I stood back, disconcerted, as he went to her bedside and most gently took her hand. "Ma Skelton, it's me. It's John. Is the man tiring you? It's time for you to rest."

She looked at him uncertainly, and there were tears in her voice. "He simply was asking about Berwick."

"Oh, ma, he's gone. I told you he's gone," he comforted her. He eyed me belligerently. "Get out, will you? Putting false hope in the old woman's head. Clear off, I said."

A wave of light-headedness washed over me as I emerged onto the street. I stretched my leg uncertainly, caught in two minds whether I could manage the ascent straight home or should I take the longer but less taxing route via King's Cross. I heard a call behind me and turned to see the weasel approaching me.

"No need for alarm, copper," he said, stretching out his hand. "I'm John Fairfoul."

I was not about to shake his hand. I walked away, but he fell in beside me.

"I was only protecting the old lady." His amenable tone took me aback.

"No doubt. And that other day, did you not lie to me?"

He laughed pleasantly. "Come off it."

"You told me you didn't know Skelton."

"You know the score. I wouldn't snitch on my worst enemy to you lot."

"Nor your brother, apparently."

"Stepbrother. Ma Skelton took me in when my folks passed on."

"All right," I said, taken with feverish optimism, "let's assume you won't talk. Let me tell you, I am concerned for him. I have no wish to harm him. I fear for what he may do. If you have any affection for him, I implore you–"

"Affection?" He laughed. "The devil take him."

I looked at him closely. "Then tell me where he is."

"Haven't the foggiest, copper."

I recognised that look from that day in the tavern. I knew with sudden certainty he was lying. Taken with impatience, I grabbed him by the shoulders and hoisted him against the wall. "Good God, man, you will tell me what you know or I will make not only your life a misery, but hers, which will pain me, for she seems a noble soul."

"I told you, I don't know."

"And you wouldn't tell me if you did."

"There's rules about these things."

"Rules? Are you in some organisation?"

"What's that?"

"Some league for reform?" When he gave no answer, I shook him against the wall with all my force. "You know where he is."

"He's gone," he burst out. He tried to remain composed by his eyes showed that he was startled. "He's went away."

"Away? From London?"

"Yes."

"When?"

"Last winter. Good riddance to him."

I slackened my grip a little, but held him pinned against the wall. "She said she's seen him."

"She's past her three score and ten. She sees things."

I was saddened to think of her as a fanciful old woman, conjuring up ghosts of her past to keep her company. I hesitated. "Why did he go?"

"Am I my brother's keeper?"

"Where, then?"

"Some said Canada, some the Cape. I heard Australia. Wouldn't surprise me. People like him, no place for them in this country."

"Meaning what?"

He shrugged again. "Always in some kind of trouble. Nobody wants that, do they? Look, copper, I need to be getting back to mother."

With that he wriggled free and was gone. I stood there, my heart stilled, the trail struck dead.

A cock was crowing up at Mount Pleasant. I walked away in a turmoil, filled with a kind of reckless indignation. Once back at the Yard, there would be little time for extra-curricular enquiries, what with the theft inquiries and my injury. If I could just get to Nellie, though. If I could only persuade someone to talk.

The day I went back to work, a man tugged my sleeve as I stepped out for lunch.

"Lawless, is it?" He was an odd-looking midget of a man, with an egg-shaped head and an effeminate air that sat ill with his deep mumble of a voice. "Jackman."

It took me a moment to place the name.

"Sergeant of the Yard, retired," he explained, discomfited. "Inspector Wardle may have spoke of me."

"Of course. Yes."

"I've been waiting a week for you. We must talk."

"I was sick." I suggested my usual lunch haunt, but Jackman preferred to stroll down to the Thames and along the splendid new esplanade that now overhung the river's north bank. Great edifices were springing up where before had been broken ground punctuated with the rickety dens of iniquity, ever on the point of tumbling into the stinking mud. I had always feared to see in that mud, amongst the discarded cartwheels and anchors, ill-fated mudlarks sinking into the sluggish loam, grasping at the coarse grass to save themselves from sinking. Now the mud was gone, and the river flowed along, washing appealingly against its new limits.

I strode along, amazed. "What became of the families who lived along the banks?"

"Bazalgette's built houses," Jackman wheezed, struggling to keep up. "Thousands of them. Trusts. Housing associations. Around the Crystal Palace hill."

"Sounds idyllic," I replied. "I never saw the Palace myself."

"A long way to go to see a greenhouse," he sniffed. "Especially as they're building a new one in Kensington."

I laughed uncertainly. "Still, it seems a healthy measure. The houses, I mean."

"Politic manoeuvre," he demurred. "Pacify the masses. One day soon, they'll have the vote. Where will our masters be then? Out on their ear, and we'll have some greengrocer's daughter for a prime minister. Can't have that. So they pay out a pittance to please the workers. Divide up the communities in the process, else you get a lot of troublemakers living together, and what will they do but make trouble?"

I chose not to comment on his negative view of humanity.

"The Dickens job," he said, licking his lips. "I was right, wasn't I?"

I nodded reluctantly.

He started mumbling to himself, "He should never have got rid of me, he knew where he was with me."

"Mr Jackman. Kindly get to your point. I am soon due back."

He recovered himself, and stood looking out across the water, stroking his chin. "These skellington jobs, tell me. Is

Wardle truly wasting his time with petty theft?"

"Petty?" I wanted to give the impression that there was a hidden story he knew nothing of.

"Don't tell me that the man who cracked the Sadleir suicide now occupies himself chasing pickpockets for tuppeny ha'penny personalities."

The man was offensive, but his claim nonetheless disturbed me.

"What else is cooking in the office, if I may ask?"

"You may not ask, Mr Jackman." I took pleasure in not calling him "sergeant", which seemed to pain him. "Though you left me a deal of refiling."

He stopped on the spot. "Tell me," he said in deadly earnest, "have you worked upon the Mary Ann Brough case?"

"The wet nurse?" I said casually, pleased to feel I knew something of Wardle's past.

"The royal wet nurse," he said.

There was something in Jackman's manner I didn't like, a suggestion that I was not truly admitted to Wardle's confidence, not as he had been. "That was twenty years ago."

"What do you know of it?"

I trotted out the facts that Wardle had mentioned: the royal wet nurse had gone mad and murdered her own children, six of them, and tried to take her own life.

"Did you stop to ask what drove her mad?"

"Family troubles, wasn't it? I forget. Violent husband."

"That's what the popular press hinted," said Jackman, his manner unsavoury. "Wouldn't you be violent if you worked hard your whole life and came out without nothing? Hmm? Tell me that! Cast out like so much scrap iron."

I was determined not to be drawn by his air of cheap mystery and walked on into the parliamentary gardens. "Servants are dismissed every day. There are hard-luck stories worse than hers, that kill nobody."

"Maybe so, but injustice rankles, wouldn't you say?" His dark eyes bored into me. "Injustice you daren't speak of. That puts terrible pressure on the mind."

"I wouldn't know, I'm sure," I said uncomfortably. "But you weren't there either, twenty years ago."

"I wasn't," he smiled eerily, gazing across to the south bank, "but I have been to see her." And he began to recite, in a querulous tone:

> *Within the prison's massive walls,*
> *What anguish will torment her breast*
> *When phantoms of her six dear children*
> *Will disturb her of her rest?*
> *Such a sad and dreadful murder,*
> *On record there is no worse,*
> *Committed by a cruel mother,*
> *Once the Prince of Wales' Nurse.*

The Parliament bells pealed as prelude to the hour striking, but Big Ben was being repaired, and in place of the great bell's two o'clock chimes a silence fell between us. "Look here, Jackman, I haven't time for your poetry," I said flatly.

"It was a popular pamphlet of the day," he said in less portentous tones. He sensed that he was losing my sympathy and went on rapidly. "There's a lot that doesn't come out in a trial. Things left unsaid. Strings being pulled. Manipulation behind the scenes. Only you never know who is the puppet-master. You'd assume the defendant only conceals things to improve their chances, to cast themselves in the best possible light. But there are things in this world more frightening than prison. When threats are presented in a particular way, when someone powerful wants information kept secret, sometimes you'll beg for a life of poverty and malnutrition."

"Please, do not treat me as a novice. If you wish to speak of dark secrets from that trial, kindly speak of them."

He looked over the railing at the dark waters. "Mary Ann Brough chose not to speak of the circumstances of her dismissal, a dismissal in no way her fault. You would admit that a wet nurse must be empowered to scold children in her charge? What, then, if the situation were reversed? If the nurse had no power of chastisement, while the child was permitted to abuse her with any amount of violence?"

"Then I call that household a madhouse."

He turned to me sharply. "Why do you say that?"

I wafted a hand. "Because it's as children that we learn our place in the world."

He breathed out. "I thought you might be referring to rumours about the Queen." He looked around to check that nobody was near us and began in a tone of earnest pleading. "You'll have heard of the Koháry curse. No? Well, well. The Coburgs, you see, have an eye for advantageous nuptials. But they're suffering for it. Our beloved Prince Albert made the most brilliant marriage; he was penniless when he crossed the Channel. But his Uncle Ferdinand scored almost as high, winning the Hungarian heiress, Antoinette Koháry, whose father was so delighted with the match he bequeathed her his entire estate. What luck! Except that one cousin, a monk no less, was aggrieved at being precipitously disinherited. So he takes his manual of exorcisms to the churchyard at midnight. Oh, verily shall the Lord Almighty visit the sins of the fathers upon the sons, intones this old monk, to the third and fourth generation. You see? The blood curse of the Coburgs!"

I looked back and forth in impatience, up and down the river. The tide was high and the reflections of the bridges, shimmering upon the turbid waters, seemed phantasmal links to another world. "Spare us the mumbo-jumbo, Jackman."

"Superstitious it may sound, but the Coburgs have been afflicted ever since by melancholic illness. Have you not read how Prince Albert's cousins are falling like flies? It's disastrous, this conjunction of royal bloodlines. It begets incurable maladies." Jackman leaned closer to me. "The Hanovers, they're notorious for brutality. Victoria's father was drummed out of the army for flogging men hundreds of times over. Her uncle Ernest, Duke of Cumberland, was suspected of murder, and incest. Of George III and his lunacy, the tales untold are countless. Now it's the turn of the Prince of Wales."

I could brook this nonsense no longer. I turned back towards the Yard.

Jackman dogged my footsteps. "Bertie is a charming enough young man, but he has a cruel streak. The stories in the clubs–"

"Enough of the tall tales," I retorted. "What happened to Mary Ann Brough?"

"Victoria's brood took their toll. She was dismissed. Heartbroken. Penniless. It is my belief, when she saw in her own children one iota of the cruelty she received at the hands of Victoria's eldest son, she decided she could not bring such monsters into the world."

"Enough of this, Jackman. What is it you want to tell me?"

He looked at me, hesitating. "He's not a bad man, don't get me wrong. Only there are decisions a man makes, early in life, that mark him, that alter his direction, so that when he has lived for many years with the consequences of that decision, he looks back upon a chain of actions he has taken that would have been anathema to his younger self."

"You are speaking of your own career?"

"I am speaking of the inspector's."

I looked at him and smelt only his bitterness. He had hinted that he had been unfairly sacked. It might be true.

"I want to warn you. There are things that go on in the force. You're young, an upstanding chap. You think you're above all that. Don't be too sure. You could lose everything, just like I have."

His look troubled me. I shook his fishlike hand and returned to work, trying to put from my mind that wheedling tone, that pleading gaze. Wardle had gone out. But I recalled his reaction when I first complained about the spout report, and I wondered if in every career the compromises and half-truths began so swiftly as they had in mine.

It took all Saturday and a series of exorbitant cab-rides to find her, but I tracked Hester down in a shabby Hoxton dance hall far from the West End. She seemed pleased to see me and lost no time excusing herself from a desultory rehearsal.

"Gone down-market?" I asked as we sat down in the tea shop opposite.

"Got to take the work that's going." She pouted. "My glamour days is over."

I smiled. "Surely not."

"Oh yes. Someone's got it in for me."

It took me a moment to realise she was in earnest. "What happened?"

"Another bleeding spout, wasn't it?"

"At the Evans?" I said breathlessly. "I didn't hear of it."

She shrugged. "Toffs and royalty are never too keen on seeing their mistresses' names plastered all over the press."

"But how has that affected you?"

"They decided I was the Jonah, didn't they, and sent me packing."

I leaned forward. "You know something, Hester."

"I know I'm no bleeding jinx," she burst out, "and I can tell you her name, if you like. Starts with an N and ends in Hell."

"Was Nellie in the show?"

"She was in the bleeding box. Safety curtain comes down at the interval and sends bloody Niagara Falls on her and her fancy man. Only I'm the one as gets the blame for it, while her with her friends in high places waltzes off free as a lark. Buy us a bun, won't you, love?"

I smiled, sad to see her disappointed. Yet there I sat, calculating for my own ends how to lead her into indiscretions. I told myself it was from admirable motives, the type of game Wardle would play without qualms, but it turned my stomach. Still, a mug of chocolate and a cream bun, and it all poured out, without my prompting.

"You could see the shillings in her eyes," she said. "All doe-eyed she'd been over Berwick while they were courting. She loved being admired, and he admired her like no other man could. He was clever, you see, and funny, which flattered her the more. They were a handsome couple, it's true. Him with his hat and sideburns, cracking some hare-brained joke; her with her waist and her bust, and that hair of hers, flailing it round like a fire torch, and putting on elegant airs. But I tell you, for all she was full of it, of how clever he was and how fascinating he talked, she couldn't bear playing second fiddle to him. All her life she's been centre of attention. Since the day she was born! They picked her up and clucked over her chubby cheeks and that flaming hair. But at those posh parties, it wasn't enough and she felt like a fool. Finding herself in a circle where words counts as much as looks, and where her filthy tongue wouldn't do, it came as a shock to her."

The posh parties she spoke of were, of course, *soirées* chez Dickens. The professional actresses of whom Miss Dickens had spoken were Nellie and Hester. She had a soft spot for the novelist himself. "Stickler for details is Mr Dickens. None too keen on the, shall we say, improvisational style I'm used to. But he's always ready for a laugh and a jape after hours. We had grand times. Played to gentlemen and ladies all over. I met the Queen, you know."

"And Berwick?"

"He came along to start, but he had his meetings and that."

"Meetings?"

"You know, all that protest nonsense."

"What nonsense?"

"Don't ask me."

"Reform? Some kind of secret society?"

"You're talking to the wrong girl, love."

"Then tell me where Nellie is and I'll ask her."

She looked at me reproachfully. I was about to push the point, but something told me that Hester didn't know, or care. "Can you tell me about Nellie's fancy man?"

"Is it that still? Well, young actresses tend to draw a lot of attention from gentlemen. At the cocktail parties, we received an embarrassment of invitations, not all of them above board. I often wonder if that was why Mr Dickens stopped re-engaging us: he wasn't confident of our morality." She raised an eyebrow. "Fair enough. We weren't too sure of our morality and all. Some of these gentlemen, I couldn't tell you the things they're after."

"Hester, don't tell me you are blushing." I had imagined the world held nothing secret or shameful for her likes, but nonetheless she blushed. Still, I had no need to hear of the indelicacies and indecencies that gentlemen demanded. "Tell me about the spout at Euston Square."

A smile played across her lips. "You know already."

"It was Berwick, wasn't it? Ho there! Another bun for the lady."

She giggled. "All right, I admit it. I tipped him the wink

about the time."

She still seemed to think I knew more than I did. "How? When?"

"There was me and Nellie and Roxton and–" She bit into the second bun. "You know who."

"Nellie's fancy man. The one she met after *The Frozen Deep*."

"That's right. Up at Roxy's place in the country we were. What a mansion! All the frills and trimmings. Though Nellie reckons it's all for show, he hasn't two shillings to his name, and the whole place is put under dust covers the moment we leave. The way he goes on, gambling and drinking and showing off and worse, I thought he had a goldmine up his *derrière*. Anywise, Berwick was distraught about Nellie. He wouldn't believe it at first. Then off he went and hid like a mouse. Half-starved himself."

A strange envy took me. "He sounds a curious fellow, Hester."

"Berwick?" She looked at me quizzically. "He's all right of a chap," she laughed, as if to describe the Koh-i-Noor as a nice little diamond. "Says what he means, which is more than can be said for most people. Thinks the best of everyone."

"Of everyone?"

"Everyone who deserves it. There's a few fools he won't suffer. I always liked Berwick. He's what I call a gent, not like some of 'em that are said to be born into it. Always a kind word he has. Makes you feel like you're worth a thousand guineas. Tell you what else, he has big ideas. Yet she dropped him like so much dirt."

"So you helped him?"

"He was cooking up a scheme to cheer himself up. I told him when we were coming up to town and he set up a welcoming party. I was expecting fireworks, or maybe a brass band."

"To embarrass them?"

"For a laugh," she said.

"Because Nellie had left him and Coxhill had orchestrated it?"

"For a laugh," she insisted, voice cracking with amusement. Hester cared nothing for industrial sabotage or syndicated espionage, or any of the tangled plots I had conjured up. "Roxy so full of himself, and Nellie turned all hoity-toity like, they needed the wind taken out of their sails. Roxy loved working out secretive times we could arrive so as nobody'd see us. What a hoot, says they, to take the late train. Why not, says us girls, expecting we'll head for their club and make a night of it."

"So how did Berwick find out?"

"I nipped out and sent him a wire." She smiled a naughty little smile. "You should have seen their faces when the waterworks started up in their faces. Serve 'em right."

I nodded, picturing the scene. Coxhill struts from the train, showing off to his fancy friends how his machine is putting the crowning glory to the greatest station in Christendom. Alongside him, Nellie with her new fellow. Skelton, tucked in some corner of the square, watches – glumly or exultantly? – as said machine pops its cork all over them. "Why the body?"

"Body?"

"I mean… What I meant was the body of the clock. Why would Berwick steal a clock's workings?"

She shrugged. "Nellie had a lovely watch he made her. Engraved and all. She used to wear it pinned to a bow on her bosom. Until she got a gold one off her new fellow."

This betrayal I somehow found the most objectionable. Besides that, Hester was the first person who had let me in on the game. While everyone else held their tongue or wove me fairytales, she delighted in telling it all, irrepressibly drawn to share the fun of it.

Her brow darkened. "It's not right, forgetting your old bestest mate, is it now? With her high-falutin' friends, living the high-life in their posh frocks and flash carriages."

"So bitter, Hester?" I smiled. "Did Coxhill not treat you well?"

She made a face. "My own fault. I had shillings in my eyes and all. Horrible little man he is, in every department." She chuckled to herself. "Not that it's got me anywhere, except bleedin' Hoxton Hall. Chucked out of my lodgings too. What was the need for that, I ask you? We're like puppets. They pull a string and up we jump; they pull another and the curtain falls forever."

"Hardly forever, Hester. You're not finished yet."

She smiled. A valiant smile, yet it made me feel glum. "Nellie don't look so clever now, either, eh? All sorts of promises he made her. We'll see if he makes them good."

The first time I spoke to her, I had actually assumed it was none of my business who had stolen Berwick's girl. It seemed unnecessary. Ungentlemanly. Now I realised what a poor detective I was.

Hester sat looking at me with appeal in her eyes. That was what she wanted from me. To rescue her. She had been dropped from a great height, all the way from the West End to the East, and she thought I could break her fall.

"Put in a kind word for me, will you?" She drank down her tea. "And look after yourself. You're thin as a rake."

"I've been under the weather."

"You've been underfed, poor boy. You should get someone in to feed you up."

I laughed. "You overestimate a sergeant's wage."

"I didn't mean a maid," she said, a little crestfallen. She took out her purse to square up. "I'd best be off."

"Hester," I said, putting my hand on hers. She withdrew it

and rose from the table, as I drew out my own money to pay. Foolish me, I almost let her go and I hadn't got my answer. "Who is Nellie's new fancy man?"

"Away with you," she laughed. Seeing I was in earnest she burst out, "Don't play your games with me. You know who. You've been sent to catch me out, so's they have an excuse to stamp me further into the mud."

"Hester, Hester, I'm not playing a game."

"They told me not to tell. You know they did."

"Who told you?"

"You know very well. Them as knows." She headed for the street.

I followed. "Did Coxhill tell you to keep quiet?"

She gave a hollow little laugh. "He didn't need to, though that Hunt made some less than friendly suggestions. But it's your man I'm scared of."

I grabbed her arm roughly. Too roughly, but I had to know. "Hester, you must tell me what you're talking about."

"That bloody inspector, wasn't it?" she cried in exasperation.

I stood in the middle of the road. "Which inspector?"

"Little bloke in the long coat."

I let go her arm, feeling the world around me spin. "Wardle?" I said in a whisper.

"Himself. Keep your mouth shut good and proper, he said and he promised that would make it all right. More of a threat than a promise, I s'pose. Must dash now, love. I'll be late for curtain up." She pecked me on the cheek and was gone.

"Fancy seeing you here, Sergeant."

I turned in dismay to see the shrewish little reporter from the *Bugle*, rolling up with a hoofer on his arm. "Scholes. What are you doing here?"

"Theatre review, my friend." He grinned at the girl. "Like a spot of culture, me. Coming along?"

"Not tonight," I said.

"Don't you like a bit of music?"

"Oh yes," I said, turning for home, "but I've no stomach for it tonight."

A Prince Amongst Men

"I have news," said Miss Villiers, leaning forward to pour me a cup of tea. "You have been too busy, it seems, with visits to actresses, to grace us with your presence in the library."

"Miss Villiers, I was injured," I exclaimed. "Besides, Hester has furnished priceless information."

"Not to mention famous novelists and their daughters."

"Ruth!"

"Mr Collins uses the library, you know. He was most pleased when I was able to show him to the particulars of the Road House murder so promptly. Detective fever, I explained to him. Detective fever? says he. Wonderful phrase. I shall steal it for my next novel, if I may."

It seemed too long a time since our last tea room meeting, and I smiled as I sliced the cake. I had told her of my discoveries, and my injury. The story of my return to the Rose and Crown enthralled her particularly.

She, in her turn, had been no sluggard. First she had popped along to Red Lion Square, where the Reform League's central office was attached to the working men's club.

"I was politely informed by a well-meaning old duffer called Kenelm Digby that the League was an association of diverse organisations with convergent interests. As such, they had no record of the millions of citizens who had attended meetings or contacted them. Even if they had such a record, he doubted whether he should make it available to any old Tom, Dick or

Harry. That is, without being openly rude, he sent me packing. You would need a warrant, I think, to persuade him that your intentions were *bona fide*."

I shook my head. Wardle had told me to end an investigation that he regarded as a personal tomfoolery and a waste of police time. "I could never request such a warrant. Not as things stand."

"Another door closed," she sighed. "But I have pursued a second line of enquiry. The British Museum is not the only institution of learning in the world. Our man, I reasoned, might have turned elsewhere to leaven his reading diet of politics and persecutions. Fearing to be a nuisance to you, I took it upon myself to make discreet inquiries. At the London Library, nothing. Clerkenwell, Camden and Finsbury, nothing."

"But?" I said impatiently.

"But I am pleased to report my intuition proven correct. Our man joined Mudie's Lending Library in 1855, before it removed from Red Lion Square to New Oxford Street, recommended by a certain Mr Digby. Besides novels, he liked poetry. Apocalyptic stuff. You know the sort, Shelley and Blake, Christopher Smart, John Skelton, right back to Dante."

"John Skelton? That was his father's name."

"John Skelton was Poet Laureate, but to Henry VIII. Not much use to us. By late last year, after we started looking for him, a new direction in his reading emerges. History, or rather drama and novels based on history. The Bastille, Cromwell, Guy Fawkes. Hamlet, Julius Caesar, the rape of Lucretia. Biblical tales, like Samson, David and Goliath. Now, several of his books had faint pencil annotations. Scribbles, they seemed like, and at first I thought them simply illegible. But I wonder if it might be code."

I slammed my palms on the table so hard I upset the teapot.

I had omitted to mention the notebook inscribed with meticulous cipher, and the secret writing that Madame Skelton spoke of.

"I knew it." She scrabbled around in her bag and passed me a book, marked with a bookmark. She drummed her fingers on the table. "I took out the Everyman Shakespeare just in case. See how he's marked passages? That's in Julius Caesar."

I stared at the margins filled with pencil lines. "That's the same hand, no doubt about it. What does it mean?"

"I don't know. But I'll have a stab at finding out." She knitted her brows. "I'll go back and copy across all I can find."

"Sounds a deal of work."

She shrugged. "No point in trying to crack a code without being thorough. All you need is one tell-tale passage. Translating a single sentence might be enough to match his code with the alphabet, although he may use encipherment beyond that."

"Is he still taking out books?"

"He has one outstanding item, a translation of the Indian epic, the *Ramayana*, a tale of princes chasing fabulous maidens." She made a face, perhaps in disdain of such tales, and of such maidens, or perhaps in envy of them. She put down her teacup with an air of finality and raised an eyebrow. "So. Are you pleased with the efforts of your industrious assistant?"

"I am." I bowed my head under her scrutiny. "Sorry I've been out of touch."

"You're looking the worse for wear."

"Close brush with a different kind of fever." I did not explain the severity of my illness. Instead I pooh-poohed her attentions, and related Hester's comment that I needed looking after.

"Applying for the job, was she?" Miss Villiers replied, rather sharply. We got up in a disjointed mood and took our leave of each other.

Hurrying back from meeting Miss Villiers, I heard Wardle's voice raised from down the corridor. I hesitated at the door, but it swung open, and out sprang Scholes, his mouth set in a grim line. At least it was not I who had incurred the great man's wrath.

"Glad we've come to an understanding, Scholes," said Wardle, following him out and holding out a hand in unusually spirited style. Scholes shook it with a certain reluctance and bustled past me.

"Trouble at the printing works, sir?" I grinned.

"Watchman!" He looked me up and down, decided I was no bringer of plague, and thrust his hands back in his pockets. "There was a difference of opinion. I believe the newsman has seen sense. Lunch?"

I had never seen him so pleased with himself as that day in the Dog and Duck.

"Good morning's work," he said, tucking into a loin of pork. "Scandal silenced, culprits confessing. And all thanks to your good work, Watchman."

I kept silent. I had done no work for a month.

"That Scholes, bloody vermin, must have seen you down the Evans while he was digging dirt. A stroke of luck for us. He connected you with me and came to check the rumours. Otherwise he might have gone ahead and printed his filth."

"Oh, yes, sir? What was it he wanted to print?"

"Won't print now. Not now I've had a quiet word."

"Won't print what, sir?"

He looked at me squarely. "Just one of my special concerns. Very important person in a tight spot. Rumours in the clubs."

I nodded, unable to muster an appetite. I was dismayed by the sudden feeling we hadn't been working together at all. I huddled into the corner of the snug, struggling to restrain my annoyance. "So you persuaded Scholes to steer clear of libellous rumours?"

"Libellous?" he replied, mouth full of potato. "Your innocence is touching, Watchman. When important persons are seen sneaking out of private boxes with young ladies they should have nothing to do with, the press may feel justified in pursuing certain rumours."

"You mean you're hushing up stories that are true?"

He snorted. "Don't give me the small town innocence, son. You know very well this city is run by money."

"I don't follow, sir."

"Paxton and his gang not only own the *Bugle*. They're big fish in the Great Western Railway, who inexplicably chose not to invest in Pearson's underground railway. I say inexplicable, but I happen to know the Monopolies Commission wouldn't allow them. That's why their pet newsrag, the *Bugle*, churns out doom and gloom about the underground trains."

"I just thought they didn't like the idea." I frowned. "What is this Monopolies Commission?"

"The government thinks it's a danger to have industries run by single corporations. In fact, it's Prince Albert who did it. He set up the Commission to watch companies like the Great Western. Stop them getting too powerful for their own good. Monoliths, he calls them, great hulking monoliths. As a consequence, the *Bugle* takes a jaundiced view of all things royal. Sticks the knife in whenever it can. Unfortunately, the young Prince of Wales is hell-bent on making himself an easy target."

"What's he done?"

"Oh, no different from any other youth celebrating his

twentieth birthday. Hard to blame him for that. But if he doesn't learn to cover his back, he'll find himself a laughing stock." He picked up the pork gristle and turned it over in his hands. "We've managed to save him today, no thanks to his fool antics."

"Have we?"

"See, now the underground train looks a certain money-spinner, the Great Western wants in. Of course they do! Link their Paddington terminus to the City, big business, a killing to be made. It's no surprise they want to muscle in on the shares." He threw the gristle to the floor, and watched with evident pleasure as the landlord's mongrel fell upon it. "Which puts me in a pickle, as I told Scholes. As a police officer, I'm obliged, morally obliged, to point out these manœuvrings to the Monopolies Commission."

"You threatened him?"

"You know how it is, Watchman. If I dine with friends on the Commission, something may slip out." He pushed his plate aside. "And yet, morally speaking, I'm not sure the underground trains will be safe without the GWR's expertise. Pearson's having problems with his engines. A word from me to the Railway Board of Safety could make all the difference, Might persuade the Monopolies Commission to turn a blind eye. Do you get my drift?"

I blinked at this pragmatism. "And Scholes was persuaded?"

"He wouldn't want an indiscretion in the *Bugle* to cause problems for his masters. Besides, I manufactured a little scoop as a trade-in-kind."

"Sir?"

He took a sip of ale. "Confessions for the skeleton thefts."

That made me sit up.

"Your cellar notion was good. Little birdy informed me that a couple of old sewer rats were living in splendour beneath a

Mayfair mansion. Had them up for small jobs before. They confessed to the lot."

"And the things? The furniture – did they have it all?"

"No."

"What did they say about the bones?"

"Didn't go into it."

"But there must have been a reason."

He drank down the last of his ale. "Watchman, I don't think for a second that they did the crimes."

I stared.

"But they've done enough over the years. Bit of pressure and they put up their hands. That'll keep the press off our back."

"Sir," I said, restraining my indignation, "it seems less than wise, if the real culprits may strike again at any moment."

"How long since the last job? Six weeks? More. I reckon they're scared off. Or they will be when they see what we do to the scapegoats. I'll make sure Worm spreads the news round his more unsavoury friends."

We lapsed into silence. I felt insulted to think how much further into his confidence he had admitted the loathsome Jackman. How much did I still know nothing of? I had been planning to discuss Groggins' story with Wardle, to tell of Madame Skelton, and ask why he had told Hester to hold her tongue. Yet I had hidden my investigations from him, and it was too late to come clean. So much concealment, so much equivocation.

And this new perversion of justice, how could he coldly engineer it? Surely Jackman's insinuations could not be close to the mark? If we lie and threaten and blackmail, are we not as guilty as those we are pursuing?

The next day, there was no sign of Wardle. I was summoned

to see the Yard cashier.

"Should be a nice day for you," he said, handing me the fare for a cab to Paddington and a return ticket to Windsor. "The inspector will be waiting."

When I stepped off the half nine train, Wardle simply grabbed my newspaper and headed up the hill toward the castle. We walked in silence as he glanced at through the pages until he snorted.

"Very nice." He thrust the page under my nose.

SKELETONS LAID TO REST

Scotland Yard today announced the apprehension of suspects, including the probable ringleader of the Skeleton Thieves. The Yard is hopeful that this puts an end to these mysterious break-ins.

Inspector Wardle will today be received at Windsor Castle to receive another royal commendation.

"Sir?" I looked at him. "I have to ask you about the spout."

He did not meet my gaze. "Why's that?"

"I was speaking to someone who seemed to think–"

"Who?"

"They suggested," I went on, "that you know more about it than you've told me."

He looked at me steadily. "Doubtless I do, son, just as you've been poking your nose where it ill belongs." Seeing me startled, he broke into what was nearly a smile. "Son, sometimes you remind me of my younger self. You've good instincts. Good heart, too, not that that's so useful in our profession."

Struggling to keep up as we climbed toward the castle gates, I held my peace.

"Look, son. I'm soon for retirement. Keep on the straight

and narrow, and there's no reason why the Prince shouldn't take you on in the same capacity as me."

"What capacity is that exactly, sir?"

"Not much to it mostly. The occasional big call. The odd moment of glory. I was there, up on stage in the Crystal Palace when he gave the closing speech of the '51 Exhibition. Do you know how many people were there? Two hundred and fifty thousand! Had them in the palm of his hand, he did."

It was overwhelming to think that Wardle had assignments of which I knew nothing. I felt like a clerk, running around in the dark after my own little mysteries, in which he indulged me, just to keep me quiet.

"Distasteful duty we have today, though. Still, good and early," he nodded, as we entered the shadow of the castle. "He likes that, does the Prince. Have you any idea what an extraordinary man you are about to meet? He single-handedly conceived the most important event in history. Do you know what effect the Exhibition has had on our country? Showed us as the leading force in every area of development. Garnered laurels round the globe, and the goodwill and flattery of countries we'd barely heard of. No need for conquering the buggers. Messy and expensive, all that. Now dagos and darkies from Peru to Peking have seen how our country works, they invite us in open-armed. We build their railways and their roads and their palaces, and they pay us in diamonds and gold. They give us islands and fishing rights and free ports for our navy. They shower us with land and with slaves – cheap labour we're to call it now, I suppose. I tell you, we had a raw deal with our kings when I was your age. But this German prince is the best ruler we ever had. All these elections and parliamentary reforms, it's all hogwash. We should make this Albert king and no more bones about it."

• • •

"Welcome, Inspector. Thank you again for dealing so tactfully with my son's boorish indelicacies. Welcome, Sergeant... Jackman, was it?"

"This is my new sergeant, Your Royal Highness. Lawless."

I was so surprised to hear Wardle use my real name, I nearly forgot to shake hands with Prince Albert. In the enormous room we were shown into he sat, utterly at home, at an immense desk in a sunlit bow window. I had known, of course, that he was German, but I was still surprised by his whiskers, and how marked his accent was.

"Of course. Delighted to meet you at last, Sergeant. I hear great reports of your diligence. I will make no secret of it, this has been a difficult year. It is no small comfort to feel oneself supported by able and dedicated men."

Thoroughly disarmed, I murmured, "Thank you, Sir."

"Thank you, Your Royal Highness," Wardle corrected me.

The Prince brushed the formality aside and poured himself a glass of some kind of *aquavit*. "My congratulations on solving those bally thefts. A satisfying riposte to the haranguing of the popular press."

Wardle coughed as if to say it was nothing special. "Once we identified the links between incidents, Sir, it was just a matter of time. Still, always pleased to strengthen the Yard's reputation." I flexed my injured knee, but kept my peace. "However," Wardle continued with a pained look, "I have more to tell about your son. Watchman, stand by the door, will you? I want no interruptions."

As I retreated to stand like a guard dog on duty, I heard urgent whispers across the desk. Albert gave a small cry, as if of pain, then spoke with controlled vehemence.

"The disgusting creature! Such vileness. With a tart!"

"Sir," Wardle replied, "it is at least an improvement on the violent behaviour he displayed as a child."

"Is it?" the Prince gasped. "Forgive my prudery, but I find it repulsive. A prince. Such things. With an actress. What is to be done?" He put his hand to his brow.

"I'll pass over the grosser details, Sir," said Wardle quietly. "I have told him off. Had stern words with him over and over. But he's overstepped the mark now. I can see no alternative. You must speak to him yourself."

Albert wrung his hands. "Filthy boy. What if she's pox-ridden? We can't have the Prince of Wales going around crazed with the clap."

"I've seen the girl. She's fair, at least."

"I care not whether she be diabolical or divine," he exploded. "She is unsatisfactory for a prince."

"Yes, but you have no need for alarm." Something about the way Wardle defended her told me: not only had he met Nellie, he rather liked her. If it weren't for Albert's prudishness, I suspected he might have been reporting Bertie's first triumph over a gamesome wench. "Regarding the pox, I mean."

"You think my reaction extreme, Inspector? Perhaps. It's this damnable curse. Makes one jittery, you can imagine. So many deaths in the family. Pedro of Portugal gone, and only twenty-five. I feel like I have lost my own son." He paused, in genuine grief. It was one thing for a wretch like Jackman to speak of curses, but another to hear it from this remarkable man, the epitome of rationality. It made me wonder if the rumours about Victoria's sanity were also not so wild after all.

Wardle coughed. "Cholera, Sir?"

"Typhoid," he replied bitterly. "Prince Ferdinand to the same, and the heir to the throne still sick. We seem terribly prone to it. And my sister, Victoire, in childbirth." No sooner had he marshalled his emotion than he fell into a coughing fit. "Excuse me. I feel quite febrile. This news puts me in the state of nervous energy." He stood up to pace around the room, and noticed me lurking in the shadows. "Your young sergeant is quite bemused, Inspector. Sergeant, there are things the country does not need to know about the Prince of Wales. Just as there are things the Prince of Wales does not need to know about the country. Bertie's propensity to laziness has been a tremendous disappointment to his mother. I never met such a cunning lazybones. I planned every hour of his studies. I ensured his society only with adults. Now he encounters his peers in Oxford and the military, and what a merry dance they lead him. Stupid *soi-disant* friends, putting all sorts of ideas into his head. I call them fatiguing bores, don't you?"

These idiomatic declarations sounded bemusing in the Prince's clipped Germanic tones. I had to recover my senses in order to murmur agreement.

"He lolls about with a cigarillo in his mouth, sinking into debauchery with an *habituée* of the most vulgar dance halls in London. I will not have it said that I have raised within these walls a second George III to heap shame upon this great Empire." He stopped pacing and frowned at Wardle. "Of course, this must go no further than these tapestries."

"The sergeant can be trusted," said Wardle. I looked at him, surprised and pleased.

"There is little I value more highly than discretion," the Prince smiled tightly.

"Will you speak to him?" Wardle said softly.

"I will write him a letter," he declared, "in the sternest of terms. That will stop this behaviour."

"If I could avoid troubling you, Sir, I would. But it has gone beyond letters. The parties and the gambling are one thing. But this actress… You must speak to him personally."

"Perhaps. On his eighteenth birthday, I wrote him a memorandum, you know, telling him that life is composed not of indulgence and pleasure but of duties, in the punctual and cheerful performance of which the true Christian, soldier, and gentleman is recognised."

"With what effect?"

"The boy burst out crying." The Prince put his hand to his forehead. "I am told he is bright. Good-natured and charming. Perhaps. His aversion to exertion is regrettable."

"There is no need for his mother to know."

A look of repugnance passed across the Prince's face. "You are right, Inspector. What a loyal servant you are." He gestured vaguely towards Wardle. "She mustn't hear of this disgusting incident, nothing beyond the merest outline. What an indescribable burden that youth is upon his poor Mama. What headaches she suffers from the anxiety. I will speak to him. I will try to exhort the boy to be an example to the nation. He will reach his majority one year hence. Let us send him to the continent to gain the German influence. I only hope that he may some day meet with a lesson severe enough to shame him out of frivolity. An early marriage is the best hope. This Danish poodle is the very thing. Alexandra is a pearl not to be let slip through our fingers. She is no fool, though. She deserves better than Bertie, truth be told. But the royal line must be served." He looked suddenly drawn. He drew a sheet from a drawer, and I watched in fascination as he signed it floridly, slipped it into an envelope and passed it to Wardle. "Your latest commendation, Inspector." He turned to me. "Remember, dear sergeant, your labours are not in vain, for this boy must one day soon be your king."

Wardle headed down the hill with an air of quiet triumph. I could barely contain myself.

"Sir," I said, "I sometimes have the feeling we're not working together at all."

He shot me an amused look. "Come now, Watchman. There

are matters I'm obliged to conceal. National security. Just as there are matters you feel obliged to conceal from me."

I caught my breath. I had no idea how much he knew of my investigations. But I could not be cowed into silence, not this time. "So you chaperone the Prince of Wales?"

"I protect him from his own excesses." He shook his head and pursed his lips. "His father doesn't know the half of it."

I shook my head. "You have little time for the young Prince?"

He raised an eyebrow. "I've seen enough types of depravity to last me several lifetimes. The boy indulges in vices I find hard to condemn. Albert had him studying continental literature when he was still in his cot. Now, his valet checks through the *Sporting Times* for him and that's all the reading he does."

"After your own heart, sir."

He snorted. "He likes a drink. Smoking, gambling–"

"Women?"

"And what of it, if he kept it quiet? He hasn't realised he's under the scrutiny of an Empire. He must at least be seen to be beyond reproach."

"But he enjoys the company of… well, the sort who tend to be indiscreet."

"Unless they're given strong reasons for discretion."

I nodded. We were walking along a broad avenue beside the green pastures of the great school. I took a deep breath. "I spoke to Hester, sir, but she wouldn't talk."

"Scholes must use methods more persuasive than yours," he said. That made me bristle. He eyed me sharply. "Got to you, did she?"

"It wasn't her who spilled the beans, sir."

"Whoever it was. Should have thought twice. Deep waters, these. The less people that hear of Bertie's peccadilloes, the fewer stories we'll need to hush up."

"Won't stop hydraulic engines going off in our faces."

A shout went up beside us, and I gazed up at a group of youths throwing each other into the mud in pursuit of a leather ball. Wardle looked at me. "What have you found out, then, son?"

"A lot that wasn't in the report."

"Should I describe it in writing? Prince of Wales, unceremoniously soaked as he struts drunkenly into town, on his arm a dancing girl wearing a fine gold watch given him by his mother."

"I would have thought you'd investigate who did it."

"That I did, son. That I did. But as long as the Prince is unhurt, why dignify the charade with official charges? I packed the Prince and the girl away from the scene before they were spotted. That's what mattered most. I told him to break it off. Thought he had. Now it seems he's been sneaking around with her behind my back. Silly tart's got a mouth on her, so now it's got to stop." He gestured down a lane. "This is me here."

I hesitated before heading on for the station. It occurred to me for the first time how strange it was that Wardle, living out here, got to the spout so swiftly. "Sir, that night, how did you come to be at Euston?"

He looked at me with a mixture of censure and approbation.

I stared at him, electrified. "You were there. You knew in advance."

He nodded. "There was a tip-off."

"From whom?"

"Anonymous. Threat, you could call it. Some nonsense about Guy Fawkes. Coxhill passed it on to us."

"You were there when the spout went off?"

"In the station. Nothing I could do. It was less serious than

I'd feared, though."

"Were they trying to hurt the Prince?"

"Don't know. Don't rightly care. No point in making a fuss over a stupid joke. Thought at first it was some trick of Coxton's, trying to impress Bertie. But his affairs are none of my concern, except as they mess with the Prince's."

"And the report was filed with no mention of the dead man? Nothing suspicious?"

"Can't have the Prince of Wales mixed up in intrigues."

"But you're no longer concerned?"

"No. He'll have forgotten about her by now, the good-for-nothing scoundrel the Prince's little trollop jilted. You know these simple folk." He turned and walked off towards his home.

There flitted through my mind the image of Berwick's desk, the political books, the articles, the strange cipher writing. I had the feeling that mixing Bertie up in intrigues was exactly his intention. Fairfoul said Berwick had gone, but the spout at the Evans suggested otherwise; it suggested he had far from forgotten. My head was buzzing as I boarded the train. I recalled Glossop's accusation, that Wardle chose me for my malleability, and it rankled. Yet at least Wardle's intentions were honourable, even if his methods left me dumbfounded. At least we were on the same side.

Philandering Princes & Crazed Cuckolds

Winter bit early. I watched in amazement out the Yard window as people stomped past, suffering through the harsh mornings. Every night I walked home by a different route, recovering strength in my knee. Sometimes I headed up York Way, with the trains from King's Cross puffing mournfully north below me. I would turn when I reached the canal, head through the dark maze of ill-designed tenements, until thankfully gaining the sanctuary of my little room. There I would sit, gazing out the grimy window at children with ragged kites, until the melancholy clip-clop of hooves announced the arrival of the costermonger, his aspect so fierce that the little ones went running before him, while his threadbare horse plodded the glistening cobbles, despairing of a return to its stable.

I took the new tram down the Kennington Road to meet Mr Wetherell, the retired underwriter, at the Surrey Cricket Ground, where he had come to renew his membership. He led me into the pavilion and lost no time in calling for two whiskies. Down on the fine expanse of turf, some hardy children practised wild bowling actions. I asked if he shared Wardle's nostalgia for the old styles.

"Quite the contrary. Only an old fuddy-duddy could hold with that antique opinion. These new boys, you should see the artifice they use on the ball. It's thrilling. They spin it, they swerve it midair, they work magic. The top players invent it, and within a year the whole country copies it. It's like business, really. One year you make a mint on railways, next year everyone's in on it. Then it's boom time until the wheels fall off the bandwagon and we all go bust. We're all children playing games at heart. Though some bend the rules a little, I grant you." He set down his whisky. "I didn't call you here to talk cricket."

"What have you found?"

"Your Coxhill," he began, "is a dreadfully lucky man. Wherever he goes there are explosions and disasters, yet the chap walks off unscathed. Amazing, wouldn't you say?" It took me a moment to grasp Mr Wetherell's tone of careful irony. "You have stumbled upon a nest of vipers, wherein the businesses with the worst records walk off with the fattest profits, in the short term at least. Venture capital, they call it. If I can convince you to invest in my company, why go to all the bother of producing anything? When somebody actually asks to see your product, much easier to burn the thing down and claim the insurance. The goods never need exist. Do you smell a rat?"

He had discovered HECC insurance policies all over. The legislation was due for reform, as multiple claims were common.

"Coxhill is still making claims for stocks in Tooley Street that nobody ever saw. By contrast, despite all his mishaps, I can't find a trace of one successful compensation claim against his company." Mr Wetherell leant forward. "These are godless times, Sergeant. At least in the past men thought there were things worth dying for; God, Queen and Country. Nobody believes anything these days. Who can blame them, when the pillars of society are built upon money alone? That bloody war, fighting with the French against our friends, the Russians; there's a deal more scandal to come out, I tell you. Someone has done very well through the mismanagement of army amenities. A man who steals two-and-six, you call him a thief. A man steals two thousand from his investors, you call him Sir. What do you call a man who throws away two million? Prime Minister."

He raised his glass and we drank each other a toast. "Something's rotten and you're on the scent, old man," said Mr Wetherell. "What other swindles go on, I can barely guess. I tell you, they'll burn the Crystal Palace down if they think it'll pay out."

A month after our visit to the castle, I stepped down onto the platform at Windsor for a second time. Wardle was sitting on a bench, staring blankly ahead.

"Sir?"

He looked up as if surprised to see me. "Watchman? Good of you to come."

"Sir, are you all right?"

"Take a walk, shall we? Nothing to be done. Might as well enjoy the air." He led me off among the playing fields of Eton. The youngsters were still hurling each other onto the now frosty ground, and I wondered if they were allowed home for Christmas. Wardle stopped at the corner of the biggest pitch, gazing up at the castle. The flag was flying at half-mast. "He just slipped away. All month they've been saying he's on the mend. Getting him out of his sick bed, tramping the stone hallways, him with that fearful chill. What use are they? This medic, Jenner, he discovered bloody typhoid. Yet one minute, he hasn't got it; the next he's dead of it. The finest man in the country."

I looked at him. Shocked though I was to think of the Prince Consort gone and the Queen a widow so young, I was more amazed by the strength of Wardle's sorrow.

"I'm sorry, sir."

"He died there, in the Blue Room. The King's Room. What'll the country do now? I shouldn't have told him. Not everything at once. Such a refined man. The shock went right through him."

"Perhaps we should have told him as it happened. Lessen the shock."

"Sometimes things have to be concealed," he barked. "I don't like it any more than you do. He expects too much, the young scoundrel. Gadding about with a tart. I've covered his back since he was a little boy. And why? For this!"

"The Prince Consort knew nothing about it before we spoke to him?"

"Nothing. Which is a miracle. Bertie's been bothering women since he was old enough to walk."

"Including his nurse?"

Wardle didn't pick up on my meaning. "This one now he's had on the go for three years. Blasted Royal Performances. Clapped eyes on her and lost his heart, he told me. Lost his brain, more like. I spoke to that Coxhill: they've houses enough between them to hide a wealth of iniquities. I told him to look after the tyke. But he's a fool of equal proportions."

I recalled how, at the spout, Coxhill had barely recognised Wardle, too incensed about his damaged engine.

He clenched his fists in useless anger. "I hired them a closed box at the music hall. Laid on special trains for him. Got him a closed view of the Tunnel fête. It's never enough, not for this boy. He wants it all. Wants to step out with the girl in public. No notion of repercussions. Having her in a Dublin barracks is one thing. Even Marlborough House, playing billiards with his cronies. But back here in Windsor! The Queen will never forgive him."

"Sir, if his father died of typhoid, it's hardly the boy's fault."

Wardle gave me a look. "Prince Albert travelled to Cambridgeshire, in ill-health, mind. He walked out in the cold, with no precaution for his health, he was that livid. Now it's killed him." Wardle slumped down on to a bench by the road. "Why couldn't it be the youngster who slipped away? I sometimes believe in this damnable curse."

I thought again of Jackman's nonsensical rantings. It was as if Berwick Skelton was making himself the agent of the curse, softening up Bertie, in preparation to exacting his vengeance.

"I don't think," I said nervously, "that the Hungarian monk is the only one angry with the Saxe-Coburg clan, sir."

"What's that?"

I took a deep breath. "Why did you allow the spout to be

hushed up?"

"What was there to know?"

"Weren't you concerned he would do something else? Something worse?"

"Of course I'm concerned. Watchman, I've been a policeman since before you were born. You can't be preventing crimes before they're committed." He sighed. "Say the prankster was the girl's previous fellow. What should we do? Catch him? Air his grievances in a courtroom?"

I gritted my teeth, annoyed to see sense in his equivocal behaviour. "Why did you conceal all this from me?"

"You didn't need to know."

"I wasn't to be trusted."

"You were new, son. We had to wait and see."

"What other secrets have you kept from me? Like this threat before the spout. Was there a threat before the Evans?"

"The Evans? Coincidence."

"Come off it, sir. Bungled hydraulics, in a West End theatre?"

"It was a burst pipe."

"I heard it was a spout. Bertie and Nellie in the box, by any chance, were they?"

"Who told you this?"

"Hester told me. And the other incidents? The Haymarket. The Embankment? The man seems able to conjure disasters wherever he feels like it."

"Well, he won't need to any more. Bertie's well and truly warned off." He turned away and sat heavily on a bench, gazing up at the castle, as if the thing was too much to think about. It made me feel ashamed to be haranguing him so.

"Sir, the man must hate the young Prince, if he stole his girl. He may be quite reckless. The affair's already caused Albert's death. Shouldn't we take it seriously?"

"We don't dignify every prank with a response. They'd have us jumping around like a cat o'nine tails." He looked at me stonily. "I thought it best to sit tight. Never thought it would come to this."

"Are you sure Bertie's under control now? It sounds like nobody's ever refused him anything before. And these high-living friends, don't you think they'll lead him back into temptation?" I tried to put from my mind the image of Coxhill's gambling hell, dotted with Madame Lorraine's ladies of the night.

"You must find me a right old stick-in-the-mud," Wardle said, looking old and worn. "Gabbling on about the crimes of yesteryear, Sadleir and Brough and the others, when all this was unfolding beneath our noses. You sometimes wonder, Watchman. You wonder why one man lives and another dies. Why are they up there in the castle and we down here? Why do I drive myself mad running around for a flibbertigibbet of a prince?" He slapped his hands upon his knees in frustration, then put his hands to his face.

I stood there dismayed. "How long had you been working for Prince Albert?"

"What's that? I don't know. Fifteen years. Twenty, I suppose, since the Mary Ann Brough case. What does it matter? I'll be out of it soon enough."

I stared at him.

"Yes, yes. It's all settled. A year hence I'm retiring. Please God this is the last shake of my time. Let's hope that Bertie sees sense. His bit of skirt can go back to the crazed cuckold of hers, and I can retire without further fussing." He sat there pondering and there was nothing I could do but walk away. He called out weakly as I left. "Watchman? Come for dinner some time. The wife would like to meet you."

I nodded, touched by the thought that he had discussed me

with her. He was right, I knew. We must make sure things settled back to normal. Yet I couldn't suppress a contrary yearning: for everything to melt down, for the lies and machinations we were burying along the way to break through in a vast eruption. I couldn't help recalling the envelope Albert had passed Wardle and wondering how much of Wardle's grief was for the envelopes. I could have no doubt. Albert had been doing him the handsome, in royal style. Still, I had heard much worse. Older officers spoke of the bad old days when inspectors took cuts from criminals to overlook crimes, and retired with their pockets lined with gold.

THE FIFTH PERIOD
[EARLY 1862]

EUSTON EVENING BUGLE

28th January, 1862

WHAT A JUBILEE!

This is not the time to criticise our gallant Queen.

The outpouring of grief for the Prince Consort is unprecedented, the mountain of flowers outside the Palace testifying to the nation's depth of feeling. We respected him. We loved him. Mr Disraeli did not overstate when he declared, "This German prince has ruled for twenty-one years with more wisdom than our kings ever showed." He had the absolute touch of a gentleman, which is that everybody takes him for one of their own. He was all things to all men.

Yet time marches on, and Queen Victoria's refusal to celebrate her Silver Jubilee, honourable though it be, casts a pall over the decade. The Prince of Wales lacks the statesmanship to step into her boots and there seems no alternative but that the new Exhibition, which the Prince planned so brilliantly, will be a crass failure. The authorities moot an "Albert Memorial" for the old site of the Crystal Palace, while this year's event is sadly neglected.

Let us mourn, by all means. But let us not make jackasses of ourselves. The workforces of important exhibitors have been decimated by sick leave taken under the masquerade of national sorrow.

FLUSHING OUT ILLS

The Marlborough Works of the Thos. Crapper Co. have monopolised demand throughout London's better boroughs for his fine apparatus. With a 250 gallon water tank on the roof, his works continuously test flushing mechanisms. For no extra charge his men install it with an airtight seal preventing the escape of noxious aromas. Detractors may deplore the apparatus' discharge into culverts not intended for such abuses, but Mr Crapper's is the sort of Great British invention to take the world by storm.

Bear in mind, however, rumours that footpads and mountebanks are using Bazalgette's sewers to access houses. Last year's Skeleton Thefts, solved by Inspector Wardle, may have links with the new network. Lock up your water closets.

The Elements of Destruction: a Series of Threats Sent Between 1859 and 1862:

Oh, fat foul false friend,
The time of judgement draws near.
Guy Fawkes was a genius.
Cromwell had the right idea.
The writing is on the wall
For the family blind in blood.
Across the Styx go I, go I,
Eyeless in Gaza, at the mill with slaves.
When you descend where you belong,
I shall know in which circle to place you.
Whom the gods wish to destroy they first make mad.
The monster is slain in his tortuous lair,
Despatched to the belly of hellfire.

The common man throws off his shackles.
Vive la république!
The Monstrous Rotundity has had its day.

And Still London Stank

Darkness fell rapidly in these times. The dusk crept in and seized hold of the smog. Together they extinguished the daylight at a glance. The lamplighters could barely keep pace.

Individual woes were forgotten in an embarrassment of emotion, as London became a prison of overwrought mourners, exuding grief for the dead Prince. He may have been the finest king we never had, but the glowing eulogies, tears and wreaths left a sour taste in the mouth.

I had my own sadness too. On Hogmanay I had word from the Clockmakers' Guild, Edinburgh division, that my father had passed away on Christmas Eve. Typical of the old beggar to miss the feast. It was too late to get back for the funeral. His friends would mutter, but what could I do? It was the last in a long series of disappointments I caused him.

I kept my own company that night. Walked myself ragged. From Primrose Hill, I looked down at the city huddling under its blanket of smog, as there drifted up to me the plaintive roar of the lions in the Regent's Park Zoological Gardens. I crossed Hampstead Heath, careless of robbers. I did not stop until the cheering lamps of the Spaniard's Inn. There I drank a solitary toast to the old man and drowsed away the wee small hours in an old leather chair, as the carousing outside died away. Then I trudged homeward, down the hill and along the canal. At the sight of my frosty home, though, restlessness overtook me and I set off down towards the river.

And still London stank. On that brisk winter morning, the

drains were frozen over with filth. Nightsoil sellers still flouted the regulations. Poor Josiah Bent. If Wardle could shamelessly pin our thefts on innocents, why should I have believed the prison warden's word over Josiah's? Where were his wife and children now, I wondered? I heard of a family given shelter against the bitter cold by a kindly landlady of Clerkenwell. Each night she locked them in the cellar, fearful of prying eyes, now we police were to enforce the regulations against cellar dwellings. One morning she discovered the whole family drowned in filth. The neighbouring cesspit wall had given way. Through the stout oak door nobody had heard their cries.

Some other things smelt none too sweet. The freezing fog that crept up oppressively from the docks could not hide the stench of two million unhappy people. But what matter? Come the summer, remove to your house by sea, and you barely noticed. After all, the Empire has made us all rich. And there is no shame in that because nobody is really poor, leastways no one worth speaking of.

As I neared the river, the streets were fuller than ever with Scots and Irish vagrants, come to look for those streets paved with gold. But the gold remained elusive, busy underwriting stocks, standing as insurance on houses, or against loans for ventures to the Southern Seas. The Bank of England's notes promised to pay the bearer on demand the stated sum, but it seemed folly to believe that the accounts would be squared at some great final reckoning.

I walked along the Embankment, considering my future. What profit was there in chasing Berwick? My pursuit was less a series of revelations than a slow confusion. Likewise, though the skeleton thefts were quieted rather than solved, Wardle had no enthusiasm for pursuing the real culprits. Devoted as he was to Albert, I would not have expected him to go and admire the sea of flowers left at the Palace by the bereft public.

I had seen his son just before Christmas. Wardle was out the day Charlie popped in to say goodbye. The cotton crisis had deepened. He could foresee no end to it.

"I'm off to Australia, me. Sick of famine, strikes and riots."

It filled me with yearning, his talk of the vast prairies of Queensland. I envied him the chance of starting again. I envisaged great green bays and cavernous waterfalls beneath soaring mountains. Leery natives and monstrous vegetables, wild horses and implausible creatures loafing across vast plains.

"One other thing now I'm off, though," he said. "Couldn't tell you before. Union regulations. There was a Skelton, you know, in the Reform League down here. Highly regarded. Great hopes held for him. Last I heard, he'd gone a bit strange. Lost patience with the movement. Taken his unit underground."

Yet Mr Wetherell's words of encouragement stayed with me, when the Tooley Street enquiry proved fruitless and a high-ranking Inspector of the Yard retired to the South of France. Clearly someone was gaining; and if somebody was gaining, someone else must be losing; and it wasn't the rich that were losing.

Walking there by the Thames, as the city drew its breath for a doleful year, I felt for the first time a swell of pride in the terrible beauty that was London. The Guild's letter mentioned certain business affairs of my father's. If I chose not to interfere, they would deal with the business, and I might expect a small stipend. Or I could return to Edinburgh, escaping London's feverish speculations. With father gone, I found myself considering a return. I could take over the workshop, live quietly there. Could I? Go back to the life I had long left behind me?

WARDLE GETS THE CALL

I knew something was wrong as soon as Wardle opened the letter.

"What is it, sir?"

He crumpled the letter tight in his hand. "He's had another bloody threat."

"May I see it, sir?"

"Just when you think you're clear," he said. "One prince is already dead from this foolishness. I won't have it any more."

"Sir, the threat?"

"You can see it when I have it," he burst out. "There are things you don't send by letter."

I nodded, unsatisfied. I was tired of not being taken into his confidence. "What about the first threat, sir, before the spout? Do you have that?"

Narrowing his eyes, he pulled an envelope from a drawer and handed me a telegram. "See if you can make any sense of it."

"That's all it is, sir?"

"That's all. That's where the whole mess started."

I read it aloud in puzzled excitement. "'Guy Fawkes was a genius.'"

"Bloody pranksters weren't."

"Why do you say that, sir?"

"Don't know their bloody history. Fifth of November, you'd expect from that, wouldn't you? That's what I expected. Spout went off on the eighth."

"Early on the ninth," I corrected him. "I wonder. Why did he get it wrong?"

"Quite simple. I kept Bertie out of town. They couldn't get at them when they wanted." For a moment Wardle looked satisfied, then his face darkened.

I looked at him. "No other threats, sir? Before the Evans, for instance?"

"Nothing."

"Seems strange. Why give warning of one and not the other?"

"Why give warning at all?"

"To make us puzzle. Make us try to understand."

"Taunt us, you mean." He stepped absently over to the window and stood silent a few moments. "The boy sounds like he's had a real scare. I just want it stopped. He's dropped the tart. What more can we do?"

"Maybe it's gone beyond that now, sir. Or…" I frowned. "Are we quite sure that he has dropped her?"

"The gentlemen," I said with curled lip, "will kindly remove themselves from the corridor."

I was stationed outside a room in the Oxford and Cambridge Club. Wardle had burst in and ejected several young men in cravats and blazers, smirking like schoolchildren. They passed me without acknowledgement, as if I were a manservant, conceiving the notion of skulking around to listen. I took pleasure in standing up to my full height, some inches above them all, and telling them to leave. They looked at me, unable to muster defiance, and melted impishly away. With their clatter gone, I could hear Wardle's voice distinctly within.

"I hope you're satisfied now," he was saying, shouting almost. "Now your father's dead and buried."

The Prince – Bertie – replied in low tones.

"But it is your fault, young man. I've watched you. I watch you cavorting around. Too long you've vexed your parents. Your father was already heartbroken, how you were carrying on with this trollop of an actress. Then he catches his death, telling you off."

Bertie asked a question.

"I didn't have to tell him. The whole of London knows. An actress! No wonder she goes round bragging she's bedded a prince of the realm."

"Old chap," Bertie raised his voice for the first time. "I simply won't have her spoke of in that way. She's a sweet girl and–"

"She's an actress. That's an end of it."

"Look, old man, I know I've been foolish, but I'm– I was so terribly fond of her."

Here Wardle adopted a softer tone. "Look, son, you've done no different from these army officer types, I know – college saps with lax morals and full wallets. But you are the heir to the throne of England. The British Empire. It has to stop."

Bertie remained silent a moment.

"Like your father said. The only hope for you is marriage to this Danish filly and early marriage at that."

"Inspector, old chap," he said dolefully, "you've been a real brick through this whole business. But let's not do anything hasty. Some days, I tell you, I wonder if I'll go mad with it all, the way mother is mad–"

"Enough of that."

"Over dear Papa, I mean."

"This new threat," Wardle interrupted. "Let's see it. Hmm. *Monster is slain… Belly of hellfire…*"

"Unnerving, ain't it, old man?"

"So much bloody mumbo-jumbo. What I want to know is why now, out of the blue? It's years since that last nonsense."

"Not so long, I think," Bertie said apologetically.

"Since the business at Euston? Two years, boy."

"There may have been one or two other incidents." Bertie coughed.

Now it was Wardle's turn to speak so low that I could not hear.

"That's right, threats too," Bertie went on uneasily. "Forgot to pass them on. Slipped my mind, you see."

"How many?"

"One or two. You know."

"How many?"

"Every few months since the Euston thingy, and the one before even."

"What do you mean, the one before?"

"When I was inspecting Bazalgette's embankment, you know. Then the Haymarket, the Evans and the rest. It's uncanny. They seem to know where I'm going before I do."

A butler came towards me down the corridor. As Wardle was shouting, it seemed best to cover their voices by humming an air. After the man passed, without a look askance, Bertie was speaking urgently, marshalling the emotion in his voice.

"You were all so incensed about it. I could perfectly well understand, but it seemed so dashed unfair. She's a darling of a girl. What kind of a world is it where a chap who likes a girl isn't allowed to see her? So I couldn't pass on the threats, because I was afraid it showed that someone knew I was seeing her, when I'd promised everyone, not least father and your good self, that I would stop."

There was silence for a moment, then Wardle spoke with a terrible withering tone. "Have you stopped now? Have you? Now that your father is dead of it?"

There was no reply.

"Don't give me that quivering lip." The door flew open, and Wardle burst out, muttering. "Bloody fool." As the door slammed shut behind him, I caught an image of the chubby Prince, face buried in his hands, sobbing.

"Where is he?" Wardle barked suddenly, as we reached Green Park.

"Who, sir?" I suppose I knew very well what he meant. But it pained me to think that, on top of the uncertainties around us, Wardle and I should still be mincing words.

"Bloody Skelton. That's the man, isn't it?"

"Why, sir?" I was sick of all the pretence, the half-truths, and I'd be damned if I told him what I knew until he took me into his confidence. "What's happened?"

He breathed out through clenched teeth. "Bloody fool of a boy. I've lost one royal and I don't intend to lose another. Where is he?"

"I was hoping you might know, sir."

"Me? Why?"

"I was under the impression that you were three steps ahead of me all the way. That you'd spoken to everyone I was looking for."

He raised an eyebrow. "Don't look so offended, son. I'm just trying to protect the idiot Prince. Have you found no more trace of him in your poking around?"

I hesitated. "Traces everywhere, but all leading nowhere. He's truly gone to ground, sir. Could be in Clerkenwell or the Cape."

He snorted. "Is he in heaven or is he in hell?"

"I don't think the heavy-handed approach will work."

"We'll just have to smoke him out."

"I think Nellie will know. If I could only find her."

Wardle made no reply. Instead he absently handed over a scrap of paper.

"'The monster is slain in his tortuous lair'," I read aloud.

I stared at it, fascinated, studying the impersonal print for hints of the handwriting I had seen in the finely bound tome at Madame Skelton's.

"Bloody fool of a boy now tells me there's been something every few months. The madman's been tracking his every move. Why play games? If he wants to do something, he should come out and do it."

"Sir, I should like to see all these threats."

"Why?" he said grimly.

I was about to mention Miss Villiers and her notion of codes and hidden messages, but I mustn't admit divulging secrets to the uninitiated. "He wants us to understand."

"He wants us afraid."

"Maybe so, but he has a plan, and if we're to understand it, I'll need to see all the threats. I'd also like to hear Bertie's version of what happened following each threat."

"I'll get you the details."

"May I not speak to the Prince?"

"I said, I'll get the details."

I looked away in annoyance. Of course, Wardle's sense of hierarchy would preclude a sergeant speaking with a prince. "Does he not understand what's happening?"

We were approaching the Yard and he looked about him before he spoke. "He doesn't know it's about Nellie."

"Hasn't he noticed how the things happen when he's with her?"

Wardle sighed. "Look, he's a contrary fool. I was afraid it would make him more pig-headed. I led him to believe it was anti-royalist protest. You know, having a go at the debauched Saxe-Coburgs. I thought it might curb his other vices and all."

As we walked into the Yard, Darlington was waiting for us in the hallway. "Inspector? Thank goodness. You're wanted in Chelsea."

"I'm busy," he barked. "It can wait, can't it?"

Darlington gave a deferential cough. "Sounds like a new skeleton theft."

Wardle put his head in his hands.

Panic in the Streets

That afternoon, Wardle handed me the envelope of threats. I was afraid to use the Worms to contact Miss Villiers, lest Wardle hear of it and ask about her. So I stopped in at the library myself and waited at our tea room.

"Ah, Detective Fever," said Miss Villiers, buzzing in like an electric storm. "On the rampage again?"

"Yes," I said. "Somebody ought to put a stop to me."

"If it's not one disease it's another."

I was surprised how pleased I was to see her. Books spilled from the satchel she hefted onto the table. "Studying hard, I see."

She laughed hollowly. "I'm so busy hunting down your man's reading habits, I've no time for my own studies. What's wrong? Don't you have books in the provinces?"

"We have our own national library, thank you very much, quite the equal of yours, in Edinburgh."

Her eyes softened. "Edinburgh? Is it pretty there?"

"Pretty? It's beautiful." I surprised myself with this outburst. I had never thought myself capable of feeling homesick. I coughed. "Are you allowed to take out so many books?"

"Ah. I was forced to borrow Aunt Lexy's card. She wouldn't mind, if she knew."

"Which she doesn't."

"Which she doesn't." Aunt Lexy was the waspish maiden aunt who was the benefactress of Miss Villiers' studies. When her father disowned her, set on her marriage, the aunt stepped in to pay the fees. She also arranged the library job, which enabled her to pay her own rent. She tapped the books. "I have almost everything that he's had from Mudie's over the past four years."

"Almost?"

"He still has the translation of the *Ramayana*. I've asked them to let me know when it's returned."

"We could set guard," I said, enthused. "Catch him when he returns it."

"That's what I thought. But he's renewed it twice."

"That only means we've missed him twice already. We must stake out the desk."

"You might watch for months. The lending period is four weeks. Even then, he could get someone else to slip it back on to the returns desk. He could renew it by post."

"It seems a long shot," I nodded, racking my brains. My head filled for a moment with grandiose notions, mounting my own operations. "Unless I set a team of Worms on vigil. Couldn't do it without Wardle's say-so. And I'm reluctant to tell him about–"

"About me?" she raised her nose. "You shouldn't be involving innocent young ladies?"

"I shouldn't be consulting anyone outside our office, not without his approval."

She glared at me briefly. "There was a chap the other day who seemed to shy away from me stamping his card. It wasn't him, though. Our man was chubby and genial. This chap was thin-faced and slight. Couldn't have been a disguise. But it made me wonder." She shook her head and fell to looking rapidly through the volumes before her. "Pay attention," she said sharply. "In every book there are pencil underlinings. Grand ideas. Fine phrases."

"What sort of phrases?"

"Apocalyptic visions. Revolutionary incantations." She stabbed at a page and I saw underlined in fine pencil something about "a family blind in blood". She looked at me closely. "Mean anything to you?"

"Rings a bell. But perhaps," I said, pulling the envelope from my pocket, "it has something to do with these?"

Her eyes lit up.

"I thought it curious," she said, poring over the series of messages Bertie had passed on to us. "Giving warning of one thing and not of the others."

"Why give warning at all? To taunt us?"

"No." She waved a dismissive hand. "He's no fool, just showing off. He wants to make us think. To understand why he's doing it."

"That's what I said."

"I'm sure you did," she nodded. "Well done."

"I did," I said indignantly. "Anyway, he's foolish enough not to know the date of fireworks night."

"Why do you say that?"

"The spout was preceded by the Guy Fawkes threat, but it went off on the ninth of November, not the fifth."

She frowned. "Why do you think he waited?"

"Wardle kept them out of town." I had told Miss Villiers as much as I felt I could, that Coxhill was on the train with Nellie and her new man, and that the other girl contacted Berwick. But I had kept from her the fact that the other man was the Prince of Wales.

"He waited till he had an easier target."

She nodded. "Then why did he let them come back, sir, if he was so anxious?"

I hesitated. It did seem surprising. If Wardle was concerned enough to be at Euston at two in the morning, why had he not simply told them to stay away?

"I know very well, Campbell Lawless, when you are hiding things from me. For my own good, no doubt, you man of mystery. Nevertheless, I am not too stupid to realise you think the gentleman in question worth protecting. Let us think more laterally. Guy Fawkes vented his spleen upon an important personage by setting Parliament on fire. Berwick embarrassed the man who thieved his sweetheart, and his accomplice, showering a railway station with water. The parallels are clear enough, leaving the date aside."

I nodded. An attack on a king; an attack on a prince.

"Am I warm?"

I nodded. "So what is his aim? To set clues for us?"

"More likely he wants to embarrass his enemy. Shame him before destroying him. He says it himself. 'Whom the gods wish to destroy, they first make mad.'"

"Destroying him?"

"It's the rules of tragedy. There'll be no dignity to the downfall unless the man understands it. Think of Caesar. Think of Macbeth. What makes it profound, rather than absurd, is that the hero understands his fall. He recognises that his own hubris leads to his nemesis. His *hamartia* leads to his *peripeteia*."

"You'll have to stick to English. I'm afraid I was useless at Latin."

"Greek," she sighed. "He must realise that his flaws have caused his downfall."

"Like Hamlet showing the play to Claudius before seeing him off?"

"The savant speaks! You really do like the theatre."

I fell silent. These messages, I reflected, would mean little to Bertie, who so hated to read. And, as Wardle treated him like a child, it seemed unlikely we would apprise him of the complexities. For Miss Villiers, however, they might provide a key.

She held up the envelope. "Can you leave them with me? I hope to match them to the scribbles. Crack the cipher."

"I've copied them out," I said, exchanging the envelope for

a hastily written sheet of my own. "They seem quite poetic, all written together like that."

"Poetic?" She stared at the sheet. "Yes, and menacing too. 'The Monstrous Rotundity has had its day.' He seems clear that he intends to destroy something, or someone. Oh, I also want that book of his, the one you saw at his mother's."

"I can't just waltz in and take it." I looked at her, smiling at me insouciantly. "Fairfoul, the step-brother, will have everyone warned about me."

She nodded, eyes wide. "You have to go back for it."

It was some time before I had the chance to put Miss Villiers' thoughts to Wardle. For, much to his chagrin, he was summoned to form part of the team responsible for the new Exhibition. The new theft was even assigned to a different office. This was guaranteed to throw him into a foul temper, as it meant putting everything aside to communicate with foreign dignitaries and ill-mannered industrialists.

Contrary to my expectations, he made a huge effort. Albert had wanted it to be another national triumph. In the face of public apathy, it was as if Wardle took it upon himself to put the late Prince's desire into effect.

"I've to take the King of Bechuanaland sightseeing. I ask you. Where do you take the King of bloody Bechuanaland? St Paul's? The Greenwich Observatory?"

I thought for a moment and pulled the envelope from my desk. "Will the Prince be showing other bigwigs the sights, sir? We'd better check each place before we go."

He narrowed his eyes. "Still thinking of Skelton, are you? He's done nothing since we warned Bertie off the girl."

"You're sure?"

"This time I'm sure."

"All the more reason to worry, sir. Think of it. You told me yourself what a profound effect the Great Exhibition had. This could have the opposite effect. What better chance to embarrass the Prince? To embarrass the country. Your son told me that Skelton–"

"Don't tell me Charlie knows Skelton."

"Knows of him. He was well-known in the reform movement, he said, considered capable of great things. But he was disaffected. He left the fold, struck out on his own."

"When did Charlie tell you this?" He stared at me.

"He came by at Christmas." I hesitated. "To see you, before leaving for Australia."

Wardle nodded for a moment. "Uncle Tom Cobbley and all know the bastard, and we can't find him for tuppence." He gestured towards the envelope, defeated. "You still making sense of that mumbo-jumbo, then?"

"I don't think it is mumbo-jumbo. You said he doesn't know his history. Perhaps he knows it better than us."

"He got the date wrong."

"The date doesn't matter. Blowing up a royal, early November. Guy Fawkes did it with fire, our man with water. Besides, why did you let Bertie come back at all, if you were so concerned?"

"He was required at Windsor." His jaw tightened. "Birthday. His eighteenth."

I shook my head in wonder. "A birthday present." I went to his desk and I emptied the envelope on to it. "And more presents to come."

Wardle sat impassive. "Why warn us? If he wants to blow up the Prince, why doesn't he do it, instead of faffing around with hocus-pocus and jiggery-pokery?" He swept a hand wildly through the notes on his desk, scattering them to the floor.

I caught one as it fluttered down. "No sense of tragedy, sir.

No sense of vengeance. Unless the Prince comes to realise, slowly and surely, that what he did was wrong, there's no satisfaction in destroying him."

"Destroying him?" Wardle snorted.

"'The monster is slain.' It's fairly unequivocal."

He flared his nostrils.

I smiled. "Don't you have the feeling he's been toying with us? It wouldn't surprise me if he wants the whole country to see Bertie, and his family, held up and ridiculed for their sins."

"What's that?" he barked.

I held up the threat in my hand. "'Whom the gods wish to destroy they first make mad.'"

"Spare us the philosophy, Watchman," he said grimly. But he stood up and began to pace back and forth. That was all the sense I could get out of him.

Later, I found him scrutinising the threats at his desk. Over the next weeks, he paid special attention to Bertie's official diary. When there were lesser functions, he cancelled them. At major events, he chaperoned him or, when the Prince grew weary of this attention, shadowed him at a distance. Though he maintained his dour demeanour with others, I could feel beneath the surface the panic that Berwick had instilled. He began to look tired and haggard. It took me some time to realise he was overwrought trying to outguess Berwick, coming up with wild suppositions from the series of threats.

"Perhaps it was a spelling mistake. Not Fawkes. Captain Fowkes, the genius Albert chose to design this exhibition hall. A threat to his Greenhouse."

To that I pointed out that Fowkes had not even been chosen when that threat was sent. Nonetheless, I couldn't deny the sense in maintaining close watch on it. Yet with twenty thousand exhibitors and a limited number of constables, there was only so much we could do. Wardle communicated to the other inspectors his concern that there was a danger of some kind of attack. But he could not be more specific, not without exposing all that he had worked so carefully to conceal. So he was restricted to vague warnings, warnings which in those times of Gas Wars and Fenian protesters made so little impact on his colleagues as to make no difference.

When I met Miss Villiers in the cafe, she looked tired. "I'm all right," she said.

I nodded. "What have you got?"

"Not much so far." She bit her lip, then opened a book. "First, all the threats have a punitive feeling. Somebody is to get what they deserve. This Monstrous Rotundity, whatever he means by it, is linked to apocalyptic imagery. This one's about Samson, pulling down the temple on the Philistines. Guy Fawkes, Cromwell, the Storming of the Bastille."

The passages she spoke of were marked in the margins with scribbles and arrows. There was the odd little drawing, too, stick figures, buildings collapsing, flames and floods.

I took a deep breath. "He's mad."

"Not at all. Obsessed, I give you. But there are clear threads running through it all." She blinked with tiredness. "If only I could unravel them."

I smiled awkwardly. "What do you make of it?"

"I think he has chosen somewhere to destroy. Some final cataclysm."

"Where?"

"It could be any number of places once you start thinking of it. The Monstrous Rotundity. One of the pleasure rotundae. Nelson's Column: that's a symbol of power. The new Parliament tower: the clock face is round, the bell is round."

I put my head in my hands. "Wardle's going to love this.

He's already boxing at shadows. Reckons the Fawkes threat was a misspelling for Captain Fowkes, and Skelton's going to blow up the Greenhouse."

She didn't smile. "Why not? It's costing the nation a fortune and distracting everyone from the country's real problems. And it's got a great big rotunda at each end."

It was some weeks later that I drew up in the early morning to Wyld's Great Globe in Leicester Square, and stepped down from my pony and trap to request an interview with the manager. Strange to say it, I was enjoying myself immensely. Wardle's advice, recalling his Mary Ann Brough case, made sense to me now. Here was I, moving up in the world, purely by being in the right place in an unexpected crisis. Some of the other sergeants had raised eyebrows at the role I had been given in the operation, but none of them knew what we were really seeking, and Wardle wasn't about to begin explaining.

Wardle's reaction, when I told him of Miss Villiers' theory about the rotundae, had been beyond my expectations. I say I told him of her theory. I must admit I allowed him to think that the idea was my own. Finally he seemed convinced of Berwick's ability, and his disaffection. The hydraulic spout seemed gentle, compared with the scenarios we were now envisaging.

Within days, he was seconding constables left, right and centre, demanding extra protection and care for all the foreign dignitaries, and so on and so forth. He had me organising teams to carry out checks on all the popular public buildings in London, the pony and trap often picking me up from home. We characterised it all as security for the Exhibition, protecting the dignitaries and very important persons flooding into town. Indeed, as spring drew on, the town was filling with colourful faces and colourful voices, as if the country, feeling itself wounded by Albert's death, had cried out for an infusion of life from overseas.

At Wyld's Globe I explained the purpose of my visit to the owner, James Wyld, MP.

"I'm glad someone thinks we're still popular," said Wyld, twiddling his moustache. "Public's forgotten us. Closing the bally thing down. Putting back the garden at my own expense. Ah well. Everything has its day. To be frank, it would be a blessing if somebody went and blew the place up."

I looked at him sharply.

"Spice up our reputation, you see. Insured to the hilt, of course. Have to be, public place like this. Otherwise any old grandmother leans out to touch Canada, loses her footing, can sue us silly. Sorry. Bad taste after Tooley Street, what?" He wiped his nose carelessly. "We had some boys, took to hiding in northern New South Wales. It's a broom cupboard, you see. Look, you can reach it from the floor or leap from the stair. These chancers would roll out when nobody was looking, yelling in agony, claiming they'd fallen from the top. Rather enterprising, I thought. Can't offer to show you round, I'm afraid I'm off to the House. St George's Day, you know, and there's a rather appetising debate on Baby Farming."

With a slap on the shoulder, he entrusted me to the manager, a dull-faced man who launched into a rehearsed spiel as he led me up the stairs in the centre of the great spherical building. "Sixty feet in diameter, a global map of the world inside-out, as it were, viewed from four landings."

I paused on the second, tickled at the notion of gazing upon the whole world. I glanced back and forth between diminutive England and majestic Australia and wondered. Was Charlie Wardle already starting his new life? I spotted the broom cupboard door and chuckled, drawing a scowl from the manager. Fairfoul had told me that was where Berwick had vanished to. How green I had been to believe him.

Even now, we were being made fools of. The International Exhibition was to start on the first of May, just over a week away, with a party for important persons the night before. The Queen, immersed in her grief, had squarely rejected public appearances. Bertie had reluctantly been persuaded to make his first significant contribution to public life. He was scheduled to attend a packed programme of functions through the summer; visits from princes and presidents; the opening of Big Ben, the Parliament bell already twice repaired; and the Exhibition party. Yet his presence gave opportunities for Berwick to act. I never doubted his expertise; surely one motive behind the spout was to show off how easily he could strike. Now that Wardle was finally convinced of his intent and his fervour, our doubts multiplied. How long could we risk Bertie appearing publicly? Should we not wheel out in his stead whatever old dukes and earls we could lay our hands on?

The manager's voice cut through my reverie. "It's the public taste, you see. Their diminishing appetite for wonders. Everyday life is ever more fanciful, what with telegrams, trains underground and who knows what next. Who wants to waste their time looking at pictures in a dark room?"

I thanked him and hurried on.

My punishing list of checks comprised rotundities, and anything that might be termed a rotundity. I checked cellars and broom cupboards, offices and boiler rooms, noting every sign of machinery, hydraulics especially, and assigning constables to stand guard, watching for suspicious behaviour. Would that ward off Berwick? Like Wardle said, fighting crimes that haven't yet happened is a way to drive yourself mad.

I headed next for Burford's Panorama, just off Leicester Square, a beautiful building, but the show terribly outdated:

Moving Pictures of the Siege of Sebastopol. I confess I was disappointed, for I expected the pictures to be moving in the literal sense. As for the figurative sense, Hunt might have shed a tear, remembering some fallen colleague; but I could not see how the thing paid.

I gave it the all clear, and moved on to the Regent's Park pleasure domes.

The Park Square Diorama had become a Baptist Chapel. It seemed sound enough.

In Burton's Colosseum, the vista of London from the top of St Paul's Cathedral was realistic enough to give me a vertiginous moment. I sent a constable.

The next day, I went good and early to St Paul's itself. An enthusiastic verger showed me enough nooks and crypts and passageways to conceal an army. By the time we climbed to the Golden Gallery, above the dome, I was not only out of breath, but in panic. As I emerged onto the outer terrace, the force of the wind shocked me. My stomach lurched as I peered out across the city.

I tried to steady my nerves, looking for places I recognised. All I could see were targets. To the south, the Greenwich Observatory, and of course Brunel's tunnel under the Thames, where Berwick's father had been ruined, the new bridges at Lambeth and Chelsea, the vaulted roof of Victoria Station.

And the British Museum Library. Its rotunda, nestled in the great museum's heart, was impressive as any. I was struck with a sudden fear for Miss Villiers, and determined to drive there forthwith.

"Some kind of disturbance down by the river," said the keen-eyed verger. I could make out nothing. "Oh yes. Parliament Square's quite full of people."

With a horrid sensation creeping through me, I flew down the steps, past the Whispering Gallery, and headed for

Westminster in the utmost haste. As I pulled off the Embankment, who should I pass but Glossop, trudging disconsolately out onto the bridge. We exchanged a few pleasantries through clenched teeth.

"What the devil are you doing down this neck of the woods?" I said.

"Only protecting Westminster Bridge. That's my lot, Yard boy," he scowled. He looked at the sky as if it would not surprise him in the least to be attacked by squadrons of hawks, or men from the moon. "Against what I'm not sure, but I'm protecting it."

I looked at him. What could be more absurd than trying to protect yourself from a terror that had no name? Glossop knew only that the powers that be feared some dark havoc.

Berwick, I reckoned, would like this description. Such was the mayhem his threats caused. It made me see for the first time quite how angry he was, angry enough to make fools of us all. Angry at the careless rich for stealing his love. Angry at a world that applauds injustices; at the System, and its grinding inescapable quirks – the same things that had left me, only months before, ready to throw up my hands and give in.

Clerks and politicians were pouring onto the grass by Parliament. God almighty, what had happened? I found Wardle inside the base of the clock tower, where I was disturbed to see a hydraulic engine.

"Sir?" I said.

"Watchman?" He turned to me, a hunted look in his eye. "I couldn't get it checked in time. It's a warren; a thousand offices, a million cupboards, wine cellars like football pitches, tunnels as far as Leicester Square." He glanced upwards. High above us a platform was swaying. He checked his watch, looked anxiously at the engine, and tugged me outside. "Five minutes now."

"You evacuated, sir?"

"They moved it forward without telling us, the fools. Wanted it up and running for the Exhibition. They went and brought Bertie without asking me."

"He's here?"

"I sent him home," he said wearily. "They're livid about it."

We took our place among the hordes. They had stopped the traffic around the square. Politicians mingled amiably with passers-by, every one of them looking up at the bell tower. Palmerston and Disraeli were playing chess. It was a shambles, an undeniable shambles.

"When did you find out?"

"Early morning. I've had people combing the place for hours." Wardle looked at me restlessly. "I had this feeling in my gut, poring over those threats. I've got it, you see. Who slew the beast? St George, weren't it? Fellow obviously sees himself as some latter day saint, riding around, slaying dragons. And what day is it today?"

"St George's Day."

"The Monstrous Rotundity, well, that bell weighs four tons. Big Ben, they call it." He put his fingers to his brow. "And it's a bloody clock, isn't it?"

I looked up, recalling that first night at Euston. Pat had spoken of clockwork affixed to the hydraulic devil, mechanisms that Berwick removed in one place, he had used to set off spouts in another.

"You see? What alternative had I? I had none." Wardle turned to the crowd. "Stay back now. Keep back!"

Darlington scurried out from the tower towards us and my heart leapt into my mouth. "No trace, sir," he said, beaming. "No sign of Davy's dust. No little Guy Fawkes. Not even Robin Hood and his Merry Men."

Wardle scowled at him.

"Hulloah, there, Sergeant," said James Wyld, MP, holding out a hand in greeting. "Didn't realise it was you lot putting on the show. Nicely done. Fine sense of drama." Just then, melodic bells pealed as prelude to the hour. "Tally-ho," said Wyld and with all the melodrama of a circus ringleader, began calling out, "Ten seconds! Nine! Eight…"

A hush fell across the crowd. It was impossible not to imagine an explosion. Would the tower shake? Would it buckle? Crumple onto the House? Or topple down upon us all?

Into the silence exploded the clang of the great bell. Once it tolled. Twice, and no explosion. By the fifth peal, the crowd burst out into applause. They kept clapping and cheering, with a few catcalls mixed in, until it reached the twelfth and long after.

The Metropolis Surgeon

That evening, I stopped in to carry out my checks at the British Museum Library.

"He would never strike here," said Miss Villiers as we settled in to our tearoom. "A man like him? He might wish terrible vengeance on his enemies, but he wouldn't destroy the greatest resource of learning in the country."

I told her of our fiasco in Westminster, outlining Wardle's interpretation of St George and Big Ben.

"Ah, no," she said. "It's very specific. 'The monster is slain in his tortuous lair.' It was always a dragon that St George slew, and you never see any pictures of its lair. Besides, why say 'his' lair? Only if it was part beast, part person."

I frowned. "One of your mythological beasts?"

"The minotaur. He's half bull, half prince, from the queen's unholy congress." She looked at me steadily. "His tortuous lair is the labyrinth."

"Which is round and monstrous." I put my head in my hands. "You have it."

"Oh, I have more than that," she said and called for more tea.

Wardle went quiet when I presented Miss Villiers' interpretation. Borrowing Ruth's turn of phrase, I explained that we had been fools. The threats, far from being random menaces, all alluded to kings, or sons of kings, slain by righteous avengers. The writing on the wall for Nebuchadnezzar. The minotaur, slain by Theseus in the labyrinth. All the way to Cromwell and King Charles, the guillotine and Marie Antoinette. It was sobering to think that it was reasonable for Berwick to believe in revolutions; after all, his own mother had fled one.

Miss Villiers reckoned that Berwick was styling himself as the East End hero out to kill the wicked prince – although I still did not speak of Bertie. Tracking him down through the labyrinth of London, he intended to bring down the temple upon all our heads on the final day of reckoning.

I expected Wardle to dismiss our ideas as high-flown nonsense. Instead he spent a few moments running his finger over his calendar, then he grunted, putting his hand to his forehead. It was as if he had come to the end of his patience with Berwick's games. He wanted to throw down his cards and call in the hand, whatever it meant paying out. "Let's clear Bertie out of it. He's a danger to himself. I'll speak to the Queen. We'll send him out of the country at dead of night without the blighter knowing. God help us, we've some work to do."

● ● ●

As we headed for the Palace, I checked through the luxury accoutrements while Wardle hunched in the corner, peering at the traffic through the smoked glass. Cupboards of physic; East India brandy and orange cordial waters; caviar and smoked salmon sandwiches; a Fortnum and Mason shaving kit; a box of Havana cigars; the *Times*, though which of them would read it I didn't know; two lady's shawls (better not to ask); a book of dirty pictures – Bertie's, I assumed; and a children's music box that played "Dainty Miss Skittles".

I descended at the Palace gates. Wardle wanted me to travel all the way to Calais with them. I had convinced him that it would be safer that only one of us was absent. The fiasco at Parliament had disturbed him. Besides, the fewer people who knew Bertie's whereabouts, the better, until he was safely on the continent, whether in "our darling little Germany", as Victoria wished, or in some faceless nightspot in the City of Light, as Bertie doubtless hoped.

"Keep working on it," he said wearily. "When I get back, we'll dig out the little rat and tie him up by his tail. I should have done it right at the beginning. Chase up that sewer notion of yours too. If there's new gangs of underground thieves in town, somebody will know about it. I'll try my contacts when I'm back, but you go the official route. Talk to the authorities. All right?"

It was more than all right with me. Compared to my usual role, this was a *carte blanche*. I had been expecting to have little to do in his absence, but now there was nothing to stop me pursuing my own ideas.

I sent the bones we had collected from the thefts to Simpson. A sorrier collection I had never seen, ribs and forelegs and vertebrae, dirty and aged and brown. "I am a physician, not an anthropologist," announced his peremptory reply, "but I will give it my attention after the university entrance examinations."

I decided against posting Worms outside Mudie's Lending Library. For what could I tell them to look for? A genial chubby man, returning an Indian epic? Instead, I turned to the sewers. My enquiries turned up Joseph Bazalgette's name at once, but his location proved harder to pinpoint. The chief officer of the Metropolitan Board of Works seemed to move from point to point as fast as lightning and rather more energetically. The Professor shuffled into the office – we used their services so much that procedures had slackened – to find me plotting the thefts on Stanford's new map, sticking pins into the wall that formed three lines progressing westward. The wee fellow stared at the map as if it were Michelangelo's David.

"What, pray, is that," he burst out, "if you don't mind my asking?"

I told him it was a representation of London; that is, a map.

"Someday," he said with conviction, "I too should like to own something akin to that particular apparatus."

He brought news that Bazalgette had finished overseeing the High Level Southern Branch and would be returning today to check the Low Level Northern. This was so much gibberish to me, and the latest in a series of conflicting reports of the man's whereabouts, but I went all the same. So it was that I found myself standing in a great trench in the middle of Fulham Broadway.

"The big man's expected this afternoon, guv'nor," said the foreman, a huge brute of a fellow with a shock of white hair. He gripped my hand as if to crush it and introduced himself as Slasher Fleming.

I nodded, staring at the maelstrom of activity around us.

"Can I do anything for you while you're waiting?"

"Thank you, no," I said. "Only I'd imagined I would have to go down some kind of mine shaft."

He laughed. "Oh, it's deep enough in some stretches. This bit's what they call cut-and-cover. The navvies cut, and we cover." He showed me how they fenced off the road ahead while the diggers advanced a channel, ten feet deep, in a rough "V" shape. Pony men wheeled the soil down to the river for the new embankments. Pumps were on hand for lying water and other run-off. To the other side, meanwhile, a team of surveyors reported on peculiarities of local drains. Smiths prepared grates and manholes. Bricklayers bricked the sides of the channel; carpenters arched it over with a timber framework; the bricklayers returned to vault over the duct; and finally the navvies surfaced the road anew.

"A lot of bricks," I said.

"Only a hundred million," he grinned, "so far. Those wee men you see with the gas lamps, inside the tunnel, they're checking the mortar work. But if you'll excuse us, I'd best be back at work."

It made me wonder what Bazalgette must be like, if this giant was awaiting his arrival with such trepidation.

"Envisage a city," boomed a voice behind me, "as a body, pumping with fluids." I turned to greet a smartly dressed man with an imposing moustache. He breathed in deeply, surveying the work around him with quiet satisfaction. "Blood, nerves, intestines, bowels. The whole kit and caboodle heaving with life." Bazalgette exuded verve and energy. Even as he spoke to me, little men began equipping us to go underground, arming us with galoshes, greatcoats and gloves. The great man shook my hand warmly and pulled on a deerstalker to top it off. "Sergeant Lawless, I take it? Pleasure. Official visit?"

"Could we call it semi-official?"

"You won't mind if I carry on working. Terribly busy. Don't require a canary, do you?"

I looked at him in bafflement.

"Regulations require a canary. Signal unexpected emissions. But I wrote the regulations. This stretch is secure enough." Without further ado, he showed me to a makeshift wooden ladder. "Now, what the deuce is this about?"

I descended as swiftly as I could. As he followed me down, I breathed deeply. "I will try to be brief, sir. Could one walk around London, vanishing in one place and reappearing undetected in another, through these sewers?"

He nodded briskly. "Let us enter the third circle of the inferno," he proclaimed, and strode into the tunnel, looking always about him with keen interest.

The entrance to the tunnel was oval, or rather in the shape of an upturned egg. That is, we walked on the narrowest part; the walls rose away from us and curved into a broad arch well clear of our heads.

"We decided early on, Sergeant," Bazalgette said, "that a sewer through which a man cannot walk is a sewer not worth building."

"Like underground roads, then," I nodded. "Is that not an invitation to loafers and footpads?"

"No right being down here, if they're not working for me. Ah, here is the first feeder junction. Good, good."

Only minutes into our walk, liquids were emerging from a grate in the tunnel wall. I avoided the questionable stream by walking with legs akimbo, but I was glad of the protective clothing, recalling Simpson's stern injunctions.

Bazalgette explained his system succinctly, but with undisguised enthusiasm. After years of debate at the Sewer Commission, with depositions from engineers and academics the length and breadth of the country, he was constructing five intercepting sewers of this size to divert the whole of London's wastes away from the river, by gravity where possible, pumping where necessary. They incorporated existing functional sewers as feeder ducts. Where they were obliged to, they rebuilt to allow a fully grown man easy access. "The cost of maintaining smaller drains," he explained, "is a menace, not to mention the danger."

Bazalgette interspersed this discourse with suggestions barked at Fleming and orders to the workmen. He wanted grates angled, flaws in the mortar fixed, manholes at curves in the tunnel.

"It was written in papyrus. The Romans discovered it by chance. The stormwater drain for the forum turned out to be quite the most effective sewerage system ever. The *Cloaca Maxima*. Gravity carries away solids suspended in water along the bottom. Natural floods serve not to overwhelm the system but to cleanse it. Now, Sergeant," he said, turning to me with impatient eyes in the dim light, "what is your business here?"

"My fear is this," I said. "Could you enter houses from here? Remove property?"

"Tell me, Sergeant," he chuckled, "you must enjoy those sensational French novels. Vagabonds and political undesirables hiding out in Parisian catacombs."

"Sometimes, sir, I feel I am in one of those novels. I have puzzled and puzzled at a series of impossible thefts, thefts where no entry has been forced."

"That skeleton lark?" he said thoughtfully. "Done and dusted, ain't it?"

A scrabbling sound announced the appearance of a small child, jumping nimbly from an opening high up in the wall ahead. He tipped his hat to us, clearly unaware that Bazalgette was his employer, and reported to Fleming. "Good and shipshape, guv. The odd gap in the upper brickwork, but nothing like that previous. I'd call it sound."

The foreman slapped the boy encouragingly on the shoulder and led him back a few yards. There was something touching in their workmanlike exchange, the little urchin and the great grey brute. Fleming lifted him in his great hands and practically threw him up to another opening. The wee fellow scrambled through with a will and vanished like a mouse into its hole.

I turned back to the engineer. "Sir, I must compare the locations of these thefts with the progress of your sewers."

He nodded thoughtfully and pointed ahead. "Can you accompany me as far as Millbank? There you will see that a fully functioning sewer cannot be easily navigated. Access to houses is a different matter. The connecting sewers are a motley affair. Some you could walk through, but only the smallest of toshers could wriggle up through the older ones. Only those little fellows know what is accessible and what is not. A thief blundering in would be unlikely to get out with anything intact."

Only the little fellows know. I could see it in my mind's eye, a curious tosher; something shiny in a cellar; things for the taking. Why not look around, up the steps, try the cellar door? I looked up at the hole where the urchin had vanished. "Toshers, you say?"

In the dim light, it was hard to read Bazalgette's expression, but he took Fleming's lamp, declaring suddenly, "Fine work, foreman. That will be all. We continue alone. You called your visit semi-official, Sergeant? Only I hesitate to cast suspicion on innocents. Unless you will give me your word that you will consider the facts in the broadest possible light, I can make no deposition."

I looked at him. There was something about the man I found intensely impressive. Noble, even. Besides, I simply wanted a solution. "You have my word on that, sir. We have punished scapegoats enough. I only wish to curtail the crimes."

"Well, then," he sighed. Bazalgette lowered his tone as we

strode on and quickened his pace somewhat. "I see your concern, Sergeant. Come to my office and I'll share a few things with you, in the light of which I hope you may take a reasonable view, should these little fellows prove to be involved in your thefts. Mischievous scoundrels, some of them, it's true." He peered into the distance. "But they're damned good workers, I tell you."

He began by telling me the story of the Sewer Commission.

"It's hard to remember what it was like back in '48. Revolutions across the continent. Five million signatures on the Chartist petition. Hundreds of thousands marching through the streets, smashing lamps at the Palace and chanting "*Vive la République*". They evacuated Victoria to the Isle of Wight, you know. Bloody awful state the country was in. Somebody had to sort it out. They passed Reform Acts, poor statutes and colliery laws and still twenty thousand a year were dying of cholera. We call ourselves civilised, yet we spend our summers bored in Brighton, while the other half are dying in ditches. It's a scandal, of course, but people don't want to know." He pulled his deerstalker on more firmly as the smell and darkness intensified. "In '48 the Commission flushed the sewers. A mistake, the cholera turned epidemic. They decided to survey the whole shambles. Only chaps kept dying in mysterious ways. I had one man suffocated, two blown to bits and more wasted away with the ague. So when I discovered a veritable army who knew the old system like the back of their hand, I took them on like a shot. Pig-headed not to."

"Do you employ these tosher children?"

"I certainly do. A pittance we pay them, but they think it a handsome wage. The taxpayer gets good value out of them. A job I had convincing the damned politicians. Had to do a little persuading work. You recall the Great Stink?"

"I've heard tell of it."

"The Thames was backed up something rotten. The city was a graveyard. But, of course, the ruling classes simply fled the city. So my little toshers orchestrated a special concoction of aromas outside Parliament." He chuckled. "They had to soak the curtains in chloride of lime. What I'd failed to achieve in ten years of meetings, they did in sixteen days. Disraeli ran from the chamber and they gave us the money. Ah, look here."

The filth beneath our feet began to swell as we approached a massive metal grate across the whole tunnel. The sewer beyond it was in full working use, deep sludge flowing away from us, fed by innumerable adjoining passages. Foul and stinking, but navigable in waders. Could you remove a Tom Thumb chair thus, without ruining it, without being afraid you would drown?

Bazalgette led me up metal rungs set in the sewer wall and pushed open a manhole. We emerged into broad daylight on the embankment, near Westminster, and headed for a makeshift cabin.

"Here already, sir?" said a small round man brightly, leaping up from his deskwork to fill a porcelain basin and put the kettle on the hob. Bazalgette wasted no time in throwing off his accoutrements and scrubbing his face and hands with carbolic soap. The small man turned to me and introduced himself as Jebb. "Glass of water, officer? And warm yourself up, now, you look proper chilled. What do you make of our catacombs?"

"Extraordinary," I said, moving over to the stove. "I can't believe the extent of it all."

"Oh, the London sewers were long enough to reach to Constantinople even before we started," said Jebb. "Thousands of millions of gallons of filth flowing into the Thames."

I put down my glass. Above the stove hung a display

cabinet, contents neatly labelled: Roman coins, pots and whale bones.

"Office is full of bones some days," remarked Jebb. "Wherever you dig, you unearth the past. Found a whole Roman bath under Parliament Square, water still in it."

I frowned. "And what do you do with it all?"

"Depends. Human remains we take off to the charnel house–"

"Thank you, Jebb," said Bazalgette briskly. "Fetch me the map, will you? And off to lunch with you."

Jebb deferentially vanished and Bazalgette unrolled before me a map of London thrice the size of mine. His great sewers were traced in different colours, continuous from the east into town but dotted as they headed on to the south, west and north.

He placed on top of the map a series of apocalyptic engravings: Daniel and the lion; Noah's Flood; the Tower of Babel. "This Royal Academy fellow, John Martin," he said, "has a penchant for mythological images." He placed a further sheet on top. "Looks like something from Dante's *Inferno*, eh? Sinners drowning in trenches of excrement. But it's a vision of London, you see. Martin's plan for trenches through the heart of the city, intercepting the old sewers perpendicular to the river, drawing the capital's filth out eastward. But you have to dig the trench before you let the sewage in." He pointed to a demoniacal figure releasing a sluice gate into an empty channel. "That's the moment for your thieves, before the sewer's fully operational. Like the stretch you saw today."

He removed the prints and I looked again at the map. The five snaky lines, traversing the metropolis, were labelled with opening dates. I ran through my mental list of thefts from Pearson's onward. Each one tallied with one of Bazalgette's lines.

Seeing my expression, he sat down heavily. "Cunning little schemers. This is deuced unfortunate. Sergeant, how can I impress it upon you? These boys have saved us innumerable injuries, deaths even. They are curing the city of its most deadly ills. They deserve the bloody George Cross, not prison." He clenched his fist in frustration. "And I need them. I am trying to make London the greatest city on this earth, and I need their help."

I nodded. Something was pulling at the back of my mind. "Mr Bazalgette, tell me. How on earth did you come to engage this group of vagabonds?"

He looked up. "Chap called Skelton." The kettle whistled to celebrate my utter confusion. Berwick seemed to be everywhere I had been and everywhere I would go. "Are you quite all right? Have a cup of tea, old fellow."

"I'm sorry, sir," I said as if in a dream, "but this Skelton. How did you meet him?"

He looked a little surprised by my interest. "At a Sewer Commission hearing. If I remember, he was pleased by my notion that we have a duty to sanitise the whole city, including the poorer regions. He impressed upon me the added duty of rehousing those dispossessed by the work, a measure for which I have convinced Parliament to pay."

"Good of you."

"There's enough ways we steal from the poor," he said impassively. "Sharp fellow, though. Surprising knowledge of hydraulics."

I nodded breathlessly. "I believe his father worked with Brunel."

"For Brunel, you say?"

"As an engineer, I thought."

He frowned. "If you say so, old man. I was under the impression he came from labouring folk. Did rather well for himself, I thought."

I thought of old Madame Skelton in her great brass bed.

Could it be that she had deluded herself about the grandeur of their origins?

"Still, I have a high opinion of the chap. Saved us a deuce of work with these tosher fellows. They were reluctant at first. Congenitally shy of all things legal. I had my own qualms: child labour, grim conditions. But I'm convinced it's for the best. At their old game, the poor souls would have ended up dead or in prison. This way, we benefit from their estimable knowledge and dependable advice. They get bathing facilities, money in their pocket and tremendous pride in work that will safeguard the capital for the future."

"Skelton organised all this?"

"The teams have their own little leaders, all answerable to the Tosher King." He gave me a little smile as he pronounced these words.

"The Tosher King?"

"There was an old duffer, a bit harum-scarum, who passed away. His brother runs it now."

"The old boy," I asked, short of breath, "did he have a club foot?"

"That's the chap. Know him, did you?"

"Not exactly. And the brother?"

"Goes by the name of Smiler. More efficiency about it, though I'm concerned he skims the cream off the boys' wages."

"Where can I find them now?"

"All sorts of little hidey-holes they have. I offered to house them but they wouldn't have it."

"And Skelton is still involved?"

"No. Bigger fish to fry. Writing for magazines. Committees. Dynamo of energy."

"Would any of your fellows still know him?"

Bazalgette took his tin cup and beckoned me outside. His

secretary was skulking at the bold new wrought-iron railing, looking down at the Thames.

"Jebb," said Bazalgette pleasantly. "Do you have an address for Skelton?"

"Don't believe so, sir. But he pops through occasionally, checking on the boys. Sergeant, you haven't any tea. Can I fetch you a cup?"

I spoke slowly. "Could you let me know if he popped through again?"

"Last saw him on the mid-level northern, sir. While back."

"We'll keep an eye out," Bazalgette assured me. He hesitated. "Will you be pursuing my little army? It will be deuced difficult to decide who is responsible for what."

I sighed. "Mr Bazalgette, I have no wish to embarrass a cause as worthy as yours. My inspector is also averse to public embarrassment. Before I can give you any assurance, however, I'd like a chat with one of your little toshers."

"I'll arrange a rendezvous. I'd leave the uniform at home if you don't want to frighten the chap witless. You'll be wanting a copy of our map, I imagine."

"Please. The Yard can pay the draughtsman's costs."

We stood for a moment looking out at the river. Gone was the debris I had spied from Waterloo Bridge two years before. The Thames splashed happily against its new embankment. I was alarmed to feel a rumble beneath my feet.

"Pneumatic train," Bazalgette nodded. "Test stretch. Plan for all eventualities, I say. There's so much shoddy work done these days, drives me potty. No wonder Pearson has the Fleet ditch bursting in every two seconds; nobody has the faintest idea what lies where. We've laid the water, gas and hydraulics into this thing ourselves."

I blinked. "You're not working with Roxton Coxhill, are you?"

"Ditched him. Bloody idiot."

"But you know him?"

"One of those for whom life never quite matches up to Eton. I imagine his finest hour was torturing some fag over a spit in the dining hall. His engine burst the day they installed it and he wouldn't take the rap. Must be off in two ticks, Sergeant. Anything else?"

I turned to him. "Good luck, sir. A monumental task you've taken on."

"Pleasure to talk to someone who sees what I'm at." He sipped his tea, enjoying the moment of calm. "A little vision, that's what's needed. Babylon, Knossos, Rome – they all had it. London could be the greatest city the world has ever seen. Of course, drains aren't newsworthy, Sergeant. No glamour. But someone has to sort out the bloody mess. That fellow Skelton saw it." He sighed. "Wife says I'm obsessed with faeces. Cloacal fixation, she calls it. I tell her I'm trying to save the country, damn it. Good day, Sergeant."

With that the great engineer shook my hand and strode off along his bold new embankment to forge the greatest city in the world.

BAIT FOR A WORM

Miss Villiers took out a file, looking around to check we were unwatched. She looked exhausted. "Pshaw," she said. "I'm fine. Behind on my college work, that's all."

I wondered if I was wasting her time with this code-breaking. If she failed her final examinations, her family struggles would have been in vain. She pressed the tips of her fingers into her forehead. Thinking she was on the verge of tears, I suddenly found myself telling all about Bazalgette and the sewers and the map.

"What am I to do?" I whispered. "There's no escaping it. The thefts must have been carried out by Bazalgette's toshers. Perhaps there was no coordinated plan. More likely opportunism. Word of mouth. Yet what did they take? Those who have nothing steal a pittance from those who have everything. Should they be transported for it?" I screwed up my eyes. "What if Worm's lot are involved? Am I to cause their downfall?"

"Scare them off, then. Have a word with Worm. Better still, catch them at it."

"Catch them? I never thought of that," I said ironically.

"Why not?" She stuck out her chin. "You have the maps. We can pinpoint the stretches at risk. They only steal from the wealthy. So we post constables in the most eligible cellars and you'll catch one soon enough. Offer him to Wardle on a platter. That should scare off the others. Better lose a soldier than the whole army be routed, don't you think?"

I nodded glumly, picturing Worm and the Professor languishing in Cold Bath Fields. "Might get the poor blighters that Wardle nabbed for it off the hook as well."

Ruth looked at me strangely. "You're a good man, Campbell," she said and locked her fingers with mine for a moment.

Bazalgette sent the map as promised, on which it was clear which stretches were at risk, and a note. One of the head toshers would meet me. Bazalgette had characterised me as an interested benefactor so as not to scare the timid fellow. Dressed for the part, I waited at Seven Dials for several hours one morning. The fellow never showed up. I did, however, spot Numpty shuffling along.

"Numpty! Long time, no see."

He curled up into his coat, like a frightened hedgehog in the dusk.

"Come, come, Numpty, it's me, Watchman. Listen, do you recall the night we met, at Euston Square? That old fellow, Shuffler. You didn't know him, did you?"

As if reciting lines learnt by rote, Numpty denied it.

"Don't panic, wee man. Ask Worm to pop in, will you? Haven't seen him for ages."

He nodded vigorously and, as Worm might have put it, scarpered.

I went directly to the Chief Superintendent to moot the notion of coordinating an operation in Wardle's absence.

"There's rumours of copycat thefts from our source, sir. Think I can nip it in the bud."

"Wardle speaks highly of you, my boy." The big man scratched his chin, while I wondered what Wardle had said of me. "How many constables do you want?"

I was assigned three giants with the unlikely names of Watkins, Atkins and Atkins (no relation), who seemed only too happy to regard me as their superior. They ran errands to Bazalgette's office, for this seemed one task I could not entrust to the Worms. When it came to our plan, they were in no way discomfited at the prospect of a week's vigil in the cellars of Shepherd's Bush.

How many early birds do you need to catch the worm? The Professor brought Miss Villiers along to the Yard one evening, and I smuggled her in under the auspices of an interview about a theft. This minor deception was amply rewarded by the look of wonder on her face on entering the Yard. Perhaps I could have made my plan of action without her; but I had seen the library stack, and it seemed fair to show her our inner sanctum.

After a decent period of nosing around our office, she fell to studying Bazalgette's sewer plans. "Think how much time must go into each of these lines, every twist and turn revised and double-checked, above ground and below, before they commit it to paper."

It struck me that other plans were being forged with such detail. How much groundwork was going into Berwick's new stratagems, whatever they might be? To what lengths would such a man go, once he decided to destroy his enemy?

The most recent thefts had exploited all three sewer lines north of the river. The low and high levels were both advancing through warrens of streets, affording an impossible guessing game. The mid level, by contrast, underpinned a wealthy mews along the Bayswater Road.

"You should plead your injury," she said excitedly, as we put the final touches to our plan. "Stay in the office while the boys do the dirty work."

I shook my head. "No, no. We need to cover as many houses as possible."

She seemed suitably impressed. "Leading from the front."

Samuel Smiles' basement in Palmer Mews, Notting Hill Gate, stank. From a discreet but thorough search, I had discovered four houses on the street with grates large enough that a boy might enter. Miss Villiers cooked up stories for the owners about routine checks on underground rivers and Roman remains. Samuel Smiles, the sage of self-help so admired by Coxhill, was an overbearing little Border Scotsman with little interest in archaeological remains, unless there was coinage involved.

Watkins, Atkins and Atkins (no relation) were posted in equally plush houses with equally foul cellars.

These were the grimmest nights I had passed since my fever.

I decreed candles impermissible. We must occupy the darkest corner, sweating away in gloves, galoshes and regulation greatcoats. Lavender posies for the stench were allowed, and beer in a wooden tankard. As I crouched in my corner, rheums surged afresh through my joints, the memory of fever ran in my veins. In the mornings I could hear the work in the sewer starting up, and I thought ruefully how we declined to visit Pearson's cellar all that time ago. I thought shamefacedly of my three hulking charges huddled down the road, far from their families with little clue what they were achieving. I could not have been a general, sending men to their deaths. Indeed, Atkins (no relation) did contract an ailment over the following weeks, despite all our protective clothing. I never knew if it was in his cellar he caught it, but Simpson could not cure him, and I felt the dismal shame of robbing his little ones of their father.

By the fifth night of our vigil, the Saturday, I was shattered. Even if they did not strike, I would have to call a halt, for Wardle was due to return Monday, and I was already too tired to be of use to anyone.

Then I heard the grate rattle.

My eyes could barely pick out the movement. From the sounds, however, I could picture the latch being expertly lifted and the grate swung gently open. Light footsteps passed me and a figure ascended the stairs. I had been expecting a boy, planning to let him strike and seize him as he returned, for I had made sure there was no other way out. But this was a man.

He opened the cellar door and swung it to behind him. I waited in high anxiety. When I heard him above, I moved over to the grate, to make sure he would not escape me. In the darkness I was not as quiet as I would have wished. I had that puzzling feeling that somebody was there with me. Sure enough, when the cellar door was pulled open again, a boyish voice behind me whispered sharply, "Esilop, esilop!" and scarpered.

The man sped down the stairs towards me, bag of swag swinging freely. As he headed for the grate, I bundled him to the ground. He looked up at me with a pained smile, as if it was indescribably boorish of me to trouble him at his work.

"You got me," he said without rancour. "No messing now. Let's be on our way."

Content that he would not flee, I reached for my lamp. When I saw him in the light, my blood ran cold. I knew that face. He was the drunken smiler from the Rose and Crown, and I knew now of whom he reminded me, the old fellow from the spout, Shuffler.

"You look like you saw a ghost," he said cheerily. I had loosened my hold on his arm, and he swung his bag and gave me a thumping clonk on the head. I went flying, and he lost no time in scrabbling through the grate and away. I scrambled to my feet, but with my knee there was little chance of catching him. I stuck my head through to see him disappearing into the distance down the narrow passage. I called out in frustration. "Why the bones?"

The figure stopped a moment and his reply echoed down to me. "Ask Berwick."

And he was gone.

I turned back to the cellar, clutching at my throbbing head. He had left the bag. It took only a moment to find what he had taken: a few coins, a silver candlestick and the workings of a clock.

Letter to Sgt Lawless, May 1862, Trieste, Italy:

How much I have enjoyed looking over these scribblings! What comfort my diary brought me through that mayhem of excitements, that maelstrom of disappointments! I shall never be a great writer like father, but perhaps one day I shall have copies printed and bound to circulate privately. This narrative, assembled from diaries spanning 1857-1860, I submit not for literary merit. Who can foretell the salient detail that will lead our gallant sergeant to the truth? What he seeks I know not, but I was pleased at eliciting Agnes' confession that day. For the delay, I can only apologise, adducing as defence my elopement. Father upset me with a remark that day, that nursing policemen was a job not for the daughter of the house but for a maid. Though I said nothing, I bethought me of a comment Mr Skelton had made.

"Are we not all people in the end?" he said. "Take Hester and Miss Dickens. Swap their clothes, and many folk would be at a loss to say which is the lady."

I took this properly to mean that people are ignorant and, in their ignorance, might not see me for the lady that I am. Father was upset, however. He has been touchy about the whole issue since his run-in with Thackeray at the Garrick.

I am glad that I nursed you, Sergeant, and I hope that these meagre notes may illuminate your investigation.

God bless,

Mrs Charles Collins, formerly Catherine Dickens (Kate!)

(More for brevity than for fear of causing offence, I have seen fit to chop Miss Dickens' narrative down to size, while attempting to retain the flavour of its naïve charm. RVL)

Excerpts from a Lady's Diary

1857: The Amateur Drama

JANUARY. The first performance of *The Frozen Deep*, in The Smallest Theatre In The World, has drawn roaring applause from the servants, and, I am led to believe, tears. Father called us magnificent. Next stop, the Champs-Élysées!

FEBRUARY. We have been invited to mount *The Frozen Deep* at the Gallery of Illustration in Regent's Street, by ROYAL COMMAND! Father attempts to pass it off as a trifle, but I know he is all a-flutter at the thought of performing for our dear Queen.

MARCH. This, as the poet says, is the start of my woes. Despite the indignities I have suffered at the hands of the cruellest of directors (father), my role is to be stripped from me and handed to, of all things, a professional actress. Father defends this decision by pure snobbery: he will not have his daughters presented to the Queen of England in the guise of coarse actresses. He is allowed to be presented as he wishes, however, the two-faced old boot. I call it shameful. Ingratitude. Exploitation.

JULY. After the play. Despite my relegation to props mistress, the play has been a thorough success. True to his word, father refused to grant an audience to the Queen. Refused the Queen! Just as well, with his ridiculous costume and make-up streaking down his face.

Our meeting with Her Majesty was brief, but her son was

more personable. Yes, the Prince of Wales himself! He snuck out the back, filched a cigarillo from one of the actresses and stood joking with us that his mother will have him hung, drawn and quartered if she discovers his filthy habit. Secret information about a prince. How thrilling! A most charming boy. The interest he took in the actresses over us ladies was lamentable, but doubtless provoked by the performance.

1858: The Semi-Professional Drama and the Soirées

I am quite distraught with the repeat of last year's travesty in casting. After the success of the *Frozen Deep* tour, father has decided that professional actresses are quite the thing. Following a number of jaunts, they have cast Mr Collins' new piece, *The Lighthouse*. Father will play opposite the actress from last year, Ellen, for whom he seems to be developing great affection. Two of the other roles are assigned to the vulgar actresses he refers to as his Haymarket hoofers.

At our rehearsals chez Colonel Waugh of Nether Stonehaugh, however, I discovered a silver lining to this cloud. Watching the rehearsal was a charming fellow named Berwick Skelton. He spoke to me courteously and intelligently, offering me tea, and asking me did I not think it daring that my father should present such a blatant attack on the maladministration of the war before the Queen. Having read the play more as domestic melodrama in two acts, and less as political allegory, I struggled to think which war he meant, let alone to deliver an intelligent reply. Like a true gentleman, he noticed my discomfort without alluding to it and changed the subject, complimenting the costumes. I blushed: can he have known I was the seamstress?

Mr Skelton's only failing is that he chaperones one of the vulgar actresses, Nellie. Nonetheless, I will prevail upon father to invite him to our evenings.

What gay times we have had!

I shudder to think what father means by his "sybaritic jaunts". Beastly. Mr Collins and Mr Skelton have become his firmest friends, sharing with him a taste not only for literature but for long walks and the low life. Still, it is hard to begrudge father his illicit pleasures, when he returns in such high spirits. If it takes a visit to a beastly music hall or public house to rouse him from the darkness that beset his spirits through the winter, can I berate him for it?

But I do like Mr Skelton. He is not a gentleman in the strict sense, but I care not for such gentlemen. I say it is the way a man acts, not the size of his stables, that counts. Last night, the conversation was being dominated by Roxton Coxhill. I used to think him a card but he was a bore yesterday, declaring there to be no substitute for breeding. Everyone nodded sincerely.

"Were everyone offered education," Mr Skelton suggested, "they might in time acquire breeding."

"Berwick," said Mr Mayhew, the *Punch* writer, "it's an admirable project, but if you expect the masses to gain taste and refinement, you may be disappointed."

"Disappointed?" Coxhill burst out. "You are deluded. Not for nothing have the ruling classes remained the ruling classes for centuries."

"Many ordinary folk buy your magazine, Mr Mayhew, and your books, Mr Dickens, and the rest would if they could read."

Father looked troubled. "Berwick, how I wish that you were right. I hope my books are popular, but a basic level of intelligence – dare I say, of breeding – is required to follow them."

Mr Skelton looked shocked.

Wilkie Collins piped up. "Dickens, what an old Whig you've become. Always the same. We who were heartfelt liberals in our youth become canny conservatives in our dotage."

"Give me an army of street children," said Berwick, "and I will deliver you in ten years an educated, well-bred fighting force to give the pillars of society such a shake as they have not felt since Samson."

Coxhill chuckled uneasily. "Why does society need to be shaken?"

"Because it is run by cankered *noblesse* and inbred royalty."

Now it was father's turn to look shocked. Indeed, the whole room fell silent.

"Beware, Berwick," Collins warned him. "Dickens will stomach insults to anything except his beloved Queen."

Everybody laughed, though, to me, Mr Skelton looked sore disappointed. As polite conversation resumed, he invited Mr Collins and myself out to the street, an impish glint in his eye. Sneaking out as quietly as we could, we met some little urchin friends of Mr Skelton's, a young vagabond with a couple of waifs in his charge. They greeted Mr Skelton on familiar terms and us most courteously, then proceeded to exchange a repartee infinitely more entertaining than the tripe being spouted inside.

"Is this how the other 'alf live, Mr Skelton?" said the young ruffian. He launched into a string of jokes about the other half, and two halves making a whole, and holes in your pockets; pigs, prigs and Whigs, swigs, swag and scallywags; and who knows what else.

Mr Collins and I were soon hooting with laughter. Before long, ten more urchins appeared, making it a street party of bows and curtseys. They serenaded us with bawdy street songs in close harmony. Agnes brought out the porter for us and lemon sherbet for them. The mood was most jocular and Mr Collins declared that he had never passed a more enjoyable evening.

It was over the detestable habit of gentlemen retiring to smoke that Mr Skelton clashed with Mr Coxhill last night.

"Why are ladies so treated?" he asked one day, as the men headed for the drawing room following a fearsome game of Pass the Slipper. "We men enjoy parlour high-jinks and word-puzzles." He himself was a regular demon at acrostics. "Why can ladies not revel in the social debate?"

"You believe in women's rights?" Coxhill sneered. "Some of us know what ladies are good for and would like to see them stick to it."

Mr Skelton, to credit him, maintained a cool silence, until he was egged on.

"Come now, Berwick," urged Mr Collins. "We cannot leave it at that."

"I have observed," Mr Skelton replied levelly, "that prejudice is its own begetter. Those prejudiced about race are often of mixed breeding. Snobs are insecure about their class. Those biased about sex – well, perhaps I had best not finish the thought."

I glared at Mr Coxhill to back up the point. After all, I had heard father's secret view of the man. How his father left him a packet of money from the White Conduit Club; how he drank away his fortune; how he was fixated on "the next big thing" to make his name in business, and all his friendliness was a sham.

I am sorry to note that Mr Skelton is still taken with his actress. Although she has striven to better herself in accents

306 LAWLESS & *the* DEVIL *of* EUSTON SQUARE

and demeanour, her plain features and over-developed bust cannot but betray her common background. It pains me that a man of such taste and intelligence can swoon before the vulgar charms of this (dare I write it?) tart.

1859: The Lighthouse

What a prism of disasters. It started during the tour of *The Lighthouse*. Now that Mama has – the shame of it – moved out of our family home, I have to suspect father's motives for his tour of the North-East.

A coldness has developed too between Mr Skelton and his fiancée. I was not sorry to see it at first, but now it seems we have lost a dear friend. How recently he and father were thick as thieves, as if they shared a dark secret. Perhaps it is simply regard for the virtues of hard work and honour, through which they have both prevailed.

Father invited Mr Skelton to write about the boroughs he grew up in, which remain to us of more fortunate birth as mysterious as the Orient. What things he wrote. Trails of woe through Bethnal Green. Misery in Clerkenwell. Disenfranchised hordes and multitudes made homeless by the advance of progress. The pieces were filled with exquisite paradoxes. The poor die of miasma, so politicians are loath to devote taxpayers' money to solve it. Projects such as the underground train are meant to benefit the common man, but instead block his roads and destroy his borough, while the empowered waft away such schemes from their vicinity.

I found it strange that father did not publish the pieces in *Household Words*, though Mr Berwick was pleased with the interest of father's friends from *Punch* and the *Illustrated London News*.

● ● ●

One night, the gentlemen sat down to a game at cards, after a particularly strenuous game of leapfrog, while we ladies retired to the bow window. The talk revolved around the financing of newspapers by businessmen, whose interests sometimes clash with the duty to report the news impartially. It used to surprise me how well a commoner like Mr Skelton held his own amongst the editors, entrepreneurs and engineers who frequent our *soirées*. But he has an unquenchable belief in his own capacities; indeed, in everyone's.

"You were lucky," said the editor of *Punch* to father, "to get out of that *Daily News* debacle before the brute Hudson got his teeth into you."

"Mr Lemon," Coxhill piped up, emptying coins noisily onto the table. "Mr Hudson was a friend of my father and I'll thank you not to slander him."

"Mr Coxcomb," Berwick smiled, "will you resolutely defend any friend of your father whether he be the local butcher or the butcher of Cumberland?"

"I know nothing of this Cumberland chappy, but loyalty was one of my father's attributes, and if your father had more of it, perhaps you'd be in better shape yourself."

Mr Skelton looked at him coldly. "I'll thank you not to speak of my father."

"The thing is," ventured Mr Mayhew gamely, "it's not simply that a financial backer has the opportunity to meddle. The power of the media is such, there's times he'd be a fool not to."

Lemon nodded. "Hudson sold a lot of railway shares that way."

"Then it's up to the discerning editor," said Mr Skelton, "to resist the backer."

"That's not always possible," father burst out.

"Is it not?" said Berwick, looking at father strangely.

"Of course it is," said Lemon, gathering up his winnings.

"I used to think so," said father quietly, "but I'm afraid the System is stronger in the end."

"One must stand up," said Lemon, "and fight it."

"Then you will lose," said Coxhill smugly.

"Should one really," said father wearily, "stand up to such forces simply in order to be mown down?"

"My dear Boz," said Mr Skelton earnestly, and looked father in the eye, "if you stand on your own two feet, unsuspected forces will appear, in admiration and solidarity, to support you. And if enough people stand up in protest then even the wheels of commerce may be turned aside."

"Those wheels will run such jokers down," said Coxhill gleefully.

"Some may fall," Mr Skelton agreed. "I see no shame in that. But the machine will run smoother if the driver yields and goes around them."

Mayhew clapped Mr Skelton on the shoulder. "You are a revolutionary of the old school, what?"

"I like to think that my school is still current," Mr Skelton quipped. But he folded his cards and got up from the table, and I caught him glancing at father strangely.

"Bloody hell," Coxhill burst out. "Can somebody lend me a couple of guineas?"

Lemon pushed two notes across the table, but kept his fingers upon them. "This how you finance your business, old man?"

"My business is sound enough," Coxhill sounded offended, his tone unnecessarily sharp. "I have the Prince of Wales' assurance–"

"Can you give me the Prince's assurance on these two guineas?"

Mr Skelton moved away from the table to sit with me and

my sisters.

"Is it true, Mr Skelton," I said, "that you are of the reforming persuasion?"

He laughed pleasantly. "I suppose I am, if you must give in to the mania for classification."

"No wonder you clash with father so," I nodded, "now that he's an old Whig and opposes improving our prisons."

"Reforming what?" asked my little sister.

I ignored her. "When will we see one of your articles in father's paper?"

"Oh, no, I've had done with that," he said. "I'm going into construction. Your father has written me recommendations to Bazalgette, Fowler, Paxton and all the best engineers. So I won't hear a word against your father's politics, young Kate, you hear?"

"Engineering, Mr Berwick? What a departure."

"Not really. My father worked on Brunel's tunnel. You know, under the Thames."

"Where they had the fête last summer?"

"The fête? Yes, that's right. In a way, constructing a piece of writing is no different from making a tunnel or a bridge."

"Is your father still in that line of business?"

"My father passed away." He looked at me squarely. "An accident, many years ago."

I murmured my condolences. We fell silent. I had to give my sister three stern looks before she understood that I wanted her to leave us together. In those moments I felt very close to Mr Berwick, so much so that I felt, had the gentlemen not been across the room, I might have forgot myself and embraced him. Thankfully, I remembered myself and thought to ask after his fiancée.

"Who?"

"The actress, Nellie? I understand she and her charming

friend are to appear in our play again?"

"I'm afraid I can't help you, Miss Dickens. Something of a distance has developed between us. Our marriage has been postponed." He stared out of the window.

Strange as it was, though I wanted to congratulate him on his fortunate escape, I managed to look sufficiently demure. "Oh, I am sorry." I flashed him my sincerest smile. "I do hope that won't prevent you from coming to see us."

He seemed not to hear me. What a change had come over him, as if his energy had been drained quite away. He stared across at the gentlemen with a tightness round his eyes. "I'm sorry? No, of course not." He gave a faint smile. "As long as I'm welcome."

Once rehearsals started, however, we saw him no more, and rather too much of Mr Coxhill. Imagine my disgust, when I noticed Coxhill slip his arm into Hester's after rehearsal. I made some comment to father.

He burst out rather improprietously, "Yes, and Nellie has a new fellow too."

He mentioned Mr Skelton to me once, perhaps a year later. It was when he was starting his periodical, *All the Year Round*, under his own finances.

"I may be doing a foolish thing," he said, "but Berwick, at least, would be proud of me."

What with *Two Cities* along with Mr Collins' *The Woman in White*, father stood on his own two feet, just as Mr Skelton had predicted.

Suffice it to say that Mr Skelton vanished from view. Nellie's name is eternally damned in our house, as she left father in the lurch in the late stages of rehearsal for *The Lighthouse*. To me, it seemed like the world was ending. When the mantel clock stopped, nothing could have been more appropriate.

Then Mr Collins introduced me to his brother, Charles, and now we are married. Father disapproves, of course. When does he not, these days, despite the questionable nature of his own conduct? Only now that Charles and I have eloped to freedom here in Italy do I feel free of the burdens weighing down my poor, estranged family.

Mrs Charles Collins

INTERNATIONAL EXHIBITIONIST

"Our machines are the apex of all that's new," announced Coxhill, brandishing a flute of champagne in front of his exhibit, "in this epoch to outdo all others."

The glory of the epoch was hard to dispute, looking around Captain Fowkes' Kensington Greenhouse during the opening shindig. A million square feet, thirty thousand exhibits, and I was the linchpin in checking them all. I had just had an unpleasant run-in with Hunt by an adjacent exhibit of taxidermy, where towering bears roared silently in a painted Alaskan glen.

"What's all this about?" the little man challenged me. "Why's the place swarming with coppers?"

"Standard security," I replied.

"Why?" He hunched up his shoulders. "Had some sort of threat?"

"What do you mean by that?"

"Don't play high and mighty, mister la-di-dah copper. You're supposed to be protecting Mr Coxhill."

"I thought he had quite enough protection with you snapping at his heels." I made to walk away, but Coxhill spotted me.

He was lecturing in front of his display of steel and hydraulic valves, convincing a herd of businessmen and their wives to invest in his scrip; that is, a kind of share in a share. It amazed me that, despite his verbosity and his glazed look, he seemed to be winning the crowd over with his relentless self-promotion.

Wardle had given us a dour talk to the effect that we were upholding British standards on the stage of the world. His talk served more to startle than prepare us. For if he was concerned, how should we remain calm? His trip with Bertie had left him tired. Probably none of the fresh-faced new constables noticed. But to me he seemed like a runner, so long in control of the race that he has grown weary of it. What he fears is not being overtaken by another – that is only to be expected – but rather making a foolish mistake, tripping over his own feet, so that he will leave the arena with laughter ringing in his ears, in place of the applause he deserves. I never saw Wardle prepare for anything so assiduously. He even studied the promotional literature, which spoke of drawing the world closer in brotherhood and commerce. We wage war on them one moment, then invite them to a show the next. It never failed to draw adverse comment from Wardle too. The '51 Exhibition, when Albert addressed the multitude, would forever be the pinnacle for him, not only of his career but of Britain's glory in the world. To him now, the light of Empire would never be as lustrous.

Of my night-time escapade, I had told him very little. I reported how I had laid the trap and been overpowered by the two accomplices, without mentioning that one was a child. Not that I was ashamed of my failure. I hoped I had scared the thieves off and there would be no need to delve deeper.

Luckily, Wardle only had thoughts for Fowkes' Greenhouse. Perhaps he had put himself in Berwick's place and decided that Albert's dream Exhibition in the heart of London was the perfect place to strike. So we assigned other targets to local constabularies, freeing our lot to comb the Greenhouse's labyrinthine intricacies.

"Do you know what the next mania will be?" Coxhill enthused, champagne dribbling down his tuft of a beard. "Piping! The future is in piping. Our network offers power outlets all along the Marylebone, Euston and Farringdon Roads. Opening any day now! Stock like hot cakes, you know. I have some scrip here. Everybody's after it."

It was the first time I'd seen him since our prodigal night out. I was keen to ask him about Berwick, and about his insurance set-up, but I had no wish to stand by listening to his old spiel, as if I was giving my blessing to the enterprise.

"Mr Coxhill – Roxton – I can't stop now, we're run ragged, but could I have a word with you later? It's about Berwick Skelton."

"Come and join the banquet, Cameron. You've worked hard enough."

"For God's sake, Roxton, let the poor fellow go." Charles Pearson emerged from the crowds, looking tired and careworn. "Officer," he said to me, "you mustn't let this blighter bully you around."

"Nonsense," Coxhill blustered on. "The poor chap doesn't understand what's on offer, that's all. Remember the railway mania? The millions people made? Rags-to-riches stories on all sides. Once our pipes are pumping, beneath the very streets, Sergeant, dividends will soar. Some are predicting four per cent. I've even heard of six!"

Coxhill continued his monologue as I stepped away with Pearson. "Thank you, sir. Are you quite all right?"

"I am fed up," he sighed. "It's an embarrassment and an insult. We're ready to open, but they've obstructed us at every turn. Board of Safety won't approve our smokeless locomotives,

and we're obliged to deal with the oafs at the Great Western."
He massaged his temples, then looked up brightly. "It runs
beautifully, though. We're having a trial in a few weeks. Did I
hear you mention the Reform League chap, Skelton?"

I blinked. "Why, do you know him?"

"Bazalgette recommended him. Did some liaising. Good
with the men."

"He works for you?"

"Long gone now," he shook his head. "Embarrasses me,
actually. We've exceeded our budget, trying to outwit the
bloody Fleet Sewer between King's Cross and the City, and
I've had to renege on my promise to rehouse those made
homeless. The Fleet has made a liar of me."

He looked on a sudden so pale and ill, I suggested he would
be better off at home. As I packed him into a cab, he leaned
out the window. "Something else I meant to tell you, officer. I
did have something go missing after all."

"That day at your house, sir?"

"A set of plans. For the hydraulics that run along the line."

"Why did you not report it?"

"It was only a set of copies. I'd rather you didn't mention it
to Coxhill. He'll think it's some competitor stealing his ideas.
Sees intrigue everywhere. Can't see what good they'd do
anyone. They were absolutely specific to our network. Now I
come to think of it, a few things from the office went astray
around the same time. Bits and pieces we found during the
diggings, you know."

I recalled the whale bone in Bazalgette's office. "Fossils and
the like?"

He nodded, rather sheepishly. "That's right. You wouldn't
believe the things you find in the old Fleet Ditch. I am under
the weather, Sergeant. I shall bid you good night."

• • •

"Certainly, I know him," said Kenelm Digby, pushing his glasses back up his nose. I had expected him to be difficult, but he seemed a man from whom all the fire has gone, his wispy hair falling away from a distracted face. "Knew him rather."

"He's not dead, is he?"

"Dear me, no. I haven't seen him lately, that's all. Do come in, officer." He led me through the Red Lion Centre, a club for working men. Posters advertised all manner of opportunities for self-improvement: classes, bursaries and legal advice.

"Quite an establishment you have here, Mr Digby," I said.

"I am merely a cog in a machine," he laughed nervously and set about tidying his papers. "The passivist wheel, you might say. Bringing change from within. Strange you ask about Berwick. It's due to him I'm giving up."

"Giving up?"

"Berwick was more of the activist persuasion. Such energy, such commitment. Sorry to lose him, of course."

"Is he gone?"

"Off to Australia, didn't you know? Had a crisis, you see. Made himself sick with it. I caught him weeping outside meetings. Shocking to see this genial chap reduced to an angular bag of bones. I feared he was consumptive, but he insisted it was simply over-exertion. Tireless activist. Gave talks, wrote papers, brought old Shuffler and his crowd into legal work."

"You knew Shuffler?"

"Amusing old chap, yes. One of the old breed with his gang of willing slaves. Like the feudal system, I thought it, but he treated them well, as far as I could see. He took such an interest in our industrial compensation seminar I actually thought he might join the cause. Many hands make light work, you know. Sad when he died. The brother, though, was a different story."

"Brother?"

"Yes. Splasher, wasn't it? They had divided it into three kingdoms: earth, water and underworld, like Jupiter, Neptune and Pluto. Shuffler with the toshers, Splasher on the river, and Smiler with the street grubbers. All over now, of course, with the new legislation. Progress at last, but people in power don't stop to think how progress hurts the little man, cast aside in its wake." Digby clearly thought he was the one to spare that thought.

I nodded dourly. "Are you in contact with the toshers?"

"They pop in once in a while, when they're in a spot of bother."

"Can you put me in touch with them?"

"No, no. Even if I knew their whereabouts, League connections are confidential."

"But you don't know?"

"If Berwick's brother comes in I'll be sure to ask him."

"Berwick's brother?"

"Half-brother, is it? Fairfoul. Bright chap." He coughed and continued tidying his desk. "Let your faith be as your stockings, Sergeant, spotless and ready to gird on. My wife tells me what a fool I am. I have been known to give the shirt off my back to poor unfortunates on the way home from church. But my wife says to me, Kenelm, they are waiting for you to visit the Kensington Arcade for the latest fashion."

I frowned. "And what has Skelton to do with your giving up?"

"Oh, that?" He hesitated. "We had an ongoing quarrel about the movement. My view was that everybody wants to end poverty and hunger. Berwick, on the other hand, lost his faith in the goodness of mankind. He insisted that the great and good have no interest in sharing wealth. They need these inequalities to promote labour and demand. Not that they're necessarily bad men, just pessimists. If humanity is such a low species, then somebody will profit from it. If someone is going to profit, it might as well be them. Reform talk is just hot air, fooling the masses into suffering in silence in pursuit of some illusory justice." He dropped the sheaf of papers he had been tidying neatly in the wastepaper basket and turned to me with a sad smile. "That's why I'm giving up. Because he was right."

Bad Odour

"More pudding, Sergeant?"

"I couldn't possibly, Mrs Wardle."

"Go on, or it's wasted. Jack won't have it and I oughtn't. I'd give you more shepherd's pie, only it wouldn't be right to go back to savoury now."

Mrs Wardle was a hard woman to refuse. In my father's house, if you were offered more, you were to say no and mean no. Pleased by their invitation, I was just a little disappointed when there turned out to be a further motive.

"Just another mouthful, Mrs Wardle, then I'll get to looking at the clock."

Wardle had gone outside, taking advantage of the evening light to work on his azaleas. While his portly wife bustled around me, I tucked into the stewed apples. We had shared a bottle of port to celebrate our recent work. We talked of the skeleton thefts, deciding further traps were unnecessary if we could just spread the word that we knew the *modus operandi*. At least we had kept these latest thefts out of the press, and there need be no more scapegoats. The poor devils Wardle had pinned it all on would just have to stay put. The puzzle that remained outstanding was the bones.

We talked of the Exhibition too. Three weeks it had been going and our panic was gradually subsiding. With a list of foreign dignitaries as long as my arm, we were calling heavily on politicians to stand in for the absent royals. Mr Gladstone was signed up for Pearson's trial run. Mr Disraeli kept giving stirring speeches. The low attendance figures were attributed to economic malaise in the wake of Albert's death. But we had fulfilled our function. Indeed, perhaps we had overreacted. Perhaps Berwick had just wanted to scare Bertie off Nellie. Maybe now that Bertie was far away, Berwick would try to win her back – though whether he was in Brisbane or Bethnal Green I could not be certain.

A little tipsy, I went to check their grandmother clock in the hall, while Mrs Wardle talked away, ten to the dozen.

"It's a great relief to me that he has an agreeable assistant like yourself. Last chap drove him potty, dotting i's and crossing t's." She unclasped the window and looked out. "Oh, he was that upset when Albert passed away. So many years he's worked for him. It makes you afraid too. What if the things you were promised get forgotten? Ever since he was your age, Jack's said he would retire at sixty and spend his dotage back in Yorkshire. There's a cottage he has his eye on, a lovely place with a garden, and a stream for his fishing. He deserves it. We both do."

I oiled the guilty sprocket and delicately set the pendulum swinging. Not too hard. I went over to stand by Mrs Wardle, looking out at her husband working in the garden. Seeing him there, away from the fight of the town, with the rich evening sun glinting through the trees, I liked him more at that moment than ever before. He too held secret dreams. Long-cherished dreams, never secure. Would he be happy away from the bustle? Why not? Why couldn't a man have two sides so different?

"Yes, Mrs Wardle. You deserve it." A rose nodded before the open window. I leaned forward to smell it, but it was dried up with blight or worm. All I could smell was the oil on my fingers.

THE SIXTH PERIOD
[MID 1862]

12th June, 1862

OUR FRIENDS FROM ABROAD

Whence this welter of strange accents prevalent across the capital today?

The discerning *Bugle* reader will identify around town exhibitionists of every extraction, hoping to cash in on a bonanza as big as the fair of '51. Sadly, our great Queen's refusal to celebrate her Silver Jubilee has cast a pall over the nation in general and in particular over the "Not-So-Great Exhibition". Nonetheless Captain Fowkes' Conservatory has attracted thirty thousand expositions and innumerable foreign dignitaries, at a cost to the nation of four hundred thousand pounds.

The well-informed money is on Bessemerised steel and its upshots, such as the HECC's new hydraulic network alongside Pearson's underground train. Their next proposal is a visionary scheme to underlie the whole city. Water, pressurised through reinforced piping to five hundred and forty pounds per square inch, will power not just dockyard machinery, but West End curtains and Mayfair elevators. Do we sniff a Royal Statute?

The biggest seller remains the stereoscope, that larksome

device which will turn us all cross-eyed.

The biggest dodo is a new type of hobby horse. Made of metal in place of wood, this "bi-cycle" employs an ingenious pedalling device to propel it forward. Shame, then, that only a circus acrobat could hope to keep it upright, and the saddle sits so high from the ground that a fall at speed would inflict grievous injury upon the intrepid rider.

The other influx of accents is due to discontent in the hungry north. The Cotton Famine caused by our American cousins' inconsiderate Civil War has brought the Lancashire mills to a standstill. Talk of riots, turmoil and a militia rising may be exaggerated, but the *Bugle* advises you to look after the shirt on your back.

What greets these incomers to the world's greatest city? Apocalyptic hoofbeats, fires, famine, and the spectre of King Cholera re-establishing court over the East End, our own Father Thames a bringer of plague.

THE PIT INTO WHICH WE ARE PLUNGING

Even the ever-optimistic Charles Pearson seems defeated. The Member for Lambeth promised us the greatest engineering project since the Hanging Gardens of Babylon. Yet the opening of his "Metropolitan Railway" has been postponed again, the Board of Safety unimpressed by his "smokeless" engines. Undoubtedly, the public will not trust the scheme until the engines are run by a well-known and trusted company, for instance the Great Western.

The *Bugle* can also reveal that "certain remains" dug up during works have been stolen from the company offices. Pearson declined to comment, but the *Bugle* has discovered that the remains include human bones. These relics date back centuries, but some are doubtless from more recent explosions of the Fleet sewer: recall the Poor House blast of 1846. Medical students purchasing cut-price skeletons should beware, lest, in saving a few pennies, they catch typhus from their own forefathers.

Nonetheless, the Metropolitan's trial run, at the end of May, impressed shareholders. Mr Gladstone, they tell us, though reluctant on entering the catacomb, seemed impressed by the 3¼ mile dash from Paddington to Farringdon.

Yet the *Bugle* received contradictory reports, describing how "a shrieking, as of ten thousand drones, rises up beneath the thunder of the wheels. One has Tartarean visions of accidents, collisions, crumbling tunnels. A fierce wind takes away the breath. This, then, is the living instantiation of The Black Pit into which we are now plunging."

Tartarean indeed. Such is the folly we like to style Progress.

Conclusion of Article in The Beehive, *by Berton Kelswick, prints by John Martin, RA:*

… Such are the degradations of Clerkenwell's rookeries.

Besides such shame, the East End is also renowned for its primordial sense of justice. "Doing the rights", they call it there. This justice is exacted any weeknight outside the borough's taverns whenever there is a promise broken, work unpaid, or profit made from another's pain. In our land divided into two nations, what will prevent this vengeance from spreading beyond the borough's bounds?

When Noah built his ark in his back garden, hundreds of miles from the sea, his neighbours thought him deluded. Reasonably so, you might say – though your scepticism would have got you drowned. The Chartists' petition of 1848 was a manifesto of delusions, we were told; ideas such as union rights and the universal franchise, we were told, are further from sense than Noah's garden from the sea. Thus were we fobbed off with diluted reforms and promises of a new Jerusalem among these dark satanic mills.

Beware! If the trusting common man, who toils unheeded to shore up the floodwaters, should open his eyes, he will lose patience. There will come such a quake as has not been felt since Samson ripped down the pillars of the temple. There will follow a deluge to wash the guilty from their palace of indolence. If the common man should also be sacrificed in this shake, at least he will die with his eyes fixed upon Noah's great rainbow, but those responsible will end deep in the circles of the inferno, enduring for eternity the punishment to fit their crimes.

There may be times to silence the deluded. There are also times to heed delusions, lest they turn out to be visions.

CODE BREAKING

Wardle came into the office white-faced. "Bloody Worms. Never get one when you want one, then they deliver nonsense like this. What do you make of it?"

He planted the note from Simpson squarely in the middle of my desk:

"Initial Analysis of Bones, requested by Sergeant Lawless. The specimens derive from many different bodies: age varied, both sexes, date and cause of death indiscernible at this remove. I can tell no more on such pitiful evidence, save that they are all human."

Wardle stood there, waiting for my explanation. All I could do was clench my teeth and screw up my eyes in frustration.

My night-time encounter with Smiler had left me with several headaches. In my exhaustion, I could barely comprehend the ramifications. As the Exhibition got into full swing, I sat down to write the report of my operation. Only then did I realise quite how much I would be forced to conceal.

I sent to Bazalgette, thanking him for his help, and mentioning in passing that his tosher had not appeared. I was taken aback to receive a frosty response. The fellow had been sent, all right, but he had never come back to work. His friends had all vanished into the aether with him. If I had not arrested the fellow, he could only assume that young Numpty had seen me from afar, panicked that their game had been rumbled, and taken his troop underground.

Bloody Numpty.

It was less than a year since Worm had saved my life, when the sewer fever took me. Besides Bazalgette's valiant plea for clemency, I was damned if I would get Worm's chums needlessly into hot water. After all, there had been no more thefts since my encounter with Smiler; they had got the message. Several men already languished in gaol for the crimes. Why bring down Wardle's wrath on a hapless gang of urchins who, for all they had led us a merry dance, had stolen nothing more than pennies, curios and sprockets?

Yet I now had it on Smiler's authority that Skelton was involved. I was shocked to discover that the two cases were intertwined, and I badly needed Wardle's help to make sense of it. But in my report for him, I determined to omit several details. I mentioned the second thief, the one who called out in backslang, but did not say that it was a child. Secondly, I did not record recognising Smiler, nor working out that he was the Tosher King, successor to his brother, Shuffler. For if I could unearth Numpty's tosher credentials, so could Wardle.

I did, however, want Wardle to realise that Skelton was somehow caught up in the business. So I stressed the importance of the stolen clock workings, declaring as resident expert that the extraction resembled the job on the Euston Square clock. Why it had been done I did not spell out, but I recalled Pat's amusement in describing how that first hydraulic spout was set off by a clockwork mechanism.

I also vowed to corner Worm as soon as possible.

Busy with the Exhibition, Wardle had brushed off my report. He seemed annoyed that I had used my initiative in his absence, and this latest news from Simpson was the last straw.

"What the hell is he on about?" he demanded. "Human bones? Are you telling me the thieves are mass murderers?"

I read over Simpson's letter in a panic. "He must be able to tell us more than that."

Wardle paced to the window, tight-lipped. "Could be grave-robbers."

"Resurrectionists," I said absently. "I hadn't thought of it like that. Leaving bodies at the scene of crime. Like the spout. I told you it was linked, sir."

He looked round sharply. "You told me nothing of the sort. What else do you know? What about this outing in the sewers?"

"I've been trying to find him, sir. He used to work for Bazalgette. But he's vanished. I've tried every lead I can. Except…" I paused as he looked at me expectantly, enjoying for once the sense that I was one step ahead of him. "If we could find Nellie…"

His brow darkened as I spoke the name, and I sensed it: he knew where she was. All this time I'd been seeking her, he'd known and kept it secret. "Leave the girl be."

"Sir, she could be the key–"

"He's sworn off her, I tell you. What does she matter?"

I held up Simpson's note. "We don't know what he's doing. He runs rings about us. He springs surprises all over town."

"You think he orchestrated the thefts?"

"Perhaps. Just to show that he could. So we'd take him seriously when he threatened the Prince. You can't shrug it off any more, sir."

"All right," he barked. "I should have nabbed him at the start. That won't help us now." He stared out into the courtyard. "Even if we could have pinned the spout on him, how would you shut him up? You couldn't transport him quick enough. Do you see it? He's no fly-by-night. What more had he to lose? I thought I'd leave him be. Let him run around like a wild chicken. I never expected this."

"We have to find him, sir. If anyone can tell us where he is, it's surely Nellie."

"I'll find her. Have words with her. Though, with money in her pocket, she might be anywhere now. How much Bertie's thrown at her, I don't know."

"Sir, trust me, I can–"

"I said no, Watchman." He sat down at his desk. He started to speak, hesitated, and began again. "I'm told you had a woman in here. You're a man of surprises, Watchman."

I stared at him, dumbfounded. "I brought a lady, sir, I confess it, who is an expert on literature and mythology and whom I am consulting about the threats."

"Get the academics in, that's right, seeing I made such a hash of it."

"It was she pointed out, after our Big Ben debacle, that the beast in his tortuous lair could not be St George's dragon, but must be the minotaur."

"Good at parlour games, is she?"

"The minotaur, sir, was a monster who required maidens

delivered fresh to sate his filthy appetites. Who ended up dead in the labyrinth on the end of a great hero's sword. He was the son of the king and the shame of the kingdom."

"And this woman knows all about it, does she?"

"Of course not," I said, though I feared Miss Villiers knew more than she let on.

"I won't have it. You're not a bloody inspector yet. You'll wait your turn to behave so recklessly." He pursed his lips. "Talk to everyone again. If he's been murdering left, right and centre, somebody will talk. Somebody has to talk before he carries out his threat."

"I've all but cracked it," said Miss Villiers. "I've matched cipher annotations in the margins of these books to two of the threats: '*blind in blood*' and '*Guy Fawkes was a genius*'. That's half the alphabet. I will keep guessing until I crack the rest. If I could compare a longer section of code to a piece in proper English, I'd have it. For instance..." She dabbed at some splashes on the table, then took from her bag a pristine edition of a periodical, screwing up her nose as she set it down gingerly. "This, I've borrowed from the stack."

"But it's a reading library, Miss Villiers, not a lending library."

"Shush and look at page twenty-four."

"The *Beehive*," I frowned as I flicked through it. "Edited by George Potter?"

"Of the trades unions, yes." She pointed to an article entitled "The Shameful Slums of the Bethnal Green". It was a polemical piece, warning of the consequences of leaving the East End to stew in its poverty – threatening even. "Very commendable, but hardly relevant."

She pointed out the author's name. "Berton Kelswick. Does it not sound familiar?" She sighed. "It's an anagram, you nincompoop. I've found several articles under that name in different papers. It has all the hallmarks. He likes Milton, he likes Dante, he likes floods and apocalypses. He's angry about socio-political injustice."

The Bethnal Green piece seemed somehow familiar. I frowned at the periodical. "But what is he going to do?"

"Overturn the System. Punish the Oppressor. The last shall be first and the first shall be last." She took a sip of tea. "That would my guess, at least."

I stared at her. "How? When?"

"I don't know." She looked at me. "He loves planning. He loves righteous tales and inflammatory literature. And he writes. I'll wager you this, your Mr Skelton will have written down his plan in as much detail as any engineer."

I shook my head. "A cunning criminal wouldn't."

"He's not a criminal. He's a visionary. He probably won't even have hidden it."

"Now you're being silly. Why would he not hide it?"

"Because he'll have written it in code." She leaned towards me. "Remember that notebook you saw at his mother's?"

When I went back to the Rose and Crown, it had gone.

"What you gawping at, copper?"

I turned to face a little tyke. Not one of Worm's, as far as I knew. "The tavern," I gasped. "The street..."

You could not simply say it had been demolished. Rather the whole slum of rookeries to which it had stood as portal had been annihilated, sacrificed to Progress. The bold new extension of the Euston Road was already swarming with traffic all the way down to the City. Between this new Farringdon Road and the gentrified centre of Clerkenwell, the engineers had left a chasm, as if they looked at the borough like surgeons and decided to excise the whole area round the cattle market in the hope of reducing infection. Cut and cover, only they had conveniently forgotten to cover.

"Oh yes." The little fellow nodded like an old man. "Gone the way of all flesh, eh? We must have this new train, you see. Pity, 'specially for them as lived here."

I turned to him earnestly. "Where have they gone, by God?"

"I moved in with relations, being on more or less good terms, luckily. Those that couldn't, some are drunk, some in prison, some gone to hell." He wiped his nose carelessly on his sleeve. "Looking for someone?"

The boy was amusing and I was happy to give him sixpence. But when I spoke Madame Skelton's name, he hesitated. For an instant I thought he was going to give the coin back. Instead, he drew his hat low over his eyes and pointed to the last building still standing beside the excavations, a great cowshed where the cattle market had stood.

"She might be in there," he murmured, preparing to scarper, "and then again, she might not."

Crossing the bridge that carried the Clerkenwell Road across the vast cutting, I looked down towards the grand new station. And to the other side, two tunnels from King's Cross emerged from the earth, the rails criss-crossing in dizzying confusion.

As I neared the shed. I spotted a lanky young man, in a long overcoat, watching the door. He was pretending to pass the time of day with a quiet smoke, but he made a point of monitoring all the comings and goings. Had Wardle set guard over the place? Or was it one of Berwick's associates? I thought of challenging him openly, asking what the game was. But instead I turned tail and hurried away, my mind buzzing.

Back over the bridge, I noticed one little shop that had survived the upheaval. I stepped into the clockmaker's, fully expecting another earful from the distasteful little man. The sight that greeted me was shocking. Ganz was wasted away.

He barely seemed to recognise me.

"It's a scandal," he muttered. "A scandal and no mistake. That's what it is. There's you and ten thousand busybodies, hobnobbing around town, yet you don't raise a finger to help honest artisans like myself. Highly trained, I am, qualified in the highest arts of clockmaking. Spent my best years studying, and paying the debts from my studies. What good has it done me? None, when the unscrupulous rip open my pieces and copy 'em. Shameless! They churn 'em out by the thousand in manufactories, assembled by wretched northerners for slave wages. I thought mine was an ancient trade and respected. I thought it would never die. I said as much to the Guild. I said, what future is there for us if we sit back while our kingdom is snatched from us?"

I looked at him. I too had thought the clockmaker's art safe from the wheels of industry. "What did they say," I asked, "at the Guild?"

He gave me a hollow look. "They laughed. Half of them are struggling like me."

"And the other half?"

"The other half own the factories."

The spy was still outside the cowshed. But, I asked myself, on whose behalf was he spying? I turned north and followed the cutting back up towards King's Cross, amazed to see the old roads gone, or hidden beneath viaducts. I passed the new Metropolitan station, in front of the Great Northern Terminus, and continued up York Way, where I chanced upon Hunt driving the chaise out of the yard gates, his master within. A feeling of unease gripped at my stomach. I should have talked to Coxhill sooner, but I felt our night on the town somehow gave him a power over me.

"Constable!" Coxhill bellowed. "Step up smartly. Looking

for me, are you?"

I told him I had business in Clerkenwell. He was headed for Mayfair, but as I climbed up he directed Hunt back the way I had come. I would only have a few moments. "Sir," I began, "do you know–"

"Have a snifter, old man," he said, brandishing a hip flask. "Don't tell me it's too early. I know you Scotch. Whisky in your porridge, isn't that right?"

"Mr Coxhill–"

"Can't tempt you?" He faced me with a charming smile, but I felt he was tensed for a shock. "You won't mind if I do."

"Not at all." I coughed. "Only tell me this. I am looking for a man named Skelton. Do you know him?"

The cab swerved, jolting us sideways. Up front Hunt cursed loudly.

"I do beg your pardon," said Coxhill pleasantly. He drew out his handkerchief and dabbed at a few spots of brandy splashed on to the seat.

There were drops on my trousers too and for a moment I feared he would mop them up as well. "Berwick Skelton," I repeated.

He frowned thoughtfully, but something outside stole his attention. "Hunt, stop the car. We're nearly at Ludgate Circus, God damn it. I am sorry, Sergeant."

"No matter. But, sir–"

"Yes, yes. Burton, you say? Name rings a bell. You'll want to descend this side, old man. Avoid the rotten traffic."

"I do not care to descend at all, sir," I said firmly, "until you answer me plainly. I'm sure you have met him."

"Oh yes?" He scratched at his neck. "Can't say where, for the life of me."

"At Mr Dickens' house, for instance."

His birdlike eyes darkened. "I can't put a face to the name.

But Dickens will invite any old johnny-come-lately. I say, you don't mean one of the servants, do you?"

The door of the chaise swung open and Hunt appeared. "Allow me to help you down," he said and fairly wrenched me out onto the pavement. Coxhill prattled away by way of taking leave, and the chaise sprayed my trousers with mud as they pulled away. Was Coxhill playing games? Perhaps Miss Kate had played up their clashes, for Skelton seemed not to have impinged upon his memory at all.

I came back at the cowshed from the Smithfield side, sneaking in while the youth was lighting up again. I found myself in a den of hopelessness. Half of Clerkenwell was squeezed in there. Bodies huddled together upon blankets and straw that smelt as if it had not been changed since the cattle left. Good God, I thought, what is this place? Have they herded the dispossessed out of sight while they build grand offices on the wrecks of their homes?

My whispered questions brought mistrustful glances. But for two farthings I was pointed towards a gloomy corner. There, to my amazement, stood the great brass bed from the Rose & Crown. Tucked up in clean linen, amidst a mountain of packing cases, lay Berwick's mother, exuding a beatific aura at odds with the disorder about her.

"Madame Skelton," I said, reining in my astonishment. "May I speak with you?"

She reached out and squeezed my fingers, the warmth of her hand surprising me. "The benign police," she said. "A pleasure. Will you have a cup of tea?"

This left me at a loss. Did the poor woman not understand where she was?

She saw my concern. "Our circumstances," she assured me, "are somewhat reduced. But look past the dishevelment and you will see we still have some graces. *Alors*, child! Tea for the gentleman." A nearby lad scurried off towards a steaming urn.

"Graces aplenty," I said. "But, Madame, what has brought you to this pass?"

"The housing they have promised is not ready. Soon, they tell me. What use is soon to me? Ah, your tea." She took a tin cup from a bedraggled child and handed it to me. "Now, tell me, young man. What news have you of my Berwick?"

My heart was ready to burst for her. The shame of it, for a life like hers to end here, in a cowshed. Despite her vivacious air, the pallor of her skin spoke of the shocks she had endured; the sharpness of her cheekbones of hunger. I managed a rueful smile. "I hoped to ask you the same. He wouldn't leave you in a place like this, would he?"

She inclined her head. "He is busy, I am sure of it."

"You don't think he has gone away? Like Fairfoul said?"

"Not at all. John Fairfoul has always been a naughty boy. Let me not speak of jealousy. But he has grown up in Berwick's shadow. I dare say, though he misses him, there is a part of him that is glad to see my boy gone. He tells me not to raise up my hopes. Let me tell you a secret." She leaned forward and spoke softly. "I saw him. He came, before they knocked down the inn. He came late at night to see me."

I nodded forlornly. I wished for her sake it were true, but I feared that Fairfoul was right, that she was deluded, summoning up ghosts of days gone past.

"Yes, he will be busy with these schemes of his. Writing. Studying. Mixing with the lofty upper sets. His father was the same, you know. When Monsieur Brunel and Monsieur Stephenson took him on, well, on grand engineering projects you have not time to waste. Everything must be drawn and redrawn, drafted and rechecked. Can you imagine? It was a struggle for his father, who only learnt his letters late in life.

Reading was a chore for him. He studied at the Red Lion College, you know. Prince Albert gave him a medal. I have it here somewhere."

Before I could assure her she need not look for it, she reached under the bed, with surprising agility, and heaved out a brass cornered wooden trunk. I hefted it up for her, wondering if it did not contain all the secrets I needed to unravel Skelton's plan. I glanced around, suddenly conscious of so many eyes fixed upon us. My arrival had doubtless been broadcast across the length and breadth of London.

"Let me see," she said. Taking a tiny key from her pendant, she unlocked the box, and drew out the faded sheet that used to hang above her bedside, by the engraving of the banquet in the tunnel. Red Lion Club, the Royal Seal and that florid signature – a signature I now recognised as Prince Albert's. Her stories were not all vain dreams, then.

She replaced it among her treasured heirlooms, and smiled, drawing out a little daguerreotype in a silver frame. She gazed at it fondly. "Happier days. Always a smile on his face. My boy."

"Is that Berwick?" I said, fascinated. I stared, trying to fix in my memory the contours of the face, the brash muttonchop whiskers, the cheeks pleasantly chubby, the bowler hat, the smile that hinted at secrets. "And his notebook? I would dearly love to read some of his writings."

She gestured vaguely. "Somewhere here."

There was no way to insist, however much Miss Villiers wanted that book. Looking about in frustration, I spotted the lanky youth loitering in the doorway. I had better make good my escape.

"I do worry for him so," she frowned. "His father died young, you know."

I could not endure more. I resolved in my heart to send to

Bazalgette. Perhaps, out of his esteem for Skelton, he could find a leafy suburb for this grand old dame. "I'll be back, Madame Skelton. I'll be back another day," I said. And yet, as she squeezed my hand and settled down for a sleep, I thought, with the panic of a thousand missed opportunities, I will never see you again.

Worm Cornered

As the summer drew to a close, I could see no way forward. Nellie had gone, Wardle said, to live on the continent. Perhaps our worries were at an end after all. The Exhibition was also drawing to a close, the public flocking to it through the balmy September afternoons.

I saw nothing of Miss Villiers through these weeks. Besides my disappointment at not recovering Berwick's book for her, I was chastened by Wardle's scolding. I was disgruntled, too, to think that our carefully planned operation had come to nothing in the end. It shamed me to think that my report was full of lies, even if it was for the best of motives, and I was loath to speak to Miss Villiers about it. Often, though, I stood uselessly on guard at the Greenhouse, wondering what she would make of the new-fangled world on show. I sent via the Worms, offering to show her round. I received no reply.

Mr Wetherell, late of Lloyds, called me to his club in Charles Street. He warned me not to come in uniform. So, in my Sunday best, I was led through an imposing hall and into a grand smoky drawing-room, where gentlemen reclined in plush leather armchairs. Mr Wetherell called for port and Stilton and informed me of fresh rumours afoot. A full investigation of claims made by the HECC and its subsidiaries was pending.

"Subsidiaries?" I said. "From what I saw there's barely enough money to keep their own yard from closing."

"That's just it, old chap. My banking friends are hinting at darker secrets."

"Bankruptcy?"

"Worse. You know, old Hudson used to pay dividends out of capital. It's a way to boost confidence, long before you sniff the real profits. Highly dubious."

"And George Hudson is Coxhill's idol," I concurred.

"Takes all sorts, I suppose," Mr Wetherell frowned pleasantly. "By the by, your man Coxhill is personally spending like billy-o, either to drum up some confidence, or just from a wastrel nature. But where's the cash from, old chap? Answer me that."

On quiet days, I took the chance to visit some newspaper offices, adding one or two from my own investigations to Miss Villiers' list from the stack. Most of the editors were impossible to find or else recalled nothing of Skelton. The *Red Republican* had been summarily closed down, the *Poor Man's Chronicle* was no more, and the *Beehive* had folded in ignominy, bankrupting the mighty Potter. In the *Punch* offices, I found Mark Lemon and Henry Mayhew quarrelling amiably over engravings for a new book about the criminal classes. The prints put me in mind of the characters I had encountered: Shuffler and Smiler, the legless singer in Green Park, Worm and the Professor.

They told me about Skelton's dispute with Dickens.

"Charles liked his articles," said Lemon, "but wouldn't publish."

"He attacked big business, you see," explained Mayhew, "specifically the railways. Fiery stuff. Only *Household Words* – Charles' paper back then – was specifically backed by railwaymen. Dickens trod a fine editorial line between his own

340 LAWLESS & *the* DEVIL *of* EUSTON SQUARE

inclinations and their requirements. I think it quite ended their friendship. Since that, Skelton's vanished from the face of the earth. Pity."

I nodded. "Did he not submit work to you?"

"He did." Lemon said.

"And why didn't we publish him?" said Mayhew.

Lemon grimaced. "He couldn't quite catch our whimsical tone."

At the *Euston Evening Bugle*, they directed me towards the ferret, Scholes. As I waited for him to finish speaking with his editor, I glanced idly through a recent copy of the paper. It hardly seemed Skelton's style. Indeed, the editorial had a report on the HECC so glowing it sounded as if Coxhill himself had written it.

Scholes surprised me, sneaking up silently. "Enjoying the rag, Sergeant?"

I pointed at the editorial. "Is Coxhill on your staff?"

He smiled an oily smile. "Mr Coxhill has made a certain contribution to our retirement fund."

"I care not how you fund your business. Did you publish pieces by a certain Berwick Skelton?"

"Name rings a bell." Scholes wrinkled his nose. "Ah, you mean Berton Kelswick, I presume? Yes. I liked one piece about the East End slums. The angle wasn't right, though."

"Do you remember him?"

"Bright chap. Writes well enough. I told him to read the paper more closely, study the house style."

"You mean compromise?"

"Tricky business, being a newsman. Navigating Skilly and Char-Bydis." He scratched unpleasantly at his nose. "Kelswick had facts, but that reformist stuff doesn't wash with us."

"Let me guess. You stole the facts and wrote it afresh."

"Officer, don't you know how this city works? Wheels within wheels."

"And I'll bet you paid him nothing for his trouble."

"Come now," he said, entwining his fingers together, "let's not be hostile. You and I should be working together."

Foolish as it was, it rankled me to think of Scholes mauling Skelton's fervent prose for his own low purposes. I turned tail and left.

It was the end of October and the last days of the Exhibition. Heading into the Yard one morning, who should I finally see crossing Whitehall up ahead of me but Worm? There had been next to no sign of him since I was in the hospital, and I was delighted to see my old amanuensis. I darted behind a cart crossing from Downing Street and caught the little fellow unawares as he was nearing the office door. I say little, but he had shot up since I saw him last. Thin as a rake and swaying in the breeze, it was hard to credit him as the wight who had summoned me so cheekily three years before.

"The early bird," I said, jumping into step with him. To my sorrow, he ducked away from my grasp and crouched down, fists cocked, ready to fight or flee. "Hold your horses, young fellow. Just me."

He stood up, holding his hand to his heart. "Bleeding heck, Watchman, you nearly gave me a turn."

"You're jumpy today, Worm. Got a guilty conscience?"

"Which of us ain't?" He presented me with an envelope. "I was looking for you and all."

I inspected the frail handwriting. "From whom?"

"Some admirer of yours." He nudged me in the ribs. "Mustn't dally. Business to attend to."

"Business," said I, clasping a hand on his shoulder, "can wait a few minutes, can't it? There's one or two matters I'd like your opinion on."

"Kind of you to think so highly of me, Captain Clocky, but

you know how it is." He wriggled free and set off with a somewhat hurried gait.

"Come, come, Worm." We fell into step again and I put my arm round him to shepherd him along. For all my height and weight, he was such a wiry young thing he might well throw me off. He would run quicker too, if need be. "Can you not spare a moment for an old friend? I'll shout you a lemon sherbet. Or is it ale you drink? How old are you now?"

He laughed as if the question was meaningless. "The river taverns is gone, old cove. Ain't nowhere to get a drink this time of day, nowhere that'll accept the likes of me." He looked me up and down. "Or you, for that matter."

We fetched up at an unsavoury pie stall that had survived by Horse Guards Parade. I ordered a steak and kidney tartlet and sat him firmly down. "Worm, which of your lot work down the sewers?"

He looked up from the pie. Rather than dive into it ravenously, he had cut it neatly in half with his pocket-knife. "Come on, Watchman. You look desperate underfed. Get some of this down you. Now, what's this?"

"There'll be no wool-pulling over these eyes, young man. You know, and I know, that friends of yours have worked down in the sewers."

He kept an amused silence.

For once, I had no patience for ironic sparring. "For God's sake, man, your boy Numpty is deep in it. I have protected him, in deference to you. If I should blow the whistle, Wardle will send out the troops in such force that your business will be presently crushed. Crushed forever. They will have his head on a platter and throw you in the Tower with as many of your chums as they can find. Into the river, why not, and be done with you. That's more the inspector's style."

Worm bit into his half of the pie. "My. Excuse me talking

while I'm eating, but you have given me something to chew on. I don't know, I'm sure. Eat up, Watchman. Good food getting cold."

With a sigh, I took a bite. "You know a deal more about all this then you let on."

"I'm a man about town, Watchman. I know my arse from my elbow. I wouldn't be no sort of gaffer if I didn't. But you're telling me young Numpty is mixed up in what exactly?"

I stared at him. Was he playing me along or genuinely in the dark? "The details I can't explain, but I have reason to believe Numpty is up to his ears in the thefts."

"The skeleton thefts?" he guffawed. The pie maker looked over in our direction, and the customers at the counter. Worm rubbed his brow remorsefully and looked at me with those eyes. "Look, Watchman. I don't know everything that goes on in this town. Besides us Worms in the north, you've got your Eels further east, your Roaring Boys out west, Filchers, Bravadoes and who knows what south of the river. We're one of hundreds. There's the 'Dilly boys, theatre lads, station luggers, sweeps and touts. All partitioned and segregated. It's a fine balance, I tell you. Continual negotiating it takes, else the whole deal falls down. And yet, despite the convoluted windings of it all, Watchman old cove, I think I can assure you that if Numpty was in on something as big as the thefts I would know about it."

There seemed sense in that. I nodded. "You know what toshers do?"

"An ancient trade, if a grimy one."

"That man we took to hospital, the night we met. He was a tosher."

Worm considered a moment. "He was that."

"You did know him after all?"

"Shuffler wasn't just anyone. He was a master tosher.

Everyone knew him."

"And Numpty worked for him?"

Worm raised an eyebrow as if pleasantly surprised how much I knew. "Shuffler was a good man, and there was many folks relied on him. Not my lot, but many folks. We was all saddened to see him done. Not to mention the end of his business."

"You know about Bazalgette and the sewer job?"

"Heard they had work. All the better for us. Don't want some new crowd emerging from holes in the ground and invading our streets."

I smiled. Worm's phlegmatic stance was not so harsh when you considered that "reputable" gas companies blew up each other's buildings in their struggle to dominate. "You'd rather see them working in the stinking tunnels?"

"It's hardly my fault."

"It's an illegal trade, you know."

"There's a lot of illegal trades around, and I don't see you putting a stop to the most of them. It's so much hot air, all this talk of reform. They say they're helping the poor. So they ban small boys from cleaning chimneys. What if you are one of them small boys? What if that's the livelihood you was brought up into, then they only go and make a law against it? Selling turds from your cellar may be unsavoury, I grant you, but where else do you turn for extra pennies when they ban that? Them toshers the same. Doomed to early death, I don't doubt, but they ain't going to live any longer if they can't eat." He had forgotten his pie and I stared at him, struck how the cheeky urchin, whose patter I had smiled at, had turned into a cynical youth. "How are we to get excited over reforms that ruin us? For this railway they're constructing underground, they invited us to vacate the Euston Road. A fairly robust invitation it was too, but they did promise us new homes some

place else. Out in the leafy suburbs, they said. Strange to say
it–"

"Don't tell me," I sighed. "The leafy suburbs haven't
materialised. Look, your place at Euston Square–"

He cut me off. "It's years since we was chucked out of that."

"Where are you now?"

"Little hole we found. No thanks to all the promises."

"Where, though?"

"That," he grinned, "would be telling."

"Don't you trust me?" I smiled.

"You?" He laughed. "No! Haven't you learned? Bad habit,
trusting anyone, even your own mother. Can't have a worm
trusting a copper!"

He was right. I was foolish to think we had a friendship. It
was a professional relationship, an exchange of services.

"Though you," he piped up, swallowing the last of the pie,
"I probably could trust."

Because I was his friend? No. As if I were a fool, incapable
of guile. Indeed I felt strangely guilty, trying to wheedle
information out of him. But I had to stop the thefts. I sighed.
"Indulge me for a moment, Worm. Picture, if you will, a little
tosher, who's learned his trade well, in the old style. Like a
magpie, can't resist a shiny thing. Let's say he now finds
himself working for the government. An ironical twist,
banned by parliament one day, paid by them the next. This
little tosher, going about his business surveying the sewers,
spots something shiny in a cellar. And he reasons that a
shiny thing abandoned in a cellar won't be missed. In fact,
in the scheme of things, it would be rude not to take it.
When he gets this shiny thing back to his friends, and his
guv'nor, they're curious as to its provenance. They
encourage him to expand his search a little, go up the cellar
stairs, try the door, why not, pick the lock if need be, because

careless folk leave other shiny things lying round their households it would be equally rude not to take. All his friends and acquaintances get involved, selecting the aptest spots and spicing up the daywork with little night jaunts. Thus is born a beautiful new scheme."

"Which ain't exactly stealing, if them things ain't wanted."

"And is not exactly legal, whether they are or no." I pursed my lips. "Do you find my little tale credible, by any chance?"

He looked at me equably. "I've heard queerer."

I laughed in exasperation. "Worm, we know the ruse."

"And you don't want Numpty going to college?" He raised his eyebrows. "Prison, that is to you, old cove."

"I need them warned off. Won't you spread the word for me?" I turned away and went up to pay. I thought for a moment he had vanished, but there he was, right behind me.

"Tell us, Watchman, do you know how Shuffler died?"

"He was bruised. Like he'd fallen."

"Fallen?" He looked at me expectantly.

"Yes, but long before the spout. Somebody put his body there."

"Oh, yes? Why did they do that then?" I looked at him squarely.

"You know, don't you? You know who did it."

He laughed. "If I did, do you think I'd say in a court of law?"

"Why not, if it's the truth?"

"Watchman, don't you know what a precarious thing the truth is round here?"

"Speak plainly for once, can't you?"

"There's influential people who don't want the truth known." He gave me a look. "The grounds for keeping mum are very persuasive."

"Are you telling me you're scared? You, Worm? I had you down for fearless."

He looked at me with something approaching respect. "Good talker you are, Watchman. You know, if I tell you, I'll be giving you my life."

"I see. And I already owe you mine."

He nodded reflectively. "Why should I help you?"

"Because I look out for you and yours. Because I need your help."

"And if one day I should require a service of you?"

I hesitated, as if on the banks of the Rubicon. Strange to say, but I had an indefensible respect for this boy. I could not believe he would demand something outwith the bounds of my duty. "Whatever you want, Worm. Tell me who killed Shuffler."

"I'll be straight with you, Watchman. If you tell a soul, I'll be dead before the week's out." He shook his head and blinked. "Who put his body there, I can't say. But who did for him, with nary a scruple, is clear as day. It was them hydrollah-rolical people. No wonder there's people on their trail. They killed Shuffler and hid the doing of it with the stupid accident. They killed him because he was an enterprising old cove. All sorts of operations on the go, licit and a little less than licit, I warrant you. One of those operations involved asking a few pounds from them in return for not blabbing, you know, keeping quiet about certain mishaps they'd had."

"Blackmail?"

"Just doing the rights, if you take my meaning, but doing them nice and civilised, like. Look where he ended up. Beaten and dead in a ditch. There now. I've said it, and I've trusted my life to you. Don't look so flabbergasted, Watchman, nor try telling me there's no such thing as doing the rights where you come from. I'm off. Ta for the pie."

• • •

Dear Sergeant,

You cannot imagine how greatly your visit was appreciated. In such a hovel as ours, tædium weighs heavy, despite one's attempts at jollity.

I fear, however, I was of little help to you. I have bethought me of a possible connection that may be of help to you. There was a priest at the chapel of St Thomas on Old Street who knew our family. Canon Symon was his name, though he may be long gone.

Fond regards,

Madame Pierrette Skelton

NARRATIVE OF RUTH VILLIERS

Hail and Farewell

I said it to Sergeant Lawless. A man who hobnobs with authors cannot help but dream of getting into print. It's only natural. You see that the authors behind these ever so popular stories are only flesh and blood. You think to yourself, why not my story? If your story is the story of changing the world, then of course people will sit up and take notice. I was sure of it, even then. Mr Skelton had looked at the world, evaluated it soberly, and decided that it must be changed. To this end, he constructed a plan. How far-reaching and elaborate this plan was, we had at that time no idea. But there was little doubt in my mind that he would have written it down, complete with historical arguments and philosophical underpinning, even if it was treasonous.

With my final examinations upon me and my studies in disarray, I only worked fitfully on the code through the summer months. Substituting the letters I had already deciphered, I wrote out the marginal annotations over and over, gradually chipping away at the rest of the letters until I had the whole thing. It was a disappointment. Despite the satisfaction of transforming it all into real words and phrases, there was nothing revelatory. His annotations were no more shocking than my own scribbles in the margins of John Stuart Mill and Thomas Hobbes. On reflection, why should there have been? He was educating himself in those years of reading; his own constructions must have come after. Somewhere he must have written his own *magnum opus* – most likely in code, if it was as incendiary as his politics.

I sent to Sergeant Lawless, asking him again to hunt out that book he had seen. He replied brusquely: he was doing his utmost. I wrote again, suggesting we could discuss it over a stroll round the Exhibition. I was puzzled – peeved, I suppose – to receive no reply. So I set aside the cryptographer antics and returned to my studies. A grim task, the set books, written by our lecturers, had none of the honesty, none of the vision of the great thinkers that had drawn me to the subject. Revising at the library checkout desk, I would find myself glancing instead through notes from my meetings with Campbell. Hence my discovery of Berton Kelswick and his agitatory articles.

It's hard to remember the indignation of those days, when even the *Times* consistently harangued the government over slum conditions. Still, Berwick's writing was too blistering. Moral outrage was ten-a-penny, even conventional, but to criticise Progress – railways, viaducts and the like – was too much. I admired his fervour, righteous anger that only highlighted the sterility of the academic texts I was being forced to swallow.

• • •

In late summer, Worm accosted me outside the Library. His dapper appearance, when acting as intermediary for my communication with Campbell, had always been remarkable. Today he looked like death. His boots were muddy, his hair matted and his eyes ringed by dark shadows.

When he saw me he leapt to his feet. "Miss, Miss, I'm dreadfully sorry to bother you." He paused, knitting his brows.

"Get on with it, young chap. I'm late for work, as always."

He looked terribly distracted. "For work? Ah, that's a pity."

"Out with it, Worm."

"Only I was wanting to beg a great favour." He looked up at me, eyes filled with such entreaty that I was fairly touched.

"Go on."

"It's my… my friend, the Professor. Had an accident. A most awful accident."

"Well, I'm no good to you," I said. "You need a doctor."

"We've took him, Miss. Straight to the Children's Hospital, we did. Only they won't let me in. So as I don't even know if… if the Professor's all right."

"Why don't you ask your friend, Sergeant Lawless?" I said, rather sharply.

His face fell. "I would, Miss, only… Begging your pardon, but is our conversation confidential, like?"

"If you so wish."

"Then, you see, me and mine have been in a spot of bother with the authorities of late. Nothing shameful, mind. Only I can't be consorting with policemen right now, not for my sake nor his. Which leaves me without my normal resources. And you being such a friendly and kind lady."

I gave him a sceptical look. But I recalled Campbell's dilemma over the thefts, his reluctance to get his friends into hot water, even if the Worms were involved. I called to the museum porter. "Withers, take a message in for me, would you? Tell them I'm sick."

"Sick, Miss?"

"Sick as a dog," I said and coughed deliberately. "You see? Off to hospital right now."

"Right you are, Miss."

I held out my arm for Worm to escort me. He squeezed my hand and off we went.

"Half-drowned, poor wight," said the ward sister. "Working down in those sewers. Shouldn't be allowed."

"It isn't allowed," I said. I would have words with Worm.

"Came in filthy as a pig," the nurse said, "coughing, puking and half-dead."

"And now?"

"Needs sleep. Doctor will be in later. My fear is the diseases: rat's pox and cholera."

There was nothing to be done. I agreed with Worm we would return that night. I would try and sneak him in on condition he scrubbed his face and hair and put on some clean clothes which I would bring for him. He nodded gratefully.

That evening I returned to Great Ormond Street earlier than I had promised, but Worm was already waiting. The doctor on duty looked at him askance and asked me to come in alone. The Professor was looking much worse, yellow in the face, greasy-haired and sweating. I demanded to know what had happened.

"Sewer fever."

"And what are you doing about it?"

"Nothing to be done. Sometimes they get through, sometimes not." He looked at me. "You're the mother, are you?"

"Certainly not. But the boy outside is a relation."

I was allowed to bring Worm in. When he saw the little

yellow face, he stood a moment in shock. I withdrew to a chair across the room, while he went up and stroked that tousled hair, emanating a silent dignity beyond his years. After long minutes, the Professor stirred and Worm knelt down by the bed. Something in their faces struck me with the force of a train.

"Worm," I said quietly. "Tell me. The Professor is not just one of the boys. You're brothers, aren't you?"

He seemed barely to hear me. He took the Professor's hand from under the covers and clutched it, whispering quiet words of comfort and urgent affection. "Forever hail and farewell," I heard him say. A few minutes later, he stood up and came towards me. "Miss Villiers, I must go now. I know not how to thank you."

"Don't think of it, young fellow. We will not give up without a fight."

He smiled and sadly made as if to leave.

"Tell me one thing, Worm, in case..." I frowned, unable to say it. "What is the Professor's real name? Given name?"

He lowered his eyes to the floor, then looked me decisively in the eye. "Molly," he said. "She's my sister."

I stared at the mop of ginger hair poking out of the covers and her little upturned nose and thought how foolish everything seemed and how awful.

That week I studied long hours. During the day I sat in the college, failing the papers set by my miserable lecturers. It seemed as well to study the evenings away at Molly's bedside rather than return to my dismal quarters and fret there alone. It gave me strength to see the fight the little girl put up against her fever. She would stir and twist and groan, as if trying to wrest some demon from her flesh.

The second evening, I spoke again to the doctor. There was nothing they could do, he said. She was too weak for leeching;

she was losing substance because they could not feed her; the longer the fever possessed her, the less chance there was. This filled me with an impotent rage.

The third evening, I stared unseeingly at my books, racking my brains. I had no money to be hiring doctors. If I asked the aunt, she would want to know everything. It would be no good dissembling that it was I who needed the assistance, as she would assume I was pregnant or worse and choose a doctor who would report back to her in full, Hippocratic oath or no. All I could hope for was to call in some favour. I wrote a furious letter to Campbell, demanding that he turn a blind eye to whatever the Worms might be entangled with, for now the Professor was entangled in a fight over meeting her Maker, and suggesting that, even if he could not come in person, he could use some influence to send along a competent doctor. Dickens, for instance, had raised money for the hospital. He must know doctors in high places.

Before the evening was out, a wonderful new doctor came. I do not remember Dr Howie's method, except that he gave us tasks, and thus inspired our confidence. We must get her system into flux again. Make her drink, and sweat, and micturate, in the hope that the passing of fluid through her slight frame might drag the fever out with it. We held hot compresses of rosemary to her temples. We loaded her bed with covers. Whenever she seemed half awake, we put water to her lips. The nurse raised eyebrows at all this. But the poor thing did seem to take some water, and I left that night, filled with hope.

The fifth evening, she had taken a turn for the worse. I cursed myself and all doctors. Uncertainly, we kept up his regimen of treatment. Just before I had to leave, fearing gravely that I might never see the little girl alive again, I was rewarded. Her lips opened to the water I was offering. A few moments later, she stirred.

"Molly?" I said and took her hand. "Molly, can you hear me? This is Ruth. Ruth Villiers. A friend of your brother, Worm."

The eyes opened heavily and she smiled a smile so weak it broke my heart. "I do know you, lady. I do. Is Worm here? I 'spect he's busy on business."

"Molly, take some water."

"Thank you. I think I just might." She drank long and full.

"Don't tire yourself now. You must rest to get better."

She looked at me reproachfully. "There is no need to fool me, Miss. I thought I was already long gone. Drownded. How he got me out I don't know. Miss Bilious?"

"Yes, Molly," I said, trying not to laugh.

"Can I request something of you?"

"Of course you can, my dear girl."

"When I die, bury me out in the green fields, far far from here. Not them burying grounds."

I stared at her in dismay.

She smiled and went on cheerily. "It's this filthy city has killed me. I ain't no foundling, I'm one of Mr Skelton's best boys, and I'd rather be buried out there, on one of them hillsides, looking at the cows and maybe a river and trees, if you'd be so kind."

With that, her eyes closed and her breathing settled. When finally I dragged myself away, her fragile little hand was still holding mine. I was late for my boarding house and had to tap on the poor chambermaid's window for half an hour for her to undo the bolts and let me in without incurring my landlady's wrath. I was also late for my exam the next day. Worst of all, I couldn't seem to care.

The sixth evening, there seemed no sign of improvement. I tried to study but couldn't keep my eyes open. I dreamt I saw a man by her bedside, a kindly thin man, whispering soothing words to her, who murmured as he passed me, "Bless you, lady," and silently left. When I awoke, I asked the nurse, but nobody had been in besides me.

The seventh evening, the yellow tinge was gone from her face. I feared at first that we had lost her. Dr Howie appeared, smiling approvingly. "What she will be needing, Miss Villiers, is affection and care and some feeding up."

I looked at him in consternation.

"Has she a home?"

"She is loath to speak of it. I can only imagine it is some windy slum."

"You wouldn't know of any philanthropic folk willing to take in such a wight while she's recovering from her close call?"

"She is recovering?"

"She is."

I smiled valiantly. "These philanthropic folk. Would they need to be kin?"

"The Children's Hospital is accustomed to unusual family set-ups. I'm sure a special dispensation can be arranged."

I smiled. The next evening I left clear word that, if anyone should ask for her, they should be directed to visit at my lodgings. Still poorly and shivering, the Professor moved in with me.

Sergeant Lawless' Narrative Resumed

Aquae Sulis

A visit to the Old Street church proved inconclusive. The priest whom I interrupted whilst working on his sermon was Canon Symon's replacement. He promised to dig out his predecessor's new address. When I said I must have it now, he left aside his sermon and our exchange became rather strained. However, I left with a scrap of paper bearing the name of a small parish on the outskirts of Bath.

Over and over I studied Mme Skelton's note, as if it could yield up secrets. The spindly writing seemed familiar. I supposed it no surprise that it should resemble Berwick's, if she had taught him his letters. Was it foolish to rush off in pursuit?

The Exhibition would close the following evening with a gathering of luminaries, but more important was the Garden Party at the Palace the day after. Although the Queen had not budged an inch out of mourning, her canny courtiers were gambling on a repeat of last year's triumph.

How different everything was now. The country seemed in crisis. Riots, famine and anger wherever you turned. The government obsessed by far-off squabbles, and not a drop of confidence in it at home. The party at the Palace must go smoothly, Wardle declared, so that the assembled aristocrats and chairmen and dignitaries would fan back across the country, spreading the word that all was hale at the heart of things. Perhaps such moments really do occur, when the hub of things must hold firm, so that the rest of us can carry on revolving happily around it.

Yet I couldn't help but see serendipity in the note's timing. Finding Nellie still seemed to me the crucial step forward. This friend of the family, far from the city, might be free from the endless webs of secrecy that had so far confounded me. The notion of winding up Skelton's story was intoxicating.

I wired St Jude's in Somerset on the Friday afternoon. After work, I took my time changing, to leave a decent interval for Wardle to catch his train, then headed for Paddington, beneath gathering storm clouds. By the time the

Bath train left the suburbs, the night was already black. My first trip out of London since my arrival, more than three years previously, and it seemed as if the whole countryside had been extinguished. I huddled in the corner of the third class carriage, going over and over Skelton's threats in my head more out of habit than in hope, and dozed fitfully. I had hoped to make sufficient queries that night to find Canon Symon in the early morning and be back by lunchtime. But I was soaked through by the time I stumbled into the station hotel. With no stomach for polite enquiries, I huddled by the fire and considered my options. Should I give up on my country excursion and head back first thing? The Greenhouse would be awash with constables all day. It was a risk, but as long as I was there by early afternoon, I shouldn't be missed.

I had counted on finding cheap transport for the day, but the cabbies turned out to be as expensive as their London counterparts and more impertinent. As I sat on the back of a milk cart, gripping the churns as we bumped up muddy country roads, the drizzle came on again and you could barely tell the day had come. The kindly fellow sat a while after setting me down at St Jude's, on a barren promontory overlooking the river.

"That be St Jude's," he said again, chewing on his tobacco.

"Thank you," I repeated, searching about me for signs of life. "And the rectory?"

The fellow frowned. "St Jude's, you said."

"That's right, my man. But it's the priest I need to speak to. Canon Symon."

"Symon." He nodded slowly, seemingly oblivious to the rain streaming over the brim of his hat. "Symon. That'll be the vicar man, will it? Him as lives on the edge of the village."

"The village?" I exclaimed.

He blinked. The rain lightened for a moment, then set in again. "The village as that we just passed through."

As I stomped back over the brow of another bleak hill, I was in a foul mood. The last roses of summer were nodding around the eaves of the cottage. The warm yellow light at the windows glowed through the haar, offering indescribable relief, and the notion took me that I must escape from the big city before it proved too much for me.

"Skelton?" Canon Symon mused in a tone that must have drawn sober reflection from his congregation. "Yes, indeed. I married them."

My eyes open wide. "Berwick and Nellie?"

"Who?" He sat back from the hearth, where my coat and boots were steaming in the heat. "Oh, now, is it the son you mean?"

Through the windows of his drawing room, I could see sunlight finally breaking through the clouds and onto the Avon Valley. I felt a swell of relief within me, not just the calm of the countryside, I think; rather the hills. I always found it strange in London that not one horizon was fringed with hills. "Yes, sir. Berwick Skelton."

"Ah, now, it was the parents I married. Unlucky couple. Perhaps it was a poor match. Astonishing, really, the people that the great city brings together. A fugitive of the French Revolution with an Irish labourer."

"Labourer? Was he not an engineer, with Brunel?"

"May have worked with Brunel. But shovelling rather than engineering."

He talked on as I looked about me, thinking of Madame Skelton's belief that her husband was a great inventor. Was she a fantasist pure and simple? I think not. She simply painted the world, and her loved ones' place in it, in glowing colours. And who can say that such belief did not instil Berwick with confidence?

"Invalided out, as I recall," Canon Symon continued. "More of a curse than a blessing, though. He took to drink and gambling." He told me his version of Mr Skelton's decline, in which he died not on a charitable visit to the Poor House, but rather living there, after his imprisonment for debt in the Clerkenwell House of Detention. It must have impressed upon Berwick that hard work was no security in itself. "The mother did well to keep the boy from going to the bad. A serious child, I recall, industrious and well-intentioned."

"And Nellie?"

"I christened a multitude of Ellens and Eleanors in those days. That's London, you see. All fashions and fads. Everything is so fast there, don't you find? Life down here has a little more solidity to it."

I burst out in irritation. "Do you know nothing of his engagement?"

"Why, Sergeant," he said, palms spread wide in apology, "I had no taste for the revolutionary fervour of the city. I left London in '49."

On the train back from Bath, one of those glorious autumn days swept away the remains of the storm and seized hold of the landscape. Yet I was late, and the sunlight dappling the gentle hillsides could not keep my mind from darker things.

I wondered exactly how much Worm knew. I thought of Shuffler, the Tosher King, returning home from a day under the ground. On a dark street corner he bumps into a small figure, a terrier of a man, a man he knows from certain dealings, as yet unresolved. The man barks for attention. Shuffler makes some amusing remark. The terrier is not amused; the blackmail Shuffler has attempted rises up in his gorge and he strikes out in blind anger. Shuffler, not so young as he once was, is thrown off balance. He stumbles. He falls. The man has chosen the place for its darkness, its silence. Shuffler falls down a flight of steps, tumbling over and over. The man follows vengefully, kicking him down to the darkest corner of hell, making sure he will not return. He checks that Shuffler has stopped breathing – though he does not check carefully enough – and he leaves.

I thought too of the foolish expense of this vain excursion. I could make no sense of it. Why had Madame Skelton sent me there, when Canon Symon knew far less than she? I studied the note again. The tone was formal: that was convincing. The message was gushing: that was convincing too. But the English was a little too correct. As the train pounded on, closer and closer to home, I studied the handwriting closely, the extravagant "*g*", the flourish of the "*f*" curling into the next letter. I should have known. It was disguised, but there was no doubt. It was written in the same hand as the threats.

FINALLY NELLIE

My cab drew up at the Yard, next to a fine carriage, at a quarter past four. I would change my boots and hurry to the Greenhouse. As I was going in, I felt a strange thrill down my spine. I thought I saw a movement within the shutters of the fine carriage – a face, perhaps, withdrawing hastily into the shadows. I stood, indecisive for a moment, until Darlington came out to greet me.

"There you are," he said. "Had the day off, have you? A couple of messages. Thought you'd want them before you, you know, went off." He gave a knowing wink and vanished inside.

In some confusion, I ripped open the first envelope. "Where are you? Wardle." I took a deep breath and opened the other, to see Miss Villiers' elegant writing. "About time I heard from you. See you at the stereoscope at 3pm." I put my fingers to my brow. It was as if she had only just received my invitation of months ago. Today, of all days. She would never forgive me.

"Sergeant Lawless?" called a voice from the fine carriage. Only the full lips speaking my name were visible.

I was struck with unease. Had one of Madame Lorraine's girls been engaged to abduct me from my duties? Was I being tricked again? Come, come, there would be hundreds of coppers at the Exhibition's closing, and I had learned nothing so devastating in these last days that I would need to be kept away.

The carriage door opened. I tucked away the envelopes and stepped up into the darkness.

"Where are you headed?" said the lady in clipped tones, as if measuring out each syllable. As my eyes grew accustomed to the dark, I studied the shapely young woman. Striking features she had too, framed by a tumble of russet hair. Whether the radiance of her face was rather a febrile pallor, I was not sure. "You are in a hurry, I fear."

"Kensington."

"We'd be most happy to give you a lift."

I glanced around sharply, afraid there was someone else in the shadows. But it was the royal plural she was using. "Thank you, ma'am. I am expected at the Exhibition."

"Business or pleasure?" she smiled.

"A little of each."

She nodded. Leaning out the window, she yelled in a different voice entirely, one that would not have been out of place at Chapel Street Market. "Oi, Foskins. Up the Exhibition, but don't shift your tired arse too quick. I want a word with the charpering homie."

The carriage pulled smoothly away along Whitehall.

"Please to excuse my yelling, officer," she said, returning to the refined tones she must have learnt from Groggins. "Only Foskins, being half deaf, is liable otherwise to get hisself horrible confused."

"Nellie," I whispered, fascinated. "Is it yourself?"

"You seem shocked, officer." She made a face. "Am I such a monster?"

I opened my mouth but could find no reply. I had the agreeable sensation that she was playing with me, but my overwhelming feeling was relief. "I am glad to meet you, Miss–"

"Call me Nellie," she laughed. "Everyone does."

"Nellie," I sighed. "It's such a long time I've been looking for you."

"Looking for me?" she said, a breathlessness in her voice. But perhaps she always spoke that way, as if what you had said had thrilled her. Or, even better, as if she expected the next thing you would say would thrill her. "What's so fascinating about me?"

I wanted to hear her version of the story, right from at the beginning. Of the glorious East End romance that Groggins had described. Of their ascent into society, as related by Kate Dickens. Of how Bertie shattered it all. I began at the end. "I'm afraid of what Berwick may do."

She clucked at me ironically. "What, start a revolution?"

"Is that what he wants?"

"That's what he always wanted, even before he met them reformist types. He was a bright one, you know, for all his generosity. I knew that the day I met him. We're a good match, I told him. We could go a long way on my looks and your brains. We could have a house in Brighton."

"But he didn't want that?"

"He wanted me to live underground with stinking sewer children. He talked about revolutions. I said, there ain't never going to be a revolution in England, Berwick. Already has been, Nell, says he. First I heard about it, says I. That's just it, Nell. They don't want you to know in case we wants another one to divvy up the riches fair and square. Don't be a fool, I says. Why do you want to go sharing it out? There's never enough to go round. We all want as big a share of the cake as we can get, and who can blame us? I told him, you want to stop worrying about the troubles of the world and think a little more of your nearest and dearest. Where's the fun in being rich if every Tom, Dick and Harry is as well?" She stared out the window, as if troubled by the memory.

I sat in silence. What she said was reasonable enough. Yet it tarnished her radiance.

"We went far enough. Me showing a leg and him meeting clever folk. Always his head in a book, that one. Said how his father made it out of the gutter that way, though he didn't talk so much about how he drank hisself back into it."

"You knew the family?"

"The old man was long gone when we started stepping out, and the old bag wouldn't have me, not distinguishing treading the boards from whoring. Maybe that's how things are in France. I've acted for this country's finest, I have. I've met the Prime Minister, and the Queen." She broke off, aware that she was entering dangerous ground. "That's the truth, not like the tall tales she'll tell you of her husband."

"Do you still see him?"

She glared at me, then her look softened. "Berwick, you mean? I thought you was talking about Bertie. Cheek of it, I thought, when it's your lot that have soured my name with him. Ruined it all." She eyed me darkly. "You think I'm a fool.

I can see you do. That a prince would never court a girl like me, even now that I talk proper."

"No, Nellie," I said, "I can see why a prince would court you."

"Think what you like," she shrugged. "You didn't see how he wooed me. He nearly wet hisself when we met after *The Frozen Deep*. Courted me proper, he did. Promised to take me off the stage and look after me. Private box at the Evans. At Roxy's country pile. Riding out down Cremorne Gardens." She cradled the words with such pleasure, I didn't have the heart to tell her that Wardle had arranged all these things for the Prince. "Have you seen the gardens lately? Flags of every nation draping the pavilion. Like the old jousting tournaments. We watched this Frenchman fly there, in his balloon, you know. A fearful crash he fell with. Killed on the spot. Marvellous." She lowered her head to give me a thrilling smile, then stuck out her bottom lip like a child. "Then you lot started interfering."

That was what Nellie wanted. She wanted exotic men falling to their death for her amusement; knights in shining armour jousting for her attentions, jousting to the death for her sport. "What did you expect? Did you think Bertie would marry you?"

She gave a wry smile. "I used to pester him, that he'd never marry a commoner like me. Only princesses for the likes of you, I'd say. Then I get this beautiful invite, summer of '58 it was. A carriage rolls up, takes me down the Thames, and he's had the tunnel fête shut for the afternoon so's we can ride the miniature railway. He gets all lovely and stroppy with it. 'I'm going to marry whom I damn well like,' he goes. We had a lark, back and forth on the train, the stalls all lit up, never mind they were shut. 'Bertie,' I says, 'build us a train under London, won't you, so's we can go wherever we like without anyone telling us no.' He smiles and says, 'You shall have your secret train, Nellie.' He takes out this gold watch and gives it me. I says, 'What, you trying to make an honest woman of me, young Bertie?' 'One day, Eleanor,' he says, 'we'll ride on your train beneath London and I'll make an honest woman of you.' And he kissed me."

Throughout our talk, I couldn't help but smile at the lapses in her vowels. It was as if she spoke two different languages, and it was always an effort to stick to the correct one. "And Berwick?"

"Fuss and drama I expected." She frowned. "All he did was stare. He stared at me and let me go."

That had clearly upset more than any amount of stomping and shouting.

"Hester told me I was a doxy haybag. That Bertie was out for improper favours. He'd never treat me like a lady. I was a fool for dropping Berwick who loved me. She was always sweet on him, though. Don't look at me like that, like you're on her side. What would you do? Your sweetheart gives you a watch that he's lifted and christened for you; then a prince of the realm only goes and buys you a gold one. You wear the gold one, don't you? Anyone would. That was what got Berwick all moony-eyed."

"You were engaged."

"S'pose I was. He asked and I'd said I might. Didn't owe him nothing. I helped him out of the gutter. Where is he now? Gone and got himself back into it like his old man after all, never mind his ideals and fancy talk." She pulled at a strand of her hair. "There was always going to be problems. He never liked my touring. I couldn't stand him wasting his time and his brains on committees of wastrels and moaners."

"Wasting time?"

"I want my husband caring about me, not Yorkshire weavers

and nigger slaves. Berwick could have got himself a position. He knew people. But he was too busy, overthrowing the System."

"Are you not afraid he's going about these plans now?"

She looked at me. "Nah. He'll have forgotten me by now."

"I don't believe anyone forgets you. I think he's plotting his revenge."

"Revenge? He's not the sort."

"And the spout at Euston?"

"Just playing up." She looked up at the window, sadness flashing over her face as a street light lit up her hair. "We're there, Sergeant."

"Where is he now, Nellie?"

"Berwick? Haven't seen him for a month of Sundays."

I gritted my teeth in frustration. She was slipping from my grasp as soon as I'd found her. Except it was she who had found me. "Then why did you come?"

She rubbed her stomach absently for a moment then smiled dazzlingly. "I'm glad it's you, you know, and not that inspector of yours. He's been a curse to me from the beginning."

I gestured at the carriage around us. "Is it him has given you all this?"

"I am far from destitute, officer," she said, drawing herself up and resorting to that false voice, "despite the indelicacies I have been put through."

I shook my head in desperation. "Why now, though, after hiding so long?"

"I wasn't hiding from you, young fellow." She reached out and touched my chin, a gentle gesture, but it could not win me over. She was sad, it was true, but somehow not sad enough for my liking. Her face was luminescent within the dark carriage, but there was a toughness in her voice. "He's asked me to leave."

"Who?"

"They're paying me off. Me! It's a liberty. Ain't it a liberty?"

"Wardle?" I looked away. "I didn't know."

"Take him a message, will you? Tell him it's not enough. There's complications needing dealt with and they'd better see me right. There's this finishing school in Switzerland I rather fancy the sound of. Need a good word from a gentleman, and a few pennies to boot. I'm sure there's an arrangement will suit us all." She smiled again, touched me on the shoulder, then turned away with a swish of her hair to tell me that our interview was at an end.

I stepped out in front of the Exhibition Hall, and watched her plush carriage sweep away. I wondered if she had understood Skelton at all. She wanted to be courted, wanted to be spoiled. Berwick fitted the bill well enough, until Bertie came along. When you turn a prince's head, how can you look the other way? And even now that it was all gone wrong, she was well enough looked after. Why should she care?

As I went into the Exhibition, Big Ben struck five. I tugged down my shirt sleeves and headed for the stereoscope.

The Greenhouse

"Ah, Sergeant," said Miss Villiers, as I entered the great forecourt, "I'm afraid I must be off."

"I'm terribly late, I know," I began, but something in her eyes stopped me. Her smile was uncertain and in her eyes was a strange look, as if she no longer felt she knew me.

"I understand," she said offhand. "A policeman's life, et cetera, et cetera."

She broke off as a young constable approached me. "Sir, here's a note one of them boys of yours brung. Oh, and watch yourself. Wardle's on the warpath."

I screwed up my eyes, trying to make sense of the spidery letters on the envelope.

"*Sir*, is it now?" Miss Villiers nodded. "My, we are important."

I smiled tightly. "Not so important I won't get a lecture."

"Best run along then," she sighed, "hadn't you, Sergeant?"

"I wanted to show you around."

"Don't concern yourself over much."

"I've spent so many days here," I sighed. "I wish you'd have come."

She pursed her lips. "You could have invited me."

"I did. Twice."

"Did you really?" She didn't believe me. "Don't worry, this is my third visit."

I looked at her in exasperation. Did she mean with other gentleman friends? I coughed and gestured across to the Exhibition Halls. "You've seen the stereoscope?"

"Two were given to me."

"The bi-cycle?"

"Yes."

"The piping? Revolutionary hydraulics," I said, aiming at a jocular reference to our first meeting.

She did not smile. "You still take an interest in that?"

"I take an interest in the case, yes."

"I imagined you'd wrapped it up."

"Not at all. Have you stopped working on the code?"

"I cracked it. I told you, I needed something more to transcribe."

"I assumed you were busy with your exams."

"I finished in July."

"Of course." I hung my head. "How did they go?"

She pointed ahead. "Have you seen the Difference Engine?

That machine could do some code-breaking for us."

I smiled. For a moment I felt the spark of the old warmth between us. Then she turned away, and I looked up to see Wardle charging towards us like a rampaging bull.

"Where the blazes have you been?"

"Sir?"

"I sent for you at nine this morning. Look at the state of you."

"I was out of town, sir," I said, acutely conscious of Miss Villiers observing my discomfort.

"Nice for you," Wardle barked.

"Pursuing the case, sir," I said through gritted teeth.

"Get my note at the Yard?"

"No, sir, I came directly," I lied.

"Bloody useless Worms," he snorted. He glanced back towards the room reserved for important personages. The sociable murmur of railway kings, piping princes and toilet lords bubbled away pleasantly. Originally there had been mooted a huge event, like Albert's address to the multitude, when Wardle so proudly stood guard. But there was no-one to fill his shoes. Bertie, even if we risked exposing him in public, could not be trusted. Victoria, still inconsolable, was not fit. Instead, things were winding up with this informal do for investors and exhibitors, with the party at the Palace the following day.

"Look," said Wardle. "Coxhill's bending my ear with some scare story Hunt's been feeding him. Run up to the gallery and keep him quiet, will you? I don't want any surprises."

He stepped back into the party. I turned to Miss Villiers, my head bowed.

She laid a hand on my forearm. "Don't worry. I have to be leaving anyway."

"I'm sorry," I began.

"Think nothing of it," she shook her head. She handed me a scrap of paper. "Come to visit the invalid, will you? And to fill me in, if you dare, on what's happened."

I nodded, too upset to think what she meant. I watched her walk away with that measured step of hers. Wrenching myself away, I hurried away towards the gallery staircase, checking in with the constables on duty as I went. There was a sense of holding one's breath, waiting for the exhibit to close so we could breathe a sigh of relief, exhausted but proud.

Pausing at the bottom of the stairs to gather my thoughts, I pocketed Miss Villiers' address and pulled out the spidery envelope the young constable had just handed me, a messy scrawl in a barely literate hand. I ripped it open:

SUMFINK
TO SHEW YOUS
SEE U AT OUR STAND
CLOZING TIME

The signature, in childish print, was Wm Hunt.

The doors were closing to the public at that moment. Hunt would already be there. What a day. Was Miss Villiers playing games with me? Or had she truly not received all those notes of mine? The Worms' delivery service might be less trustworthy than I had realised. Still, here was a chance to put some pressure on Hunt. Coxhill had the smooth talk, and I might never tie him down to any admission. But Hunt, with his foolish belligerence, was more volatile. If I hinted that I knew his dark secret, mightn't he crack? I could say that I knew about the fraud; that I suspected him of killing Shuffler. There would be no way to prove it after so long, not without witnesses. But Hunt was the sort of fool who might blurt out an indiscretion.

I headed up the stairs.

"Sergeant?" A small ferret-like man appeared behind me. "What a pleasure."

"Scholes," I groaned. "Are you not sufficiently occupied rubbishing the underground railways?"

He grinned as if I had complimented him. "We're changing track on that one, as it were. Great Western's done a deal with the Metropolitan, supplying locomotives in return for a share of the business. Access to the city from Paddington, you see."

"And how does that change your opinion?"

He laughed. "I've no opinions, my friend, beyond the GWR's holding in the *Bugle*."

I shook my head. "How do you live with yourselves?"

He chuckled again. "I could ask you lot the same question."

"I beg your pardon?"

He tapped the side of his nose and pointed towards the engineering section. He too was clutching a note in his hand. "Heading this way, are you? I have an urge to view a few last things."

"Hadn't you better be leaving?"

"I'm invited to the cocktails. Why, aren't you?"

I turned away.

Coxhill was heading towards us at full steam. "Cameron, old man."

"Speak of the proverbial," murmured Scholes. "I'm off."

Coxhill pushed impetuously past the newsman. "Glad to see you. What the devil is going on?"

I was disappointed. With Coxhill around, I would get nothing indiscreet from Hunt. "I could ask you the same question. I just got a note from Hunt–"

"Me too. Damned strange. Fellow can hardly write a line."

Scholes was still skulking nearby, so I guided Coxhill towards the gallery. "Hunt wrote you a note as well?"

"Delivered to the door," he said, looking anxiously about him. "Not like him. Straight as an arrow, all things being equal."

"Has he been behaving oddly?"

"We've all been under a spot of pressure."

"Anything particular, Mr Coxhill?"

He put his fingers to the bridge of his nose as if in pain. "What an effort it's been," he sighed. "A success, of course. A tremendous success. But these problems with the Metropolitan. Bloody Fleet sewer bursting in. Dreadful business. We need a boost. Is young Bertie back yet? I'm so hoping to hold a little bash for his birthday. Keep in the royal good books, what."

"I see," I nodded. I had never seen him so out of sorts. Mr Wetherell must have it right, Coxhill's schemes were coming unravelled and he was just opening his eyes in time to see it.

He fretted silently as we rounded the stuffed animal exhibits. November already, I thought, the first today. Golden lamplight was beginning to spill across the gallery. The cupolas normally needed only natural light, but with the drawing in of autumn they had taken to lighting the chandeliers for late viewing. Down below us, the murmur of the party spilled out into the great hall. I spotted Wardle looking up at me, hands thrust in coat pockets. I gave him a workmanlike nod.

"No sign of the blighter?" Coxhill harrumphed. "I couldn't see the chaise outside."

His nerves were beginning to affect me. I glanced rapidly across the HECC display case. Steel pipes and intricate diagrams, in front of a great map of London.

"Everything looks in order," I assured him.

"I'm not sure," said Coxhill, biting at his nails. "Some of the fixtures are missing."

As the lamplight grew stronger, we heard a groan behind us.

"Jesus God," said Scholes in a rasping whisper.

Poor Coxhill saw it before me. He shrieked like a distraught girl. All conversation below was silenced for a moment. Then there was hubbub, footsteps on the stairs, shouts of anger and distress.

I ran to the case where Scholes stood struck dumb. There, instead of the stuffed Alaskan bears, stood two figures in a horrible parody of action. In place of the zoological label was a scrawled replacement: "COMMERCE CONQUERS IDLENESS". One figure crouched, with hands aloft, as if in his death throes, but his face turned towards us. I recognised Smiler from our sewer encounter.

Above him loomed another man, holding a rifle, his face so dreadfully burnt that the features were unrecognisable. His clothes were familiar, his stature lean, but it was the hat perched on his head that I recognised from the little daguerreotype that Madame Skelton had so proudly shown me. There could be no doubt in my mind about that bowler hat. It was Berwick Skelton.

THE VENGEANCE

"Are you sure it's Skelton?" said Wardle impatiently. We were in the hospital morgue, waiting on Simpson's arrival.

"I never met him, sir. I can't be quite certain." I looked at the body, remembering that night at Euston three years previously. Was this really the man I had been seeking for so long? The body seemed so small: somehow less than human. It struck me that in my heart of hearts I had wanted his plot to come to fruition, whatever it was. That somehow I had more faith in him than in Wardle, and I was saddened to see the renegade hero laid low. "But I recognise these clothes, from a photo his mother showed me." I shook myself, and set about checking the pockets, trying to master the strange sense of wonder I felt. I suppose part of me was hankering for answers, hoping that the *magnum opus* Miss Villiers had imagined might be hidden about his person. There was only a scrap of paper.

"His mother?" said Wardle. "Enough of your Celtic intuitions. He could be any old fool in a bowler hat. Bring the mother in to identify him."

"I can try, sir." If I told her, she might give me that old leather-bound book. Yet I couldn't bear the thought of Wardle haranguing her. "But her home's been knocked down. Who knows where she's gone? Even if I find her, she's old and frail. She wouldn't know her own reflection." I narrowed my eyes. "How about Nellie?"

He ignored me. "The stepbrother, then."

"You couldn't take his word for it."

Wardle stared at the burnt face. It was as if Skelton had held such a spell over us that we had barely been able to think about him, until this. Now he lay there dead in front of us, as if he had fallen from another realm, a magical place. The spell was broken, and we couldn't look away.

"I want no doubts," Wardle growled to himself. "I'm tired of these games."

"This other man, it was him in the sewer. He's the brother of the old corpse from the spout."

"How do you know this?"

"The Reform League. They also told me he worked with Skelton. I'd even met him, in a Clerkenwell public house."

"When you were sniffing around?"

"That's right." I thought of Madame Skelton, of Numpty, of

Shuffler, and all the convolutions of those last months. I would have to choose my words carefully. I had promised Worm I would tell nobody what he had said of Shuffler and Hunt.

Wardle nodded. "Skelton's accomplice, eh?"

"The first old tramp, maybe he tried to get something out of them. A few pennies' compensation. But these two will have wanted more."

"Revenge."

"Smiler for his brother. Skelton for… I don't know. For everything." I turned over the scrap of paper in my hand. There was a series of symbols in Skelton's inimitable code. Yes, it was him, all right.

"What is it?" said Wardle.

"Just scribbles," I shrugged and held it up for him to see.

He looked at me closely for a moment, then nodded, as if content I was keeping nothing from him.

"Sir, you've known where Nellie was all along, haven't you?"

"I have kept things from you, Watchman." He turned back to the bodies. "But I promise you, only things as it seemed dangerous to tell."

"I don't doubt you, sir. But if you want a proper identification, it has to be her."

"She's gone."

"She hasn't. That's why I was late. She says to tell you, it's not enough. She wants to go to a Swiss finishing school."

"Does she now? I'll send her to a Swiss bloody bedlam."

An assistant bustled in. Dr Simpson would be along in a moment, and he had to prepare the bodies for examination, which entailed stripping them. We withdrew to the outer room.

"Is there no end to it, Watchman?" he sighed. "I need some rest before tomorrow's party. We'll take no chances. Get through tomorrow safe and sound and that'll be an end to it."

"Yes, sir." I was just tired, but he seemed to take this as a reproach.

"Look, Watchman. I own I made a mess of it. It's not the first mess of my career. I only hope to God it's the last. It's only in those novels of yours you'll find policemen above making mistakes." He closed his eyes for a moment, pressing his fingers to his brow. "Still, there's only a few dead from it. We can be proud of ourselves for that at least. Tomorrow, I'll go to the Palace. You speak to Coxhill. He's played a canny game. Bang some sense out of him. I'll wager that Skelton took it into his head to derail Coxhill's operation. He and his friend must have chosen tonight as the perfect moment to humiliate him. They've cooked up some little stunt, Hunt's got wind of it, and lost his rag."

"Can't we put out an alert to catch Hunt?"

He curled up the edge of his mouth. "A man like that, he won't get himself caught. Even an animal like him knows when he's gone too far. We'll send word to the ports, but he'll lie low a long time. And to be frank, when rough justice has been served, why trouble yourself?"

I looked at Wardle and saw in his eyes something I would never have expected, the light of a fanatic. The world had come to revolve around his precious royal family. Perhaps it was from motives of personal gain, but I think more from blind prejudice, or perhaps just habit and fatigue, from all those years in their service. They were all that mattered and, in his eyes, the two people lying dead in the next room had no rights at all.

He picked up the bowler hat. "That display he left, it's a message, see. A warning. You know the Cockney slang for hat? Titfer. A tit-for-tat. To tell us it's due revenge, see, for Skelton messing them around. You have to understand the criminal mind, Watchman."

"Gentlemen." Simpson rolled in, looking pleased with himself. "An unexpected pleasure. Sergeant, I had a further inkling on those bones of yours. I date them to 1846."

Wardle glared at him. "How so sure of a sudden? Insufficient evidence, you said."

Simpson handed me a newspaper clipping from his pocket. "If you'll excuse me," he said and proceeded into the inner room.

The piece spoke of bones found along the railway diggings. In the days before they flushed the sewers, the Fleet ditch was full of fetid gas. Explosions were commonplace. A whole Poor House had gone up in smoke in 1846. I blinked at the date: that must have been when Berwick's father died. He made himself ill building a tunnel that was barely used, fell into ignominy and debt, and died in a filthy explosion; then they go and dig him up for another stinking tunnel. Just like laying Shuffler's body at the door of the HECC, Berwick left bones in the houses Smiler and Co. were robbing as an accusation.

We heard a cry of surprise from the next room. We hurried in.

Simpson looked up from the bodies, surprised at our intrusion. "Allow me to explain my surprise, gentlemen. This fellow…" He pointed at Smiler, now doubly disturbing, being still in that crouching pose. "…died some days ago. Rather like that old tramp, you remember. Bruising and head injuries."

"And the other?" barked Wardle. "Burnt to death?"

"The burning is simply superficial. He was shot. Shot at close range with a rifle. Here. And here." He pointed to the head and the groin, both bloody messes.

"A rifle," I nodded. I had to fight back a wave of nausea. "How did they come to be standing up?"

"Your killer is an odd one and no mistake. This one, see, is embalmed. Rushed job, I'd say, and amateurish with it. The second – I cannot put it delicately – has metal tubes inserted to keep him upright."

Wardle led me without a word into the public house at the corner of Ossulston Street. He ordered two whiskies and two pints and did not speak again until he had finished the short. "If the press ask, we hint it's underworld killings. The skeleton thefts wrapped up for good. You send harsh words to Bazalgette. We can't have more thieving. If the Prince Consort hadn't been so set on that sewer scheme, I'd have him bloody well shut down." He shook his head and looked around him.

"What will you do now, sir?"

"Off to Yorkshire for Christmas," he said. "Not coming back. Go on and dig up secrets, if you want to make sense of it all. I'll be leaving a recommendation for you, son. You'll be an inspector yourself one day."

We fell silent, nursing our drinks. I hid my disappointment. When he bade me good night, I sat there watching him go, holding down my bile, until I headed home in silence.

THE SEVENTH & FINAL PERIOD
[EARLY 1862]

EUSTON DAILY BUGLE
[INCORPORATING THE CLERKENWELL HORN]

2nd November, 1862

DIABOLICAL MURDER IN THE GREENHOUSE

In a sour finale to the Kensington Exhibition, two bodies were found dead yesterday on the closing night of the seven-month extravaganza. Scotland Yard hinted that the killings mark a final end to the affair which so thrilled Society last season, the Skeleton Thefts. Inspector Wardle was reticent. "We are still tying up loose ends, but we are confident there will be no further trouble." It seems that the investigation put pressure on the criminal elements. Rival underground leaders met in a fearful showdown over territorial issues, choosing the Greenhouse in a daredevil display of criminal bravura.

These events will not affect the social calendar's most glamorous event, the Palace announced this morning. This afternoon's garden party will provide a glittering finale to the summer, as dignitaries gather to celebrate the Exhibition's close. The Queen disdains to cast off mourning, but rumours are afoot that the Prince of Wales may be back from the continent to preside with his famed hospitality.

The Prince's return will give the Queen something to smile about, as his engagement to Princess Alexandra of Denmark is now confirmed as something more than court gossip. The wedding will take place in Westminster Abbey as early as March of next year. The Queen must be relieved at this long hoped-for (long despaired-of) sign of the heir to the throne's maturation. Nonetheless, the Prince's cronies were secretive about his birthday plans. We can expect a few last bachelor indiscretions before his coming-of-age.

KNOW-HOW

The trouble-beset Metropolitan Railway is to be rescued by the mighty Great Western. The late Charles Pearson passed away a disappointed man, his project still in the balance with its smokeless engines a costly failure. The Board of Safety's objections proved well-founded when the Fleet Sewer burst into the works between Farringdon and King's Cross. Mr Gladstone and those who braved the trial run in May cannot have known the risk they were running. Imagine the scandal, at the underground banquet planned to celebrate the opening of the line, the great and good might have been deluged with filth as they tucked into the pheasant.

Thankfully, the Great Western has stepped into the breach, offering matchless know-how, in addition to engines with chambers that hold smoke and steam for release at the ends of the run. Promised an opening on 1st May, 1st September, 1st October and 1st November, the public have lost patience with the Metropolitan. Under the new management, we can breathe a sigh of relief and expect a prompt opening in the New Year. A passageway already links the GWR's terminal to the Underground platform, at last an end to the madness of the trip from Paddington to the City taking longer than that to Bristol.

Excerpt from THE KIND-HEARTED REVOLUTIONARY *by BS*
(Deciphered by RVL)

"What need for change?" say the powerful few. "Everyone is satisfied with the status quo; at least, anyone with any sense."

Such insular perspective leaves no option. Too long have we fought amongst ourselves, passivists and activists, arguing moral force against physical. Too many, indeed, have ceased from mental fight, naively trusting that our masters share our goals of equality and justice. Yet what we have builded here? Not Jerusalem, but hell.

For my single self, too far steeped in blood already, my sword shall not sleep in my hand. When a nation is so cast down that it does not even know it is oppressed, violent remedies must be tried. Such a pass have we reached. Fawkes used fire; so shall we. Rama fulfilled his destiny; so shall we. Samson cast down the pillars of the Temple; so shall we.

For the death and destruction, I shall be sorry; but I do not repent of it. Even though I should fail, I dare to hope that the legend of my revolt may live on. (I imagine the Russian serfs overthrowing their Tsar, the Balkans boiling over, even the Irish regaining their own land.) Should I succeed in starting the quake, the floodgates will open for the people to walk into the Palace of Westminster and seize hold of their own country for the first time and forever.

SPEAKING ILL OF THE DEAD

I rose early, despite macabre dreams, and headed for Farringdon beneath skies that would not brighten all day. I would not ask Madame Skelton to identify the body, but it was my duty to let her know that her son's long struggle was over.

The cowshed had gone. The great space it had covered was already pockmarked with new foundations.

A newspaperman on the corner saw me standing, mouth agape, in the rain. "Lost somefink?"

"I was looking for somebody."

"In the old shed? All gone. Last week."

"Where to?"

"God knows. Some other purgatory."

I wrote her a brief note, saying I had grave and urgent news, and gave it to the man, with a half-crown. I walked away in vexation. I had no way to find Fairfoul, and Nellie I had promised to leave to Wardle. I might find Hester in the musical halls, but first I would question Coxhill. If he maintained the fiction that he hardly remembered Skelton, he wouldn't do for identification, but an interview might be revealing. He had been a wreck after we found the bodies, sweating abundantly and whimpering nonsense. The one thing he had managed to confirm was that the gun in Skelton's hand belonged to Hunt, his rifle from the Crimean dragoons.

Coxhill was only too ready to confess. The HECC yard was quiet as the grave, with no sign of activity and Hunt's little hut apparently burnt to the ground. Whether Pat was late or had been sacked, I didn't ask. I found Coxhill in his office, already murmuring away to himself in a fever of penitence. He was still in the same clothes as the night before. He hadn't slept, I reckoned, or washed.

"Dear God, dear God," he muttered, gazing down on his kingdom, while sickly smoke from his pipe filled the room. I coughed to catch his attention. He stared at me as if I were a ghost, and for one moment I thought he would fall against the window.

"Dear God, Sergeant. I thought for a moment... I don't know what I thought." He slumped against the wall, giving an unconvincing chuckle. "Standing there silhouetted with your blasted policeman's hat."

I set him upright at his desk, where he curled up, holding his pipe to his forehead. Poor man, I had little fondness for him, but I couldn't wish that anyone be turned to such a gibbering fool.

"You cannot imagine the shock, Sergeant. And the guilt. I'm tormented."

"Guilt?"

"I know! I shouldn't feel guilt, should I? It's not my fault, not legally, not in any sense. But one still feels this moral culpability."

"For what Hunt has done?" I sat down across from him. "Why should you feel responsible?"

"You know, Cameron... May I call you Cameron?" He continued before I could put him right. "I had a high opinion of Hunt. A man of simple principles, but he's served me deuced well." He spoke on feverishly, explaining how Hunt had come into his service. A fusilier in the Crimea, Hunt was a wild soldier. Certain black rumours circulated about his untoward behaviour in battle. I can only assume that he was downright barbarous, for the army are not in the habit of criticising their own for killing the enemy.

Around the time of his court-martial, Coxhill was looking for a valet-butler. Due to certain problems with his new company's solvency, he rather fancied a tough right-hand man.

"Look, Cameron, I don't mind telling you, now that Hunty's vanished. Out in the desert, he got to know some mad Turks, known as Gilzais. They taught him the methods of the Hashisheen, a lunatic band who nerve themselves to fight by drinking hashish, which the Indians call bhang. Hunt learned how to concoct it so as to fuel himself to any lengths of passion." He drew deeply on his pipe.

"The Assassins?" I said sceptically. It sounded like a story from the penny press.

"That's right, old man. Hunty boy used the stuff to great distinction in the storming of Sebastopol, but he overstepped the mark and was disgraced. His nickname was the Dentist, he so loved to extract the source of his enemies' pain, that is, their lives." He laughed, an ugly heaving guffaw, then sat back, suddenly pensive. "I heard he was in a pickle from a mutual friend, Eton and the Guards, you know, and I pulled a few strings for an unconditional discharge. I suppose he regarded me as something of a saviour. He'd stop at nothing for me. Protected me to the hilt."

"In the same style as his military service?"

Coxhill pulled at his beard. "I am responsible, morally. I do see that. But the fellow must have said something quite out of order to drive Hunty to such extremes."

"Which fellow?"

"Last night," he said discomfited. "The smiling one."

The image of the corpses in the display case flashed before my eyes. "Did you know him?"

"Not as such." He started filling his pipe again. "He'd been bothering us, saying he was going to squeal on us to the authorities."

"Squeal about what exactly?"

"Hmm? Oh, I'm not entirely clear. Hunt was dealing with it, you see, as normal." He relit his pipe, then licked his lips nervously. "Hunty's been under a deal of pressure. We all have, with the Exhibition and the uncertain market, you know. We're launching new shares, any day now. Perhaps you–"

I cut him off. "Hunt dealt with such complaints?"

"I deal with professionals. Hunty takes care of the rest. This fellow was a real joker, he talked about some injury done to his brother. Claimed we'd given him his dashed limp, and then he'd died. Such theatricality! He'd been limping from birth."

The stories no longer added up. "Enough half-truths. You met Smiler. You know about Shuffler. And you know Berwick Skelton better than you know me."

"Knew," he retorted, fixing me with those birdlike eyes. "You're right, Cameron, of course. You must excuse me for pretending not to know Skelton. Your fellow, Waddle, told me categorically not to breathe a word about it. Sorry, old man. Thought you'd been sent to test me! Must accustom ourselves to the security game, eh, if we're to gad about with a future king."

I found his over-familiarity galling. "So, before he was found dead, Shuffler asked you for compensation, is that right?"

"It was nothing to do with us. Why did they go upsetting poor Hunty by putting the bally corpse there? Then his brother turns up making unpleasant insinuations."

I lowered my eyes. "And you asked Hunt to shut him up?"

"No, no." He drew on his pipe and smiled. "Not in so many words. I asked him to have a word in his ear. Deal with it as he saw fit."

I turned away in disgust. A word in his ear, and there he lies in the morgue.

"I am morally at fault. I own that. My father... Have I told you about my father? He was unflappable in a tight spot. Revelled in 'em. Hunty, though, got himself into such a state. The Crimea, you know. It's no wonder he's finally cracked." He sniffed valiantly. "One has to be firm, Cameron. At times you feel the whole world is out is to take a piece of you."

"Firm?" I gasped. "It seems Hunt has been a little too firm."

He stood up, nodding seriously. "It's a terrible show he put on. Must have quite blown his top. No other way to explain it. As if he meant it as a warning. Do you see? Protecting the company even as he ran."

"You're sure he's gone? Where to?"

"The colonies, I'd imagine. Australia, or the Argentine." He paused for a moment. "I recall reading him a call for mercenaries from the *Times*. Some Frenchman's setting up a kingdom out there. He was tickled pink at the thought. Thinks a lot of the French, since the Crimea. That's it, I'll bet. He'll be on some steamer set fair for the Southern Seas. Shame, really. If he'd gone to Australia, he could have watched the cricket." Coxhill gazed out at the dismal sky above his deserted yard and I almost thought he was going to cry. As I rose to leave, he recovered himself suddenly. "By the way, you don't know if the Prince of Wales is back, do you? If I could only get a message through, he'd let me know himself. Only I'm planning this rather exciting birthday do with a few chums." He tapped the side of his nose.

It might well be Wardle blocking the channels of communication. Coxhill had never proved the restraining influence he had hoped for, and Bertie must have been warned off him. "I can't help you."

He fixed me with those birdlike eyes, then reached suddenly for my hand, shaking it with a damp two-handed grasp. "I like you, Cameron. Liked you from the first. Now that the thing is over, one is inclined to reflect. What a senseless waste." He shook his head. "Is it worth it, the casualties that fall by the wayside in the jostle for profit and preference? The great struggle for life. Who knows? Damn it, I don't."

I returned his grasp, managing a half-hearted smile before I disengaged myself, murmured my farewell and made my escape in contrition and disgust.

GARDEN PARTY

It was difficult to credit the possibility of revolution in the Palace gardens, as the quadrilles got under way, punctuated by cucumber sandwiches and cake. The gowns were flowing, and the champagne. I wondered if the Queen was peeking out of an upper window at this extravagance. Would she find it immoral? Would she envy it? Footmen flitted to and fro, lighting torches to spread warm pools of light in the gathering gloom of the great lawn. I spotted Wardle, enveloped by bewhiskered dinner jackets.

"Caught those bally thieves, old chap?"

"We have."

"I heard you'd thrown 'em in the river."

Wardle grunted. "Don't go giving me ideas, sir."

"The wife didn't sleep for weeks. Longing to be robbed."

"Then my apologies to her, sir, but I couldn't retire without finishing the job."

"Jolly good work."

That's right, I thought, jolly good work, pinning the crimes on a few unfortunate old marketeers. If I told him that Numpty and Co. were involved, he would string them up without a thought. At least I had kept my word to Worm and told no one it was he who enlightened me as to how Shuffler died. As far as Wardle was concerned, Hunt had solved all our problems at a single stroke.

As we were checking the invitations of the early birds, Wardle had seemed filled with an unusual excitement. I thought at first he was nervous after the fiasco with the Parliament clock. Then I realised that this was his swansong. In his long service of the royals, he had encountered countless luminaries. I could not doubt their respect, as they bade him good luck for the future, Palmerston and Gladstone, Trollope and Thackeray.

It struck me, as I looked on, that Wardle had succeeded less through brilliance than a mix of perseverance, self-confidence and good fortune. Though I was beginning to believe in my investigatory abilities, I felt cursed by doubts. They say that in some countries the police are popular heroes, the guardians of the people. Here in England, with constables peppered around the Palace walls, we seemed instead the strong arm of privilege.

"Cameron. Good to see you." Coxhill clapped me on the shoulder, looking around nervously. "Must have a word with your inspector. Have a cigar, won't you?"

He gave me a puny cigarillo and moved off to buttonhole Wardle, doubtless begging to know if Bertie was back. Wardle turned to him tight-lipped, as if obliged to suffer his attentions.

As the ladies began drawing their menfolk away, and the single men became rowdier in their cups, I wandered away from the lights towards an ornamental pond. Toying with the cigarillo, I leaned against a stone palisade that rose from the paved walkway up to a pretty stone bridge. In the pale pink light of evening, I saw in the water what I took to be my own reflection, only my reflection was at the wrong angle, and it seemed to be wearing a hat.

At a cough from the shadows above me, I turned abruptly. On the parapet of the bridge sat a figure, legs dangling jauntily, like Humpty Dumpty ready to fall. Except this Humpty Dumpty was not so round, as far as I could make out in the dim light. He seemed to have a weary smile upon his face, framed by cheery muttonchops.

"Want that thing lit, old chap?"

I looked at the cigarillo. "Why not?" I said. "You're only young once."

"If ever. Toss it up, then."

A match flared and the cigarillo seemed to float down to me, surprisingly easy to catch, except it had turned into a grand Havana cigar. I laughed. "Thank you."

"Welcome, old man. Might as well live a little, eh?" He lit a cigar of his own. "I understand you are the young sergeant working so hard to keep scandal at bay."

I blinked in confusion. "I'm not at liberty to discuss such things."

"Quite, quite, old chap. Wouldn't dream of inviting an indiscretion." He coughed in embarrassment. "I'd just like to thank you for all your resourcefulness."

I stared, but he kept his face in the shadows. I could just make out the eyes, flashing above his whiskers. He was gaunter than I expected, for tales were rampant of his insatiable gluttony. Perhaps the past year had curtailed his excesses. But it could only be Bertie, back from abroad on the hush-hush, benevolently watching over proceedings from a hidden corner.

"Do you have a drink? Let me offer you a drink." He tossed me a hipflask. "I think you've gone about the whole thing with a darned sight more sensitivity and consideration than you might have done."

I was at a loss. "Just doing my duty, sir."

"Quite, quite. Do you think the thing's blown over now?"

"I'd love to assure you that it has, sir, but–"

"Best watch out, eh?" He gazed out over the pond. "Look, I have a request for you. It's out of the common run, and I'll quite understand if you don't feel up to it."

"Ask away, sir."

"It's just," he began, and his voice trembled an instant, "it's Nellie. You know, of course, who I mean."

I breathed in. "I do, sir."

"Good. How is she, would you say?"

"I've only met the lady briefly, sir. She seemed well enough."

"Oh." He seemed taken aback. "What a shame. I was rather hoping you could give me a full report."

"I think, sir, they've kept me away from her."

"Why have they done that, do you suppose? I had you down as inner circle."

"The less we know, the less we can let slip."

"I see. Yes, I do see. Look, I can't speak to Wardle about it. He'll have my head off for evincing the least bit of interest. Regards her as a fortune hunter and a lowlife. All wrong, you know." He scratched his head briefly, and I couldn't help thinking what a likeable young man he was. Was this really the same fellow I had heard wheedling with Wardle at the club? But then people change, of course. They grow up. It appalled me to recall how the inspector had lectured him like he were a child. Although he seemed tired, or just disappointed, I sensed a well of good humour underneath, of optimism even. Indeed, his manner was quietly inspiring, and I would go so far as to say that I felt myself in the presence of greatness. "Sometimes a chap can't follow through with his plans. He makes promises – has dreams – that fall through, and he feels like a cad and a cur. I would most dreadfully like to know she's all right."

"I'm trying to find her, sir."

"She hasn't left the country?"

"I don't think so, sir. Not yet. If I do find her, should I send word?"

He thought a moment. "No, no. No need to report back. I have a tremendous regard for you, Lawless. It would mean a lot to me just to feel you'd check up on her."

I lowered my head, overwhelmed by this unlooked-for approbation. "Sir, that's kind of you." I looked up again, but he had slipped away.

As the last stragglers were herded into cabs by weary footmen, Wardle stood with the pride of a victorious general after a battle. "Thank God that's over. Now I can retire with peace of mind."

"You make it sound like you're about to depart from this life, sir," I said.

He gave me a look and asked me to walk up to Paddington. "What's left to be done?"

"I thought I'd track down Hester, sir, the other hoofer."

He thought for a moment. "Don't see the need. Have another look for the mother, then write up what you got. We deserve a rest." As we headed up Rotten Row, a fine drizzle began to fall, the drops glistening in the streetlights. "I know you're puzzled by some of my ways, Watchman. We could have dealt with Skelton at the start. Paid him off, had him transported. But that's a dangerous game. He was smart enough to blow the whistle."

"Not to mention having friends in high places," I remarked.

Wardle snorted. "I thought he'd see sense. Let it drop; even better, take the girl back. We'd have paid their way out to Canada like a shot. I never expected him to go native. Pose such a threat. For all his lunacy, I respected him for that."

"Well," I sighed, "he won't be telling tales now, sir."

"You were right to chase it up."

"For God's sake, sir, it was you yourself that warned me off."

"Maybe that was wrong. I'll grant that now. I thought it was under control."

"You thought wrong."

"Look, son," he said, his voice sharper, "You've a good heart. That's important. That's why I want to leave it in your hands. But you need to be tougher. Trust your instincts and cover your own tracks."

"You mean, go on investigating behind your back?"

"That's what you did, isn't it? Only you weren't so subtle about it. Could have been more thorough too. Should have been." He gave me a look. "Let me tell you a story. When I was a young copper, they had a problem with the royal wet nurse."

"You told me. Killed her own children. Six of them."

"That's right. She had a discipline problem with the little prince and princesses. She was black and blue from their maltreatment. But we can't have servants accusing the royals of such cruelties."

"Why not, if they are guilty of them?"

"You don't know much, Watchman. If you knew all of it, you'd be shocked. They're a mad lot, there's no denying it. The inbreeding, must be. Bertie could be the worst of the lot, given rein."

I recalled Jackman's insinuations. "Then why defend them so?"

"They're royalty." He looked at me and I could see in his eyes no shadow of doubt. "Without them, the whole thing would collapse. Would you have the country ruled by some shopkeeper? These reforms are bad enough, but don't think for a moment that the common man can be trusted with decisions about the world. All he cares about is the food on his table and the wench in his bed."

"Doesn't sound so different from the Prince."

He stopped abruptly and I thought for a second he was going to slap me, as if I were a miscreant child. "The Prince will do well enough. His father was tough on him, maybe too tough, and he has a stubborn streak of rebellion. But he will make good, and he'll be king, don't you doubt it."

I looked away. "I'm sorry, sir. I'm just disappointed in myself. That we didn't get to the bottom of it before–"

He patted me on the shoulder. "Don't worry, son. I thought you'd dig something up. That's why I left you to it. They had to trust you were acting off your own bat. Like Worm, he trusts you, I thought you'd get something from him."

He still had no idea that the Worms were involved with the thefts. Better that way. I stopped and looked at him squarely. "Sir, why won't you give me Nellie?"

He screwed up his eyes. "We want nothing further to do with her. *Persona non grata*. We've paid her for her troubles. If she's still in London, she'd best watch out." He headed on up the Edgware Road, leaving me there at the Marble Arch, shaking my head.

THE HOUSE FOR FALLEN WOMEN

I arrived late at the Yard the next morning to be told by Darlington that two serious-looking insurance detectives were waiting for me.

"Insurance associates," they corrected me. One was large and looked dull-witted; the other was thin with a face like a flint. I wouldn't have been surprised to see them burst into a music hall routine. I showed them into the office.

The large man spoke in rapid, measured tones, his colleague

murmuring assent. They were private detectives, hired by a group of insurance companies to investigate Coxhill. It had begun as a query about multiple policies on machinery that subsequently malfunctioned. Now larger questions were looming, and they had received an anonymous tip-off mentioning a Scotland Yard investigation. I wondered from whom. Not Mr Wetherell. Smiler, then, or Skelton.

"We quite accept that this Coxhill may be a singularly unlucky man," said the burly one, "but this ill-luck proves rather fortunate for him in the long run. We suspect he is insuring hardware that never existed. Several of his claims were for losses underground. Devilish hard to inspect."

I was only too happy to add the tuppenceworth I had gleaned from Pat, about old machines being passed off as new.

"Probably insuring them as such," the man nodded. "They break down, and he ends up in the black. We've also discovered shadow companies which we're trying to trace to him. One Tooley Street claimant was a small components manufacturer, utterly destroyed with all the documents, save for the insurance policy submitted by a certain Mr Sachs-Cahill of St Albans, return address the post office, who continues to prove elusive."

I recalled Hester's talk of the country mansion, put under dust covers the moment they left. "I may be able to point you towards some hidden assets." Perhaps it was worse than Roxton Coxhill had admitted. If he knew of this Tooley Street intrigue, Skelton could have driven Coxhill into disgrace before destroying him. Perhaps he threatened exposure. That would explain why Hunt had acted so brutally. "Where does the money go?" I asked.

"He has no trouble running up debt. He spent his way through his father's fortune in gambling dens and houses of ill-repute. All his previous ventures have gone bust. It's a wonder he can sell shares at all."

"Oh, he's vociferous about the dividends he pays out," I explained. "That must be persuasive. Keeps the stock high. In fact, he's issuing new shares soon. Why not pick up a few, and keep a close eye on your investment?"

They both shook my hand. We understood each other. Coxhill was on the rack. By the look of him, he knew it. With these bloodhounds on his trail I didn't give him much hope. I doubted that even he could squirm his way out of this nest of vipers. It was as if Skelton had got him after all. Tit-for-tat, doing the rights. Only it was too late to tell Hunt that his master was beyond protecting. And too late to save Berwick.

I went to six different theatres before I heard a squeak about Hester. This appalled me. A girl might not show up for work and nobody batted an eyelid. They might be married, missing or murdered, nobody cared. Finally a pockmarked seamstress at the Lyceum advised me to look in the institution behind the old St Pancras Church.

I went into the grim building beside the St Giles burial gardens, and asked sceptically if they had a Haymarket hoofer in the house.

The white-starched marm at the desk sniffed at me distastefully. "One of our fallen ladies?"

"I dare say," I replied. "I'm a police officer."

She led me out through the hall, decorated with slogans: "God is truth." "Fear God and he will look upon thy lowliness." They couldn't have sent Hester here, I told myself, not without the risk of her telling tales.

In the scullery, scrubbing obsessively at one flagstone, knelt a sorry-looking wreck of a maid.

"Hester?" trilled the woman. "A man to see you. Speak clearly now, and remember godliness."

She looked up at me with half-remembering eyes. Her hair had lost its lustre, as if soaked in carbolic soap. On her face I saw not a trace of the impish smile I remembered.

"God Almighty, Hester, what are you doing here?"

"If you please, sir," she said softly, "you shouldn't curse like that."

"Hester, it's me. Campbell."

She broke off her scrubbing and looked at me, the old brightness trying to shine through. "What do you want with me, sir?"

I hesitated. "I wanted you to know that Berwick is dead."

She crooked her head against her shoulder and looked aside, as if afraid I might hurt her. "Sir, you ain't going to talk to me about the old times, are you? I should rather you didn't talk about the old times. I have a terrible time remembering to have only good thoughts. They tell me I must forget the old times which was sinful and filthy."

"Hester, they–" I broke off, cursing in my mind. Could this be Wardle's doing? Could he have arranged for her to be kept here? "Never mind that, Hester." I lowered my voice. "It's over. There's no need for you to be shut away here. The Prince is finished with Nellie. He's to be married next year to a Danish princess. I just want to find Nellie. I want to tell her."

"A foolish one, she is. I told her, sir. I told her not to trust them. Takes you out riding, they do, showers you with gifts. Flowers and carriages, she had from him, and a gold watch. There's only one thing they want, sir, and that's the one thing a girl must refuse."

"Oh, Hester."

"She told me, you see, about an indecent suggestion he made, down in that tunnel. I know their ways," she said, her eyes darkening. "Dreadful things I saw in those clubs. Filthy appetites, gentlemen have. I said to her, Nellie, have you gone and compromised your honour, have you? I have, she replies, and a more pleasurable compromise I never did make." The corners of Hester's mouth bent into a smile and, to my delight, she giggled. But she bit back her amusement and returned to her scrubbing.

"Hester, tell me, is it Wardle who sent you here?"

"I deserved everything has happened me. And I'm grateful to them for showing me the error of my ways. I didn't know, you see," she said wide-eyed. "I didn't know what wicked and shameful paths I was walking in, not until I got here, I didn't. My heart was the province of the devil. It was my own fault. I'd asked for it, you see, with my wanton ways. The man was doing God's work by doing the devil's."

"What man?" I stared at her. "What are you talking about?"

"I only got what I deserved," she said in a singsong voice, mumbling and rubbing the flagstone like her life depended on it.

"Hester," I whispered. "Tell me."

"What I got," she said, her voice growing shriller, "what the man done to me, that was God's wrath. God's wrath with my filthy ways. I see it now. At the time I was sore enough I'd have scratched his eyes out, if he hadn't had a gun."

"Who did it, Hester?"

She brushed away a tear. "He told me not to tell nobody."

I reached out to her but she shrank back from my touch.

"He's not here now," I said.

"Military gentleman like that?" she said. "No, no. He'll live to be a hundred."

"Military?" I narrowed my eyes. "Was he a short man?"

"He was, sir, in every department," she giggled.

I smiled to see this hint of her old self. "He's gone."

"Dead, is he?" she said hopefully.

"Gone," I repeated. "Far, far away."

"Not dead, then," she nodded. The giggles took her again, then she coughed, and I thought she would burst out crying. Instead her face went blank and she looked right through me. "I don't think I should talk to you, sir. You bring back my old wickedness." She smiled at me, then the fear returned. "You bring back my old life. Nurse! Nurse?"

She began to call out, and the starched marm hurried in, giving me a disgusted look. By the time I left, Hester was screaming.

I strode back to town, sickened by it all. Grown men playing games with people's lives, like boys torturing flies. If only I had asked her to identify the body, I could have taken her from that wretched place and she could have gone free.

I never saw her again.

Apologia Calamitatis

I spent some time asking around for the Worms, but there were none to be had. Nor any sign of Wardle coming in to work. After all our labours of the summer, it felt as if the world had suddenly fallen apart. I sat restless at his desk all day, poring over his paperwork, filling in the things that had not been committed to paper. I could see no way to write a meaningful report.

"What's eating you, eh?" asked Darlington, popping his head round the door.

I gestured at the mound of paper. "Back on the old refiling."

"No peace for the wicked," he said brightly. "I prefer it like that. Takes your mind off all the gloom and doom. Still, don't sweep all his misdemeanours under the carpet, will you? I mean it. He's a menace, your Wardle, when you ask for information on his cases. Don't get rid of anything important."

I nodded. "I sometimes feel like an accomplice in erasing history, throwing away files on fraudsters and interviews with murderers."

For a moment he looked shocked. "You're joshing me, aren't you?" he smiled. "There's strict Yard regulations about that kind of thing, and acres of space in the basement."

Disquieted, I wondered if I had somehow tainted myself, doing Wardle's dirty work for him. Darlington was right. Perhaps even Jackman's insinuations were justified. I had been erasing Wardle's misdeeds from the record, wiping miscarriages of justice from the slate. I imagined challenging him about it. "Sir, why did you have me destroy so many old records? Is that what you call covering your tracks?"

I could hear just what he'd say. He would look at me dismissively. "I've nothing to hide, son. Nothing I'm ashamed of."

"There's plenty of storage room in the basement. Why go against Yard policy?"

"Yard policy? Nonsense!" he would snort. "There's a multitude of sins I've committed, son. You won't find an officer who hasn't. But it's all in the line of service."

There was too much unexplained for my liking, not least why we had taken such risks to keep royal scandal at bay. Would Nellie go abroad as instructed or wait till she got what she wanted? Even now, could we be sure that Skelton did not have accomplices, skeleton thieves and more, who would carry on his work with more fervour now he had been martyred?

Midweek, I became impatient. The Worms had gone to ground, as if in fear that a passing bird might pick them off. I decided to send Wardle an abrupt missive.

Sir,

> *Body still to be formally identified.*
> *Must see Nellie.*
>> *Sgt Lawless (Watchman)*

There. I had finally put Nellie's name in writing. He must understand that I would not stop till he told me where she was. Of course, he might not be relaxing at home after his endeavours. He might be up at the castle, ironing out the details of his pension. After all, he had done well for them. Kept the scandal out of the press, managed the Exhibition smoothly, and seen off the madman. The Queen must be well pleased.

The next day I found two things at the Yard. First, a package containing Skelton's leather-bound notebook. In my astonishment, I almost missed the note: *"For the kind policeman, with thanks, Mme S."* No address. I cradled the thing in my hands, gazing at those familiar hieroglyphs in wonder. Perhaps, now that he was gone, we had the key to his plan. It was hard to credit after so long a chase.

I also stumbled across an address in Wardle's accounts, an address to which money had been forwarded: *N, 44 Shepherd Market*. Could it be that Nellie was staying with the whimsical elocution teacher? Was he a trusted confidant of the Yard? Or just a personal admirer with a spare room?

I dropped in at Miss Villiers' place on my way. She looked pleased to see me, if a little surprised, and prevailed upon me to come up. The stairwell was dank and dirty, but she had created an oasis of gentility in her flat. I was in a fearful hurry, but she led me straight into the inner room. I was astonished to find that the convalescent she had mentioned was the Professor, and more astonished still to discover that the Professor was a girl.

"What happened?" I said. The lass looked worse than I had after my excursion in Dickens' cellar. "You've been down the sewers, haven't you?"

"It wasn't his fault," she said in feverish confusion. "We was playing with the switches." Then she seemed to think better of it, and rolled over back to sleep.

I felt ashamed at the sight of the consumptive little face. Poor little wight. She and Worm had saved my life. If I had known, I would have done anything to help. When I said as much to Miss Villiers, she looked angry. But I had no time for quarrelling. In my hurry to get to Nellie, I simply dropped off the cryptic tome and left, wondering how we had failed to communicate for so long.

I turned up at Groggins' door and there she was, dressed in silken finery.

"What on earth do you want to see me for?" said Nellie.

"Berwick is dead. I'd like you to identify the body."

"You got a nerve." She led me up to the drawing room. Two cases lay open and clothes were strewn about the sofas. "If you'll excuse me, I'm in somewhat of a hurry."

"Why the sudden rush?"

"You know very well. I'm off to pursue my career on the Continent."

"Which career is that, actress or kingslayer?"

"You don't like me very much, Sergeant." She laughed. "Hoofers ain't so well paid we can let opportunities go a-begging, you know. I don't know about a policeman's wages, but I heard tell there's some of you behave likewise."

"Berwick is dead. Does he deserve no consideration?"

"If he's dead, he'll hardly notice." She saw my anger and sighed. "He said to me, when I told him about Bertie, he says,

Nellie, dear Nellie, how cruelly you have stamped upon my heart. He was always excitable, making dramatic declarations. Not at all, says I. Plenty more fish in the sea for you, but it ain't every day a girl gets proposal from a prince."

"Berwick might have kept his promises."

She rounded on me fiercely. "Sir, I have been badly dealt with by enough fellows. If Bertie welched on his promise, who's to say the fault was all his? Berwick was full of promises too, grand talk and universal schemes. Had he offered a bit more of what a girl needs, perhaps I would have stuck with him." She fell to coughing, and sat down, clutching at her belly. "Besides, I have what I wanted. The Prince's loss is Groggins' gain."

"Have you no shame?" I muttered. "Or would Berwick not have taken you back?"

"I wouldn't have gone," she retorted. "Excuse me, I have to finish my packing."

I stood up, filled with indignation. "You refuse to come and see the body?"

"Why do you try and trick me? I'm sick of it. I don't know what you want, but Worm just brought a letter from him, and he ain't dead." She pulled a sheet of paper from her bosom and held it out to me like a talisman.

My darling Nellie,

I must bid you farewell. I often wonder, had I won you, if I would have had the strength to pursue this path now coming to its end.

A hundred years from now, when all wars are at an end, struggles such as mine will seem unbelievable. When hunger is vanquished and all live content with their just share, there will be no need for such protest and destruction. Unseen forces are already uniting, using education and generosity, violence and fear, to secure that goal yet distant, but certain.

Certain too, that I loved you. You may consider my action simple vengeance exacted upon the Monstrous Rotundity. Think what you wish, bewitched as you are by ancient privilege. How, in this world, can a man outdo a prince?

If he has thrown you over now, I am sorry for you. For me there is no way back.

Farewell,

B

From The Criminal Prisons of London, *by Henry Mayhew and John Binny, 1862*

There is the Cadgers' (beggars') cant, as it is called – a style of language which is distinct from the slang of the thieves, being arranged on the principle of using words that are similar in sound to the ordinary expressions for the same idea... Again, we have the Coster-slang, which consists merely in pronouncing each word as if it were spelt backwards... Lastly comes the veritable slang, or English Argot, ie, the secret language used by the London thieves. This is made up, in a great degree, of the mediaeval Latin, in which the Church service was formerly chanted, and which indeed gave rise to the term "cant" (from the Latin *cantare*), it having been the custom of the ancient beggars to "intone" their prayers when asking for alms.

Ruth Villiers' Penultimate Narrative

Our Nation Underground

Six weeks already Molly – the Professor, that is – had been in my rooms when Sergeant Lawless finally came to visit. I had seen him only briefly at the Exhibition, when he turned up hours late, behaving rather oddly, after sending me the most abrupt invitation. I put it down to his work, of course, but still. To make no mention of the messages I sent through the summer, nor the merest inquiry after the Professor's health. Then he turns up on the doorstep, fresh as a coot, holding out a package.

"In a hurry?" I said. "Come up for a moment, do."

"I can't," he said. "I've just found out where Nellie has been hiding."

"There's someone upstairs who would love to see you. And I must hear the story behind those murders. The papers are useless."

"Wardle has them hushed up entirely," he nodded. He gazed abruptly about him, as if any number of people on the street might be listening in. "I'll come up for a minute."

Upstairs, I drew the book from the package. I stared at Sergeant Lawless, as if he were Moses come down from the mountain. Upon seeing the cryptic inscription on the fly leaf, I let out a little yelp. "But I can translate this. I have the cipher cracked." I pulled out my crib sheet from my desk and transcribed aloud. "*The– Kind– Hearted– Revolutionary– by–*"

"Miss Villiers," called a little voice from within. "Can I have a drink of water?"

"Of course, dear," I called. I gave the sergeant a look. "That's my convalescent."

"You mentioned something," he frowned and followed me into the bedroom. His shock was palpable. "Professor!"

They exchanged a few words. When I brought in the water, she gulped it down and hid away under the covers as if afraid she had said something she shouldn't.

"She's been terribly ill," I said. "But she's a tough one. She'll pull through."

"Why didn't you tell me? I could have helped. Called for a doctor. Something."

I sat smoothing her hair for a moment, but she was already asleep. I ushered him out of the bedroom. "I sent hundreds of notes and you never even replied."

He looked aggrieved. "I received nothing."

"Worm took message after message–"

"Worm?" he interrupted me. "Have you seen him? I must talk to him most urgently."

"Of course I've seen him," I said. During the darkest stretch, when it was far from clear if she would make it, Worm visited almost every day. He seemed almost fearful that she might settle in our world, like some kind of changeling. It does credit to him, looking back, that he took the risk of leaving her with me. "They're brother and sister."

"When was he last here?"

"A few days ago." I frowned. My mind skipped back over the summer. It seemed Campbell and I had been at cross purposes for so long. "Do you suppose they've been unreliable messengers?"

"Wait till I get my hands on that boy," he glowered. "I must go now, Miss Villiers."

"Not so soon," I said. "I'll translate the code for you here and now."

"That's not so urgent any more."

"Why? Is Berwick–" My eyes widened. "Those murders!"

"I will tell you everything later, I promise, but I must catch Nellie before they spirit her away. They're all playing games. Even Wardle. I don't know who to trust."

"I'm glad of it." I had not found the inspector at all ingenuous at the Exhibition, lording it over the whole place – especially as murder was committed under his very nose. In a flash, my gallant sergeant was gone. Another thought struck me. If he had not received my messages, who was it that solicited Dickens to find a new doctor for the Professor?

I sat by Molly's bedside with the gas lamp dimmed, transcribing Berwick's tome, *The Kind-Hearted Revolutionary*. Although I had decoded the full cipher, by matching the threats with annotations in his library books, the transcription was hard going, for he often used abbreviations and nonsense words I could make neither head nor tail of.

Although Molly still slept much of the day, she enjoyed sneaking out of bed. "Back to bed with you," I would cry, "you in your pyjamas and stockinged feet."

"I's only taking a look at the world, Miss Bilious," she would say most humbly, trotting back to curl up beside me on the little ottoman, from where she knew I would not have the heart to remove her.

That night, I caught her pressing her little nose against the windowpane to stare out at the passing bustle. She gripped my hand, and whispered urgently, "I didn't say nothing amiss to the sergeant, did I, Miss? Only I'd been dreaming about the Worms." She looked about her nervously. "I was afraid I might have mentioned something that I oughtn't."

"No, child," I told her. "Go back to bed."

She nodded, relieved. "What's that you're reading? Homework?"

"Not any more," I laughed. I had told her little of the

disastrous end of my studies. "I am free from the college and them of me. This is a special notebook from a certain Mr Skelton."

She looked from the book to me and back at the book again.

I looked at her closely. She had mentioned his name only in the height of her fever, and it seemed somehow a breach of confidence to talk of it openly. "It was handed to me for safekeeping."

"Ho," she nodded with that grown-up style of pondering she had. "Already. And can you make sense of it, Miss?"

I narrowed my eyes. "It's tricky. I don't suppose you could help?"

"I know my letters, you know." She looked anxious. "I can even read."

"I'm sure you can."

"My brother was mean about it. Called me the Professor. But now I can read, so it's not rightly fair." She squinted gravely at the book. "Don't be daft. That ain't English."

I laughed. "You're right. But I can translate it."

"Can you?" She looked at me sharply. "Miss Bilious, would you be so good as to kindly tell me the date, if you please?"

"The fifth of November, Molly. Fireworks night. Do you know what that is? Would you like to see the fireworks? We shall watch from our window, but I'm afraid the main celebrations will be at the weekend. If you're well enough, we might go out."

She beamed. "Miss Bilious, if you please, is the underground train working yet?"

"No, Molly, I don't believe it is. They keep postponing it. It was due to open for the Exhibition. Now they say the New Year. I'll believe it when I see it."

She nodded seriously. "You been kind beyond reckoning, Miss, and I shall never know how to thank you for it. But, if

you'll excuse me, I'd better be getting back to my people."
Blow me down if she didn't jump up and look purposefully
around as if to grab her hat and coat. Except that left her so
dizzy I had to catch her in my arms.

"Oh, Molly," I said. I lifted her back to the bed without any
difficulty, she was that light. "Just a few more days. We'll feed
you up good and strong. Next time your brother comes we'll
see if you're well enough to go."

I commenced to making some thick nourishing broth. If the
little one had set her heart on leaving I could not defy her. I
was concerned, however, about her lodgings. With the winter
nearly upon us, she could easily lose the health she had fought
so hard to recover. I said as much as gently as I could.

"Not at all, Miss," she called out, happily tucked up again,
as I worked in the kitchen. "Our new lodgings is practically a
palace. Forgiving your pardon, but I had rather expected your
own place to be a bit more extravaganter. Being as how I seen
a few great houses and bearing in mind all that talk about how
the other half live."

"The other half, am I?" I laughed.

"Our place was donated by a certain Mr Basil Jett," she said.
"It's brick top to bottom, and we've been furnishing it with the
finest accoutrements."

"Obtained how, may I ask?"

"Various means, Miss," she said tetchily, thinking better of
her confession. By the time the stew was made she was sound
asleep.

That night, I carried her to the window, wrapped in Aunt
Lexy's tartan rug. It was raining, and we strained our eyes to
make out a poor fireworks show far off over Islington. I forced
out many an "ooh" and "ah" as the desultory flames popped
and fizzled, and I had to promise her that we would go and

see the real show at the weekend. Afterwards, she insisted on sitting up with me while I translated Berwick's notes. Surprisingly enough, she was a good companion, silent and thoughtful, and I made great strides.

It was soon clear that, while not a complete text, these were notes for a major work. Berwick had organised his thoughts into chapters, on society, labour and capital, education, prisons and the like. His thought was cogent and unusual, with an admirable capacity for envisaging a radically different future. I had spent the year buried in small-minded treatises by embittered academics who proposed only solutions that would benefit themselves, *viz* better-funded universities. Berwick was aiming higher. His was a book of fiery challenges, to stand beside the Americans' Declaration of Independence and Thomas Paine's *Rights of Man*: a book to spark revolutions. His literary themes were vengeful, but they were epic themes. He wrote beautifully, with a vision of the future clearer than any college lecturer. He might be fanatical, he might be foolish, but he had extraordinary dreams. Whatever the crimes which kept Campbell pursuing him, Berwick was full of conviction, and I began to feel a grudging admiration for him.

It was by chance that the Professor solved my difficulties with Berwick's text. "Bother and fiddlesticks," I burst out, "what can he mean by the 'esilop'?"

"That ain't English, either," Molly replied.

"What the devil is it, though?" I said.

"What that is, Miss Bilious, is that it's the backslang–"

"Oh yes? Which is what exactly, Molly?"

"It's quite simple," she said, with the pedantry of a school teacher, "you take a word and say it backwards. 'Esilop' is P-O-L-I... erm – police!"

"I thought you could spell!" I poked her tummy, and she poked me back. "All right," I laughed. "What, then, does 'stall to in the huey' mean?"

She gave an understanding sigh. "That, Miss, is the argot. Don't you know anything?" Within half an hour she had apprised me of such a range of dialects as I would never have dreamed could coexist within two miles of my rooms, and me not understanding a single word. That was the whole point, of course. These were secret dialects for people who did not want to be understood, backslang and argot for card-sharps and tradesmen; rhyming slang and parlyaree for clowns, dockers and circus folk. Within the hour I could count up to ten in Thieves' Latin, Romany, and Lingua Franca.

"There's a book about it. By a man named Mayhew," she announced proudly. "I met him."

Mayhew, I thought. Henry Mayhew, one of the *Punch* brotherhood, mentioned in Miss Dickens' narrative and a user of the library. I might take the chance to speak to him.

Under Molly's able tuition, I began to make sense of my transcriptions. I also began to worry about the life she would be returning to, a life I pictured in fearful colours. So it was that I learned about the Nation Underground. It began with a simple question.

"Tell me about this palace of yours, Molly."

The Euston Square Worms, she told me, originally lodged in a lean-to by the New Road. When this was abruptly cleared in the building of the underground, it was Mr Skelton who organised a new place, with the help of a Mr Basil Jett, out of harm's way beneath King's Cross.

So they moved into their palace, and Mr Skelton with them, as he had some problems with his own home. They vowed it should be a fine residence, worthy of the company that dwelt there. Everything was decided by vote. There was a tidying committee, a furnishing committee, and so on and so forth.

All the Worms contributed, and Mr Skelton suggested taking things a bit further. He told them about the Reform League, meeting across the country to discuss things that needed improving. Meanwhile, across Europe, similar groups were meeting and discussing similar problems. These organisations were beginning to communicate, comparing their grievances and exchanging solutions.

"Now, there was Worms as didn't believe that talking could do more than heat up the room," said Molly. "But Mr Skelton told us as how not fifteen years back there was revolutions in every country in Europe. Even here in England, which just goes to prove."

The Worms were so entranced with his stories that they persuaded Skelton to give them lessons. He began with history. Now, the Worms were accustomed to long hours on the street and down in the sewers. Hard workers by nature, they considered it the height of entertainment to sit down to classes when they got in from their labours. The older children taught the younger how to read and write, and it flourished into a full schooling system. As legend of their organisation spread, individuals from across the capital turned up to join. Realising they would not be able to take everyone in, they sent goodwill messages to all the rival gangs. Soon enough, other Worm-like organisations sprang up, organising themselves in great underground cooperatives.

A model community, then. Self-educating and by its very nature activist. At first, I listened to Molly's tale as one would to feverish delusions, but she told it with such matter-of-fact detail it was hard not to credit her. Could there really be a Nation Underground at King's Cross?

"And this Skelton had you working in the sewers, did he?" I had never asked for an account of her accident, and I was shocked at how quickly she became agitated.

"Wasn't his fault, Miss. We was playing with the switches. He'd told us not to. It's quite safe if you don't. If he hadn't come to save me, I'd be–"

"Hush, now. Don't fret, Molly. Don't think of it."

I mustered my courage to talk to Mr Mayhew. By good fortune, he was in that Saturday, and I made sure that I took his request for books from the stack. Declaring an interest in his own writing, I mentioned the Professor's picture of an underground kingdom and asked if he thought it credible.

"People live in the most unlikely interstices. Why, there are tales of subcutaneous lodgers in this very museum. What is particular in your story is the planning."

When I mentioned Berwick's name, his eyes lit up.

"Skelton? I know the fellow. Wonderful chap, wicked sense of humour. Quite vanished from view."

I attributed my urgency to Molly's health. "My concern is this, should I allow her to leave?"

"Not all illegal dwellings are dens of iniquity, young lady. Your underground nation intrigues me. I would be glad if you would lead me to it, especially if it unearths Skelton. I'm working on another book, you see, and he has invaluable contacts."

That evening, Mr Mayhew met me outside the library. Perhaps it was an impropriety, meeting with a gentleman like that, but I was careless of propriety in those days. I almost didn't recognise him, for he was dressed as a street trader. He brought a cape to cover my dowdy library clothes. I was glad of it too, as the first chill of winter was in the air.

York Way looked a dark and uninviting prospect. I was embarrassed to admit that I had no idea of the exact spot. "I'm dreadfully sorry, Mr Mayhew. I've dragged you here for nothing."

Mayhew gave me an engaging smile. He approached a couple of beggars in front of the station. "G'night," he said in a strange northern tone.

They nodded their heads impassively.

"Could you 'elp us?" he said. "Where do the Worms stall to in the huey? We're from out of town, see."

The first man grunted.

"He said drop the main toper," Mr Mayhew went on, "and slink in the back drum."

"Who said?" muttered the second man.

"Mr Skelton," said Mr Mayhew undaunted. "It's him as told us to visit."

This effected such a transformation as to set my mind on fire. The irascible drunkards leapt up from their makeshift beds and clapped friendly hands to Mr Mayhew's shoulder. They fell over themselves to show us the way to a discreet entrance off Battle Bridge Road.

Arriving at a plain wooden door, set into the brickwork of the warehouses backing onto the station, we found a young Worm sat on guard. He nodded to us both warily. Mr Mayhew, as luck would have it, knew the boy, and easily enough engaged him in conversation.

"Ah, Mr Mayhew, I would, only as that I can't, because I'm told that I mustn't."

"Come, Numpty. I shall include special mention of you in my next book." His books must have caused something of a stir in the underclasses, for the boy took him most seriously. "Posterity, boy, if you know what that is. Let us say, you will be famous."

"It's kind, sir," the boy said, obviously torn, "though I'm not sure as I'd like that. Seem full of troubles, the famous people I've bumped into. Still, and besides, seeing as it's you and they're mostly out organisin' for tomorrow, I'll give you a peek at the lodgin's."

Through the low doorway, down two precipitous flights of stairs, and there it was. A great cellar room stretched away from us, bigger than you would believe possible underground, like a great palace squashed beneath a low vaulted ceiling. It was doubtless earmarked for storing barrels of beer, not activist brigades. Yet it was elegantly furnished with accoutrements from London's finest houses, and lit by gas lamps. Paintings hung on the walls; fine carpets graced the flagstones; assorted bookshelves ran along the far side of the room. Numpty pointed out archways at the sides. This one, he told us, led to schoolrooms; that one to dormitories; a third to a music room.

After this cursory glance, we hurried away for fear of being spotted. I had seen enough. And I imagined they might be like birds, to flee the nest if they found it disturbed. My mind blazed all the way home. Skelton had not only theorised beyond the thinkers I studied; he had put his plan into action, sharing his hard-won knowledge with the dispossessed, harnessing the Worms' entrepreneurial spirit to the demands of communal living.

If the underground nation had proved real, what of the darker threats?

I had some questions for Molly before she vanished back to the Worms. The next day, the ninth of November, she slept very late.

I too was tired. I had slept poorly after my excursion with Mr Mayhew, dreaming of subterranean kingdoms peopled by urchin princes. I glanced over my notes from *The Kind-Hearted Revolutionary* while baking a cake to soften Molly up. There was a thread of apocalyptic imagery through Berwick's book that mirrored the threats. Vilified were all manner of hypocrites, flatterers, frauds and fawners, and the solution was expressed in terms drawn from Dante, the Greek myths and the Bible. The wicked would be righteously drowned while gorging themselves on their ill-gotten fruits, whereas those not invited to the feast – the ridiculed, meek and oppressed – floated on to the new world. He had pasted in two engravings along these lines. First, the picture excised from the *Illustrated London News* of the grand banquet held in Brunel's Thames Tunnel; second, a Boccaccio illustration from Dante's *Inferno*, the first ditch of the eighth circle, where flatterers and fawners eternally drown in ditches of excrement.

Worm arrived after lunch in a highly excitable state. He was polite, as always, but I'd never seen him so jumpy. "How's the invalid, Miss?"

"Where have you been? You've been missing your sleep, young man."

"That's right, Miss," he grinned. He waved a little box, wrapped as a present. "I've brought chocolates, to cheer her up. She's a good girl, for all her whining. She'll be feeling low after all her shirking."

"She can go home soon, if you promise to keep her warm and well-fed. Though I shall be sorry to lose her." I was full of questions for him but I kept my peace.

He hurried in to talk to her. I hovered close to the doorway to hear, but they were speaking their special slang, fast and in low tones. I could understand nothing.

The bell rang again. Campbell. I asked him in, surprised to find him also in a state. I had so much to tell him. of the Nation Underground, the Worms' extended network, and all of it led by Berwick. I had barely begun when, without warning, Worm burst out of the bedroom, rushed past us and headed straight out the door.

"How strange," I said. "Does he have something to hide?"

"When has he not had!" Campbell cried. He set down his

plate with such force that it broke, though the slice of cake proved tougher. Spilling his tea over the aunt's travelling rug, he dashed out in pursuit.

Molly looked bemused. Her chocolates sat unopened on the bedside table.

"What has happened, Molly? Has your brother been found out at long last?"

Molly sighed with gravitas. "I shouldn't tell you, Miss Bilious. But being as how you saved my life and all, and I've told what I shouldn't about the Nation Underground, not mentioning that you've read it all in Mr Skelton's book, I may as well spill it all now."

And she told me. She told me the plan and I didn't believe her. She told me that Mr Skelton had long ago envisaged a plot not just for retribution but for revolution. He showed them the etching of the banquet in Brunel's tunnel, where his father had lost his health and his livelihood. That was his image of the two nations.

"His da didn't get invited, you see. That's what upset him, I think. That's why he's wanted to drown them all."

"All who?"

"Now Worm tells me Mr Skelton's not so well, and all from saving me. So he's not waiting for the opening of the railway. He's going to drive the train himself."

"Don't be silly, Molly. You can't go driving trains willy-nilly."

"Mr Skelton can. His brother works for the company. He's one of their drivers. Besides, everyone knows Mr Skelton."

I stroked her hot little brow as I listened to all this and decided I had to tell her, even if it would be a shock, even if it was he who had saved her. "Molly, I'm sorry to tell you, but Mr Skelton is dead."

"Miss Bilious, could you make me some tea?"

She gave no sign of a reaction. That worried me more than

any amount of tears. I stood by the kettle. Poor thing: what a curious connection she must have to this elusive genius. She had kept silent about it for as long as she could, and now that she had finally given in and mentioned him, I had to go and tell her that he was dead and gone. What could I do to soften the blow? I would feed her a hot supper, wrap her up in blankets and take her by hansom up to the Regent's Park to watch the fireworks. I set about warming the broth, and brought her in a fresh cup of tea.

She had vanished.

I rushed to the door to follow her, but it was locked. From the outside.

Sgt Lawless' Narrative Resumed

Worm's Final Fling

Wardle responded tersely to my abrupt note without mentioning Nellie. We met at the office on the Sunday afternoon. I came in to find him at his desk, looking over my draft report, which I would rather he had not, for I was not sure I had sufficiently obscured hints about Numpty and Bazalgette's toshers. Nonetheless, he seemed in an unusually jovial mood, a man whose demons had melted away overnight.

"Working on a Sunday, sir? Whatever next?"

"For the last time, son, unless it's in my own garden. Where I'm going, there's them as frown upon working on the Lord's Day. I could get used to such holy idleness. Come on, then." He led me out and over towards Piccadilly. "Know what day it is?"

I frowned. "Ninth of November. The day of the spout."

"And the Prince's birthday. Twenty-one today. I remember him when he was a baby. Right little tyrant. Spoilt, of course." He sighed. "I've allowed him back, now all seems safe. He seems to have behaved well enough out there, and his mother wanted him home."

I frowned. Surely Wardle knew that Bertie had been at the party. I wasn't about to give the game away. I had seen Nellie and there was no more I could do. And yet it left me with an unsatisfied feeling, like a child at a fireworks show, waiting for one last great rocket.

"I know what he's like, though. I urged the Queen to summon him to a sedate dinner, but she likes her tea at six. I've told him there's to be no extravagant behaviour. But he's that contrary, and I can hardly lock him up. So we're going to impress on his cronies, there's to be no impromptu jamborees."

"Coxhill mentioned a surprise do, sir. He's still after that Royal Seal."

"Did he now? Let's visit the clubs. Make it clear that anybody involved with high-jinks tonight will be dealt with heavy-handedly." He shot me a sideways glance. "I looked over your report. Seen Worm lately?"

"No, sir. I was hoping you might have."

"Gone to ground, eh?"

"I know where the Professor is, though. Taken poorly, working down the sewers." I don't know why, but I hesitated to mention that the Professor was a girl; it would feel like betraying a confidence. "The youngster is convalescing at a friend's house. I was thinking of putting a few questions to h– to him, when, um, his health improves."

He thought for a moment. "Go and ask them now. I'll chastise the toffs on my own. Find Worm. He knows my ways.

If he tells us what we want to know, we'll see him right. Meet me back here, six o'clock." He thrust his hands in his pockets and stomped off to visit the Oxford and Cambridge Club.

"Twice in a week," Miss Villiers exclaimed. "I shall cut you some cake."

"I need a word with the Professor," I mumbled.

"I think you should," she said brightly. "She's been making extraordinary revelations. Did you know that they live in a sort of underground palace up at King's Cross?"

"I did not."

"The Nation Underground, she calls it, built by a certain Mr Basil Jett."

"Bazalgette?"

"The sewer man! I knew I'd heard the name. He built it by dint of a deal with none other than Berwick Skelton."

"Skelton?" I blinked in consternation. "The Professor knew Skelton? Worm knew him?"

"Not only that," she said, handing me a large slab of cake, "they were his right-hand men, as it were. It's no wonder our messages were unreliable."

I cast my mind back. That would explain it all: they engineered my losing touch with Miss Villiers, and my trip to Bath. How much more? "Has she talked about his plan?"

Before Miss Villiers could say another word, the bedroom door opened, and Worm bolted across the room to freedom. I somehow knew this was my only chance. If I didn't catch him now, I would regret it.

Worm made a slippery quarry. My knee was weak and I had been too long at my desk, but what I lacked in agility, I made up for with my long legs. He hove down Longacre and across St Martin's Lane. I felt the first stabbing pains in my leg as he crossed the new Charing Cross Road, ducking into the discordant tumult of street-sellers in the maze of streets behind Leicester Square.

I could not afford to lose sight of him. Through farmyard smells and speckled eggs in wicker baskets; sausages fresh from Kent and birds twittering resentment at their cages; among dogs running wildly and the small children chasing them he weaved. Across the broad square, the lamps of the public houses were already lit, sputtering as if to complain at their early kindling.

Worm headed unerringly for Wyld's Great Globe. He darted beneath the half-dismantled portico, squeezing under the disused turnstile. Inside the great chamber, there were voices and a dim light from above. I started following the clunk of boots up the stairs until I heard a voice. "Hulloah? Who's there?"

"Stop that boy," I cried. "I'm a police officer."

"It's you, old man!" called James Wyld, looking over the upper rail. Beside him stood a young lady, somewhat flustered. "We've seen nobody, officer. Is he dangerous?"

I shook my head, exasperated. He could not have vanished. Then I saw it. Just out of reach from the stairs, Queensland was jutting out from the rest of the continent. I tiptoed back down, clambered over the stair railing, and gently lowered myself down to the South Pole. I crept up the sloping wall towards the cupboard door, struggling to keep the hollow metal from reverberating.

As I put my eye to the doorway, the young lady's voice rang out, shrill and grating. "James, I don't like this in the slightest."

At this, the clang of a manhole cover echoed from inside the cupboard. Worm leapt out of the shadows and threw back the door, knocking me sideways. I staggered, but I managed to trip the little blighter as he hopped out, and I fell upon him, pinning him down against New Zealand.

"Bleeding heck," he sighed. "How did you know I was there?"

I smiled. "I'm not so stupid as you think, young cove."

With a jerk, he pivoted away from me, throwing me off balance. We fell heavily against the Tasman Sea and rolled down towards the unexplored heart of the Antarctic. The tumble gave me a scare, what with my knee, but I held on for grim death.

"Steady on, old bean," called Wyld. He was watching from the steps above, as if it were the new sport in town. "Just a pickpocket, is he?"

"No, sir. This wee fellow's a criminal mastermind."

With the aid of two Leicester Square bobbies, I escorted Worm to the Yard and put him in a cell with three chairs and a little table. He played innocent at first, but his very desperation to escape showed me I was right: he had been playing us false.

I called for some tea and settled in to wait until Wardle returned.

"He has a few things to ask you," I began, "and so he should. For instance, why have you been interfering with my correspondence?"

He looked up at the ceiling.

"What's wrong? At a loss for a ready quip, my friend?"

He fixed me with that quizzical stare of his. "Let me express my sincere regret, Watchman, that we were unable to deliver some of your correspondence to your lady friend, due to a conflict of interests, shall we say."

I shook my head, quietly incensed. "You were afraid Miss Villiers might unravel your schemes?"

"Miss Ruth has a sharp mind," he nodded, looking at me squarely. "But you can rely on us in future."

"You don't know how much I've worked out, wee fellow."

I smiled. "If I didn't owe you my life–" I hesitated. "Look. I know your lot have been working down the sewers. I also know that Mr Bazalgette considers their contributions invaluable."

"Invaluable is right," he grinned.

"He tells me you orchestrated the Great Stink."

"Don't like to brag." He chuckled. "Shuffler was on good terms with the mudlarks, see. We were able to concentrate certain effects. Our friendly parliamentarians wouldn't cough up the dough for Baz's scheme, not until our aromatic treat. After all, there ain't no stink on their country estates, is there? Poor Mr Disraeli and his delicate nose. I heard he spewed up on the speaker. Still, Baz got his cash, eh?"

I clapped. "Future generations will venerate your contribution, I'm sure."

"I'm hoping for a brass plaque," he nodded. "Come on, Watchman. What's your game?"

I sighed. "Worm, I shall always be grateful to you–"

"But you're going to send us down."

"I've done my best," I insisted, "I've protected Numpty and his chums, but–"

"The bleedin' thefts." He clicked his tongue. "Is that all? I told Smiler it was more trouble than it was worth. People are robbed blind every day on the stocks and shares. We lift a couple of footstools from a baronet and all London's agog. I ask you."

"You upset a lot of people."

"I should hope so. Come on, Watchman. I actually thought better of you."

Worm was right. I had told myself that Wardle was dealing with the thefts because he could sniff bigger intrigue lurking behind them. Yet house thefts happen every day. The outcry was disproportionate only because it affected the rich and famous.

"Anyway, Smiler's dead and Numpty's halfway to France. You going to arrest me as an accomplice? Because I don't know nothing about it."

"Then how do you know Smiler was involved?" I sighed. The poor boy was shaking. "Worm, you look terrible. What have you been doing to yourself? I'll get you a bite to eat and a cup of tea, shall I?"

He looked at me as if I were mad. "What kind of lilly law are you, Watchman? You're meant to be roughing me up, not feeding me sandwiches." He tutted. "You won't get nowhere behaving like this."

"And why should it matter to you," I said sharply, "where I get to?"

"No secret about it," he grinned. "I likes having friends in high places."

"Like Wardle."

"Not exactly like Wardle." His smile soured. "Speak of the devil."

"Worm," said Wardle, slamming the door shut behind him. "What a pleasure."

"All mine, Inspector, old cove," Worm replied. But he avoided Wardle's eye, and there was an aggressive tone in his voice I hadn't heard before. "To what do I owe today's little invitation?"

"Shut up until you're spoken to," Wardle barked. "There's something afoot, Watchman. Disgruntled toffs waiting on Coxhill to give the word where and when, only he's nowhere to be found, and there's sleuthhounds baying for his blood. You'll want to steer him clear of Coxhill's type." It surprised me that he spoke of Bertie in front of Worm. He did not seem to realise how deeply our little friend was involved in it all. "Now, have you emptied this scoundrel's pockets?"

"Must we really–"

"Have you or haven't you?" He stared at Worm as if he were any old criminal.

Worm glanced at me. "I could have told you about him, Watchman, right from the start. And we were having such a civilised little chat, Inspector." He narrowed his eyes and said, with a strange emphasis, "Reminiscing."

"Shut your mouth," said Wardle and pulled Worm up on to his feet. "Empty them."

Worm returned his gaze evenly. "With what, pray, am I being charged?"

"Empty your pockets, child!" Wardle noticed my dismay. "I don't want him making things worse for himself, trying something foolish."

"Only, by my understanding of the law, Inspector," Worm continued, "I'm *habeas corpus* till charged and innocent unless proven guilty. Ain't that so, Watchman?"

I waited for Wardle to explode.

"Or is that law only for flash harries and royalty?"

For a moment, I thought Wardle was going to cuff Worm about the head. Instead, he bent down and grabbed Worm's ankles. He upended him and shook him like he was a rag doll. Worm chose not to struggle. He only raised his hands to stop his head from banging on the floor. Various items tumbled from his waistcoat and trousers on to the floor: a watch chain, pencil and paper, some coinage.

Wardle dropped him carelessly to the ground. "Poor pickings today, Worm? This pencil looks familiar. When did you filch that?"

Worm picked himself up and sat down, scowling. "I only take from those who has spare."

"Literary ambitions, have we?" said Wardle, unravelling the scrap of paper. "Oh dear. Still picking up the alphabet, I see."

He handed it to me and I looked at the sheet inscribed with familiar symbols: Skelton's cipher. I frowned at Worm but held my tongue.

Wardle spoke rapidly. "I'll tell you why you're here. Because you're a thief. A liar. A menace to society. And when I've left this place," he glanced at me, "I don't want to hear distant rumours of you and your misdeeds. Watchman tells me your lot had a hand in the skeleton thefts."

Worm looked at me, without accusation. "Don't know nothing."

Wardle grimaced. "Numpty, wasn't it? And this Smiler fellow."

"Who?" Worm raised his eyebrows. "Oh, the cove what got stuffed?"

Wardle sighed. "All right, Worm. If you're going to be like that. What about this friend of yours, Skelton?"

We were a long time sitting without saying a word. Worm seemed to be considering his options. When he finally spoke, it was in slow deliberate syllables. "I– don't– know– nothing. Get it?"

Wardle snorted. I felt again he was about to hit the boy. I found myself trying to appease him. "Worm, we know how they did it. In through the sewers before each stretch was opened. No trace left but the bones. I even know why. I know about Skelton's father. I know about the Poor House in '46."

Worm looked at me. "Well, well. Pleased you've taken an interest, old cove."

"Shut up," said Wardle. He looked at me pointedly. "And the other nonsense?"

"Why the clocks, Worm?" I said. "All those stolen mechanisms."

"I haven't the foggiest what you're on about. Told you. I wasn't in on it. What if Numpty was? Am I my brother's keeper? You've got nothing on me, however you try and fit me up."

I looked at him in admiration. He was right. We had nothing to incriminate him. Yet I knew he was lying. I knew it and Worm knew that I knew. I knew that Berwick had used the mechanisms to set off the spouts, even if I couldn't see why he needed so many. Wardle, by contrast, didn't really care. He just wanted someone blamed. He wanted it all done and dusted. "You've been leading us on, Worm," I said. "Withholding messages. Sending me on wild-goose chases."

"Did you like that note? Wrote it myself."

"Don't give us that," said Wardle. "He doesn't know how to write, Watchman."

"I've better schooling than you," Worm replied with quiet dignity.

Wardle snorted again. "Clever game you've played. Little turncoat. It's over now."

"Is it?" Worm murmured. "Yes, I s'pose so."

"Why you did it I don't know," said Wardle. "Bloody fortune we paid you as well."

"And did I ever let you down? Aside from one or two letters, that is."

Wardle leaned forward and whispered through clenched teeth. "What line did he feed you? Pay better than us, did he? Spill the beans and we'll see you right."

"Why," Worm chuckled, "has the great detective not worked it out?"

Wardle tried to govern his agitation, but the boy just kept laughing.

"All your cleverness and you can't see it. Still, that's how Mr Skelton wanted it."

"We know enough," I said, annoyed now too. "Shuffler and his toshers. The deal with Bazalgette. Smiler and Skelton blackmailing Coxhill. And Hunt…" I trailed off. "Forget the clocks. I know what mischief you were up to. But what's this about your new home?"

Worm eyed me keenly. For the first time, I felt he was discomfited. Why? What was there still to hide? His carelessness seemed somehow affected. "I don't know about no clocks," he said.

"Enough," Wardle snorted. "He's a nobody whose floozy ran off with a toff."

"With the heir to the throne."

"What's that to do with you?"

"It's plenty to do with us," Worm answered quietly. "They killed Shuffler."

"Hunt," I said. "It was Hunt killed Shuffler. He killed Smiler too, and Skelton." The name hung in the room for a moment. I glanced at Wardle. "Come on, Worm."

"I can trust him, can I?" Worm said to me. "Deal with paupers same as princes? If you know so much, why all the fuss at Big Ben? Don't you know who the Monstrous Rotundity is?"

"I'm about to find out," Wardle growled. "I'll happily beat it out of you."

"You should know, of all people, you spend enough time wiping his arse."

"You're going to tell us about your treasonous little plot." Wardle leaned forward. "Or I'm going to take out your windpipe and tie it round your bleeding neck."

Worm burst out laughing. "It's so touching to hear you, Inspector. Such loyal sentiments, don't you think, Watchman? So deeply felt. I hope it's a hefty pension you're getting, because if you did it from love and loyalty you must be disappointed. The Queen an old maid, one prince dead and the next an embarrassment."

"Don't give me your slander."

"Hang me, then," Worm chirped, "but I'll raise a few eyebrows in the dock on the way. Bought and sold for royal gold." He leaned forward, as if testing Wardle's limits. "Or is your devotion waning? The Prince is only following family traditions, poor chap. Let's hope he doesn't go pox-ridden loopy and all."

Wardle struck the boy a savage blow across the cheek.

Worm called out, more in surprise than pain. He touched the back of his hand against his lip and gazed at the blood in puzzlement. "Sorry, Inspector, did I say something to upset you? Hope not." And, blow it all, he winked at me. "Because that's nothing beside what I've got left to say."

"Don't push your luck, son."

"You see?" Worm looked at me, maniacally exultant. "I tell the truth and he threatens me. I haven't even mentioned Roxton Codswallop yet."

Wardle stiffened, as if in strange fascination.

The boy was irrepressible, filled with wild carelessness. "Did it seem odd, Watchman, how quick those hydrollah-rolical incidents was passed over? To me it seemed a little odd. No charges pressed. No outcry in the papers. You'd have thought the royal inspector might have paid especial attention, what with the Prince being close by and the hydrollah-rolical proprietor a particular stooge of his."

Wardle bristled, as if trying to cow him into silence.

"Unless," Worm persisted with a look of mock surprise, as if he were just thinking it through, "that proprietor made it in your interest to overlook the incident. That would be shrewd. Whatever other qualities we may attribute to him, he is shrewd, this proprietor. Devious, too. Those insurance claims. Those fires. Dividends paid out of capital investments, which is fraudulent practice, I'm told."

"What do you know?"

"Sorry, Inspector. You must be concerned for your investments. Scored a hit, have I? I'm not suggesting for a moment such perks would make you act with anything less than integrity. You must be due a payment next month, eh? How much does a blind eye cost these days? You'll have to admit, Inspector, that's more crookeder than anything my Worms done."

Wardle grunted.

"So it seems to me," Worm went on brightly, "that you have rather more to hide than we do. That royal nurse you sent down, for instance. Before my time, but we both know that certain factors didn't merit a mention in court. I mayn't have grown up with maids but I'd have thought it ain't proper to beat 'em. Wouldn't you, Watchman?"

"She murdered her children," Wardle roared.

"She was crazed," said Worm.

"She'd have gone to gaol anyway, whether they were mentioned or not."

"Like Mr John Sadleir?"

Wardle froze. "Speak ill of the dead, would you?"

"Wouldn't dream of it, old cove." Worm turned to me. "Heard of the gent, Watchman?"

"The Hampstead financier. Suicide." I said. "He's told me."

"Has he?" Worm nodded. "Speaking ill of the living ain't so bad, is it, Inspector? See, contrary to what the coroner's report might say, Mr Sadleir is not dead, and, what is more, your inspector knows it."

Wardle seemed to shrink into his chair. "You can't prove that," he whispered.

"By the way," Worm chirped, "he sends his regards from Canada. Enquires if you're still getting the cheques. Hopes your wife is well."

The inspector exploded. He threw the table aside and picked Worm up by the lapels of his jacket.

"Go on and kill me," said Worm with heart-breaking resolve. "There's others know."

"I will," Wardle shouted, "and who'll remember you then?" In a flash, he had him up against the wall. To my horror, he shook him, knocking the boy against the stone, over and over.

And I stood by and did nothing. Worm curled up, making no effort to fight him off. He had a strange look on his face that seemed to say, I knew it would come to this. Worst of all, it seemed somehow that Wardle was doing it all for my benefit.

"For God's sake!" I started forward.

Wardle stopped for a moment.

The boy looked up, wild-eyed. There was blood on his hair, blood around his mouth. "Beating up an innocent?" he said with desperate triumph. "I could have you arrested."

Wardle laughed. "And who do you think will believe you?"

Worm smiled. "That ain't so smart, Inspector."

Wardle tightened his grip.

"Oh, beat me all you like. Kill me. I wouldn't be the first to die in order to hush up police peccadilloes. But whatever you say, I know that he'll tell the truth." Worm nodded in my direction. "Don't looked so shocked, Watchman, old cove. That's why we chose you. I can depend on you, can't I?"

We all stood frozen for a moment. Then Wardle redoubled his fury. With an animal roar, he smashed Worm's head against the wall, and laid into him, pummelling him with his fists as if to pound the life out of him.

Before I knew what I was doing, I had pulled Wardle off him. I picked him up, clean off the ground. I span him around, and threw him against the wall beside Worm, threw him so forcefully all the breath went out of him.

I let go, frightened of what I might do. He collapsed at my

feet. I felt like a puppy who has opened his eyes to find himself a full-grown dog, to realise how lightly he could tear his own master to pieces.

Wardle cowered beneath me, clutching at his chest with one hand and holding the other ineffectually above him.

"Is this the thanks I get?" he muttered.

"It's you," I said with disgust. "You've done it to yourself."

Wardle looked up at me, suddenly old and tired. He picked himself off the floor and stumbled to a chair, then put his head in his hands and began to shake.

"Good God," I said to myself. "Is there nobody pure of heart?"

"I know one cove who is, more or less," said Worm. "I'll tell you about him, if you like."

Worm's Tale

We sat in silence. It seemed like an age passed by.

"I might as well tell," Worm began on a sudden. He stroked his chin and nodded to himself. "Now that we're at the final curtain. What harm in it? Mr Skelton wanted it secret, but that's all wrong. I want people to understand.

"We had it all planned. The underground train was meant to be opening in May, you'll recall. All the great and good, not just of London but the world, would be banqueting down the station. Has a thing about these banquets, does Mr Skelton. So we planned to set off another of Coxcomb's engines. Flood the place. Have a few princes and presidents swimming for their lives, you know. See how the rest of us feel.

"Best laid plans and that. They kept postponing and so we did too, until Mr Skelton took ill in a mishap below ground. Rescuing the Professor, it was, the two of them all but drownded. Mr Skelton decided he'd better not hang about.

He'd move it forward, do it at the Exhibition.

"He heard Coxcomb banging on at his club – Mr Skelton's a member of several clubs, you see. Codswallop's given to bragging, as you know, and he was boasting how he would throw a grand party for the Prince. Now, Mr Skelton enjoys the odd light-hearted deception. So he dons a disguise, quick as you like, and sidles up to Foxhole. Posing as a well-connected gourmand, he offers to do him a slap-up feast there in the Greenhouse, after the Exhibition closes. Give the Prince a treat, impress all and sundry, do his business a favour.

"Cotswold swallows it hook, line and sinker. We go along to nail down the details. We send in Smiler, as he knows both of us. I suppose the mongrel, Hunt, can sniff that something ain't right. Mr Skelton would have called it off. Smiler ain't so smart. He's greedy, and he must've dropped a hint. You know, that we knew everything. We hear a bit of argy-bargy. Me and Berwick looks at each other. 'I'll see what's happened,' he says. 'If I'm not out in five minutes, scarper.'

"In he goes in. I hear a gunshot and the hut is all flames and smoke. I duly scarper. When I finally creep back, there ain't no sign of anyone, living or dead. The rest you know.

"We planned it to look like an accident, see. Everyone would blame the Exhibition for killing their future king. Commerce. Industry. Progress! We're not Luddites, though, nor Puritans. Here's Britain, where a million philanthropists spout nonsense about our sceptred isle and our illustrious history while they send us down mines and into battles to keep themselves in clover. Your lot are being used. Think you're defending law and order? All you're protecting is the status quo. You may have doused the flames this time, but it'll burn soon enough. The nation's like a tinderbox. Don't tell me you don't know it. All it takes is one spark and it'll go up. I tell you, 1666 wasn't nothing, and this time it won't just be London."

The Plot

Wardle stared at him, face twitching, betraying no more anger. I sat silent, but my mind was racing.

"Disappointed in me, are you, Watchman?" said Worm.

I shook my head. I couldn't bring myself to look over at Wardle.

"Well, string me up or send me to the madhouse. I'm ready to go."

Wardle suddenly leaned forward. "You think you're so smart, boy, full of big schemes and high ideals. Let me tell you, if you and your lot tried to run the show, the Empire would collapse in a week."

"All the better for it," Worm grinned. "I trust all the colonials will revolt the instant we take over."

"Deranged fantasies," Wardle snarled.

"It's happened before and it'll happen again."

"Don't give me history," spat Wardle. "I won't be lectured to by an upstart street-sweep that's never been to school."

Worm bridled at that.

"Should we not," I declared, "all have some tea? I think we stand in need of a cup of tea."

Worm shot me a reproachful look. "Do you think it wise to leave me here with the inspector? We might get up to mischief."

Wardle glared at him. He stood up. "I'm sick of his nonsense. I'll be in the office, Watchman. Throw this charlatan in the jug for the night."

"What are you holding me for?"

"For cheek. Give him a book, if you like, Watchman. We'll test him on it in the morning. I'll call for your bloody tea." He stomped out.

I sat down and heaved a sigh of relief.

"Don't worry yourself, old cove. It'll all turn out for the best."

"You think so?"

"No. Just trying to cheer you up."

I laughed.

He raised a nonchalant eyebrow. "I have been to school, you know. St Blane's Poor School, Somers Town. Did rather well, prior to joining Mr Skelton's operation."

"You left school to join him?"

"Well, I'd been working for Shuffler since before I can remember. His best tosher, I was. We were on the sly for years. A precarious profession, I tell you, toshering on the hush-hush. When Bazalgette offered to turn us legitimate, we didn't need no second invitation."

"And that was the start of this Nation Underground?"

"My, my," he said, "you have done some ferreting. It works, you know. We eat more, we can read and write, and there's just enough space for dreaming." He frowned suddenly. "Say, the old cove doesn't know about that, does he?"

"If half what you said is true, he couldn't lift a finger against you." I shook my head. "What kind of policeman am I, ready to blackmail my own inspector?"

"Don't be daft." He leaned forwards. "We need the likes of you in high places."

"So you can thieve with impunity?"

He spread his hands with a conciliatory grin.

I was not grinning. "You lied about the clocks."

He looked hurt for a moment, then he shrugged. "Seemed silly, I s'pose. Presents for Mr Skelton. Loves his old watches, he does. We always filched bits, here and there. Gave him the whole collection. Pleased as punch, he was."

I chuckled at the picture of our adversary, rejoicing in his underground workshop, surrounded by the whirring hum of springs and cogs. Then I recalled what he had wrought with those mechanisms, and I stopped chuckling: the spouts that had so long terrorised Bertie, that had frightened even Wardle, that had set all London on edge.

"What is it, old cove?"

"I just wondered, what was he like, this Berwick Skelton?"

His eyes opened wide. "I'm always forgetting, you ain't met him, have you? Get on famously, you would. Holds you in high esteem."

"He didn't know me."

"Mr Skelton knows a lot of surprising things," he chuckled. "I'm glad it's you that's been after us. Gives the whole thing a sense of… What can I say? Of dignity."

"Enough of your toadying," I said. "Did you not find something undignified in Mr Skelton's concealing his own personal revenge under the guise of revolution?"

Worm sniffed. "He says to me once, he says, 'Worm, old cove, do you think I've led you and your friends astray? Have I got caught up in petty vengeance instead of working towards the future?' 'Buck up, old cove, I told him. What higher motives than a broken heart? Besides, without you there wouldn't be no Worms, nor no future neither. If the show is about doing the rights on the grand scale, I've no complaint with you settling your own score along the way.'"

I shook my head and walked over to the little barred window. He was in earnest, there was no doubt of it. Yet there was something that didn't ring true; some kind of clash, between Worm's story and Coxhill's boastings. That party for the Prince's coming of age, that should have been today.

There was a rap at the door. I opened it to find a tray laid outside the door, heavy with teapot and sturdy mugs. I bent to pick it up.

Worm hit me at full tilt, hurtling into my back and bundling me to the ground.

I flew forwards, tea things crashing everywhere. My head cracked against the wall. Tea soaked my shirt and scalded my shoulder. I lay there a few moments, just trying to comprehend what was happening.

You may have doused the flames this time, Worm had said. May have. Berwick holds you in high esteem.

I should have added it up. Hunt could barely write to save his life, while all Skelton's lads could. Worm especially did a nice line in forged notes. Nor would Hunt have left his Crimean rifle in the display cabinet. It was too elegant by half, too ostentatious a crime for a furtive thug like him.

The burnt face. It wasn't Skelton at all. Worm kept referring to him in the present tense. Worm was free, Berwick was alive and the plot was on.

RETURN TO EUSTON SQUARE

The tea-boy, who had long stood in awe of Worm's privileged position at the Yard, had heard the commotion. He was standing uselessly in the hallway, gazing out the entrance through which Worm had just fled.

"Which way did he go?" I called, rising weakly and hobbling towards him.

The boy shrunk back, moon-faced, as if he thought me mad. "Was he not on an errand?" he said. "I thought he was on an errand."

I grabbed him by the shoulders and shook him. "Which way did he go, damn you?"

Pale with alarm, the boy pointed up the road to the right. And there was Worm, leaping aboard an omnibus headed back along Whitehall towards us. The place I would least expect him to run, past my very nose, a typical Worm ruse.

I would call for help and step out to halt the omnibus. Worm would leap from the contraption into our waiting arms.

It was then that my mind went into a state I have experienced all too rarely. I was acutely aware of everything around me, yet I felt myself calm, detached, supremely rational, as if the universe had slowed to a standstill. I could see my actions and their effects with a devastating clarity. Capturing Worm would be useless. He had run, it was true, but, when I caught him in Wyld's Globe, he came quietly, inured to his possible detention. *Ergo*, Skelton's plan would go ahead with or without him. Worm would never tell us where, not in a million years. The only way to find out would be to follow him, without his knowledge. He must lead us right to the crime, or we were lost.

I stood at the entrance, acting flummoxed. If Worm were watching, he would see me looking defeated.

His omnibus swept past, horses straining, and mingled with the Whitehall traffic.

I nabbed the tea-boy's flat cap. "Tell Wardle, Worm's escaped," I said. "It's on. Their plot's on." Worm had been unnerved at my mention of the Nation Underground. I would follow him, but I could give Wardle no better directions than to head for their base. "Tell him to go to King's Cross."

I ran down the pavement. By good fortune, an altercation between a hansom and a milk cart hindered the omnibus' progress, and with a few bounds I attained the back board. I clung to the corner pole as it pulled away. It was the new style, with gents riding up top, back to back against a sandwich board. I was ready to swing myself up the ladder to the roof. But I spotted one of Worm's patched elbows jutting out above me. He was perched on the end, beneath the top seat, his legs dangling off the back, as he scanned the road behind for pursuing cabs. If he had chanced to look down at that moment, he would have seen me. I pressed my face against the vehicle, praying that I would be rendered invisible by the cap, an article I had never worn before in my life.

Dusk was descending. There was nothing I could do but keep an eye on Worm's boots as they swung there above me. I passed that journey elated, but with a strange calm. I was suddenly sure of everything. Skelton was still alive and Worm was going to him. The second body at the Exhibition, shot, stuffed and mutilated, was not Skelton, killed by Hunt in a moment of madness, but Hunt killed by Skelton in retribution for the violence he had done, not only to Shuffler and Smiler, but to Hester too. He burnt the face off to lead us astray, with perhaps a sly reference to Hunt's arsonous practices from Balaclava to Belgravia. It was a trick I had too easily believed. The tidy ending we had so long sought, but a false ending.

Worm rode all the way to the terminus at Euston Square. He descended carelessly, rather pleased with himself. A slow fog was creeping up the streets as the darkness deepened, and I was able to follow him at a discreet distance into the station. He took a chair at a pie-seller's, and bided his time, seemingly cocksure now. I found myself an observation post on the other side of the great concourse, skulking in the shadows of a flower stall.

I couldn't help reflecting how it had all started right there, three years before. 'We chose you,' Worm had said. A strange notion. I had been selected to bear witness. And those coded messages in Worm's pockets. 'I want people to understand,' he said. Did he write the threats himself? Had he deliberately led me through the labyrinth to witness the slaying of the monstrous one? That first night at the spout, it was he who had summoned me; and again, months later, for the thefts. Could it be that he had suggested my name to Wardle? Reminded him of my good offices? I preferred to believe that than Glossop's accusation, that I had earned my place through my malleability.

He glanced up with increasing regularity at the clock above the platform gateway. His earlier composure had deserted him and he was in a state of high agitation. What could I do but wait? Apprehend him now and our chance would be gone. Send word to Wardle? There was nothing clearer I could say. He would be fuming and cursing me; but with him at King's Cross and me at Euston, there was still a chance we might be in the right place to intervene at the dreadful finale.

At nine on the dot, Worm stirred himself. He tossed a coin to the pie man and sauntered off. I pulled the cap low on my brow and followed. He headed for the outside, whistling a gay air, as if he owned the grand hotels flanking the square. What the devil was he doing? I had a sudden fear that he was leading me a merry dance, that he had known all along I was following him and would any moment quicken his pace and vanish into the crowds. Or, worse, that he would turn round and laugh at his success in diverting me from my duty, while diabolical vengeance was being executed elsewhere.

He passed the grand colonnade, traversed the square, and continued over the Euston Road. At the next crossroads, he darted into a peculiar tiled entrance on the corner, marked GOWER STREET STATION in maroon and white tiles. One of Worm's chums was guarding the wide lattice gate of articulated iron. By the time I came up to the little tyke, Worm was nowhere to be seen. I approached with a friendly gesture and an indeterminate grunt.

"Who's yourself, then?" muttered the child. He held the grating closed, peering out wide-eyed through the gaps.

"I'm with Worm," I mumbled, glancing past him. Behind him stood two pairs of turnstiles. Beyond them, a flight of steps descended into the earth. There was no sign of Worm.

"Beggin' your pardon." He scratched his head. "I'm not 'specting nobody else."

"I've a message," I hazarded, "for Mr Skelton."

Momentarily convinced, the boy drew back the grating latch, then hesitated.

I seized the moment. I threw the lattice aside, pushed the boy to the ground. He cried out, his hand caught in the metal, but I leapt the barrier and went on. The footsteps ahead of me stopped a moment, then redoubled. Worm knew at last that he was followed. He increased his pace to a run and I mine, flying down the steps and on, down a dimly-lit passageway.

There was a fearful noise up ahead, a great echoing roar in the distance. Rounding the corner I found myself in a vast underground cavern. I blinked in consternation as my eyes adjusted to the light. What godless place was this? Part of their Nation Underground? A vast hall for assembling revolutionaries beneath our unsuspecting feet?

The tiled wall to my left gleamed in the gaslight as far as the eye could see. The great brick roof arched overhead and down to the opposite platform, beyond the tracks. Worm was already far off down the platform. He looked back at me, seemed to smile for an instant.

The noise grew deafening. To my astonishment, from out of the very earth a train hove into sight, belching steam and sulphurous fumes. It sounds banal now, but I cannot describe the horror of those moments, when a thing such as trains under the ground was an astonishment.

Two great lanterns speared towards me. I stood stupefied at the foot of the stairway, seemingly caught in their path. With the shrieking of the rails and those lights bearing down on me,

I feared that my last moment had come.

Worm leapt from the platform and on to the thundering train, greeted with cheers.

As the thing swept closer, the wheels a-rattling devilishly, I came to my senses. It was not heading straight for me. The tracks ran parallel to the platform, of course. The squat engine drew near, and I saw that its speed was not so terrifying. Worm had leapt onto it; so could I. There was a running board round the engine. One great leap and I would be on.

I steeled myself to run at it, but my knee, swelled from the chase, buckled beneath me. I fell to the platform.

I twisted around, and my heart leapt into my mouth. It took only an instant for the whole train to flash past and roar on into the darkness, but the image remained, imprinted on my mind.

The driver of the train was the weasel, Fairfoul, aided at the furnace by a team of little helpers. At the far end was a closed carriage, humming with activity, little hands arranging trays and decanters, passing bottles and plates.

In between, the central car was a glorious open compartment, complete with dining table and white linen. Bustling silently around, urchins in starched uniforms served from glittering salvers, carted off crockery and kept the feast in order, unnoticed by the guests.

The guests. At the far end of the table sat Coxhill. He was in his element, in his vainglorious pomp. He was attended by two personal urchins. No sooner did they fill his glass than he raised it, shouting out grandiloquent toasts, only for them to be swallowed by the din of the echoing tunnel.

In pride of place at the centre of the table, a rotund young man was tucking into a mountain of seafood. Oil dripped from his whiskers. He wiped it off with his shirtsleeve and took a slug of wine. This was Bertie, and no mistake.

At the head of the table stood a third man, smiling broadly. He nodded genially, as if to acknowledge my presence; perhaps he was welcoming Worm aboard, though my quarry vanished smartly from view. The man had swapped the whiskers he had worn at the Garden Party for a full false beard, a waistcoat, a bow tie, and a red and black magician's cape. Of course, his mother had told me how he loved disguises. His thin, saintly face was eclipsed by the beard, but finally I knew him. The same height as Hunt, it was true, though a deal broader in the shoulder. The disguise must have fooled Bertie and Coxhill, or they would have steered clear. And yet they had met him often in times gone by. How did I know him for sure, when we had met just that once face-to-face, and that in darkness? He had allowed himself one tell-tale divergence from a magician's costume. He was wearing a bowler hat.

Coded Note Found in Box of Chocolates (Deciphered by RVL):

For the attention of her good self, the Prof

My Dearest Dolly,
   Your presence is cordially required at the Moveable Feast, where BS's vermicular troupe shall present larksome sprees, glees and merriments for the Monstrous Crumbo and his Blabbing Spooney.
   The itinerant extravaganza departs Notgniddap at nobber o'the clock this very notchy.
   Tug on your cover-me-properlies, your stampers and fumbles and bonarest fakements, and toddle along.
   Shift your crabshells, you doxy old fishbag!
   Your ever affectionate
      Worm

Ruth Villiers' Final Narrative

What could I do when I realised that I, a grown woman, had been locked into my own apartments by an eight year-old girl? I laughed. I seethed. I tried and retried the handle in disbelief until my wrist hurt. I returned to the bedroom to see if Molly wasn't hiding underneath the bedspread. I raged and cursed in language unsuitable for a lady, for I had learnt a good deal in my weeks with her. And I marvelled at how, in the blink of an eye, the convalescent I had so long fed and nurtured had returned to her people, leaving me in the soup. Could I blame her? Of course not. She had got the call, poor thing, and moved pretty sharply.

In the minute it took me to decipher Worm's note, I was seized by anxiety. This was little relieved when I identified "Notgniddap" as backslang. I had so readily discredited Molly's description of their plot to destroy the Monstrous Rotundity.

I wasted precious time in panicking and uselessness. I could bang on the door, shout and wail, or call to passersby from the kitchen window, but anyone bold enough to break the door down would be unlikely to let this maiden in distress run off. More likely they would dose me. As for telling the truth, no one in their right minds would believe me.

The vegetable broth boiled over. I could do nothing right. I curled up on the ottoman and gave way to weeping. To think of the hours, the days, I had wasted on this tangled web of lost causes! This Skelton we had so long pursued began to transmogrify in my mind. His writings had entranced me, I confess, with radical ideas and poetic statements. More substantially, the Nation Underground seemed a genuine boon for the Worms. In Molly's telling of it, he was a benign dictator, the absolute monarch of Hobbes' *Leviathan*, to whom the people readily subject themselves. But could I trust a little girl's judgement? How many signs pulled the other way? He had them breaking into houses, thieving, working down the sewers, God damn it. He had threatened the Prince, thrown London into panic, not just with diverting spouts but with murders. Now he had left his little charges to carry out some unnamed atrocity. No, this was no kind-hearted dictator. This was instead a Leviathan of the depths, calling to him all the little Jonahs and Jobs, to swallow them up in one final disaster. And how we ran, all of us, still at his beck and call. Was the Prince, unsuspecting, even now being summoned by some ruse to this Feast of Fools, this macabre Last Supper?

A distant explosion drew my eye to the window. Far to the north, a bright rocket lit up the early evening, foretelling the fireworks to come. The window, I thought. I recalled some heroine of literature climbing to freedom by means of her sheets. I tore mine and Molly's from the beds, knotted them round the stout kitchen table and tugged until satisfied. It would hold my weight, if I could climb down it.

I formed a plan. The urchin Numpty had taken me for one of his own in Mr Mayhew's cape. I threw on my drabbest clothing, jammed the table beneath the sill, and wrapped the aunt's travelling rug around me.

As I hefted open the window, an evening chill was already in the air. I looked down. Living on the fourth floor was in the main pleasant, high above the noise and smells, with a view over Regent's Park. The prospect of shinning down forty feet to the street, however, was less appealing. A fine thing it would be to tumble past my landlady's window to my death.

This would never do. Too long I had sat puzzling at codes and bookishly studying. Bravado took me down the first few feet, wedging my toes into ledges and crevices. I was aided by a stout drainpipe, which led me to the outcrop of a second floor window. Through the lace curtains, I saw a family gathered round a fine high tea, laughing and joking. My shoulders were aching, my hands sore. My impromptu rope slipped with a startling creak. My stockings tore against the wall, and I thought I was falling, but I came to rest on the lintel of the first floor window. I pressed on, realising too late that the sheets gave out ten feet shy.

I dropped from the sky like a stone, landing at the feet of a bemused passerby, by luck a small boy who used to run errands for me. I was bruised all right, but the aunt's rug saved my skin. Should I run to Scotland Yard? Campbell might be at Paddington already, putting a stop to the whole foolish business. His sour-faced inspector would hardly be at the Yard on a Sunday evening, and I would have to explain all to some flat-footed drudge who would take me for cracked. "Fiendish plot, dear? How nice for you."

I took out Worm's note, with my scribbled translation, and wrote Campbell's name on it, gave the boy a shilling to take it to Scotland Yard. If Campbell hadn't wheedled the plan out of Worm, that would summon him with reinforcements. Whatever differences we'd had, I might yet be of help.

I dusted myself off and ran for the omnibus shelter. Never one when you need it, then they all come at once. I paced up and down, in such agitation that a gentleman approached me.

"May I entreat you to accept this good little book?" he said, proffering a New Testament filled with cautionary bookmarks. "I feel sure it will benefit you."

"Dear me, you're mistaken, sir," I retorted. "I am no social evil, I'm awaiting the omnibus."

Arriving at Paddington Station as the evening drew in, I spotted an unofficial-looking little chap slumped at the head of a new passageway, the entrance to the Metropolitan. Abandon hope, all ye who enter here.

It was still early evening. Nobber o' the clock this very notchy, Worm had written: nine o'clock tonight. I bided my time, spied on the chap from a distance. He seemed asleep, but I could see no way to squeeze past his outstretched legs without waking him. I mustn't be seen, not before Campbell appeared. Besides, we had to catch them red-handed. If they knew we'd got wind of them and called the thing off, it would all be in vain. With Berwick martyred, they would go to ground, mull over the lost chance, and strike again another day. Worst of all, we would never convince a soul that such a preposterous plan had ever been afoot.

After a time, a pair of Worms rolled up with a cart of clinking crates and hampers. They coughed for attention, spoke some kind of password. The little chap sat bolt upright, alarmed to be caught catnapping on duty. As they squeezed the crate through the gap, a couple of lettuces fell to the ground.

I dug my hands in my pockets and scuttled over, trying to walk Molly-fashion, a mix of humility and affectation. I scooped up the lettuces as if I were the cart-pullers' help, and thrust them under the guard's nose. Blinking wildly, he broke into a smile, tipped his hat, and let me pass unhindered.

Descending the dark steps, I seemed to enter the realm of fairy tales. I arrived in a great chamber. Long platforms stretched away in either direction, bordering a sunken railway that disappeared into black tunnels. The chamber was vaulted over, with sleek tiling above the platform, brickwork over the tracks. Light filtered through skylights, and gas lamps flickered, illuminating a train that stood proud in front of me.

I drew back into the shadows of the stairway. I could smell food cooking. To my right, fumes rose from the squat engine. Dark fears assailed me. It looked diabolical, a banquet for cannibals.

I breathed deep and looked again. Turning on the spit was a

boar. Come along, I told myself, there will be no human sacrifices here. The aromas of smoked fish and cheeses mingled with the roasting meat. A weaselly engine driver appeared on the backboard and set two Worms a-shovelling.

The final carriage held but a handful of Worms, engrossed in their chores.

The cart boys I had followed were unloading their cargo to the central carriage, a fine open car adorned with baubles and tinsel, the rude wooden sides draped in opulent red velvet to give the impression of luxury. The carriage was mostly taken up by a dining table covered by a white cloth. Their chores quitted, the boys retired to the end carriage.

I had to hide. I could never maintain my disguise under close scrutiny. Emerging from the shadows, I scurried across the platform and scrambled on board. To my surprise, there were only three chairs round the table; it could have seated sixty. An extra serving table stood by the end nearest the engine. On it lay chopping boards and carving knives, a platter of cheeses under muslin, and elegant decanters. This table too bore an elegant white cloth.

I glanced at the group huddled round the engine's furnace. The driver was schooling the Worms in using the bellows, the chefs basting the hog. I ducked under the tablecloth. Though elegant from above, the table was nothing but planks on stacked crates. I settled on a spot in the corner, resting against the crates where the cloth hung low. I could peek out down the length of the table. I would see anyone who boarded, and I should remain invisible.

I had to trust that Campbell would appear in time. I steeled myself to stay attentive, and to wait. It was a most peculiar sensation, secreted there in the world's latest marvel, waiting for the plot to unfold. Cataclysmic imagery flashed through my mind, as a delicious warmth emanated from the engine behind me. The strong aromas, distant babble of urchins, and the shovelling of the coal – it all seemed strangely agreeable.

I came to my senses to find myself amidst a hum of activity. Sheer exhaustion had fuddled my wits. There was babble all about me, somebody checking off the items on a menu. Forequarter of lamb? Yes, sir! Veal and salmon, lobster and pigeon. Ham, tongue, duck, cherries, strawberries, blanc-mange. Whipped cream and coffee. Did they intend to feed him till he burst? Then I heard Molly's voice.

"Ho, there, youngster! Opened that wine yet?"

"Yes, Professor."

"Well, get it decanted. It has to breathe, you know."

Molly might be a little girl to me, but she must be prominent in the hierarchy, though it seemed implausible that she should know the finer points of wine.

"No hanging about now," she insisted.

Wine bottles clinked, and the table above my head quivered. I curled myself up in fear and alarm. I would be discovered. Molly would sense I was there. But the bottles were decanted right there above me, and nobody the wiser.

When they moved away, I peered out. An army of Worms went about the preparations with a festive air. The time must be nigh, for they bore wine and caviare to the table, platters of meat, fresh baked bread, and fruit baskets.

A bell sounded far off. I nearly died of fright as an answering bell rang out behind me. All of a sudden, the hubbub was silenced. Only a handful of immaculately presented waiters remained.

I heard adult voices approaching. The lights brightened, showing off the marvel of the train. Two rather portly gentlemen stood looking about in amazement, with a good number of "Ho-ho!"s and harrumphing. The third man came up the carriage towards me. He was slighter, bearded, and dressed as the Master of Ceremonies. He stepped directly up to my table. My heart was pounding so, I would not have been surprised if he had snatched up a carving knife and run me through. Instead, he spoke quietly to his helpers. A cork popped, summons enough to bring the other men hurrying towards us.

"Gentlemen," said the third. "Your health."

The three men drank a toast. All I could see was trouser legs. I concentrated on the voices.

One of the three kept gabbling away, mingling boasts and excuses. "I can't apologise enough, Your Royal Highness. The fellows from your club, you know, and the college johnnies, they could have come, but, dash it, I thought it too risky."

"Really, old chap?" The second chap sounded amused.

"Risky," repeated the first fellow, too anxious to pick up his friend's playful tone. "I was anxious they'd blab. And I wanted it to be your special birthday treat, Your Highness."

"For God's sake," rejoined the second, "call me Bertie after all this time, won't you?"

It really was the Prince. I peered at the royal shoes, as he shifted from one foot to the other.

The first man I knew at once for Roxton Coxhill. Campbell had often enough impersonated his plummy accent and foppish demeanour. To my mind, the tremulous tone in his voice suggested a man on the brink of collapse. "Of course, Your Highness. Bertie, I mean. What I mean is, one can't be too careful, eh?"

"We'll have a hoot all the same. Quite a set-up you've got here."

The third man began to say something, but Coxhill interrupted, basking in the Prince's favour. "Oh, I assure you, you've never had a surprise like it."

Of course. The spout was for the Prince's eighteenth birthday, three years back, now this for his coming-of-age. Should I leap up and shout, "Dear Prince, you are played false?" Ridiculous, me in my ragged clothes, shabby and exhausted, like some madwoman. They would spirit me off and explain it away to the Prince with some half-cock excuse. No, I would have to wait for the cavalry to arrive.

"You've gone out of your way," said the Prince. "I can see that. Jolly kind of you."

"Nothing but the best for Bertie. This is the latest word in engineering science."

"Bosh and tripe to that, Roxy. Can one tuck in?"

"You must be famished," said the third man, quietly exultant. "Please, take your places. Off we go, John!"

The little helpers guided Coxhill and Bertie to their seats, and commenced to serving the banquet. Behind me, the whistle gave an almighty toot. There followed a hissing, a screeching and a series of groans, as the engine roared into life. Fear surged through my bones as we started moving. I had travelled by train before, and I had no fondness for it. But this was worse. Sulphurous smoke billowed out around us, and I clutched the tablecloth to my mouth, trying not to cough. What use the cavalry now?

We entered the darkness of the first tunnel, lit only by occasional lamps. The door of the final carriage opened, and a chorus of Worms struck up a song, their voices echoing above the engine's roar like the harmony of angels.

Fast, oh, fast fade
The roses of pleasure ...

As we emerged into a second station, the rasping smoke receded a little, before we plunged again into the darkness. I stared out at the phantasmagoric feast, frightened out of my wits, convinced we were hurtling towards our final end. Yet they had done nothing barbarous yet. They were not attacking the Prince. They were feasting him, treating him to a private show of the eighth wonder of the world. Perhaps it was all over. Perhaps, with Berwick's death, they had decided to bury the hatchet and abandon the grudge. The singing came to a climax with a rendition of that tuneless ditty, "God Save the Queen", at which the diners must have risen to their feet, albeit reluctantly.

I could hear Coxhill, shouting from the far end of the table. Bertie I could just make out above the salvers of pink crayfish. He tucked his lace napkin under his chin and merrily tore the legs off the hapless crustaceans. "Well, well!" he cried and, "I say!" as the little helpers bustled about, serving platter after platter. I have never seen anyone attack their food as the Prince did on that journey. If I had screamed out that he was in danger of his life, he would have asked me to wait for dessert.

The third man sat only feet away from me. I studied him in the intermittent gaslight: a pale thin face; a thoughtful expression. And though the food was piled high in front of him too, he barely touched a morsel. Strange that the others seemed not to know him. They treated him as a glorified servant, a major-domo. As we passed through another station, he frowned, then smiled broadly, clapping his hands as a youth leapt aboard right in front of my eyes. Worm! The little chancer had escaped Campbell.

My hopes of rescue were in vain.

Worm ducked under the dining table, out of sight. Moments later, he crawled out at my end of the table, and looked about him. The thin man bent down to clasp him by the shoulders. "Well done, old cove," he said.

"All present and correct, Mr Skelton," Worm replied brightly. "Full steam ahead, eh?" He glanced in my direction, and I shuddered.

The train lurched, the lights were extinguished and a scream of excitement went up from the little helpers as we accelerated into the darkness.

I clutched at the crates to steady myself. So this was he, Berwick Skelton, sitting not two yards from me. What kind of man was he? They killed him, and he came back from the dead. I tried to shake off my foolishness. If it was he, it was not some diabolical resurrection, but because he had never been killed. It made sense. A master of tricks and deceptions, nothing would serve him better than our believing him dead. How calm he looked, now the moment of reckoning drew near.

The sulphurous smoke grew oppressive. There were bones glowing in the tunnel walls, skulls hung from the vault. We were roaring into the pit of hell. But as I looked up, I glimpsed pale light high above. We emerged into a mighty cutting, overarched by bridges and monstrous pipes, buildings silhouetted against the sky, as if we were buried in the ground, looking out of our graves. The brakes shrieked, and we drew up in a broad station, deserted of people. The Prince clapped and shouted to the thin man, the man I now knew to be Skelton, what a terrific jape it was. I wanted to believe him. I wanted to believe that he was making peace with his enemies, forgiving them everything. But I could not credit it.

The magician's cape flashed past me, and Skelton disappeared from my view as we drew to a halt. I was tempted to run for it. I could whisper a warning to the Prince and pull him away. Except that two rather burly Worms were standing in front of my table, one of them dandling a lettuce. Had I been seen?

With a clunk and a grinding hiss, light shone in under my table. I feared I was discovered, but no. The door behind me, that led to the engine, had come ajar: a serendipitous exit?

I peeked through the gap. The station was alive with activity. The engine had been decoupled. It stood ten yards from my carriage, its furnace glowing dimmer now. There was a great grinding of gears, and the glow began to move sideways. To my astonishment, the entire engine began to rotate, the funnel end drawing nearer and the driver's board turning away from us.

"Ho-ho, look at that!" Coxhill brought Bertie up to my end to watch the spectacle. "Turntable's powered by HECC hydraulics, y'know."

"Pass the gateau, won't you, Roxy?"

"The smoothest of mechanisms–"

"Hush," said the Prince. "The show's starting."

The moment the engine stopped rotating, perpendicular to us now, the Worms draped a curtain between the funnels and down over the running board facing us, then formed into tidy rows in front of me. My view left something to be desired, but I have been less comfortable in the West End.

A hush fell.

"Ra, ra!" called Bertie, thoroughly enjoying himself.

"Yes," echoed Coxhill, somewhat less sure of himself. "Jolly fine show."

Gas lanterns were trained onto the makeshift stage, and little Worms burst across it, crisscrossing acrobatically in front of the engine, as a jolly trio – drums, accordion and tuba – struck up an oom-pah refrain. The scene was filled with colour as they did cartwheels and back somersaults. One teetered back and forth on a wooden cask; another spun a top into the air and caught in on a string. My breath caught in my throat as I recognised Molly.

Then came Skelton. Uproarious applause broke out as the makeshift curtain swished open, and he strolled along the running board, skipping up on to the engine, quite as if it were the Haymarket stage. His cape swirled, coloured handkerchiefs poked from his pockets, and his twirling cane gleamed under the lights. He despatched the little acrobats with a clap of the hands, like a circus ringmaster, and launched into stock tricks, rolling his bowler hat up and down his arm, and making his handkerchiefs appear in unlikely places. He fanned a deck of playing cards from hand to hand, set it down, and, with a show of concentration, drew it unsupported into the air. That done, he promptly walked off the engine into midair, looked around comedically as if surprised at these levitations, and fell back to the engine with a clunk. The trio accompanied his antics with jolly tunes and the odd drum roll.

"That's kind of you, little fellow," said Bertie. The smell of fresh coffee drifted past me. "Any chance of a drop more port?"

I pinched myself, trying to shake off the lurid clutch of the show. There might be a moment when all were engrossed and I could spirit Bertie away. No, it was hopeless. The burly Worms sat perched on the carriage wall, goggle-eyed. One last little helper was still attending the revellers, plying them with drinks and desserts.

"For my first trick," Skelton began, his voice cutting through the air like a knifeblade, "I require the loan of a banknote. Would a gentleman be so good as volunteer one?"

"Here you go," shouted Bertie, mouth full of cake.

One of the burly Worms bore Bertie's offering through the audience.

"Ten guineas," said Skelton, testing the note against the light. "That ain't from the cheap seats. Must have royalty in tonight."

Laughter all around.

Without a scruple, he ripped it in two. Gasps all round. He lifted the cap of the funnel with his cane, releasing a cloud of steam, and popped in one half. The other he folded, and threw into the air like a paper dart. It fluttered and took flight, up and away from the Worms' outstretched hands, transformed into a dove.

As we applauded, Skelton rapped his cane on the engine. The funnel spouted steam again, and out flew a banknote. He snatched it from the air and tugged it straight. "Please, return the money to the gentleman. And might I borrow his watch?"

I had to dive for my corner, as the burly Worm hopped up onto the end of the carriage.

"Here you go," said Bertie gamely. "Careful with that, my mother gave it me."

The boy jumped back down, and I peeked out again.

"Careful, you say?" said Skelton. He took the watch, and at once feigned dropping it. But it was still in his hand, glinting in the light. "Don't worry, sir, I wouldn't dream of being careless with–" Whereupon it fell from his hand down the side of the engine and smashed on the turntable for all to see. Skelton looked up. "Oops-a-daisy." He coughed awkwardly. "Moving on, can I have a little volunteer to be sawn in half?"

I peeked back to see how the show was being received. Coxhill was trying to restrain his giggles. Bertie was stroking his whiskers. He poked his friend in the stomach.

"I say, you don't think–"

"Not at all," Coxhill tittered. "He wouldn't dare."

I took hold of the tablecloth, ready to pull back it back and whisper my warning. The voice that volunteered stopped me short. It would have to be Molly. I glued my eye to the peephole as she clambered up to Skelton. He placed a wooden box on the running board, and she climbed in eagerly. The musicians raised the tempo. I watched, sick to my stomach, as he took up a saw and severed the box quite in half. Had she recovered her health only to meet her end at the hands of this madman, deep in the bowels of the earth?

I cried out. I couldn't help myself.

But the whole audience was shouting now, and I remained undiscovered. I was ready to run out and take on the lot of them myself. But no sooner than the box was severed, he spun it to show us Molly's little legs waggling gaily. He picked up the other half and out popped Molly's head, still alive and giggling. Indeed, I'd never seen the little girl as happy as when she was receiving our applause.

"What have you got there, Professor?" said Skelton. He reached out and extracted from her ear the Prince's pocket watch, back in one piece.

"Ho, ho," said Bertie, clapping behind me. "The old devil!"

"Return the watch to the gentleman, if you'd be so kind, Professor," said Skelton, shutting her back in the box. He rapped on the lid and opened it up. She had disappeared entirely. Not the first time today, I thought, amidst the applause and hilarity.

"For my penultimate trick, I need a very special volunteer." He looked around with mock drama, then lighted on the carriage. "Sir, would you be so kind?"

"Me?" spluttered Coxhill. "Oh, I couldn't possibly."

"Go on, Roxy!"

"No, I'm absolutely stuffed, and a bit tipsy, to be honest… Eh? Whoah, there. Unhand me, you brutes. I do say! Your Royal Highness. Bertie. Help, ho, someone!"

A wave of Worms boarded the carriage, shunting my table aside. The cloth fell, and I was revealed. Nobody noticed. They were busy carrying Coxhill down, through the door that had been my lookout post, onto the edge of the turntable. Bertie sat tight, chortling merrily, only too glad to get his own back after Coxhill's laughter. The music took an agitated turn.

"Please," Skelton called above the hubbub, "do not be alarmed."

"Sir," I began, crawling out from my corner.

Bertie glanced down and gave me a friendly nod. "Cracking show, ain't it?" he said, chuckling to himself.

"Your Highness, you must flee this place."

"All in good time," he said. "Looks like Roxy's going to get it in the neck."

I turned back. Coxhill had given up the struggle and acquiesced, pinned down by the Worms on a strange wooden contraption, not unlike the mediaeval stocks. A hush fell over the mighty chamber.

"How hilarious," Coxhill called out. "How very, very droll."

Skelton leapt down towards him, blackly illuminated in the light of the lanterns. I shall forever remember the image of him, poised to exact the vengeance he had so long planned. With consummate showmanship, he shut Coxhill's wrists and neck into the grooves of the stocks. He stepped back and locked Coxhill's ankles in hefty manacles.

The retributive verses of Skelton's tome began running around my head. Did anyone else know the depth of his anger?

"You stand accused," said Skelton, "of crimes against humanity."

"What's he done?" called Bertie gamely.

"Such dreadful crimes, sir, I do hesitate to name them here."

Bertie guffawed.

"Have you anything you wish to say?"

"Now you mention it," Coxhill began, stretching his neck, "this thing's dashed uncomfortable."

There was a shout from the darkness of the station. Skelton

looked up and gave a theatrical signal. The Worms drew back, and the great grinding hiss of the turntable gears reverberated again. The engine began to move.

Coxhill started muttering. He could not see what we could. His head and arms were affixed to the solid rails in front of my carriage. But his legs were chained fast to the turntable, now beginning its inexorable rotation.

Coxhill struggled at his bonds in earnest. His whining set Bertie laughing at the comic spectacle. The Worms went about clearing up. Skelton gazed impassively at Coxhill, then looked up at the Prince.

Coxhill scratched at the stocks. He tried to turn and make sense of what was happening, but he was held fast. "Help. Somebody. God help us!"

Bertie spoke at my shoulder. "Terribly convincing, ain't it?"

"Sir," I said, tearing my eyes from the awful show. "We're in grave danger–"

"Look at that," said Bertie admiringly. "You'd almost believe they were doing him mischief."

Out of the darkness of the station Worm appeared. He ran straight to Skelton and laid his hand on the man's forearm, conveying some urgent message. Skelton looked away across the station. Energised anew, he led Worm to the engine.

"Mr Prince, sir?" said a familiar voice. "You'll be wanting your watch back, will you?"

Bertie looked down at Molly. In those dreadful moments, I was surprised at the way he addressed her, respectful and gentlemanly. "Kind of you, little fellow," he said.

She wrinkled her nose in disappointment. "Shame."

"Molly!" I said.

"I'd love to give it you," the Prince smiled, "but Mama would have my guts for garters."

The engine rumbled back into life. Coxhill screamed. He had

been gently stretched at first, but now the rotating turntable had him drawn out full length. His arms were strained to breaking point, his eyes bulging in their sockets.

"Molly," I said desperately.

"Sorry, Miss Bilious," Molly frowned. "I don't think this show is fit for ladies."

"Have they no mercy?" I cried.

Bertie shook his finger knowingly. "Don't worry," he chuckled. "It's doubtless the same trick as with my watch. Fooled us good and proper, mark my words."

I never thought that I should see such cruelty. I do not know by what infernal power the turntable was driven, but I can tell you that it pulled that man apart as easily as you or I might shell a pod of peas or break bread into our soup. His shrieks as he was dismembered I will never forget. I turned away, struggling for breath. I no longer thought of saving the Prince, or myself. A foul smell stained the air, and I thought I would faint. The engine belched a mighty blast of steam and began rolling towards us. Coxhill fell silent.

There was a great cry from the depths of the station.

"Here comes the Heavy Brigade," said Bertie. Even he looked troubled now, like a child who fears the joke has gone too far. "Best make ourselves scarce, had we? I say, are you quite all right?"

I found myself taken up by strong arms. These are not children, I thought, as the Worms lifted me from the carriage. These are tough young men, an underground army. I watched in awe as they coupled the engine back onto the carriages and bolted. At once the train eased away, rolling back down the line towards the tunnels. I turned my weary head to see Campbell and his inspector appear from the shadows, followed by a troop of policemen. Too late. The train headed for the tunnel. The furnace was stoked high, Worm tending the engine. Bertie remained at the end of the table, smiling uneasily. The last thing I saw was Skelton walking calmly up the running board. He strode through the door of the open carriage, closed it neatly behind him, and stepped up to the Prince.

REPORT OF ALBERT EDWARD SAXE-COBURG-GOTHA, PRINCE OF WALES, AS TRANSCRIBED BY SGT LAWLESS

A most extraordinary birthday. This time next year I'll be married and sensible. Seemed silly to miss out on one last blast of foolishness.

Roxy's mishap, though, did leave me feeling distinctly queasy. Then the organiser chap, who'd been absolutely top-ho throughout the escapade, heads us back into the tunnel and strolls up to confront one, man to man, you know.

What an ass Roxy made of himself. Deuced unfortunate, but I remain convinced it was his own stupid fault. Flailing around like a bird in a cage. It's no wonder the apparatus got tangled around him. It did rather tarnish what was otherwise a frightfully rousing birthday treat.

Poor old Roxy. Pretended to me that he hadn't invited the others for fear they'd blab. Not true, of course. Nobody would go near him. Messed things up good and proper, he had. He wasn't a bad sort. Never harmed me, at least. Just tried too hard. I don't know. Life seems hard enough to me. I used to say, that chap's a German, I don't like him. Then I thought, that man's a bounder, it's him I'm against. Nowadays I think everyone's got a tough enough trot of it, and we should bally well pile in and be civil to each other, as far as we're able.

So Wardle rolls up with his henchmen and puts an end to

the magic show. Off we set into the darkness again. Back to Paddington, I assume, and I'm ready to say my thank yous and head for Buck House. I sit down at the table again, as it seems a shame to waste the blancmange. Then, hey presto, the magician chap appears beside me, all thoughtful-like, you know. He takes off the beard and the magician's garb, and I'm dashed if I don't know him from somewhere. Couldn't say where, but I know we've met before. He looks at me in a most peculiar way. In he starts about this plan he had to have hundreds of men at the banquet, all the top sorts, only he's settled on me and Roxton as the cream of the crop.

"Very good of you," I mutter, beginning to think the chap's a bit potty. "Care for a drop of Chablis?"

He fixes me with this blue-eyed stare. "Don't you know me?" says he.

"You do seem familiar," I confess, trying to inject a bit of jocularity back into proceedings, "but you meet a deuced lot of fellows in my line. Have to help me out, old man."

"*The Frozen Deep*," says he, all tight-faced.

True enough, the tunnel's damnably chilly, and I'm about to offer him my greatcoat. Then I recall that dashed play that dear Nellie was in when I met her. "What kind of set-up is this?" I ask, as he has me quite nonplussed. "I say, who put you up to this? Not one of Wardle's cronies, are you?"

At this, the chap smiles, shakes his head. Doesn't give me much relief as we're accelerating into the pitch black. I hear Papa's voice in my head. What you need, you cunning lazybones, is an almighty scare to frighten some sense into you. Suppose it's the champagne and the phantasmagoric surrounds, but I start to take the notion that this chap is acting on Papa's behalf.

True to form, the chap starts banging on with a list of my weaknesses – fecklessness, recklessness, carelessness – and ends up with a cutting remark about Nellie. I finally get it, this is the chap Nellie stiffed when she started to step out with me. And he's still sticky over it.

"Look, old chap, I was just an impetuous youngster with more spunk in me than I knew what to do with, and she is a fearful seductress of a woman, as you well know. The world and his wife are besotted with her, and I fell as readily as the next man. I had a true fondness for her. Never intended any compromise of her honour. Besides, it's all over. I've learned my lesson. I'll soon be married and sensible, like the good son father wanted."

The fellow looks at me with a plaintive, elegiac expression. The train lurches with a jolt to tighten the old testiculars, and we're into the darkness again. There's a fearful bang, and the walls seem to explode. Yet this fellow's still looking at me, sizing me up.

"Gosh," I find myself babbling, "you must really despise me, old man. I can see that. But I really did like Nellie. Does that count for nothing?"

The chap's face falls.

At this point, something flies past my face and I look down to see my blancmange covered in muck. There's a terrible din and a stink to rival the Palace compost heap. There's dung raining into the carriage. I cry out like a damn fool, and hold up my hands. I thought the sky was falling in, I tell you.

The fellow glances around, then looks back at me sadly, as if he rather regretted the whole shebang. I can't help but feel tremendously sorry for him, even though he has me scared half to death.

"Look, old man," I say, the wits frightened out of me. I hold out my hand. "Please accept my sincerest apologies, won't you?"

He shakes my hand, with this strange expression as if it's

the end of the world. Next thing, I'm being tugged from the train, floating in filth, and swimming for my life. That's the last I recall.

Sgt Lawless' Final Narrative

The Ghost Train

I was furious with myself for missing the train at Gower Street. For precious moments I sat on the platform, listening to the engine carry the Prince away. All our efforts had brought us so close; and at the critical moment I had fallen.

Except I knew where they were headed. The end of the line. What more fitting end than there, where his borough – his world – had vanished in the name of Progress?

The Euston Road of a Sunday night was as busy as ever. I promised the driver a handsome tip to spirit me to Farringdon fast as the wind. The traffic was blocked solid at King's Cross. As the man urged the horse through the vehicles, we all but crashed into Wardle, standing disconsolately by his hansom. He had closed the station, acting on my words to the tea-boy. Darlington was reporting to him when he saw me. Wardle started in at once, lambasting me for my carelessness.

I had no time for his protests. "Get in or be damned," I told him.

He climbed up. "What wild goose chase is this?"

"Send men to the Farringdon Road Metropolitan station," I shouted to Darlington. "Pray God we're not too late."

As I raced down the steps to the platform, I felt I was entering a labyrinth. The bellows of the engine echoed up the passageways. To one side lay broad platforms, partly open to the sky, and the tracks that headed back up the line. But the engine's roar came from deeper in beneath the station. I sped down the dark walkways, Wardle straggling behind me.

All at once I emerged into a broad open space, alive with activity. There in front of me lay a great turntable. The strange squat engine was just beginning to push the train back down the line. To the right, little figures ran off into the shadows.

On the platform in front of me, Miss Villiers was being attended by Fairfoul and a few Worms. Near her was some kind of ruined body, attached to the turntable. On the departing train sat Bertie, still at his ease, still eating. Wardle called out to him, but Bertie shaded his face, like a child whose parents have embarrassed him in front of his friends. Miss Villiers' attendants upped and fled after their chums. She was unharmed as far as I could tell, thank God. I left Wardle to deal with the mischief on the turntable. I had missed that train once already and I was not about to let it leave without me again.

It was sheer luck that let me leap onto the running board without Worm seeing me. He was stoking the furnace to build up steam for that final run. As we picked up speed, I edged my way down the running board. I reached out to steady myself, but the burning hot engine scalded my hand.

The rush of wind stung my eyes as we drew out of the station. I crawled towards the carriages, trying not to picture what the wheels would do to me if I slipped.

The ground below us suddenly fell away, and I saw another railway line far beneath us. I looked around in panic. We were passing over a bridge, even in the depths of that monstrous cutting, a railway upon a railway. It was all I could do to cling on.

Up ahead in the open carriage, Bertie looked up as Skelton

appeared beside him, removed his bowler hat and nodded cordially. They fell into earnest conversation. I was struck by the absurd thought that the two of them were alike, able young men whose dreams the world has decreed impermissible. Both of them loved Nellie, the Prince and the pauper, and both of their loves were doomed.

Accelerating towards the tunnel, black and forbidding, we passed under a great wrought-iron pipe, as broad as a man is tall, then plunged into the darkness. I recalled certain other tunnels I had crawled in. I am no wizard at geography, but I knew that this train line crisscrossed any number of pipes, rivers and sewers on its path across the capital. I tried to put from my mind the tales of miners perishing up north the year before, unable to breathe in the underground depths. Yet Pearson had assured us that his tunnels would be safe.

I grasped at the handrail beneath the funnel and rounded the engine. We emerged from the tunnel, and I called out to the Prince. My words were lost in a rush of wind. I glanced around in wonderment. We were again in a cutting, the sides rising sheer above us. The roar redoubled as we entered another station. King's Cross.

I pulled myself upright as Worm peered around the end of the engine, his face aglow. He was astonished for a moment, but it was too late for him to stop me.

I turned back. Up ahead, the station ended in the broad flat arch leading the underground tracks gently left, under the Euston Road. I had to leap across to the open carriage before we entered the tunnel.

The train shook, and we veered off to the right. We were headed for the wall and destruction, I was sure of it. I clung to the handrail and awaited the final crash. Instead we plunged into the narrowest of openings, a siding, rank and ill-lit. A gate clanged shut behind us, blocking out the lights of the station.

A blast sounded above us, and the train shuddered. Foul sludge sprayed down on me. I shielded my face, spitting and coughing. I could just make out where it came from, the vast iron pipe that ran above us, built into the apex of the tunnel. Alongside it ran a lesser pipe of gleaming steel. This second duct had mechanisms attached at intervals. As I stared through smarting eyes, these began to blow open, water spraying out of them.

A huge blast echoed ahead. I looked up to see the great iron pipe cracking apart, discharging its sludge on to us.

In that moment, I could see it all with desperate clarity. I knew that the mechanisms stolen from London's finest houses were no gift, as Worm had dissembled. I knew that Skelton had used them as timing devices, booby traps springing hydraulic spouts across the city. But now I saw that he had kept some in reserve for this, his masterpiece, to set off charges along the Fleet Sewer itself, cracking open the ironwork, with the valves of Coxhill's hydraulics rigged to sluice water into it, pumping the foulness out onto us, drenching us, covering everything.

I reached across to the open carriage. The wood was wet. Everything was darkness and dirt. The waters were rising, filling the siding, yet the train ploughed on. I could barely see, with excrement in my hair, on my face, in my eyes, but in disgust and anger I clambered across.

Skelton saw me first. It was he I had spoken to at Buckingham Palace, not Bertie. For an instant, I looked in his eyes. There I saw no malice, no fury. Only a resigned smile. He seemed to me almost a ghost already.

There was no time for more. I tugged at the Prince's arm. He turned to me in utter horror. Berwick made no effort to stop us. Quite the contrary, he let us go.

I pulled the Prince with me into the frightful flowing

blackness, shutting my eyes against the foulness. The tunnel had become a river, already deep, and I strained to hold the Prince above water. The train roared on with a dreadful screeching, as if the tunnel were on the verge of collapse. I did not know where the train was headed; I only knew that I must get away from it, down the tunnel, and back to the open air. The Prince was a useless swimmer, and I could barely buoy up his dead weight.

The waves of sludge swept us down, the current battering us against the tunnel walls. I had one arm around the Prince, and one hand out in front of me. He clung to me, coughing and spluttering, driving me under the foetid water. It was unendurable.

We washed up against the sluice gate. The end of the tunnel must be at hand, for there was light high above. That would not save us if the waters kept rising. Even now the Prince was losing consciousness. Good God, I thought, he's brought us here to drown in filth and ignominy.

I braced myself between the metal grating and the tunnel wall. The Prince was still breathing. The waters rose, lifting us higher, and my shoulder bumped against a box affixed to the sluice gate. I stared at it in the deathly light: a large steel panel, cogs and springs, affixed to an iron bolt. A release catch. I peered closer, my eyes stinging. The maker's name was inscribed on the panel, Allnutt & Ganz. The workings of the Euston Square clock.

An almighty explosion reverberated around the tunnel, and an unearthly light gleamed far behind us, the train and its finishing end.

I clutched the gate for purchase. My hands ached, and I could barely breathe. Before long the tunnel would be inundated. There was no time for delicate fingerwork. I raised my good leg, aimed my boot at the beautiful mechanism, and smashed it to pieces.

With a great swoosh, the sluice gate gave way.

A wave swept down the tunnel, flushing us out into the open air. Tumbled in the flood, I lost hold of the Prince.

I awoke to find myself being hauled out of the water by sure hands. I was back at King's Cross. Darlington's crowd heaved me up onto the platform and laid me down, gasping for breath. I tried to sit up, spitting and retching, but could only raise myself onto my elbows. I looked around desperately. I tried to speak, tried to tell them that somewhere under the filth was the Prince. Worm, still at the engine. Berwick on the train. The words would not come.

There was a shout further down the platform as they pulled Bertie out of the abating flood. He was covered in excrement and looked like he had seen the devil. As he came to, the Prince started upright and splashed back into the tide of filth.

I jumped down and caught hold of him. "Your Royal Highness, you need to rest."

"Fiddlesticks," he blurted out, trying to shake free, and turned back towards the dark mouth of the tunnel. "We must go after him. Goddammit. He saved my life."

"Who?"

"The little fellow." He glanced past me and with sudden strength broke free. "I'm damn well going back for him."

I caught him and held tight until he explained. In the final surge, a little fellow had swum up and kept him afloat. He had been drowning and the little fellow had saved him. I shouted to Darlington's crowd that they must go in, up the tunnel, to look for survivors.

"My friend," Darlington intervened, "it's half an hour ago we pulled you out. You'd fainted quite away. We can't go sending nobody in there. It's a death trap, that is. Heaven knows what else is waiting to blow."

And yet, I thought, Shuffler and friends used to work in those foul sewers every day, on the off chance of spotting a half sovereign.

Bertie plumped himself down on the platform beside me with a look of despair. He put his head in his hands, mindless of the grime in which he was covered. I warmed to him as we sat there, dirty and disgusting. He would have gone back in, this prince, if we had let him, to try and save Worm of the Euston Square Worms, public company as yet unlimited.

"That little fellow," said Bertie, "he was as valiant as those bloody Scots at Balaclava." He pursed his lips. "I believe he has given his life for me. The little fellow."

The Prince began talking, ten to the dozen. He was dreadfully shaken, and babbled of things I did not understand. Of his childhood. His father. He seemed to see it all as a punishment organised from beyond the grave by Prince Albert. It had given him the scare of his life, he said. He rose on a sudden and vomited over the edge of the platform.

I sent the Prince back to the Palace. He said his chaise was waiting at Paddington. Damn the chaise at Paddington, I told him. I would deal with that. He must go home and never speak of this night again.

At the platform, there was no sign of Worm. Exhausted from our journey into oblivion, I had no tears to weep. The flow of debris was ebbing now. On the last surges, flotsam and jetsam from the banquet washed out: empty crates, wine bottles, ruined fruit. I stared, sore-eyed and stinking, at Berwick's bowler hat bobbing on the water at the mouth of the tunnel.

AFTERWORD
[1863, 1911, 1888]

*The Bugle — Words & Trains — Sometimes a
Person Gets Desperate*

Euston Daily Bugle

10th January, 1863

METROPOLITAN TRIUMPH

As the *Bugle* predicted from the start, the opening of the Metropolitan Railway today was an enormous success. Despite a delay of twenty-one months, the public were united in their enthusiasm. Thirty thousand Londoners flocked to the latest in our city's great panoply of wonders. From nine o'clock in the morning till past midday it was impossible to obtain a place on the upward line.

What a tragedy that the Hon Charles Pearson MP, who endured such derision over the scheme, died before its fruition. How jubilantly would he have looked upon the throng of working men exulting in this new service. The first-class carriages were filled with London's elite and famous, although there was no royal patronage at last night's banquet in Farringdon Station, despite the Queen's predilection for novelty trains. (The Prince of Wales will, however, open Bazalgette's sewerage works next year, where the fourth of James Watt's monumental pumps is to be named for the Royal Fiancée, Princess Alexandra.)

Dissonant notes were nonetheless sounded amid the fanfare. Some deplored the crush, like the first night of a pantomime. A few expressed regret that ten thousand were made homeless during construction. Others complained that the sulphurous fumes and flickering gaslight gave the sensation of plunging into unknown and infinite danger. Just two months back, a drunken driver overshot the works in a siding beneath King's Cross; the Fleet Ditch burst in, drowning workers in sewage; and a hydraulics manager was killed while testing out the system. Since the GWR's intervention, however, these teething problems have been firmly resolved, and the Board of Safety have withdrawn their concerns.

Another step towards the modernisation of the capital. The Bugle predicts a tremendous impact. There is talk of using wind power or dried sewerage ordure as fuel. Besides the line being built into the Victoria Embankment, lines could be laid along the Regent's Canal and the bed of the Thames. Such a raft of proposals faces Parliament that, if all the schemes were effected, nearly one-half of the City itself would be demolished, every open space in the metropolis would be given up for the erection of termini with their screaming and hissing locomotives, and we would find ourselves living in a junction yard.

Instead, is not the moment ripe for a glass-covered double-decker thoroughfare spanning the heart of the world's greatest city, the *Bugle*'s own Crystal Way?

WORDS & TRAINS

Were we right or were we not? They enjoined us to keep silence, cited reputations at stake, and lives to be ruined by scandal, not least those of Campbell's superiors. One thinks too of Mr Dickens. One thinks of the King, or the Prince, as he was then.

It is fifty years since those dreadful events. Now that all the principal players are dead, Bertie the last to go, I have assembled this memoir. Principally it comprises Campbell's recollections, written in the 1880s. I have interpolated relevant cuttings, snippets of Skelton's writings and notes of my own, where gaps needed filling.

For my failure to publish, I make no further apology, except to say that even in this flippant day and age when we are told that anything goes, I preferred to excise references to certain nefarious practices in gentlemen's clubs and gambling hells, which point to a range of royal peccadilloes that cast unnecessary slurs on the late Edward VII. In my work, I have had occasion to discuss the case with the odd aspiring novelist, but I will now bind the memoir and print a very limited edition, to be discreetly catalogued in the publication libraries, where I pray that some diligent scholar may one day stumble upon our story.

Bertie, as we all know, has presided over an era of change. Many lamented the passing of Victorian standards, but I find something honest about our Edwardian frivolity. They say he loosened our morals with his gambling and mistresses. Yet all were agreed that he loved Queen Alix fondly.

Wardle retired. There seemed no sense in exposing his compromises, but he felt the scandal keenly. He and his wife did not retire to Yorkshire, as planned, but instead set sail for Argentina, where they purchased a thriving plantation, only to be ruined by the abolition of slavery. His son, Charlie – in fact Albert Charles Wardle – found success in Queensland, Australia, though ever in conflict with the authorities as a leader of the fledgling trades unions movement. Campbell liked to hear tell of him, I think he always envied Wardle

Junior his great adventure.

Nobody knew at that time about the problems between Catherine Dickens' father and mother, sparked by another actress. She escaped the broken home by marrying Wilkie Collins' invalid brother, a desperate move, as they were forced to live in Italy in penurious exile.

Madame Skelton, it transpired, did not lose everything in the destruction of Clerkenwell. She moved to Willesden, dutifully tended by Fairfoul, and became the hub of a thriving community rehoused by Bazalgette. Whether or not Campbell's plea was responsible for this good fortune, heaven knows.

As for Hester, by the time Campbell returned to the Home for Fallen Women, it was too late. She had hanged herself in her dormitory. She had a pauper's burial in St Giles in Camden, with not one friend or relative. Campbell was uncommonly upset about it, and erected a small headstone for her at his own cost.

The Nation Underground vanished into thin air. By the time the police unearthed the vault off Battle Bridge Road, the books, furnishings and accoutrements were gone, save for one Tom Thumb chair. I imagine the Worms voted to disband and went off to join other groups; a few, with Campbell's help, found gainful employment at the Metropolitan Board of Works. How long the wider cells associated with them survived, I do not know, nor how broad their effects, only that Campbell took to reading the international news pages. I remember his amusement at an account of robberies in the style of the skeleton thefts in the Berlin sewers of the late Seventies. If a new generation of Worms had set up there, Campbell did nothing to blow the whistle on it. Sometimes I'd catch him studying reports of riots in Paris or Balkan uprisings. I believe he thought they had a hand in it all. For neither

Worm nor Skelton were ever found, and Campbell harboured a notion that one or both of them escaped. After all, they knew those underground passageways as nobody else, and losing your hat is no proof that you have died. It would have pleased him to imagine an aged Berwick heading the 1905 revolution against the Tsar, with Worm marching beside him. The Professor has never said a word, but the glint in her eye suggests she knows something.

Of course, Campbell did not witness Skelton's most barbarous act, as I did, rending Coxhill on the turntable like a villain of Greek tragedy, and he never quite believed him capable of such a dark deed. Worm's suggestion that Skelton originally planned to drown hundreds also haunts my dreams. The authorities never let a word of it be breathed; I suppose even those who repaired the tunnel believed the story given out that it was another accident. Exactly two months after Skelton's attack, two hundred important personages rode on the train to a feast on that same Farringdon platform.

Campbell was fond of telling other stories from his career, but of this case he remained loath to speak. Always one to put on an unwavering front, he was anything but cold. If anything, he felt things too deeply. I urged him to write it all down, as a form of catharsis more than anything else. He would reply with some claptrap to the effect that our words are just trains, moving through the underground passageways of the mind, past things that can never really be named.

I was surprised, then, to find among his papers and case notes when he passed away this long account, neatly filed along with the newspaper cuttings. I dare to hope that he wanted it read, to convey to future generations something of the horror that faced us in those dark times. His final meditation I include hereafter.

I have omitted to mention three of our players.

Among Roxton Coxhill's private effects were found objects that suggested he was on the verge of suicide: prussic acid, razors and drafts of an intensely remorseful suicide note. Let me quote:

> *I cannot live – I have ruined too many – I have committed diabolical crimes, still unknown to any living being. I cannot live to see them come to light, bringing me and my late father into disrepute, causing to all shame and guilt that they ever should have known me. I attribute all this to no one but to my own infamous villainy. I could go through any torture as recompense for these crimes. No torture could be too much, but I cannot live to see the tortures I have inflicted upon others.*

These monstrous crimes, it transpired, included fraud and embezzlement to the nth degree. Besides the crimes that Campbell unearthed, Coxhill had defrauded a Wicklow bank, in which he had an interest, of £23,000, oversold shares in the HECC to the tune of £150,000, and represented his assets at thousands when he was in fact in heavy debt. In the end he was preparing to raise money by means of forged cheques. Even had the Prince of Wales agreed to back his venture, as he dreamed, it is hard to see how he could have been saved from ignominy. Whom the gods wish to destroy, they first make mad. Coxhill was already half-crazed from his opium habit, which Campbell was too naïve to recognise. It almost seemed that Skelton made himself the agent of a greater justice in putting such a punishing end to Coxhill's despicable grasping.

Of Nellie, reports differ. The ungenerous say she died in Paris – consumptive, alcoholic, or worse – and that her unborn child died with her. A different report places her in Geneva, living in quiet luxury on roast duck and cherry liqueurs, looking down on Lac Léman from a chalet filled with servants, styling herself a gentlelady widow as she brought up a child whom many suspected to be Bertie's son.

Finally, the Professor. Molly made a full recovery and chose to leave London with Campbell and myself. My gallant young husband was hell-bent on leaving the police at first. But I persuaded him that he had a great future, perhaps far from London. We moved to Edinburgh with Molly as our adoptive daughter. She and I took to the place like a shot, and I'm happy to say she married and had a family here. To this day she runs a popular ghost train in the Portobello funfair, delighting children along the seafront with hair-raising stories of her days in the London underworld. Her wish to be buried out in the green fields seems also secure, as we have a plot purchased in Rosslyn Glen, by the chapel there, for us both to lie beside Campbell when our time comes.

Ruth Villiers Lawless
National Library of Scotland, November 1911

FINAL THOUGHTS OF CAMPBELL LAWLESS, CHIEF-INSPECTOR, c. 1888

Sometimes a Person Gets Desperate

I picture him still, Berwick, hurtling headlong on the train towards the underground nation he had spent so long in building, smashing into the siding as the waves of oblivion rise around him.

I kept his hat for a while, thinking it might stand as evidence, should the thing ever come to trial. Until I admitted to myself that such things never come to trial. Like Shuffler at the beginning, so Berwick at the end, the little man never merits an inquest. So I took the hat one day and went with the Professor up to the Regent's Canal, said a quick prayer and tossed it into the water.

Even today, so many years later, I cannot excise his image from my mind. My wife has tried to calm the ghost. Darling woman, she asks questions to try and conjure the thoughts away. Don't you think of him as a lunatic, she asks, and cruel with it? Is it not lucky for all of us that he blew himself up? I do not answer.

Berwick Skelton was no lunatic. His disappearance has been an incalculable loss to the world. For I cannot shrug off the feeling that, whatever this cruel life drove him to, he was a man much greater than myself. A man with the heart of a lion, with an appetite for people and for life that I will always envy. With integrity, understanding, and vision that fired him to efforts beyond my imagining.

I recall Worm's image of the spark that would set off revolutions. I picture Skelton bestriding the continent, reaching down to light the tinder across Europe, to burn away the dead wood and keep warm the hopes of the poor, downtrodden and despised. I suppose I hold him a symbol of the ever-elusive future. A man much greater than myself.

Could it have worked? I mean if he had stuck to changing the world instead of doing the rights, as Worm put it. Were people all like him, I think it might have. But sadly, people are more like me, plagued with equivocation and uncertainty, not to mention greed and carelessness. Wardle, whom I trusted, even loved, was corrupt as any criminal, while Skelton was vilified as a demon. What does it mean to be a watchman if we are the ones that need to be watched? The years pass so quickly now and all these disappointments merge together: that I never squared things with my father; that I never properly met Berwick. What it would have been to spend some time in that bright company! The one act of Berwick's that seemed inexplicably barbarous took on a different hue in the light of the revelations that followed. Perhaps evil is not something you are but something you do. In my latter years, I am inclined to pity every poor soul as a fellow sufferer in life's trials.

Sometimes a person gets desperate. He gets desperate and he does something that in the normal run of events he would never countenance. Something happens, trivial or world-shaking, and for the rest of his life he can never escape the consequences. Berwick fell for Nellie, and she left him. He was a man with dreams that could have shaken the earth, but those dreams turned to dust. Crushed by carelessness and ill fortune, he set out to create a mythological terror. Condemn him if you wish. I believe I understand him, or at least forgive him. A part of me even wishes he had succeeded. So it is that, sitting here with my good and gentle wife in our Edinburgh home, committing these incoherent fragments to paper, I end with weeping. I miss Berwick Skelton, for all his sins, and I curse the world that drove him to despair. It is poorer without him.

Author's Disclaimer

Although it would be foolish to dissemble that some figures are not intended to bear resemblance to historical figures, the main characters are my invention, and their nonsenses mine. Where I have used real people and events, I have been slovenly in my researches and feel confident that this is reflected in the incongruous intractabilities of the text. I have allowed myself to stretch credulity so far you may find it all just stupid fibs.

Acknowledgments

Thanks to Caroline; to Emlyn and to Phil; to Mum and Dad; to Seán, Tom, Caroline and Vikki of the erstwhile Mercat Press; to John, Doris and Nina; to Jason, Noel, Hugh, Mirko, Suzie, Peter, Alice-Rose, Francesca, Shannon, Ruth, Jeremy, Charlie; to Dallas and Victoria, Robin, Shomit and Melissa; to Susan, Pedro, John Milton (in São Paulo); to Kenny Wright, Harry and Frank, Peter and Laura, Jane, Jill and Roger; to Lenny, Mike Greaney, Adrian Odell, Geoff, Lester, Ludo, Jasmine, Tata, TubePrune and *victorianlondon.org*; to Philip Jeays, Ken Campbell, Philippe Gaulier, Tim Crook and IRDP; to Peter Burnett, Sam Boyce, Thirsty Lunch; to Kay Hadwick, New Writing South, the Portsmouth Writers' Hub, and the ReAuthoring Project.

ABOUT THE AUTHOR

William Sutton comes from Dunblane, Scotland. He has written for the *Times* and the *Fortean Times*, acted in the longest play in the world, and played cricket for Brazil. This story of a gleaming metropolis mired in corruption came to him while living in São Paulo.

He writes for international magazines about language, music and futurology. His plays have been produced on radio and in London fringe theatres. He has performed at events from the Edinburgh Festival to High Down Prison, often wielding a ukulele. He teaches Latin and plays accordion with chansonnier Philip Jeays.

william-sutton.co.uk | twitter.com.WilliamGeorgeQ

DAN O'SHEA

Introducing Detective John Lynch

PENANCE

One dark secret is about to rip a whole city apart...

"A non-stop adrenaline rush, beginning, middle and end; half Stephen Hunter, half American Tabloid, *Daniel O'Shea's* PENANCE is a bona fide blockbuster."
Owen Laukkanen, author of The Professionals

"Ex-cop Sean Lynch delivers a hell for leather, wild ride of a debut with the 'been there done that' authenticity that lifts it above other thrillers."

JMatt Hilton, bestselling author of the Joe Hunter novels

"The narrative is fast-paced and the
frequent action scenes are convincingly
written. The smells and sounds of
Cambodia are vividly brought to life.
Maier is a bold and brave hero."

Crime Fiction Lover

No child should ever stay missing...

KAREN SANDLER

CLEAN BURN

INTRODUCING DETECTIVE JANELLE WATKINS